Thirty days hath September.
Seven heroes we remember.

PO

The League of Seven. They were always seven, and always the same: a tinker, a law-bringer, a scientist, a trickster, a warrior, a strongman, and a hero. Seven men and women with incredible powers from all parts of the known world who joined forces to stop the Mangleborn from enslaving humanity.

Different Leagues have saved the world over and over again, but few people know that. Only the Septemberists remember, watching for signs that the Mangleborn might escape the elaborate prisons the Ancient League built for them, and waiting for a new League of Seven to be born. . . .

Starscape Books by Alan Gratz

The League of Seven
The Dragon Lantern

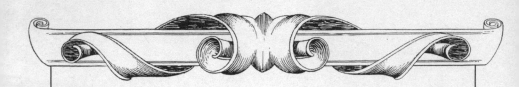

THE LEAGUE
OF SEVEN

ALAN GRATZ

Illustrations by

BRETT HELQUIST

A TOM DOHERTY ASSOCIATES BOOK
NEW YORK

THE LEAGUE OF SEVEN

Copyright © 2014 by Alan Gratz

Reader's Guide copyright © 2014 by Tor Books

The Dragon Lantern excerpt copyright © 2014 by Alan Gratz

All rights reserved.

Interior illustrations by Brett Helquist

Map by Jennifer Hanover

A Starscape Book
Published by Tom Doherty Associates, LLC
175 Fifth Avenue
New York, NY 10010
www.tor-forge.com

The Library of Congress has cataloged the hardcover edition as follows:

Gratz, Alan, 1972–
    The League of Seven / Alan Gratz ; illustrated by Brett Helquist.— 1st ed.
        p. cm.
    "A Tom Doherty Associates book."
    ISBN 978-0-7653-3822-8 (hardcover)
    ISBN 978-1-4668-3850-5 (e-book)
    1. Adventure and adventurers—Fiction. 2. Secret societies—Fiction. 3. Monsters—Fiction.
4. Science fiction. I. Helquist, Brett, illustrator. II. Title.
    PZ7.G77224 Le 2014
    [Fic]—dc23

                                                                                    2014015435

ISBN 978-0-7653-3825-9 (trade paperback)

Starscape books may be purchased for educational, business, or promotional use.
For information on bulk purchases, please contact the Macmillan Corporate and Premium
Sales Department at 1-800-221-7945, extension 5442, or write to specialmarkets@
macmillan.com.

First Edition: August 2014
First Trade Paperback Edition: June 2015

Printed in the United States of America

0   9   8   7   6   5   4   3   2   1

For Wendi, again and always

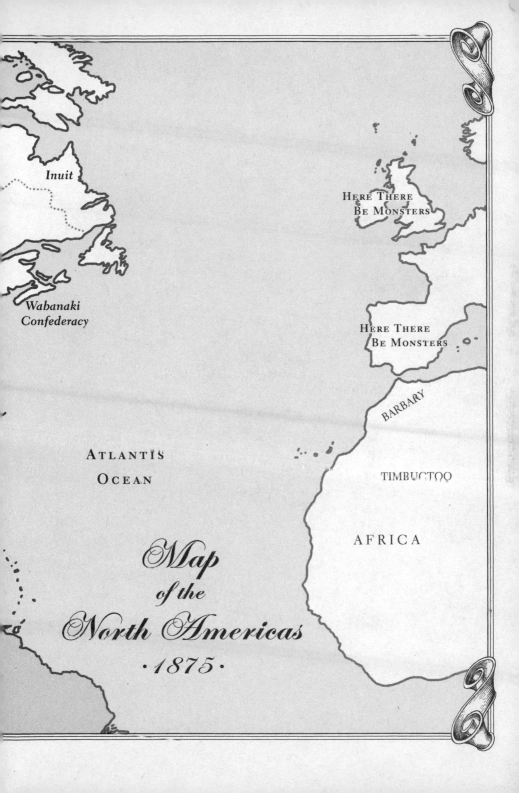

Inuit

Wabanaki
Confederacy

Here There
Be Monsters

Here There
Be Monsters

BARBARY

ATLANTIS
OCEAN

TIMBUCTOO

AFRICA

Map
of the
North Americas
· 1875 ·

THE LEAGUE
OF SEVEN

1

The secret entrance to the headquarters of the Septemberist Society could only be reached by submarine. Twelve-year-old Archie Dent had been there a dozen times before and still he had no idea where it was. Mannahatta? Staten Island? Breucklen? Queens County? For all he knew, the submarine they took to the group's secret headquarters didn't go to any of New Rome's boroughs at all. It might turn right around from the Hudson River Submarine Landing in Jersey and head back to Hackensack territory. And asking didn't help either. His mother and father either didn't know where it was, or they wouldn't tell him.

"I'll bet the Septemberist Society is under the big statue of Hiawatha in New Rome Harbor," he told his parents as they wove their way through the crowd down to the submarine docks. "That would be so brass!"

"We don't talk about the Society in public, Archie. You know that," his mother told him. "And I've asked you before not to use that awful slang."

Archie sighed. His parents were such square cogs. They were researchers for the Septemberists, both of them, and they spent their days with their noses in old books and their nights with their eyes glued to telescopes, looking for signs that the Mangleborn might be breaking out of their underground prisons. That's why they had left their observatory and come to New Rome today: The stars were right for Malacar Ahasherat, the Swarm Queen, to break free of her prison in the Florida swamps, and the Society had to be warned.

"There," Archie's father said. "The red submersible. That's the one we want."

The red submarine was dwarfed by its ocean-liner cousins—the massive four-hundred-foot-long, seven-thousand-tonne gray behemoths that carried passengers up and down the East Coast, from Acadia in the north to New Spain and Brasil in the south. Men in heavy frock coats and neckties and women in crinolines and petticoats waited for clockwork porters to load their steamer trunks onto the subs. As much as Archie was looking forward to seeing the Septemberist Society's secret headquarters again, he wished he were boarding one of the enormous submarines, setting off on an adventure that would take him all over the United Nations and beyond. But no. After his parents delivered their warning to the Society, it would be back to the family estate in Philadelphia again. Back to the books and the telescopes.

The little submarine was whale shaped, with great fins at the back that controlled its position in the water. A white plume of smoke and steam rose from a hole on its back like water from a whale's blowhole, and it had great round eyelike windows at the front for the pilot to see out of. Its name, painted along its side, was the SS *Seven Seas*.

"Ahoy there," the Dents' Tik Tok servant called to the

machine-man pilot who stood sentry at the wood-and-rope gangplank to the sub. "I am Mr. Rivets. This is Mr. and Mrs. Dent, and their son, Master Archie."

"Thirty days hath September," the Tik Tok captain said.

"Seven heroes we remember," said Mr. Dent, giving the Society's secret pass phrase. He lifted the lapel on his jacket to reveal a pin with an image of a human eye atop a pyramid, set inside a seven-pointed star. The symbol of the Septemberist Society.

"Permission to come aboard, Mr. Hull?" Mr. Dent asked.

"Aye. Permission granted." Mr. Hull was a brass Emartha Mark II Machine Man like Mr. Rivets, but instead of a riveted metal vest and bowler hat like the Dents' machine man, he'd been customized with a copper sailor's cap and captain's jacket, both of which had turned green over time. Mr. Rivets had talent cards that could be switched out to give him different skills, but Mr. Hull's Submarine Pilot card was permanently installed.

"Why do we have to give the Society's secret pass phrase and show him the pin?" Archie asked his mother. "Mr. Hull's been our captain every time. Doesn't he know us by now?"

"It's protocol, Archie. What if we weren't really ourselves this time?"

Archie frowned. "Who else would we be?"

"Hurry along, Archie," Mr. Dent said from the hatchway. "Time and tide wait for no man."

Inside, the submarine was all riveted steel and brass pipes and fittings. To the aft down a narrow passage was the hissing, steaming boiler room. To the fore was a small lounge with two red-cushioned couches. Beyond that, through a small open door, was the pilot's cockpit. Archie's parents and Mr. Rivets had already taken seats in the lounge and were fastening their safety harnesses when Mr. Hull closed the tophatch and screwed it shut.

Archie headed for the cockpit.

"Archie, I think we can leave the piloting of the ship to Mr. Hull this time," his father said.

"But I always sit up front," Archie said. As a kid, he'd begged to sit up front and watch Mr. Hull pilot the submersible, and Mr. Hull had always let him.

"Don't you think you're getting a little old for that?" his mother said.

Archie was crestfallen. Slag it. He was telling his parents all the time that he wasn't a little kid anymore, and the one time they agreed, he didn't want them to.

"It's all right by me, Mrs. Dent," Mr. Hull said as he walked through the lounge to the cockpit.

Archie grinned and hurried into the cockpit with Mr. Hull before his parents could tell him not to. Next time he'd ride in the back. Maybe.

Archie sat down in the copilot's seat beside Mr. Hull. The Tik Tok flipped switches and turned dials and checked gauges. Archie had no idea what any of them did, but he loved the sound of them clicking and whirring and spinning. One day maybe he'd have a submersible of his own, and run missions for the Septemberists.

With a metallic clank and a lurch, the SS *Seven Seas* disengaged from its mooring on the dock and turned in the cavernous underground port.

"Hold fast now," Mr. Hull announced. "We're ready to dive."

The machine man flipped a switch, and the submarine shook as air burbled out of the ballast tanks. Sloshing water rose on the window until the cave disappeared, replaced by the black of the Hudson River. The Tik Tok captain flipped another switch, and a keel-mounted carbide lamp lit up the water in front of them. The *Seven Seas* passed underneath the huge steel hood that protected the submarine landing from New Rome Harbor, and the ghostly, shimmering light of the gray New Rome morning filtered down to them through the choppy sea. Ships had once traveled on top of the water, not underneath it, Archie knew. Mr. Rivets had shown him pictures in old books. But all that had changed when the Darkness fell on the Old World a hundred years ago. Now the Atlantis Ocean was too rough to sail above. It could only be navigated *under* the waves, and every submarine sent to Europe to find out what had happened never came back.

"How long can you stay underwater?" Archie asked.

"About two hours at normal speed," said Mr. Hull. "Then I have to come up for air and stoke the furnace. But we'll have you to Septemberist headquarters long before that."

"Because it's just under the statue of Hiawatha on Oyster Island, right?"

Mr. Hull adjusted a dial. "I'm afraid I couldn't say, sir."

Archie smiled. That's what machine men said when they'd been ordered to keep a secret. Mark IIs were fundamentally unable to lie. It was built into their clockworks. Instead, they just said "I'm afraid I couldn't say." It had been worth a shot though.

True to Mr. Hull's word, the SS *Seven Seas* soon surfaced in a gaslit cave. This port was far smaller than the Hudson River Submarine Landing, but still big enough for two other small submersibles to bob at the unadorned and empty dock. Mr. Hull pulled them up alongside, and Archie helped him tie off the boat before following his parents up the stone steps to the great hall of the Septemberist Society.

Archie loved the great hall. It was round and tall, with domed steel arches to hold up a ceiling carved out of rock. Leading out of the room were seven doorways, one of which led back the way they had come from the submarine landing. All around the hall, in between the seven doorways, stood seven stone statues—one for each member of the Ancient League of Seven. Wayland Smith, the Norse tinker who invented the raygun, with his hammer. Maat, the Aegyptian princess with her talking staff, who brought justice to the world. Daedalus, the Greek scientist who taught mankind how to fly in airships. Anansi, the Afrikan trickster who stole the Mangleborn gauntlet. Hippolyta, the Amazonian warrior, whose arrows had taken down legions of Manglespawn. Heracles, the hulking, half-naked Greek with his club, whose dark, angry fury had brought the League to its knees—but saved it too. That statue had always frightened Archie, and still did. But last there was Theseus, Archie's favorite, the Athenian hero with the curly locks and the neat tunic and the short sword, who had brought this League of Seven together and led them to victory over the Mangleborn.

It wasn't the original League of Seven, of course. The original League's names and faces had been lost to time. There had been more Leagues before the Ancient League and more since, but they were always seven, and always the same: a tinker, a law-bringer, a scientist, a trickster, a warrior, a strongman, and a hero. Seven men and women with incredible powers from all parts of the known world who joined forces to stop the Mangleborn from enslaving humanity. Different Leagues had saved the world over and over again, but few people knew that. Only the Septemberists remembered—*septem* for "seven" in Latin, September having once been the seventh month, and named in their honor—watching for signs that the Mangleborn might escape the elaborate prisons the Ancient League had built for them, and waiting for a new League of Seven to be born.

"Archie, we'll be meeting with the chief and her council in their chambers," his father told him. "You and Mr. Rivets wait out here. Mr. Rivets, I don't want him getting into any trouble."

"I shall do what I can, sir," Mr. Rivets said. Before they'd left the family airship in Hackensack territory, Mr. Dent had replaced Mr. Rivets' Airship Pilot talent card with his Protector card. Or, as Archie liked to call it, the "Babysitter card."

Mr. and Mrs. Dent went through the door next to Theseus, which led to the council chambers.

"Odd," Mr. Rivets said, the clicking of his internal clockworks echoing faintly in the tall round room. "I would have expected someone to greet us. Mr. Pendulum, at the very least." Mr. Pendulum was the head Tik Tok at Septemberist headquarters.

"If a Mangleborn is rising, they're probably all in the council chambers worrying about it," Archie said. "So . . . can I have it?"

Mr. Rivets tilted his mechanical head. "Your father directed me to keep you *out* of trouble, Master Archie, not to abet it."

"Aw, come on, Mr. Rivets! Don't be clinker. It's just a toy."

"Language, Master Archie," the Tik Tok scolded, but he opened a door on his brass body disguised as a vest pocket and revealed a toy raygun stowed inside. Archie snatched it up. It was made to look just like a real aether pistol, but when you pulled the trigger all it did was rev and spark.

"I'll be Theseus! You be Lesool Eshar, the Deceiver in the Dark."

"As you wish, Master Archie. I shall endeavor to be monstrous, gigantic, and cruel. Roar."

Archie clicked the trigger a few times at Mr. Rivets, peppering him with an imaginary heat ray as the toy gun sparked, then ran through the door beside Heracles. Sometimes he would visit the workshop through the door beside Wayland Smith to marvel at the Society's latest gadgets. Another time he had explored the archives through the door beside Daedalus, but he got enough of libraries and books at home. Once he had even sneaked into the weapons room beyond the statue of the warrior Hippolyta and gaped at the arsenal of aether pistols and oscillators and wave cannons stored there until Mr. Pendulum dragged him out by the collar. But it was the catacombs underneath the Septemberist headquarters that he really loved playing in.

Like the statue of Heracles that guarded their entrance, the catacombs had always creeped Archie out a little, but fascinated him too. The catacombs were where the Society stored all the bones from the monsters they had fought over the centuries. Not the bones of Mangleborn like the Swarm Queen or the Deceiver in the Dark. Mangleborn were immortal—or at least no one had figured out how to kill one yet. The bones in the catacombs were Manglespawn. Creatures descended from the Mangleborn. Monsters that did their masters' bidding. The Septemberists could handle Manglespawn. Usually. But to deal with the Mangleborn, the Septemberists needed the superhuman powers of the League of Seven.

Archie ran through the maze of crypts, ducking and hiding and shooting at pretend minions. *Kzzz kzzz kzzz.* He was Theseus—but not in the labyrinth fighting a man-sized minotaur. That's not what had really happened. Archie's parents had taught him the real story. He was Theseus, fighting the twenty-story-tall Mangleborn Lesool Eshar, the Deceiver in the Dark. A giant with bull horns and cloven feet who could make you see things that weren't real—like make you think you were in a dark, claustrophobic labyrinth when you were actually in the wide-open grasslands of Afrika. The minotaur was the popular version. The safe version. The truth—that there was a race of misshapen giants imprisoned inside the earth and under the sea—was a little too much for most people to handle.

People didn't want to know there really were monsters in the world.

"Theseus!" Mr. Rivets' voice boomed in the underground passageways. "Theseus! I come for you!"

Mr. Rivets made a pretty good Mangleborn in their backyard adventures. He was tall, for one thing, almost six and a half feet from his brass spats to his painted black bowler hat. He was heavy too—almost a thousand pounds—so that his clockwork legs made an impressive *chi-koom chi-koom chi-koom* sound when he walked. Where any illusion of a monster broke down was in his face, with its shining glass eyes and brass handlebar moustache shaped into a smile.

Archie crept through the dark tunnels, lit here and there by flickering gaslights. Shadow flames played on the stacks of crypt-like boxes set into the walls. Archie kept his toy aether pistol raised, ready to jump out at Mr. Rivets as soon as he heard the soft tick-tock of his clockworks. Water dripped slowly from the ceiling nearby as he held his breath, listening. *Drip. Drip. Drip.*

Scritch.

Archie leaped around the corner. "Ha-HA!"

But it wasn't Mr. Rivets. It was . . . something else. Something black and shiny and big, bigger than Archie, with too many legs and too many eyes and a curled, segmented tail with a thick stinger at the end. It hung on a thick nest of white web that covered the corridor in front of him from floor to ceiling. It wasn't a giant spider or a giant scorpion or—were those human hands under there? It wasn't a spider or a scorpion or a person but something in between. Something unnatural. Something monstrous.

Something Manglespawn.

"Oh, slag."

The thing looked up at Archie with its dozens of eyes, and he realized he was still pointing the toy raygun at it. He lowered it, his hand shaking. He wanted to step back, to turn and run, but he was too scared. His feet wouldn't move.

At the base of the web, near the floor, a small ball of webbing shook like something inside it was trying to get out. Archie watched as a little stinger like the one on the big daddy-Manglespawn tore through the web ball, and a baby Manglespawn clawed its way out. It landed upside down on the stone floor, righted itself, and scrabbled toward Archie. *Scritch scritch scritch scritch.*

Now Archie's feet moved.

He stumbled back away from the thing, but it was fast. Faster than he was. He turned to run and clanged right into the brass chest of Mr. Rivets. The Dents' machine man lifted Archie into the air like he weighed nothing at all and stomped a metal foot on the black bug. *Splurch.* Green-black blood spurted on the stacked crypts.

An egg sac shivered on the web, and another black stinger poked its way through. Then another. And another.

"Run," Mr. Rivets said. He let Archie go, and Archie ran. He sprinted back through the crypts, running as fast and as hard as he could without paying any attention to where he was going. He didn't know how far or how long he'd run before he realized he was lost. Slag it all, where was he? He had to get upstairs and tell everyone there was a Manglespawn in the catacombs! He stopped. Spun. There! That crypt, there—he recognized it. He knew where he was. Four turns later he was running up the stairs, into the great hall, past the statue of Theseus, and into the offices where the Society's leaders worked.

No one was there. Not even Mr. Pendulum.

Just beyond the offices, the double doors to the council chamber were closed. Archie wasn't allowed in there.

Slag it—this was an emergency!

Archie burst into the council chamber. "Manglespawn! There's a Manglespawn—in the catacombs!" he said, breathing hard.

The Septemberist council sat at a big, round table with the

Society's all-seeing pyramid eye emblem carved into it. There were seven of them, one representing each of the seven guilds within the Society. Archie knew the lawyer Frederick Douglass with his wild, frizzy hair, sitting in the law-bringer's seat; General Lee, wearing the dark blue jacket and Hardee hat of the United Nations army, sitting in the warrior's seat; and of course he would have recognized the famous actress Sally Tall Chief in the trickster's chair and the lacrosse star John Two-Sticks in the hero's chair anywhere, even if they hadn't been Septemberists. The others he didn't know so well, except for Philomena Moffett, who was the head of his parents' guild—the scientists—and the current chief of the Septemberist Society.

Not one of them turned to look at him.

Archie ran up to the table. "Did you hear what I said? There's a . . . a thing in the basement! A monster, with little monster babies. Mr. Rivets smushed one, but there were more of them hatching, and—"

The Septemberist council finally looked at him then, and Archie shuddered like a braking locomotive. The council members turned their heads slowly, all at the same time, like they were all one. But that wasn't the creepiest thing. The creepiest thing was, they were smiling. All of them. Great big stupid smiles, like they were pretending to be happy. Like they were smiling through some great pain. Even the woman in the shadow chair was smiling, the ugly New Rome gang leader they called Hellcat Maggie, who kept an eye on the slums. Archie had never once seen her smile. Now she was smiling so wide he could see her teeth were filed down into points.

"*Jandal a Haad*," they all said, all at the same time. "They brought the Jandal a Haad."

"Who did?" Archie asked. "What's a Jandal a Haad? That thing in the catacombs?"

The Septemberist council stood up, all at the same time, and turned toward Archie. He didn't know what was going on, but something about this was totally clinker. He took a step back as Mr. Rivets ticked into the room, his brass feet stained green black from squashing the bug things.

"I have sealed the catacombs, Master Archie," Mr. Rivets said, "but I fear my efforts may not be enough to contain the creature."

"The Jandal a Haad will stay," the council said as one. "There is something in the basement we would like you to see."

"Master Archie?" Mr. Rivets said.

Archie backed toward Mr. Rivets, never taking his eyes off the advancing council members.

"Where are my parents?" Archie asked.

"They've gone already," Philomena Moffett said through her fake smile. "You're to stay here with us."

"They wouldn't leave without me," Archie said. "What's going on here?"

"There's something in the basement we would like you to see," the council said again, still advancing.

"Yeah. I saw it already," Archie said. "Run, Mr. Rivets!"

Archie took off for the submarine landing at a sprint. If his parents were leaving, that's where they'd be. But they would never leave without him. It didn't make any sense. None of this did. What was wrong with the council?

"Mom! Dad!" Archie called as he ran. "Mom! Dad!"

He came through the arch at the top of the steps that led down to the submarine landing, and there were his parents—following Mr. Hull onto the SS *Seven Seas*.

"Mom! Dad! Wait!" Archie called. He went down the steps three at a time, twice almost falling and breaking his neck. What were his parents doing? How could they be leaving without coming to find him first?

Archie caught his mother by the arm as she reached for the ladder up to the *Seven Seas'* hatch.

"Mom, wait! Where are you going?"

And that's when he saw it. A thick black bug, like the little baby Manglespawn that had hatched and come after him in the catacombs. It sat on the back of his mother's neck, beneath her swept-up hair. Its insect legs wrapped around her neck, like it was holding on, and its scorpion-like tail was buried deep inside her. His dad had one on the back of his neck too, half-hidden by his high collar.

Archie's parents turned their heads around together slowly, and he saw the same awful smile on their faces that he'd seen on the faces of the Septemberist council. His skin crawled like he had those bug things all over him, and he let go of his mother.

Whatever that thing was in the basement, it had already gotten to his parents. And the rest of the Septemberist council too.

2

Mr. Rivets climbed aboard the SS *Seven Seas* and closed the hatch just as the Septemberist council emerged from the arch at the top of the steps. Archie could see their smiling faces from the cockpit of the submersible.

"Let's go, Mr. Hull!" he told the machine man at the controls. "Hurry!"

"Readying a submersible for departure is a strict and complicated procedure, sir. To rush the process would endanger you and the other occupants."

Archie watched the smiling Septemberist council walk down the steps toward them at the same maddeningly slow pace they had come at him in the council chambers. Just walking after him was scarier than if they had chased him at a run. It was like they knew they were going to get him, and didn't have to hurry.

"Don't you have any kind of emergency override or anything?" Archie asked Mr. Hull.

"Master Archie?" Mr. Rivets said, joining them in the small cockpit. "What's wrong with Mr. and Mrs. Dent?"

"The same thing that's going to be wrong with me if we

don't get out of here!" Archie said. The Septemberist council was at the bottom of the steps. Archie couldn't hear them through the thick glass of the bubble windows, but he could see their mouths moving. They were probably still telling him there was something in the basement they wanted him to see.

Mr. Hull kept flipping switches and turning dials, but they weren't going anywhere. The council would be on top of them any second! Archie scanned the console and recognized the switch that controlled the mooring clamps. He knew he wasn't supposed to, but—*slag it*. They had to get out of here, *now*. Archie flipped the switch. *KaCHUNK*. The submersible let go of the dock and bobbed on the water.

"Sir!" Mr. Hull protested. But Archie wasn't finished. He flipped the switch to release the ship's ballast, and the SS *Seven Seas* rocked as it burbled and sank beneath the water's surface. Archie let go the breath he didn't know he'd been holding as they left the Septemberist council smiling on the dock.

"Sir!" Mr. Hull said, struggling to make up for all the steps Archie had skipped. "This is highly unsafe!"

Archie staggered as the submersible hit the rocky bottom of the cavern, but Mr. Hull soon had them to rights.

"You are not a licensed submersible operator! You are not allowed to manipulate the controls!" Mr. Hull told him. "I'm afraid I must ask that you leave the cockpit at once."

"In a minute," Archie told him. He reached around Mr. Rivets, took a long look at his parents in the passenger compartment, sitting there with the same empty smiles on their faces as before, and slid the cockpit door closed.

"Mr. Rivets, Mom and Dad—they've got bug things on their necks!"

Archie told the Tik Tok what he'd seen and how the Septemberist council had acted when he'd run in and told them about the Manglespawn.

"Do you think they have those bug things on them too?" he asked.

"I think it highly probable," Mr. Rivets said.

"But what are they doing to them? The bug things, I mean."

Archie heard Mr. Rivets' clockworks ticking as the machine man thought. "The only similar experience I have had was in service to your great-great-grandmother, Willoughby Dent, when we encountered a Manglespawn in the forests of what was then known as the Massachusetts Colony, the year the Darkness fell."

Archie blinked. He sometimes forgot just how old Mr. Rivets was, and how many Dents he'd served, all of whom had been Septemberists. Mr. Rivets was a walking, talking Septemberist Society archive.

"In that circumstance, the Manglespawn had the ability to control the behavior of human beings by laying eggs in their stomachs," Mr. Rivets said. "Rather a messy business."

"Ugh," Archie said. "So those bugs are controlling them?"

"The Manglespawn in the catacombs would be the central brain, I would think," Mr. Rivets said. "Communicating telepathically through the creatures on your parents."

"Telling them to do what?"

"That I could not say, sir."

"We have to try to snap them out of it," Archie said.

"Agreed," said Mr. Rivets.

Archie opened the door to the passenger cabin. His parents still sat there, smiling.

"Mom? Dad? Can you hear me?" Archie asked. He stood right in front of them, waving his hands in their faces. He poked them. Nudged them. Snapped his fingers. Nothing. Archie pulled Mr. Rivets aside.

"We have to pull those things off them," Archie said.

"Doing so may be dangerous," Mr. Rivets said. "In 1802, on an expedition with your grandfather—"

"I don't care about any of that right now!" Archie said. "I'm sorry, Mr. Rivets, but I want you to take them off. That's an order."

In theory, Archie was just as much Mr. Rivets' master as his parents were. He was human, and Mr. Rivets was a Tik Tok servant. In practice though, Archie's parents made Archie do whatever Mr. Rivets said, not the other way around. That gave Mr. Rivets a lot of latitude as to which commands he would accept from Archie, and which ones he wouldn't. He didn't, for example, go jump in a lake as Archie had once told him to do when Archie was ten.

Archie heard Mr. Rivets' clockwork brain clicking as he considered the command. Finally Mr. Rivets nodded. "As you say, Master Archie."

Archie was relieved, but scared too. "Mom first," he said.

"Beg pardon, Mrs. Dent," Mr. Rivets said as he turned her head. It sent shivers through Archie to see his mother sit there and be posed like a rag doll.

And then Archie saw it again. The bug on his mother's neck. It was black and shiny, with a segmented body like a spider. It throbbed, in and out, in and out, like it was another part of her. Like it was another organ.

Mr. Rivets bent forward to examine it. "You were right, Master Archie. This appears to be one of the same creatures that came after you in the catacombs. If so, that would mean its not-inconsiderable tail is buried some way into your mother's neck. Perhaps all the way to her spinal cord. That may be how it is able to achieve control over her."

Archie closed his eyes. Sometimes he wished Mr. Rivets *could* lie. Or at least not be so honest.

"Just get it off her," Archie said.

Mr. Rivets raised a brass hand, maneuvered his fingers with clockwork precision to an inch on either side of the bug on Mrs. Dent's neck, and snapped them closed on it.

Mrs. Dent flailed like a puppet, making Archie jump. Her legs lurched and her arms jerked, but Mr. Rivets held fast. Was she in pain? Were they hurting her? She looked like it, but she didn't cry out. Archie wanted to yell at Mr. Rivets to stop, but he wanted the thing off his mother more.

Archie's dad turned to Mr. Rivets, that slagging smile still on his face. "Mr. Rivets, go to your rewinding station."

"No, Mr. Rivets! Don't let go!" Archie cried. "Get it off her!"

Mr. Rivets ignored Archie's father and did as Archie said. He pulled the thing away, its little legs wriggling, its tail sliding farther and farther out of her neck. Impossibly farther. There was so much of it buried inside of her, it had to hurt. It *slurched* as it slid out, and a trickle of black-red blood oozed from the edge of the hole. Archie thought he was going to be sick.

"No!" Mrs. Dent screamed at last, making Archie jump again. She sobbed as she screamed, a sound that wrenched Archie's heart right out of his chest. "No! Can't be here. Have to run, Archie! Don't let them—"

The thing was almost all the way out of Mrs. Dent's neck when Mr. Dent reached around Mr. Rivets, lifted a small brass flap on his back, and switched him off. The tension immediately released from the springs inside Mr. Rivets, and the machine man went limp. His hand released the bug, and his arms and head lolled uselessly.

"Mom! No! Mom!" Archie cried. Mrs. Dent slumped forward on the bench, and Archie caught her in his arms. He could hear the bug slurching back into her neck. Mrs. Dent grabbed him by the lapels of his jacket with desperate strength. "Archie! One, two, buckle my shoe. Remember! One, two—" She stopped suddenly and stood, letting go of his jacket. The pain was gone from her face, replaced by a tear-stained smile and a blank stare.

"Mom! Mom, come back! Please!" Archie said. But she was gone. The thing was back in her neck, its tail buried deep inside her again. Pulling it out had hurt her, badly, but it could be done. If Mr. Rivets could pull out both bugs at the same time, they couldn't stop him.

But as soon as Archie had the thought, his father stood and moved to the bench on the other side of the small compartment. It wasn't far, but it was far enough that Mr. Rivets couldn't reach them both. They could do it if Archie pulled one of them out, but he didn't know if he was strong enough—physically *or* mentally.

Archie switched Mr. Rivets back on. The machine man

whirred and straightened. He peered back and forth at Mr. and Mrs. Dent, and then at Archie.

"I take it we were unsuccessful," he said.

"Yeah," Archie said, drying his own eyes. "We're slagged."

The submersible arrived back at the Hudson River Submarine Landing, and Archie's parents stood to leave.

"Mr. Rivets, what do we do?" Archie asked. He was twelve years old. Wherever they went, he went. "I know they're being controlled by that thing, but they're my parents!"

"And my masters," Mr. Rivets said. "I think all we can do is follow them, try to discern what plan the Manglespawn has in mind for them, and do our best to prevent it."

How? Archie wondered. But he didn't say it. His parents were already climbing out onto the busy sub landing docks. He and Mr. Rivets had to hurry if they didn't want to lose them.

As they made their way through the busy terminus, Archie spied an Algonquin in a New Rome policeman's uniform. He tugged on Mr. Rivets' brass arm. "We could go to the police!"

"And tell them what?" Mr. Rivets said. "That your parents are being controlled by a monster in the catacombs beneath the headquarters of a secret society they have never heard of?"

Mr. Rivets was right. The police would think he was a blinking flange. And they couldn't go to the Septemberist Society. They were under the same spell.

Archie and Mr. Rivets were on their own.

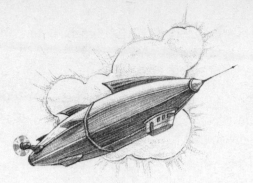

3

Archie and Mr. Rivets took a carriage with his parents to the Palisades Airship Park, where the family airship was anchored. The *Hesperus* was small, as far as airships went, a family-sized aeroyacht that had been in the Dent family for at least two generations. Unlike the huge whale-shaped airships that crossed the continent, the *Hesperus* was a small cone-shaped metal capsule with steam-driven propellers, suspended from a net full of hydrogen balloons. The *Hesperus* had been painted bright yellow to match its namesake star's brilliant evening glow, but decades of sun and use had scratched and faded her. The cockpit and cabin were all one round room, with the ship's controls and windshield at one end, and basic kitchen, bathroom, and sleeping facilities ringing the rest of the inner wall.

Archie's father stood at one end of the round room, his mother at the other, by the controls. Without a word, she weighed anchor and stoked the airship's steam propellers. New Rome slid by through the windshield as the *Hesperus* rose into the clouds and turned south. To go anywhere in the *Hesperus*, Archie's parents usually installed Mr. Rivets' Airship Pilot card and had him do the navigating. Whatever the bug thing controlling them was, it apparently knew how to fly an airship. Archie installed Mr. Rivets' Pilot card anyway, so he could tell where they were going.

"Florida," Mr. Rivets told Archie. "That would be the terminus of the flight path your parents have set. Unless they mean to take us on to New Spain or Brasil."

"Florida. Where Malacar Ahasherat is buried," Archie said. Malacar Ahasherat was the Mangleborn that Archie's parents had gone to warn the Septemberist Society about. "The Swarm Queen—isn't that what they called it?"

"Yes, sir," Mr. Rivets said. He and Archie were whispering, but it hardly mattered. Mr. and Mrs. Dent acted like the machine man and their son weren't even there. "Malacar Ahasherat is imprisoned in the swamps at the end of the peninsula. And as her name suggests, the Swarm Queen is master over the insect kingdom."

Archie watched the bug thing on his mother's neck throb. It couldn't be a coincidence. A Mangleborn with a thing for insects, and now his parents and the rest of the Septemberists had bugs on their necks, telling them what to say and do. Wait—maybe not all the Septemberists. Just the ones back at headquarters!

"Uncle John!" Archie said. John Douglas. He was another Septemberist, one who wasn't on the council. He wasn't Archie's real uncle—Archie didn't have any aunts or uncles—but his parents had always called him Uncle John. He came to visit the Dents at their home in Philadelphia a couple of times each year. In all the worry over his parents, Archie had forgotten him. "Mr. Rivets, we have to get in touch with Uncle

John. If he hasn't been to headquarters, he may not be under the Swarm Queen's control. He could help us."

"He might indeed, Master Archie. But how to reach him? We would have to land the *Hesperus* to send a letter by pneumatic post. Your parents have been docile until now, but I worry what their insect masters might make them do to you should we try to stop them."

Archie couldn't believe he hadn't remembered him earlier, back in New Rome. "This is so clinker, Mr. Rivets! We can't just sit here and do nothing!"

But nothing was all they could do now. Archie climbed into his hammock, which hung at eye level in an alcove off the *Hesperus'* round cabin, and watched his parents from underneath his blanket. They never moved, never spoke, never ate or slept. They just stood there, staring straight ahead and smiling, while the *Hesperus'* propellers drove them all south at full steam.

As day turned to night, Archie realized it had been breakfast since he'd last had something to eat. As scared as he was to come out from under his blanket again, he forced himself to cross the cabin and search the compartments in the airship's small galley.

"I'm afraid you won't find much, Master Archie," Mr. Rivets told him. They were over Cherokee territory now, and the machine man was paying close attention to Mrs. Dent at the controls. "Your parents thought we would be back in Philadelphia by now."

So had Archie. He remembered the sub landing, where he'd wished he could go off on a trip around the United

Nations. He'd gotten his wish, he realized. Just not the way he had imagined it.

Archie found an old saltine tin in one of the cabinets in the galley and popped it open, but it didn't have crackers inside.

It held an aether pistol.

It was old, from the look of it, like something from the pictures of the Pawnee Wars in Archie's history book. It was squat and round, with a pointy fin on top like antique rayguns had. Archie had no idea if it still worked, but it seemed like the real thing. He looked up at his father. Mr. Dent was still staring straight ahead and smiling. Wherever his parents were taking them, he was sure he'd be safer with the raygun than without. As innocently as he could, Archie walked to his hammock with the raygun tucked into his jacket. He was so nervous he almost tripped over his own feet, but at last he was to his hammock, where he hastily stuffed the raygun under his blanket.

"I think I'll just go to sleep now," he announced. He was still hungry, but he had to pretend it was food he'd found in the cabinet, not something else.

"Very good, Master Archie. We should be in Florida by midday tomorrow. You'll want all of your energy then," Mr. Rivets said. All of his energy for *what* he didn't say, because neither of them knew. But Mr. Rivets was right. Archie needed to be ready for whatever was coming.

He climbed into his hammock and pulled the blanket over his head, holding the raygun close so he could see it in the half-light. He'd never used one before, but Professor Torque used one a lot in *The Adventures of Professor Torque and His*

Amazing Steamboy, his favorite dime novel. Somewhere there was supposed to be a switch that activated the aggregator. There. The raygun vibrated and hummed. Archie hugged it to him, hoping his parents didn't hear. A big round gauge on the side of the raygun showed when the pistol had collected enough aether to fire. It was slow, but it worked. Archie quickly shut it down, worried he might accidentally set the thing off. He didn't know exactly what he would do with it, but it made him feel better to have it.

Archie stayed under the blanket hugging the aether pistol close like a stuffed animal. He knew he needed to rest, but he was too anxious and too scared. How could he sleep with those things here in the airship with him? What if one of them crawled off his parents and came after him? He would have to stay awake all night, just to be sure.

Fifteen minutes later, he was fast asleep.

As he slept, he dreamed. He wasn't in the airship anymore. He was in a dark, man-made cavern with rock walls and a stone ceiling supported with tall iron buttresses like the Septemberist Society headquarters, only bigger. Much bigger. But maybe built by the same people. At the center of the room, low to the ground, was a circular stone wall like the top of a well, but much larger—almost the size of the center circle on a lacrosse field.

Ksshoom. White-blue lightning flashed down from a metal rod sticking out of the ceiling and arced into the well, lighting up the chamber. In the flash from the lightning, Archie saw a vast clockwork machine set into the far wall of the cavern. But that wasn't what drew his attention.

The floor was alive.

The ground was covered with bugs, a six-inch layer of them, all climbing and crawling on top of each other. Centipedes and beetles and mantises and roaches and a thousand more creepy crawly things. A million more. It was a jungle full of bugs, right here in this room. All around him.

Archie jumped back in horror, but the bugs weren't crawling on him, and they didn't crunch when he stepped on them. He was there, but not there, like a ghost. The insects scrabbled and chittered and buzzed through him, marching along with the rest of their creepy-crawly friends toward the low wall of the stone circle, where they climbed up and over.

Archie wanted to see what was down in that hole. He needed to. He could feel the pull of it, just like the insects. He couldn't resist it. He slid a foot forward, still afraid of the bugs, but they passed right through him.

Archie crept closer and closer to where the insects poured over the wall, then peeked over.

The abyss was covered with an enormous stone, like a lid. No, two stones: half circles that met in the middle, each with a huge letter X on it. XX. It was a door. A seal. An old one, with cracks in the stone. That's where the bugs were going. They wiggled and pushed and scrunched down through the cracks to whatever was below.

THOOM. The ground trembled. Was it an earthquake?

THOOM. Dust and rubble shook loose from the ceiling.

THOOM. The stone seal on the well shuddered, knocking insects onto their backs.

There was something inside the well. Underneath the stone seals.

Something trying to get out.

Ksshoom. Lightning flashed again, and Archie woke up with a start on the *Hesperus,* the antique raygun poking him in the stomach.

"The Mangleborn wakes," his father said, making Archie jump. His mother and father were both staring at him.

"I'm glad you were able to sleep," said Mr. Rivets.

Archie felt like he'd been asleep for hours, but it was still dark outside. Mr. Rivets had said they wouldn't get to Florida until midday. Thunder boomed outside, and the *Hesperus* shook and rattled. Rain splattered the windshield, and Archie understood. It *was* morning. The *Hesperus* was just in the middle of a thunderstorm. So much for staying awake all night. Archie put a hand to the back of his neck, just to check, but there was nothing there.

He slid out of the hammock, the aether pistol stuck in the belt of his trousers under his shirttail. Through the windshield, he saw the center of the storm dead ahead. Dark clouds swirled and lightning flashed—blue-white lightning—and suddenly Archie remembered his dream, saw the cavern and the clockworks and the stone seal and the bugs. Ahead of them, deep in the storm, the lightning flashed again and again, all striking the same place: the tip of a metal tower poking up through the clouds.

"I do believe," said Mr. Rivets, "we have arrived at our final destination."

4

Mrs. Dent dropped the *Hesperus'* anchor just beyond where the lightning was striking.

"Stay with the airship," Mr. Dent told Archie and Mr. Rivets.

"Mom. Dad. Don't go," Archie said. They had to be able to hear him. But Mr. and Mrs. Dent said nothing more. They were still in there somewhere; he knew it. But they were buried too deep. Without another word they climbed into the elevator basket, pulled a lever, and descended into the dark, stormy sky.

"Mr. Rivets, we can't just let them go!" Archie said.

"I am loath to be separated from them, Master Archie, particularly in their current state. But they did command us to stay with the airship."

"That's clinker, Mr. Rivets. *They* didn't tell us that, those bug things did!"

Mr. Rivets clicked and whirred as he processed that. Archie knew it was difficult for him. He was programmed to take orders from humans, but nothing in his programming allowed for humans controlled by evil bugs. Archie, on the other hand, had never been good at doing what he was told, no matter who was doing the telling. He ran to the coat closet and pulled out his leather duster, a pair of brass goggles, and leather gloves.

"Master Archie, I believe our safest course of action is to fly back to New Rome with all due speed. Technically, that would also not violate our orders."

Archie put his arms through the sleeves of the duster. "And do what?"

"Seek help. Your Uncle John—Mr. Douglas. Other members of the Society."

"We don't *know* any other members of the Society. And it'll take more than a day to get back to New Rome, and at least another day and a half to get back." Archie put the goggles on, then slid them up into his messy brown hair. "My parents may be long gone by then. We'd never find them again."

"We don't know that, sir."

"We won't know anything unless we follow them," Archie said.

The empty elevator basket came back up and locked into place. All Archie had to do was step inside and throw the lever and down he would go after his parents. He hesitated, not sure Mr. Rivets wasn't right. He was a twelve-year-old with an antique raygun stuck in his belt. What good was he, really? He had always wanted to be a hero. Always imagined that he was Theseus, the leader of the Ancient League of Seven. In his daydreams he fought Mangleborn the size of mountains and won. But he wasn't a superhero. Not really. And now that he had to be brave for real, he was scared.

But he had to go. He couldn't leave his parents behind and

fly back to New Rome. If he did, he would never see them again. He knew it.

Archie stepped into the basket. "I'm going, Mr. Rivets, with you or without you."

Mr. Rivets ticked again as he considered the ultimatum.

"I would be more use to you if you exchanged my Airship Pilot card for my Protector card," he said finally.

Archie hadn't realized how much he needed Mr. Rivets until the machine man had decided to come. Relief washed over him as he disengaged Mr. Rivets' Airship Pilot card from the slot on his back and put it in the trunk of talent cards they kept on the *Hesperus*. There was a lot more to Mr. Rivets' decision than just wanting to protect Archie though, and he knew it. Mr. Rivets had decided not to take orders from Archie's parents anymore, which meant that he thought Mr. and Mrs. Dent were really and truly lost.

Archie would just have to find them again.

Talent cards were big, heavy brass slates with holes punched in them for Tik Tok clockworks to read. Archie had to stand on his toes to tip the card into the slot, but it slid in with a click.

Mr. Rivets straightened and stood tall. "Protector card engaged. I am ready, Master Archie."

For the first time in his life, Archie was glad Mr. Rivets had his Babysitter card in.

Archie pulled his goggles down to keep the rain out of his eyes as they rode the elevator basket down into the swirling gray sky. Below them was a marshy green swamp overgrown with ferns and vines, and shrouded by trees with broad, sloping roots. Tall grasses swayed in the wind as the basket settled on a soft, muddy patch of land. Something nearby sloshed into the water.

Archie pulled the aether pistol out from under his shirt and activated the aggregator.

"Where in Emartha's name did you get that?" Mr. Rivets asked.

"It was in a saltine tin in the galley."

"It looks like your grandfather's. I always wondered where that had got to. Have you any idea how to use it?"

"Well . . . you just point it and shoot it, right?" Archie said.

"Essentially, yes. The gauge on the side tells you how much aether has aggregated. At partial strength, the ray it generates will only stun your target. At full strength, it can kill."

"How do you tell when it goes from stun to kill?" Archie asked. He wiped rain off the round glass window on the gauge so he could read it, but there didn't seem to be any marks for that kind of thing.

"I'm afraid it was something of an art with aether pistols from that era, sir."

Oh, that's just brass, thought Archie. "Which way do you think they went?" he asked over the howling wind. If there had been any footprints to follow, they were washed away by the driving rain.

Lightning flashed in the near distance, bringing daylight to the nightmare around them.

"That way," Mr. Rivets said.

It was slow going. Having a thousand-pound machine man next to you in a fight was a good thing; getting him through a mucky marsh was another. Mr. Rivets sank in past the tops of his riveted spats, and had to use all his clockwork strength just to pull each foot free and take another step. Archie kept winding Mr. Rivets as they went with the key on his back so he would stay at full strength.

The marsh gave way to firmer ground, and the soft earth began to rise away from the water. Not very high, but they were definitely climbing what amounted to a hill in the Everglades.

"It is unusual for any place in this region not to lie at sea level, Master Archie," Mr. Rivets said, noticing the same thing. There could be any number of reasons there was a hill here, but Archie knew Mr. Rivets was thinking the same thing he was—that this was where a Mangleborn had fallen millennia ago, and was buried alive.

Lightning crackled and boomed close enough for Archie to taste the metallic tang of it in the air, and he and Mr. Rivets pushed their way through a last thicket of mangrove trees toward where it had struck. They emerged into a bright, mossy clearing filled with activity. The light came from glowing glass bulbs atop tall metal stands. Archie had never seen anything like them. They blinded him if he looked directly at them, even with his goggles on. Beneath the lights, perhaps a dozen people worked—some Iroquois, some Powhatan, and some Yankees like him, from what Archie could see through the rain. They wore long leather jackets and goggles like his own, doing what they could to stay dry in the driving rain while they ran a big steam-powered engine and worked at metal consoles filled with dials and switches. Thick black rubber hoses ran from the steam engine to the lights, and from the consoles to the giant dripping metal tower that stood high above them—the one Archie had seen peeking up through the clouds from the *Hesperus.*

Lightning struck the top of the tower again, *kazaak*ing down a central shaft into the ground. The blast made Archie's hair stand on end. It wasn't just the lektro-static discharge that gave him goose bumps. He suddenly understood where that lightning was going. He had seen it in his dream. He didn't know how, but he knew this was what he had seen from underground. From inside the prison the Ancient League had built.

"They're feeding it, Mr. Rivets. That lightning. They're funneling it down into the hole where the Swarm Queen is trapped. They're making her stronger so she can get out."

Mr. Rivets pointed. "Master Archie—there."

Archie's parents were the only ones without jackets, goggles, or hats, their good city clothes already drenched through to the skin. They looked like the bookworms they were—two skinny scholars totally out of place outside their observatory. They didn't belong here. Archie hurried after them, Mr. Rivets calling to him to wait. But nobody was paying Archie any attention. They were all more worried about their work. Archie hid behind a console near his parents and peeked around.

"Thomas Alva Edison," they said together. "Thomas Alva Edison. Thomas Alva Edison."

"What is it?" said a man flipping switches and turning dials at one of the consoles. He wore a long black cloak, rubber boots, and rubber gloves.

"Thomas Alva Edison. Thomas Alva Edison," Mr. and Mrs. Dent said.

The man Archie figured was Edison pushed his goggles up into his thin black hair. "What what what? I'm busy here! Who are you?" He turned to one of his workers. "Take over here."

Mr. Rivets clicked up behind Archie. Archie motioned for the machine man to be quiet and peeked out again. Edison was short and pudgy, with a distracted look in his eyes. Behind him stood a tall black machine man unlike anything Archie had ever seen before. It wasn't made to look human like Mr. Rivets was. Where Mr. Rivets had broad shoulders that tapered down to a thinner waist, all of which was molded to look like he was wearing a servant's vest and tie, the black machine man had a long, thin, unadorned body like a test tube, with abnormally long arms and legs. Its face had no human resemblance either. Mr. Rivets' head was shaped like an upside-down bucket with a bowler hat on top, and his wide round glass eyes and brass handlebar mustache gave him a friendly working-class look. The black machine man, on the other hand, had a head like an upside-down bowl, and a blank face whose only features were two glowing red eyes. The thing scared the steam out of Archie.

"We are the Motasalat Hamad," Mrs. Dent said.

"The Overbearing Mother-in-Law?" Edison said. He turned her to see the bug on her neck and frowned. "Why have you come here?"

"Malacar Ahasherat calls," said Mr. Dent.

"We will go through the puzzle traps to her," said Mrs. Dent, still smiling.

Lightning crackled and boomed down the tower, making everyone jump except Edison and Archie's parents.

"We've tried that," Edison said. "Nobody we send in there ever comes out. I'll get the Swarm Queen out my own way. The Archimedes Engine is working. By the full moon she'll be powerful enough to break free."

"We will go through the puzzle traps to her," Mr. Dent said.

"These bloodfoods have the knowledge," said Mrs. Dent.

"One, two, buckle my shoe," said Mr. Dent.

Archie pulled back behind the console. "One, two, buckle my shoe. That's what Mom said to me on the *Hesperus*, when we got the bug out of her long enough for her to talk. It must be the code to getting through the puzzle traps in the prison. Mr. Rivets, they know enough to set the Mangleborn free!"

"Continue your work," Mr. Dent told Edison.

"Malacar Ahasherat grows stronger. You are a drone in the swarm. Together we will free the queen," said Mrs. Dent.

Archie's parents turned and walked away from the tower, toward the darkness.

"I don't need your help," Edison said once Mr. and Mrs. Dent were gone. "*I* will be the one to free the Mangleborn. Me, alone. And once they're free, science will finally advance. *Humanity* will finally advance. *I* will be the one to take us out of the dark age of steam and into the bright, shining Age of Lektricity. The future! *A drone in the swarm*. Ha. I'll be a hero. The world will worship me! Build statues of me! They will sing songs about me!"

Edison went back to the console and pushed one of his assistants out of the way.

"Though I hate to speak ill of any person," Mr. Rivets said, "I do believe that man's mainspring is sprung."

"Forget that," Archie said. "What do we do about Mom and Dad, Mr. Rivets?" Archie's parents were almost beyond the light generated by Edison's machines.

"Edison's work here must be stopped, Master Archie. We

cannot allow him to free this Mangleborn or any other. Nor can we allow him to continue his experiments with lektricity. But the more immediate threat, I'm afraid, is your parents. They know too much. Enough to free the Swarm Queen on their own. They cannot be allowed to enter the complex that imprisons the Mangleborn."

"But how do we stop them?"

Mr. Rivets looked down at the raygun in Archie's hand.

"*Shoot them?*" Archie pulled the aether pistol out of Mr. Rivets' reach. "You want to shoot my parents?"

"My programming forbids me from purposefully causing injury to human beings, Master Archie. I cannot do it."

"Oh. But *I* can. That's what you're saying. You want me to shoot my own parents, Mr. Rivets? That's clinker!"

"Language, Master Archie."

Archie growled in frustration and ran after his parents. They were headed for a rock wall that stood up from the hill in the darkness. *Shoot his mom and dad?* Mr. Rivets must have slipped a cog. Archie couldn't do that! But his parents did seem to know some code to get through the puzzle traps the ancients had left behind to keep anyone from getting to the Mangleborn they'd imprisoned. What if Malacar Ahasherat used his parents to get all the way in and let her out? The Swarm Queen would be loosed on the world without a League of Seven to stop her. Thousands of people would die. Hundreds of thousands. Maybe millions. And then more and more Mangleborn would get free and take over the world. Maybe if he just stunned them. He flicked the raygun's aggregator off and on and watched the dial reset and begin to rise again.

Archie caught up to his parents just outside Edison's circle of light. "Mom! Dad! Please! You can't do this."

His parents kept walking. He checked the aggregator—still not to halfway.

"You have to stop. I know you're in there! You have to fight it. You can't set the Mangleborn free!"

His parents kept walking. The dial kept rising. Archie couldn't be sure what was enough aether to stun them, and how much was enough to kill them.

He raised the aether pistol.

"Stop. Stop, or I'll shoot! I will!"

Archie shrank to the ground as his parents came closer in the dark, and suddenly he was a little boy again, waking to the same nightmare he always had, the one where he was a statue, where he was helpless and couldn't move, and all he could do was cry out for his parents. And there they were, both hurrying to him in the night, his mother to run her fingers through his hair, his father to whisper that it was all just a bad dream. The way they had always come to him, whenever he needed them. The way they loved him.

Archie's parents were on top of him. They weren't going to stop. The raygun needle was right at the halfway mark. All he had to do was point and shoot. It was now or never—

And it was never. Archie lowered the raygun, and his parents walked mindlessly past. He was never going to shoot his parents. He couldn't take the chance that he would hurt them. Mr. Rivets was a Tik Tok. He saw it as a logic problem: shoot two people, save millions. But Archie wasn't a machine man. He was a human being, and those two people were his parents, and he loved them.

Archie turned to see where his parents were, and found Edison's tall black machine man looming behind him, its red eyes blazing in the dark.

"Gaaaa!" Archie cried.

Something glinted in the machine man's hands—a long, curved sword. The Tik Tok slashed it at Archie's chest. *Shink!* Archie fell backward onto the wet ground, dropping the aether pistol. His jacket and shirt were sliced clean through, but the sword must have just missed cutting him. The black Tik Tok loomed over him in the darkness, sword held high to strike again, and there was Mr. Rivets. *Clang!* The two machine men grappled over him like steambots in a Tik Tok prizefight.

"I thought Tik Toks couldn't hurt people!" Archie cried.

"Obviously this machine man was not built to the same exacting standards," said Mr. Rivets.

Archie snatched up the aether pistol and ran to where his parents had been, but they had disappeared. Wherever the entrance was to the Mangleborn's prison, they had gone in.

"Mom! Dad!"

The black Tik Tok rolled backward and kicked Mr. Rivets—all one thousand pounds of him—over its head and off into the darkness. He landed somewhere with a rattling *thump.* Archie aimed the aether pistol at Edison's machine man, closed his eyes, and squeezed the trigger. *Bwaaaaaat.* The Tik Tok dodged the ruby red beam and jumped over Archie, knocking him down again with its sword as it passed. Archie kept his finger on the trigger and swung around. *Bwaaaaaaaaaaaaaaat.* The red beam missed the black Tik Tok again and hit the lightning tower instead. Its metal beams turned red hot and began to melt.

Archie felt his skin prickle. Blue-white lightning flashed in the clouds, and a bolt struck the top of the buckling tower. *Shhhh-kooom.* The tower lektrified, and white-hot tendrils of lightning jumped from the broken tower to the consoles on the ground—

KaBOOM.

Workers and equipment went flying from the clearing in an explosion of fire and sparks. Archie flinched from the blast, his raygun spluttering out. He looked back in time to see the dark silhouette of the killer Tik Tok rise up over him, its sword raised again to strike, and then—*thwack*—Archie's world went black.

5

Archie was dreaming again.

His parents were there with him, wearing the same torn and dirty clothes they had worn in the swamp. They were in a small square room made of brass—floors, ceilings, walls, all of it brass. The strangest thing was that every inch of every surface was covered with what looked like empty picture frames. Archie didn't understand what they were or why they were there.

THOOM. The room shook. *THOOM.* The sound came from below, somewhere beneath his feet. Malacar Ahasherat, the Swarm Queen, trying to get out.

"Three, four, knock on the door," said the smiling Mr. Dent.

"Mom! Dad!" Archie cried, but they couldn't hear him. He reached for his mother, and his hand passed right through her.

Something shook him, and Archie woke with his face pushed into the damp, mossy ground of the Florida swamp. "Mom. Dad," he said, still muddleheaded. He remembered now. He had followed them into the darkness. Threatened to shoot them but couldn't do it. And then the black Tik Tok had come and—

He looked up to see that same frightening machine man toss somebody next to him—a First Nations girl a little older than Archie. She was thin and tall—taller than Archie, at least, but then most kids his age were—with dark brown skin and black hair. A Seminole, Archie guessed. Maybe Muskogee. A thin red scarf was tied around her neck, and over her simple blue dress she wore a brown bandolier with half a dozen little leather pouches on it. Archie tried to help her up, but she batted him away and sat up on her own.

All around them, the clearing looked like a war zone. Fires still burned among the broken consoles, even in the rain. Dark shapes that looked like bodies were scattered here and there, and the twisted, still-glowing hulk of the tower loomed over them like the skeleton of a giant monster. The bright lights were gone—most of them destroyed in the explosion—but a few survivors moved among the wreckage with regular old hurricane lamps.

"Is he awake?" Edison asked. He stood over Archie and the girl, holding a dark-stained handkerchief to his neck. "You're lucky Mr. Shinobi didn't kill you," he told Archie. Edison looked at the black machine man. "It should have. I don't know why it didn't."

Mr. Shinobi stared at Archie with those glowing red eyes, and Archie put a hand to the place on the back of his head where the machine man had knocked him unconscious. It felt like he was going to be lucky: no lump.

"So," Edison said. "The Septemberists send children to do their dirty work now, is it? One of you takes out my tower, while the other one tries to kill me?"

Edison pulled the handkerchief away from his neck, and

Archie could see now it was covered with blood. There was a long, deep cut along the side of Edison's neck. Archie turned to look at the girl. Had *she* done that?

Edison signaled for Mr. Shinobi to take the bandolier off the girl, and he emptied the pockets onto the ground in front of them. It was filled with little brass wind-up animals.

"Toys," Edison said, kicking one. "They send children with toys."

"Why are you trying to free a Mangleborn?" Archie asked. "Where are my parents?"

"Mr. Shinobi," Edison said.

The black machine man's torso spun while its head and legs stood still, its long, inhuman arms snapping around like bullwhips. *Crack!* One of Mr. Shinobi's metal hands knocked Archie onto the ground.

"Who else is with you?" Edison asked.

Archie pulled himself back up, holding the side of his head. He stared at the ground, his ear ringing.

"Where did you come from? How did you know I was here?" Edison asked.

The girl said nothing, and Archie certainly wasn't going to say another word.

"Mr. Shinobi," Edison said.

The black Tik Tok stepped forward again, but a small group of workers with hurricane lamps interrupted them. A short, thick Iroquois man with jet-black hair pulled back into a ponytail spoke for them. "Mr. Edison, sir. We've got the rundown on the damage."

Edison waved Mr. Shinobi still and beckoned the workers forward. There were five of them, all men and boys, three

First Nations and two Yankees. They wore goggles and gloves and coats like Edison, but theirs were sooty and torn and bloody from the explosion.

"Report, Mr. Henhawk," said Edison.

The Iroquois man held the strap of his brass goggles in his hands, turning it nervously. "It's gone, sir. All of it. The lektrical surge destroyed the Archimedes Engine, and the tower did for the rest."

"Seven months," Edison said. He turned to stare at Archie. "Seven months of work, and a rare old artifact, gone. And the full moon less than two weeks away."

There was cold, hard hatred in Edison's face, and Archie shrank back. *This Edison person might actually kill me,* he thought.

"Good riddance, I say," said Henhawk. "Mucking about down here in this gearforsaken swamp. We should go back to Jersey, work on your idea of a moving picture projector, sir. If people could just see the practical uses of lektricity, maybe they wouldn't be so afraid of it."

"Nae, wait." A tousle-haired Yankee boy stepped forward. He couldn't have been more than a couple of years older than Archie. Beneath his long, open leather coat, he wore a white button-down shirt, tall white socks, and, Archie was surprised to see, a blue-and-green plaid skirt. "We could build another Archimedes Engine. I'm sure of it," the boy said.

Henhawk cleared his throat and smiled. "My apprentice, Mr. Edison. Fergus. And no, Fergus, we can't just build another. There was only one of them things in the world, and we barely understood how it worked before it got melted."

"Nae. I had a look inside it back at the lab, and—"

"You looked inside it?" Edison said quietly.

Henhawk glanced protectively at Fergus, but the boy charged ahead.

"Oh, aye. I know you said not to, but I figured if I could just understand how the dingus worked, we could integrate it with our machinery better."

Edison stepped closer. "And did you? Did you understand how it worked?"

"Well, not entirely," the boy said. "But I began to see what those Greek nobs who built it all them years ago were up to. It's really just a series of relays and switches activated by lektrical impulses, innit? With a bit of tinkering I think we could work up a prototype of something like it in just a few months. I drew up plans and gave them to Kano. Mr. Henhawk, I mean."

"He mentioned this possibility to you before?" The question seemed meant for Kano Henhawk, but Edison still stared at Fergus.

"I . . . well, yes," Henhawk said. "But the boy's dreams outweigh his experience, sir. Always have. I was just telling the missus the other day. I said to her—"

"Kill him, Mr. Shinobi," Edison said. He pointed to Henhawk. "That one."

"What?" Fergus said. "Nae—"

Mr. Shinobi whipped a short, curved blade out of a hidden channel in its arm and buried it in the Iroquois engineer's chest. The wide-eyed Henhawk burbled and fell to his knees, and Archie jerked away.

"Kano! Nae, Kano!" Fergus cried. He ran to Henhawk. "Kano, please. Say something. Kano!"

But like Archie's parents in his dream, the Iroquois man didn't respond. He couldn't. Kano Henhawk was already dead.

Fergus' eyes were wild. He scrabbled backward, and the workers parted for him. He stumbled to his feet and ran for the darkness of the swamp, his legs pumping. *Go, go, go,* Archie urged him. But at a word from Edison the black machine man was after Fergus, running faster than Archie had ever seen a Tik Tok move. Mr. Shinobi's short sword flashed again, and Fergus cried out and tumbled to the ground.

While everyone was watching Mr. Shinobi and Fergus, the girl beside Archie picked up one of the little brass toys Edison had dumped out of her bandolier and hid it inside her dress. Her angry eyes told Archie not to say a word.

Mr. Shinobi carried Fergus back. One of the boy's legs ran with blood where the Tik Tok had cut him with its sword, and he was sobbing.

"I regret that Mr. Shinobi had to hurt you, Fergus, but it's all for the best," Edison said. "I've been looking for someone who understands the Archimedes Engine the way I do. You're right—we could, perhaps, build a new one. But not in less than two weeks. Not before the stars are right. If we miss that moment, we won't have another chance to raise the Swarm Queen for another one hundred and fifty-seven years. I don't know about you, but the only way I'm going to be around that long is if Malacar Ahasherat makes me into a god. And she might. But first I'm going to have to turn you into an Archimedes Engine."

6

Edison was crazy. Archie saw that now. Absolutely off his rails.
But Archie didn't know what he could do to stop him. Edison
ordered Mr. Shinobi to put Archie, Fergus, and the girl in a big
wooden crate that some of the equipment had been shipped
in, then set his assistants to getting the lektric generator back
up and running. Mr. Shinobi shut them inside, its red eyes
watching Archie the entire time.

As soon as the Tik Tok slid the bar over the door to lock
them in, the girl began pacing the walls of their small cell.
Archie hurried to Fergus.

"Are you okay?" he asked.

"Oh, aye. I'm brass," Fergus whispered. He winced as he
said it, his first words since Mr. Shinobi had run him down.
His face was ashen, and he was breathing hard.

*Of course he's not okay, steambrain. He just got cut by that
Tik Tok.* Fergus' leg was coated in blood. Archie cupped his
hands under some of the water dripping between the cracks in
the wooden ceiling and poured it on Fergus' leg. Fergus hissed
in pain.

Whack! Archie and Fergus jumped as the girl kicked at the wall of the crate.

"Are you going to help here?" Archie asked her.

"I am helping," she said in a quiet, raspy voice. "I'm trying to get us out of here." *Whack!* She kicked the wooden wall again, but it didn't crack.

Forget her, Archie thought. The cut was behind Fergus' knee, and it was deep. Very deep. Archie pulled his handkerchief out of his jacket pocket and wrapped it around the cut, then took off his belt and looped it around the handkerchief until he could buckle it tight.

"I'm sorry. It's the best I can do," Archie said.

"S'all right, mate. Thanks. Name's Fergus."

"Archie. Archie Dent."

"Who's your friend?" Fergus nodded at the girl. She had given up kicking the walls and was sitting cross-legged on the other side of the box now, muttering something under her breath while she worked a beaded bracelet in her fingers.

"No idea. Your boss said she tried to kill him. Hey, girl. What's your name?" Archie asked.

She ignored them, and Archie let it go.

"Edison said he was going to turn you into some kind of engine," he said to Fergus. "What did he mean?"

"I don't know," said Fergus. "The Archimedes Engine is a machine. An ancient Greek artifact. Edison's agents, they found it in old Aegypt, in Afrika. It's a . . . a math engine, is I guess the best way to put it. It does sums automatically. It computes data."

Archie had no idea what Fergus was talking about.

"It's difficult to explain," Fergus told him. "I'd never seen anything like it until I went to work for Edison."

"Yeah. About you working for Edison," the girl said. So she had been listening after all.

"Look, I had nae idea what he was doing. I still don't. I'm good with machines. I always have been. So my parents back in Carolina, they asked around, and a friend of theirs knew somebody up in Iroquois territory who knew Kano, and . . ." Fergus choked up when he said his friend's name. "It's my fault he's dead. If I hadn't said anything—"

"You didn't kill him," Archie said. "Edison did."

Fergus sniffed and shook his head. "Kano took me on as an apprentice, working for Edison in his lab. He and Mrs. Henhawk were like family to me. I'm just fourteen. I been on the job for three months. I was all excited because Edison was working with lektricity, when nobody else wanted to touch it."

"What's lektricity?" the girl asked.

"The energy in lightning," Fergus said. "Powerful stuff. More efficient than steam, if you know how to handle it, like Edison does. More useful too. Made them bright lights burn. Made the Archimedes Engine work too. Edison was using the Archimedes Engine to regulate the lektricity, send regular charges down into the ground. But I have no idea why."

Archie knew why, and he knew all about lektricity and why nobody wanted to experiment with it. But this was no time to get into all that.

"What are you doing here?" Fergus asked him. "Why did you melt down the tower?"

"Well, I didn't mean to," Archie said. "But it stopped Edison, so that's good. But I didn't even know what he was doing until I followed my parents here. They went down into the puzzle traps."

"What, you mean down into them caves? Underground?" Fergus said. "Oh."

"What?"

"Well, it's just that Edison sent lots of folks in there before we set up the tower, and they never come out."

"My parents are different."

"No, they're not," the girl said. "If they went in that hole, they're dead. You're better off accepting that right now and moving on."

"You don't know what you're talking about," Archie said, his voice rising. "They know how to get through the traps. They're still alive. I've seen them."

"Not for long," the girl said. She fingered her beads again. "You should have shot Edison with that aether pistol instead. At least then you could have killed the man who killed your parents."

"Who *are* you?" Archie demanded. "And if you want him dead so bad, why didn't *you* kill him?"

"I was trying to, until somebody dropped a seven-story tower on me!"

"Oy. Would you two mind holding it down?" Fergus said. "I'm trying to die in peace over here."

The door to the box opened. Mr. Shinobi stood silhouetted against two of the lektric lights Edison's men had salvaged, along with the generator.

Archie and the girl backed away as the black Tik Tok came inside and picked up Fergus. Archie hated himself for his cowardice. Theseus wouldn't have just let an enemy take one of his friends.

"Stop," Archie said. "I won't let you take him." He took a step forward, his fists clenched.

Mr. Shinobi flipped the short sword up out of its arm and held it to Fergus' neck. It still had blood on it from where the Tik Tok had run it through Kano Henhawk. The machine man didn't have to explain—if Archie took another step, it would slit Fergus' neck.

"It won't do it," the girl said. "It won't kill him. Edison needs him. He said so."

Mr. Shinobi pushed the sword into Fergus' neck, just enough to draw blood.

"It will! It will!" Fergus said.

Mr. Shinobi backed out of the crate and closed the door. The girl ran to it and pushed, but the Tik Tok had already dropped the wooden bar that locked them in. She kicked at the door in frustration.

"'I won't let you take him,'" she said, mimicking Archie's voice. "I don't know why it even bothered pulling out its sword. It's not like you could do anything about it."

"So? You couldn't either."

"Could too."

Archie wondered what a teenage girl could possibly do to a walking death machine, but he wasn't in the mood to argue with her anymore. He found a wide space between two of the wooden slats on the crate and watched what was going on outside.

Edison had Mr. Shinobi lay the boy out on a stone altar in the middle of the clearing and bind him to it. Watching through the slats beside him, the girl began to mutter to herself again.

This time Archie could hear what she was saying: "Talisse Fixico, the potter. Chelokee Yoholo, father of Ficka. Hathlun Harjo, the surgeon . . ." It was a string of names and descriptions, but he had no idea what it meant or why she was doing it.

Archie tuned her out as Edison's men brought over a small table with two jars on it. One was empty. The other was filled with a black, tar-like liquid. His men attached rubber hoses to the jars.

"This is the blood of the *Arkiteuthis elektricus*," Edison told Fergus. "The lektric squid. It is found only in the arctic waters north of the Japans, halfway around the world. I acquired it at the same time as I acquired my meka-ninja, Mr. Shinobi. As invaluable as Mr. Shinobi is, ichor of *Arkiteuthis elektricus* is even more rare and expensive. As far as I know, this is the only vial of it in the United Nations, perhaps all of the west."

Fergus cried out as Edison's men—men Fergus had once worked with—slid needles into his arms and attached the rubber hoses to them. One of the men activated a small steam engine that worked as a bellows, and the empty jar began to fill with Fergus' dark-red blood. The other jar, the one filled with the thick black liquid, started to lower.

Edison was replacing Fergus' blood with the blood of a lektric squid.

Two more workers brought giant metal gloves with wires attached to the fingertips. Edison held up his arms like a surgeon, and the workers slid the gloves on.

"I had hoped not to have to do this, Fergus," Edison said. "I'm not really sure it will work. The last person who volunteered for the transfusion went mad and tore her own skin off, and this is all the ichor I have left. But now that the Archimedes

Engine is destroyed, I need something to replace it. I'm afraid I must take the chance." He nodded to his assistants, and they fired up another generator, this one humming with an energy different from steam power. Tiny arcs of lektricity crackled along the wires to the oversized gauntlets Edison wore on his hands.

"*Icthy rimick, ab ru-mous gor'mary,*" Edison chanted. "Malacar Ahasherat, Queen of the Swarm, I call on your power. Create in this human vessel the means to open your prison! *Icthy rimick, ab ru-mous gor'mary. Icthy rimick, ab ru-mous gor'mary. Icthy rimick, ab ru-mous gor'mary.*"

A ghostly green energy collected around Edison's lektric gloves, burning like an ethereal flame in the twilight. He aimed them at the stone altar, and the green flames engulfed Fergus. They didn't seem to burn him, not like real fire would, but they were doing *something*. As the black blood filled Fergus' veins, the green energy lifted him, his bonds the only thing keeping him from rising up off the slab.

"Four and twenty blackbirds, baked in a pie," Edison cried, his eyes alight with the roaring green flame. "And when the pie was opened, the birds began to sing!"

"He's crazy," Archie said. "We've got to get out of here. Kick the wood."

"I tried that," said the girl.

Archie jabbed at the wall with his toe. *Crack!* His foot punched through.

"I did it!"

"Must have been a weak spot," the girl said. Archie bent down to try and pry the broken wood away, but the girl stopped him. "Wait," she said. "Mr. Lion, I need you."

The little brass toy she had hidden away burst from a pocket in her dress, fluttering in the air between them. It was a little wind-up lion with wings. The wings beat madly, almost comically, making the toy wobble in the air as it hovered, like a bumblebee. Archie gaped at it. He'd never in his life seen clockworks so small. So advanced. There was nothing so incredible in even the best Tik Tok shops in Philadelphia, but a Tik Tok it was. He could even see the little key sticking up out of its back, turning slowly as its mainspring wound down.

The lion clicked and chattered at the girl with little *roar-roar-roar* sounds. "Not now, Mr. Lion," the girl said. "Go find the others. Raise the bar so I can get out. And bring my bandolier."

The little lion flitted off through the hole Archie had kicked in the wall.

In a few moments Archie heard the scrape of wood on wood—the bar to their crate lifting away. The door creaked open, and five little brass toys, all of them different animals with wings, flew inside. One of them, a little gorilla, carried the girl's bandolier.

"What *are* they?" Archie asked. "They're amazing!"

The girl slipped the bandolier on and whistled, and the little toys hid themselves in the leather pockets.

"Good-bye," the girl said.

"Wait! We have to save that boy, Fergus."

"You save him," the girl said. She drew a dagger from a hidden place in her dress. "I'm going to kill Edison."

7

The girl took off across the dimming glade, her skirts flying. Archie thought about calling her back, but it was too late. The black Tik Tok had already seen her. It pulled a long, two-handed sword from somewhere in its back and sliced at her, but the girl ducked and parried, her dagger clanging off the thing's body.

Archie blinked. Maybe the girl *could* do something to the walking death machine.

Speaking of Tik Toks, where was Mr. Rivets? Archie looked around for him. Mr. Shinobi had thrown the Dents' machine man off into the darkness. Archie remembered the sickening crunch of clockworks. Was Mr. Rivets broken? There was no other reason he would leave Archie behind.

Archie didn't have any more time to think about it. Fergus' body was straining at its bonds, the green flame lifting him and crackling all around him. The girl, amazingly, was keeping Mr. Shinobi busy, and the rest of Edison's assistants had run scared.

It was just Archie and Edison now.

This was what he had always wanted, wasn't it? To be a hero? The Theseus of his own League of Seven? It made him sure he should do something, but it didn't make him any less scared.

Archie waited until Mr. Shinobi's back was turned, then sneaked around the small circle of light to the other side of the stone altar. Edison's eyes were wide with whatever he was seeing through his lektro-magic. He didn't see Archie at all.

"Icthy rimick, ab ru-mous gor'mary," Edison chanted. His lektric gauntlets crackled with sparks. Fergus' body fought against his bindings, but he wasn't awake. Archie didn't know if he was dead or just unconscious, but it didn't matter. He had to get him out of there.

Archie put a hand out to test the flames. They weren't hot but cold, like plunging his hand into an icy lake. Archie took a deep breath and pushed his hands into the green flames.

Immediately Archie was somewhere else, like in his dreams. This time he was in a great swamp like the Florida Everglades. But this wasn't any Florida Archie knew. Black wires dangling from tilting wooden poles sparked with lektricity. Crumbling skyscrapers—buildings taller than any in New Rome or Standing Peachtree—stood like shattered stumps, their top halves lying beside them in piles of shattered glass and twisted steel. Fires smoldered in their hulks, dark-orange glows that lit the smoke-filled sky like a dozen funeral pyres. In the water all around him, Archie saw the bloated bodies of dead people.

A storm swirled overhead. A bolt of lightning split the air—*krakoom!*—and Archie saw a giant sitting atop a suspension bridge like it was a throne. At first glance she looked human, a giant so big her head touched the clouds. Then Archie saw the spiny bones that stuck through the skin of her arms and legs, the locust wings tucked away on her back. She sat like a mantis, long arms bent, hands held in front of her, serenaded by the rising and falling cicada call of insects and human screams.

Malacar Ahasherat. The Swarm Queen.

The Mangleborn turned her head slowly in Archie's direction, like she knew he was there. Her face was human, but her eyes were big, black, and shiny, like a fly's.

JANDAL A HAAD, she said without moving her mouth, the words thundering in Archie's mind.

Archie pulled his hands out of the fire and reeled. He was panting, sweating, even though his hands and arms felt like ice. He stared at them as though they didn't belong to him.

He shook his head, trying to clear it. Those words . . .

Lektricity surged into Edison's gauntlets, and the green flames surrounding Fergus burned brighter. The girl was saying names again as she fought the Tik Tok, shouting them now: "Claiborne Lowe, twelve times a grandfather. Pompey Yoholo, seventh son of a seventh son. Woxe Holatha, the banker!" She was still holding her own against the Tik Tok, but she was slowing.

Archie had to get Fergus out of there, and he had to do it now.

He closed his eyes and plunged his hands back into the flame. The image of the Swarm Queen on her throne came again, but he pushed it away. Screamed at it. Held up an imaginary shield to keep him from staring into the Gorgon's eyes. His real eyes still squeezed shut in the real world, he groped for Fergus. Untied his ropes. Yanked his floating body free.

The green flame *whooshed* and went out like a gas lamp, and Archie and Fergus hit the ground. Edison staggered back, his eyes still elsewhere, the lektric gauntlets crackling angrily. With no one there to turn off the generator and set him free, he was trapped in his own machine.

Archie shook off the shivering terror of the Mangleborn and grabbed Fergus, dragging him away. Something black and snakelike crawled across Fergus' skin and Archie jumped back, but it wasn't something *on* Fergus' skin, it was something *in* it. A shifting, changing labyrinth of black lines like moving tattoos.

Fergus groaned as the black tattoos drew and redrew themselves on his skin, but at least that meant he was alive. Archie grabbed him again and dragged him into the darkness beyond the lektric lights. But then what? How far could Archie run into the swamp at night, dragging Fergus behind him? And where would he go? The *Hesperus* was anchored out there somewhere, but he didn't even remember which way he'd come into the clearing.

Whoom. A bright carbide light flooded the dark glade from above. It moved from Mr. Shinobi and the girl, still locked in battle, to Edison crawling for the generator, his big wire-covered gauntlets still sparking with lektricity, and then finally swept over to where Archie and Fergus lay in the grass. Archie put a hand up to shield his eyes from the light, and something smacked him in the head.

The elevator basket!

That's where Mr. Rivets had gone—to fetch the family airship! Archie hefted Fergus inside and climbed in after him, grabbing the talking horn that led to the ship above.

"Mr. Rivets! You came back!" Archie said.

"But of course, Master Archie. My only regret is that I took so long. Without my Airship Pilot card in, it took quite some guessing."

Archie felt the basket begin to rise. "No! No! Mr. Rivets, not yet," he called into the talking horn. "We have to rescue that girl. Swing us around!"

She was still fighting, but she had cuts on her arms and legs and her dress was torn and ragged. Her little brass toys fluttered around the Tik Tok, distracting it. One of the animals, the gorilla, had yanked open a panel on the machine man's back and was banging on the clockwork gears inside.

"Get on!" Archie called to her. "Let's go!"

The girl looked at Edison lying helpless on the ground. The elevator basket swung closer. The meka-ninja lunged at her and she ducked, but its sword grazed her neck. She put a hand to the cut and came away with blood. She stood staring at it. She had a dozen cuts all over her, but this one left her frozen.

Mr. Shinobi leaped at her just as the elevator basket hit it. *Thwack!* The meka-ninja went flying off into the darkness.

Archie threw the door to the basket open. "Get in!"

The girl came to life enough to stagger into the elevator basket. She collapsed next to Fergus, her clockwork animals fluttering around her worriedly, and Archie screamed for Mr. Rivets to take them up. The black machine man jumped out of the shadows, its sword slashing a cut in the floor of the elevator basket as it leaped at them, but they were already out of reach. Archie watched over the side as the *Hesperus* lifted away into the dark Florida sky, Edison and his meka-ninja staring after them

Fergus lay on the folded-out medical bay in the *Hesperus*. Mr. Rivets, his Surgeon talent card engaged, was just finishing the delicate work of stitching together the nasty gash at the back of Fergus' leg. Archie watched with a slightly queasy interest. He'd never in his life had a broken bone, or even a cut that needed stitches. The Seminole girl sat on the other side of the small round cabin with her back to them, winding her clockwork animals. Out the airship's front window, the gibbous moon glowed bloodred in the sky, just as it had ever since the Darkness had fallen on the Old World, long before any of them were born.

"If you would be so kind as to hand me those bandages, Master Archie?" Mr. Rivets said.

Archie obliged. "Why do you think he's wearing a dress, Mr. Rivets?"

"Kilt," Fergus murmured. He sat up with a start. "Kano!"

"He's dead," the girl said in her curt, raspy voice.

"Aye, I remember now," Fergus said. He buried his head in his hands, and Archie frowned at the girl's callousness.

"What's happened? How did we get here?" Fergus asked.

"Last thing I remember, that infernal Tik Tok was tying me down to a stone table. No offense," he said to Mr. Rivets.

Mr. Rivets straightened. "None taken, sir. That abomination is a discredit to the service."

Archie told him about the lektric gauntlet and the green fire, and how he'd pulled Fergus out.

"I owe you then, mate," Fergus said. "You saved my life. Not that it's worth saving." Fergus put a hand to the back of his leg and pulled away smarting. "I can't lift it."

"I've closed the wound as best I can, sir, but I'm afraid the tendons have been cut. There is nothing that can be done to repair them," Mr. Rivets told him.

"Will I—will I be able to walk?"

"No, sir. I'm afraid not. Not without some means of assistance."

Fergus looked devastated, and Archie felt devastated for him. He couldn't imagine what it would be like to lose the use of a leg. To know he would never walk normally again. Just the idea of it frightened him.

Fergus choked back tears. "I thank you for what you've done . . . Mr. Rivets, is it? Much appreciated."

Mr. Rivets touched a hand to his brass hat. "All part of the service, Master Fergus."

"There's more," Archie said, though he was loath to. "I don't know why he was doing it to you, but Edison—"

Fergus' skin flashed again with the black lines Archie had seen on him in the glade, and Fergus cried out. "Crivens! What was that?"

"That's what I was trying to tell you," Archie said. "I think it's from the lektric squid blood."

Fergus looked ashen, remembering what Edison had told him. "That stuff—that stuff's *inside* me now?"

The black lines shifted and rearranged themselves. Fergus held his arms away from himself, staring, then pulled his shirt up to see the rest of his body. "Is it all over me? Is it on my face too?"

"Yeah," Archie said. "What I don't understand is how doing that to you was going to help Edison free a Mangleborn."

"That word," the girl said. "You used it before, like you knew what Edison was doing. What does it mean?"

"The Mangleborn? Oh." Archie wasn't sure he should tell them. "They're—*twisted pistons!* Did that Tik Tok do that to your neck?"

The girl had a long ugly scar on her neck, stretching almost ear to ear. She turned away quickly, pulling the scarf back up to cover it. Archie closed his eyes and cursed himself. *Of course* the Tik Tok hadn't done that. You didn't get a scar like that in a couple of hours. Whatever had happened, *whenever* it had happened, it must have been as awful as the cut on the back of Fergus' leg. And the mental scars must have been worse. That nick Mr. Shinobi had given her back in the swamp, when she'd frozen—it must have reminded her of that long-ago trauma. Just like Archie's clacking outburst.

"Smooth, mate," Fergus told him.

"Edison," the girl said when her scarf was back in place, bringing Archie back to the matter at hand. "The Mangleborn."

Archie cleared his throat. He looked to Mr. Rivets for guidance, but the machine man said nothing. Archie hated it when adults kept secrets from him, so he decided to tell them the truth.

"The Mangleborn are ancient, giant monsters imprisoned underground who want to get free and rule the world."

Fergus laughed out loud until the pain in his leg made him suck wind and stop. "Wait a mo'," he said when the pain subsided. "How come I'm the only one laughing here?"

Archie wasn't laughing because he knew the Mangleborn were real. If he hadn't believed the drawings in his parents' old books, he certainly believed now, after his dream of the Swarm Queen sitting in the burned-out ruins of a city.

For whatever reason, the girl wasn't laughing either. She looked lost in thought.

"The Mangleborn are real," Archie said. "They've been around since the dawn of time, before humans. They're . . . they're not right. Like things from nightmares, made real. That's why the ancients called them 'Mangleborn.' They look wrong, like they've been through a mangle. Scrambled. Parts that don't belong together. One has skin like a frog and a tongue as long as a freight train. Another has horns like a bull and cloven feet," he said. "And they feed on lektricity. That's what Edison was doing with that lightning tower. He was trying to raise Malacar Ahasherat, the Swarm Queen."

"You're not joking," Fergus said.

Archie shook his head.

"And lektricity—you're telling me in the history of the world nobody's just stumbled onto it until now. Experimented with it. Found a way to use it."

"Quite the opposite," Mr. Rivets said. "The Greeks and Romans knew the secrets of lektricity well. As did the Atlanteans before them."

"The Atlanteans!" Fergus cried. "From Atlantis. The city

that sank beneath the Atlantis Ocean in the stories, you mean. This gets better and better."

"Why do you think Ancient Rome fell?" Archie asked.

"Overexpansion into the Americas, economic inflation, reliance on barbarian mercenaries in the Roman Legion, and the rise of the Germanic tribes in the Old World," the girl said.

The boys turned to stare at her.

"Well that's what I heard," said the girl.

"It—no," Archie said. "I mean, the real reason Rome fell was because they built lektric generators and covered the world with lektricity and woke the Mangleborn again."

"And you know all this pretend history how?" Fergus asked.

Archie had already told them too much—but after what they'd been through, he thought they deserved to know. He glanced at Mr. Rivets, who apparently agreed.

"Master Archie and his parents are a part of a secret society that has fought the Mangleborn for generations," Mr. Rivets said. "They have also worked in secret to keep the world from rediscovering the practical uses of lektricity."

"Worked to keep people from . . ." Fergus' eyes went wide. "There was a fire. At Edison's lab. Last month. We were just about to create a battery—a chemical storage jar for lektricity. But the lab burned down. We lost everything. Did your secret society do that?"

"Undoubtedly," said Mr. Rivets. "Men like Edison, once identified, are watched. Their work suppressed."

"But you don't know for a fact they did it?" the girl said.

"The Society is, as I said, miss, a secret. Only a few of its members know all its agents; most know only two or three others besides themselves. Beyond Mr. and Mrs. Dent and the governing council in New Rome, I myself am aware of only two active Septemberists."

"Septemberists?" Fergus asked.

"Yes, sir. That is what members of the group call themselves."

"That's why we went down there," Archie said. "My parents are researchers for the Septemberists. They know all about the Mangleborn from old books, and they watch the stars for signs that the Mangleborn are getting stronger. Like this one." He got quiet as he thought about his parents at Septemberist headquarters, those awful bugs on their necks. "They just didn't know how strong."

"Sorry, White," Fergus said. "Giant monsters trapped in the earth is a tough sell."

"'White'?" Archie said.

"No offense, mate," Fergus said. "But don't tell me it's the first time you've heard it. Not with that snowball on your head. Guess I didn't notice it before in the dark."

Archie didn't understand.

"Yes, Master Archie," Mr. Rivets said. "I neglected to mention it after your rescue as there were more pressing matters to attend to with Master Fergus, but . . . perhaps it's best you see for yourself."

Mr. Rivets pointed to a polished metal mirror on the cabin wall. Archie went closer to look.

"My hair—my hair is white!" Archie cried.

"I'm afraid I'm at a loss to explain it, sir," said Mr. Rivets.

"It happened after you put your hands in that green flame," the girl said. "It was brown before. White after."

Archie ran his fingers through his hair. It was white as steam. All of it. White to the skin. His eyebrows too. Mr. Rivets might not have understood, but Archie did. Seeing the Mangleborn, *hearing* it inside his head had done this to him. It had touched his mind. *Jandal a Haad.* He remembered the words now. The same words the Septemberist council had spoken to him. He had no idea what they meant, but they scared him to the bone.

"We have to go back," said the girl.

"What?" Archie asked. He was still staring at his white hair and thinking about the Mangleborn's terrible voice flooding his thoughts. Assaulting him.

"And do what?" Fergus asked.

"Kill Edison," she said. "Kill this monster."

Archie tore his eyes away from his white hair. "You can't kill the Mangleborn, or else somebody would have done it. That's why they're in prisons."

"Then just Edison," the girl said. "I need to finish what I started."

"Why? What did Edison do to you?" Archie thought it might be the scar, but when would Edison have cut her? And why? But the girl didn't say. She just sat there with her arms crossed, staring at him.

"This is a job for the Septemberists," Archie told her. "There's one person we know in New Rome who's a member of the Society. We'll let him know my parents are still alive, and what Edison's been doing."

The girl gave Archie a tired look. Fergus coughed and looked away.

"They *are* alive," Archie told them. "I've *seen* them. I know."

"If we're going back to New Rome, I want to go to Jersey first," Fergus said. "I need to see Kano's wife, Joanne. Tell her what happened."

"If you're not going back to Florida, I'll go back alone," the girl said.

"We don't have time for that," Archie told Fergus. "And there's no sense going back alone when you'll just get killed," he told the girl.

She stood suddenly. "There's a wasp on the ceiling."

Archie and Fergus looked up. A solitary hornet crawled up near the gaslight chandelier.

"So what?" Archie said.

The girl glared at them. "Didn't you just say Edison was trying to raise something called 'the Swarm Queen'?"

"It's just one wasp," Archie said, and then he froze. He had thought the front windshield was black because it was dark outside, but now he could see that wasn't it at all.

The *Hesperus* was covered with wasps.

9

The wasp on the ceiling was joined by another two, then another five. Soon the airship cabin was buzzing with them.

"The wasps are coming in through the air circulation system!" Archie cried.

"Actually, sir, they appear to be *Vespa crabro*," Mr. Rivets said, examining one that was trying to sting his brass hand. "Hornets, not wasps."

Fergus leaned back on the medical bay bed, swatting the hornets away from him. "I don't care what they are. They've got stingers and I can't run. Help!"

"There's nowhere to run *to*," the girl said. She batted hornets away as more came in through the air ducts. Soon they would be covered in the things. "Circus, showtime!" she said.

From the pouches in her bandolier burst her five winged wind-up animals—a lion, gorilla, giraffe, elephant, and zebra. The girl pointed at Fergus. "Keep the wasps off him!"

"Hornets, miss," Mr. Rivets corrected her.

The flying animals swooped into action, biting, clawing, stomping, and kicking the insects around Fergus. He leaned back on his elbows and watched them work with the wide-eyed appreciation of a tinker, all thoughts of mortal peril suddenly gone.

Archie wanted some help too. The hornets were all over him. He pulled a blanket from one of the sleeping hammocks and swung it at them, but there were too many.

The girl pulled a fire extinguisher off the wall and aimed it at him. "Duck," she said.

Archie hit the deck just as the fire extinguisher's chemical bath soaked the insects above him. They fell all around him, writhing and dying on the floor.

The chemical bath was a good idea, but it couldn't take care of all of them. Archie's eyes searched the cabin. There had to be something else they could use to fight the swarm! The only time he'd ever killed wasps back home was in the late fall, when it got so cold they stopped flying and slowed down long enough so he could smack them with a shoe. . . .

"Cold air. Mr. Rivets! We need to go higher! Take the *Hesperus* higher!"

"If you would just insert my Airship Pilot card, Master Archie, I shall endeavor to do so."

Archie muttered a few words his parents would ground him for and scrambled for the talent card chest across the cabin. The girl was still pumping juice out of the extinguisher, but more wasps were coming in by the minute. Archie disengaged Mr. Rivets' Surgeon card, swatted a swooping hornet with it, and quickly replaced it with an Airship Pilot card from the case. The machine man immediately strode to the steering console, brushed some wet, wriggling hornets out of his way, and brought the airship under control.

"The extinguisher's running out!" cried the girl.

"I got an idea—I got an idea!" Fergus said. Wincing in pain, he hopped across the cabin, the girl's flying circus protecting him the whole way. Fergus slammed painfully into the wall and pulled away a brass panel, revealing a network of ducts and fittings and tubes.

Archie swatted at more hornets. "What are you doing?"

"I'm just . . . rerouting . . . a couple of things," Fergus said. He grunted as he worked, trying to keep himself balanced against the wall on his one good leg. Archie ducked to keep away from the swarm and ran to Fergus. The tinker was taller than Archie, just like everybody else, but Archie was still able to hold him up. Fergus worked faster, disconnecting one hose and switching it out with another.

"There!" he said.

Smoke poured out of the ventilation shafts.

"You broke it!" Archie said, already starting to cough.

"No. I've seen beekeepers do this back home in the Carolina mountains. Smoke calms bees."

"Hornets, sir," Mr. Rivets said.

Hornets, wasps, bees—it didn't matter what they were. The smoke was working. The insects stopped attacking and hovered around Mr. Rivets, away from the smoky vents. The only problem was that Fergus was smoking himself and Archie and the girl out too.

"We can't breathe this smoke for too much longer," Archie said, coughing. He looked out the front window and saw the familiar bloodred moon in the night sky. The *Hesperus* was up high enough that the rest of the hornets had fallen away!

Archie ran to a porthole and wrenched it open. The smoke and the hornets were sucked outside, replaced with the thin, frigid air of the upper atmosphere. The girl ran to Fergus and helped hold him up while he switched the pipes back to normal, and when the last of the smoke was gone Archie closed the porthole, slamming it shut so hard the glass cracked.

"We did it," Archie said. He collapsed to the floor like a switched-off machine man, and Fergus and the girl flopped down beside him, absolutely exhausted.

"Smart thinking on the fire extinguisher," Archie told the girl.

"Taking us up where it's cold was a brass notion," Fergus told Archie.

"Pumping smoke in the cabin is what saved us," the girl told Fergus.

"Those little clockwork gizmos of yours saved *me*," Fergus said.

The girl whistled, and her circus flew back to their places in her bandolier.

"Shall I bring us down, Master Archie?" Mr. Rivets asked.

"No. Keep us up here for a while, just in case those wasps come after us again."

"Hornets, sir."

"How far d'ya think we'll have to go till that Swarm Queen can't send insects after us no more?" Fergus asked.

"I do not know, sir. The Swarm Queen's influence over the phylum *Arthropoda* means that as she gains strength, her mastery over insects everywhere will only become stronger."

"Clinker," Fergus muttered.

"I shall vent some heat in from the engines for you," Mr. Rivets told them. "But at this altitude the cabin will still tend to be cold."

"Whatever you can do, Mr. Rivets. Thank you," said Archie.

"Might I also inquire, sir, where it is we're going? At present, we are holding station over Port Hibernum."

Archie looked at the two other people shivering on the floor with him. Apart, they were weak, wounded, and alone. Together, they had stopped a mad scientist, survived a killer Tik Tok, and overcome a swarm of hornets. They were *good* together.

"I think we should go to New Rome," Archie said. "All of us. Together."

"I'm in," Fergus said. "As long as we stop in Jersey first. I have to tell Mrs. Henhawk her husband is dead."

Archie nodded. "What about you?" he asked the girl.

She stared at the floor for what seemed like an eternity, the only sound in the cabin the soft tick of Mr. Rivets' clockworks and the low drone of the *Hesperus'* twin DaVinci aeroprop engines.

"All right," she said at last. "As long as we come back. With rayguns. Big ones."

"We'll come back with an army," Archie told her. "Mr. Rivets—New Rome. Best possible speed."

"Yes, sir."

Archie and the girl pulled each other up off the floor, then helped Fergus to stand.

"Hachi," the girl said.

"What?—I don't—Is that a Seminole word?" Archie asked.

"It's my name," said the girl. She climbed into one of the hammocks and turned to the wall to go to sleep.

"Is it me, or did we just make a new friend?" Fergus stage-whispered.

"Blow it out your blastpipe," said Hachi from under her blanket.

Fergus winked at Archie, and they climbed into their hammocks to sleep.

Archie woke with a yelp. He was sweaty under his blanket despite the chill in the air.

"Master Archie?" Mr. Rivets asked from the steering console. "Is everything all right?"

"I just—I just had another dream about my parents." He remembered bits and pieces of it—his parents, still controlled by those bugs in their necks, were in another brass room. A different brass room than before, without picture frames all over the walls.

Across the cabin, the dark shape of Fergus stirred in his hammock. "Archie?" he asked.

"I'm sorry. I didn't mean to wake you."

"Nae. It was—I had a dream. About these two people, a man and a woman. They had these . . . these insect things in the backs of their necks."

Archie sat up. "Were they turning big knobs with letters on them?"

"Aye! And there were clockworks spinning behind them."

Archie got goose bumps. He remembered the clockworks now. "And the floor. The floor was . . . moving somehow."

"Aye! And there was this noise. A great booming sound from below."

"Malacar Ahasherat. The Mangleborn. She's trying to get free. You saw my parents in the puzzle traps that keep people from getting to her. We just had the same dream! My parents are still alive. I told you. We have to get help. We have to rescue them!"

"But how is it possible for us to have the same dream?" Fergus asked.

"It's the Mangleborn. We must share some kind of connection with it."

"That green fire," Fergus said. "That flame Edison used on me. It came from that insect woman. I remember now. I could see her. A great big woman with bug eyes and grasshopper wings."

"Yes! And bony arms and legs, like a mantis. I saw her when I reached in to grab you. Did she talk to you too?"

"Talk to me? Nae," Fergus said. "She just sat there on that bridge like a throne, lording over a wasteland."

Archie shrank back into his hammock. He was sure the Mangleborn had spoken. She had turned to look at him, said "Jandal a Haad" directly to him. But why hadn't Fergus heard it too? And if Fergus got his connection to the Mangleborn from the ritual on the stone altar, why had Archie dreamed of his parents *before* that, when Mr. Shinobi knocked him out? And how had he seen the big stone well and all the bugs underground before they'd even flown all the way to Florida?

"You're both crazy," Hachi said, making Archie jump. He hadn't realized she was awake too. "Go back to sleep," she told them. "We'll be in Jersey by morning."

Archie turned over in his hammock and pulled his blanket up, wondering exactly how he could be connected to a Mangleborn buried in a swamp in Florida when he'd never set foot there before in his entire life.

10

The Jersey territory just beyond the sprawling metropolis of New Rome kept its Yankee name after the Darkness fell, but little else. The countryside was dotted not with Yankee towns but First Nations villages: clusters of Iroquois longhouses, fields, and factories as far as the eye could see. Edison had set up his laboratory outside one of these villages, and it was near there that Fergus had lived with Kanokareh and Joanne Henhawk, his family away from home.

Mrs. Henhawk was a square-shouldered woman with light-brown skin and a beak-like nose to match her name. She met Archie, Hachi, Fergus, and Mr. Rivets at the door of her longhouse and gave Fergus a welcoming hug. After the introductions were made Mrs. Henhawk ushered them inside, fussing over Fergus' bandaged leg and the makeshift crutch he'd cobbled together from spare parts on the *Hesperus*.

"And your skin! What is this? Did you get yourself tattooed on that trip? Your mother will kill me for it, and I'll kill Kano in return! But where is he?"

Archie wanted to be anywhere else in the world right then, but he didn't know where else to go.

"Mrs. Henhawk—" Fergus said.

"'Mrs. Henhawk'?" she said. "I haven't been 'Mrs. Henhawk' since the day you got here. It's Joanne," she told Archie and Hachi. She led them down the narrow central hallway of the longhouse, toward the stone fireplace that rose up through the roof in the middle of the building.

Archie grabbed Hachi by the arm and held her back. She flinched and twisted, her fist raised like she might hit him.

"What?" said Hachi.

"Let Fergus do the talking on this one, all right?" Archie whispered.

Hachi looked like she might argue, then relented and nodded.

Along the way to the kitchen they passed small rooms to either side: bedrooms, and living rooms, and pantries filled with food and stores. In one of the compartments was a woven mat with blocks and toys on it.

Hachi stopped. "You have a child?"

"Yes. And there she is!" Mrs. Henhawk said in a happy voice meant for her toddler. "There's my Della!"

The baby sat in a high chair at the end of a long wooden table in the kitchen, making an absolute mess of her oatmeal.

"Fungus!" she squealed when she saw Fergus. She kicked her legs in excitement. "Fungus Fungus Fungus!"

"Hey Della Bella," Fergus said quietly, though he couldn't help but smile at her.

Hachi was all scowl. She glared at Fergus like he should have told them the Henhawks had a baby daughter, though Archie couldn't understand why.

"Fergus? Fergus, what is it, hon?" Mrs. Henhawk said, finally gathering that something was wrong.

"Joanne—Mrs. Henhawk. There's . . . something . . . something's happened," he said.

"Who wants to play, hmm?" Hachi said brightly, making Archie jump. He stared at her as she lifted Della out of her high chair and nestled her onto her hip. "Oh! What a big girl you are, Della! Will you show me your toys?"

Hachi nodded for Archie to come with her.

"Go, Master Archie," Mr. Rivets said. "I shall stay with Master Fergus and help explain."

Archie gave Fergus a last sympathetic glance and hurried after Hachi.

"Why take the baby away?" Archie whispered as they walked back down the corridor. "She's just a toddler. She can't understand anything."

"She'll understand," Hachi said. "She'll know when her mother cries."

Behind them, they heard Mrs. Henhawk cry out once, loudly, followed by a low sob. Archie stared back down the corridor but couldn't see into the kitchen.

Hachi set Della onto her playmat and sat down beside her. Straightaway Della tried to crawl off toward the front door.

"Whoa! A little escape artist already, I see," Hachi said. "That's good." Her voice was raspy as always, but she injected a light happiness into it that Archie knew was all for the baby's benefit. Hachi snatched Della up and put her back on the mat, but Della just took off again. This time Archie picked the baby up, holding her out away from himself a little nervously as he returned her to the playmat.

"She's not a stick of dynamite," Hachi told him.

Looking around at the way toys were scattered all over the play area, Archie thought maybe she was.

"I see we'll have to do something else to keep you here," Hachi told Della. "And I know just the thing. Circus, showtime."

Hachi's little menagerie burst out of their compartments on her bandolier and hovered in the air. Della was immediately mesmerized, and so was Archie. He sat down beside Della, and to his surprise the toddler crawled into his lap.

"Don't be afraid," Hachi told her. "Circus, parade!"

The little brass animals landed, stilling their wings and tucking them back along their bodies. The lion set himself up first, and all the others fell into line behind him: the zebra, the elephant, the gorilla, and finally the lanky giraffe. When they were all in a line, a music-box circus tune began to play from them—not the same notes from each animal, but different parts of the tune played in unison to form one song. Together they marched in a silly high-step around Archie. Little Della clapped and laughed. When the last of them disappeared behind Archie's back, Della twisted so far out of his lap to watch that he had to catch her to stop her from falling.

The clockwork animals marched around to the front, but the giraffe lagged behind with its slow, loping stride. Hachi nudged its bottom and it trotted back into place, making Della giggle. The music came to a triumphant if tinny end, and the animals bowed. Della clapped again, and Archie couldn't help but join in.

"Do you know what these animals are? Have you seen them in books, Della? My father took me to a circus once, when I was very little, and afterward he made these for me.

Would you like to know their names?" Hachi asked. "This is Mr. Lion. He is very brave."

The little lion made his little clockwork *roar-roar-roar* sound again, trying to look so fierce it was cute.

"This is Zee. She is a zebra. She is very fast, and thinks she is very pretty."

Zee pranced and preened, throwing her head back like a real horse.

"Horsie!" Della said.

"Next is Tusker." Hachi made her voice deep and low. "Tusker is an elephant. Boo-hoo-boo-boom. He is big and strong."

Tusker lifted the zebra with his trunk and set her back in line, then stood on his hind legs and trumpeted.

"Jo-Jo the gorilla. He is stubborn, but he is very good at climbing things and using his hands."

The wind-up gorilla crossed his arms and stood in line without doing anything special. Hachi flicked him on the bottom and he scooted out of the line, turned, and pounded his chest at her.

"Yes, Jo-Jo. Very impressive. And last but not least is Freckles, the giraffe. Don't let her clumsiness fool you; she is very sneaky."

Freckles bowed her long neck in a graceful curtsy, then tripped over her own long legs trying to stand back up. Della giggled again.

Mrs. Henhawk, Fergus, and Mr. Rivets came and found them. Mrs. Henhawk's face was streaked with tears and her eyes were red, but she had a smile for her daughter as she picked her up and hugged her. Della kept watching the wind-up animals, perhaps waiting for them to sing and dance again, but Hachi whistled them back to their places and stood.

"Mrs. Henhawk said I could use Kano's workshop, fix up something for my knee," Fergus said. He sniffed like he'd been crying too. Mr. Rivets helped him walk to the back of the longhouse, where Mr. Henhawk had a private work space of his own. His workbench was neat and tidy, with wrenches and screwdrivers and saws and hammers hung on pegs. Barrels of metal, wood, and wire scrap were arranged along one wall, with smaller buckets of nails and screws along another. Fergus limped over to the barrels and began to fish out thin strips of copper and brass.

"If I can assist in any way, Master Fergus, please say so," Mr. Rivets told him.

Fergus pulled a few tools from their pegs, and added a few of his own—tiny screwdrivers and wrenches from a purselike bag on his belt. Within minutes he had clamped, bent, and shaped the metal strips into a small, hinged cage.

"Ratchet piston? Do you see a ratchet piston anywhere?" Fergus asked.

Archie had no idea what a ratchet piston was, but Mr. Rivets pointed. "Here, sir."

Fergus took the part and fit it to his cage, lifting it up and turning it this way and that before drilling a hole to attach it.

"This will be your workshop now," Mrs. Henhawk told Fergus. A tear rolled down her cheek. "From the day you arrived, Kano thought of you like a son, Fergus. He was so proud of you."

Fergus turned his head away so they wouldn't see his tears. He shook his head. "I can't stay. I have to go."

"Go?" said Mrs. Henhawk. "Go where? Back to Carolina? You're no farmer, Fergus."

"No. Not home. But I can't stay here either." Fergus

searched through the barrel of metal and found a railroad spike. "It's too dangerous. Edison may come looking for me." He looked up, a sudden horror in his eyes. "You and Della might not be safe either."

"But—"

"He's an awful, awful man, Joanne," Fergus said. "You have to run."

"I—I suppose we could visit my sister. She lives with the Mohawk. But—"

"Just as soon as we're gone." Fergus handed the spike to Mr. Rivets. "Can you heat that end up for me in the kitchen fire?"

"Of course, sir," Mr. Rivets said.

Fergus worked quickly while the machine man was gone, laying out leather straps and hammering grommets into the ends. Archie was amazed. In the short time they'd been standing there, Fergus had built a complicated leg brace out of scraps. Mr. Rivets returned with the glowing hot spike, and Fergus took it from him in a pair of tongs.

"Anything else I can do for you, sir?"

"Aye," Fergus said. "You can bend over, mate."

Mr. Rivets' astonishment subroutine made the Tik Tok raise an eyebrow, but he did as Fergus asked. Using Mr. Rivets' hard metal backside as an anvil, Fergus hammered the red hot spike to the ratchet gear on the side of his leg brace.

"Hot—coming through," Fergus announced, and Archie and Hachi cleared out of the way for him to dunk the contraption into a big bucket, where it hissed and popped. When it was cold to the touch, Fergus attached the leather straps to it and sat down in a chair. He slipped off his left boot, slid the thing up his leg, and buckled it around his knee.

"Here goes nothing," he said. Fergus pushed on the welded spike attached to the ratchet gear. *Chink-chink-chink-chink.* His leg kicked out straight and stayed there, held rigid by the apparatus he'd built.

Fergus got up with Mr. Rivets' help and gave the knee brace a test. He was wobbly, but he stood. He practiced walking with his left leg locked straight like a peg leg, then came back to the chair. He sat heavily, his leg still out straight, but with the flick of a catch on the ratchet gear, the brace released and his knee bent freely so he could sit naturally again.

"Well, it's not the Emartha Mark IV Machine Man, but it'll do."

"I think it's rather astonishing," Mr. Rivets told him. Archie thought it was more than that; it was miraculous. He'd never seen anybody build anything like that so quickly and easily. Fergus was like one of the tinkers in the old stories. . . .

Archie gasped, and everyone looked at him.

"What?" Hachi said.

"It's . . . nothing. I'll tell you later," he said.

"Fergus, come with us," Mrs. Henhawk said. "I promised your mother I'd look after you. You're fourteen. I can't just let you go running off by yourself."

"I'm not by myself."

"No, you're with two other children who should be with their parents."

Hachi looked away. Archie opened his mouth to say something, but he didn't know where to start. It was Mr. Rivets who finally spoke up.

"I am the children's guardian until they can be reunited with their parents, ma'am. I assure you I have considerable experience with young people, having raised four generations of Dents."

"I have to go, Joanne," Fergus said. "Whatever Edison did to me, he'll want me back. I can't stay with you and Della. I'll only put you in danger. And I can't go home."

Mrs. Henhawk didn't look entirely convinced, but she didn't argue the point. Instead she pulled Fergus into a one-armed hug, still holding Della in her other arm. Della beat on Fergus' head.

"Fungus!" she squealed happily.

"Ow, Della Bella. Ow. Ow. Ow."

Mrs. Henhawk gave Fergus a kiss on top of his head. "At least let me send you with some food. Can I do that?"

"The airship's stores *are* bare, madam," Mr. Rivets told her. "It would be much appreciated."

Fergus collected his few belongings—barely a knapsack full—while Mrs. Henhawk loaded up Archie, Hachi, and Mr. Rivets with sacks of food.

"One last thing," Fergus said before they left. He went back to Mr. Henhawk's workshop and found the blueprints he'd drawn for a new Archimedes Engine, the plans he'd told Edison about that had gotten Kano killed. He stared at them for a moment, then wadded them up and stuffed them into the fire in the kitchen.

Mrs. Henhawk went with them to the door.

"I'll come back one day," Fergus told her. "And I'll write. I promise."

"I know you will. And Fergus—" She paused and gathered herself. "Fergus, Kano knew there was something wrong with Edison. Knew there was something . . . *dark* about him. Maybe

- 93 -

bad. But he ignored it. Kano did the work because he loved the science, even though he knew it might be wrong. And now he's . . . now he's . . ." She wiped her eyes with the back of her hand. Della watched her, trying to understand why she was sad. "I see that same love of science in you, Fergus. That same thrill of knowledge. And that's *good*. But you can't close your eyes to the rest of the world, Fergus. You can't ignore what's right for anything. Do you understand? Learn from Kano's mistakes, Fergus. Be a better man."

Fergus nodded, sniffing back tears, and they hugged one last time. Della looked back and forth between her mother and Fergus, frowning at their tears.

"Zee, I need you," Hachi whispered, and the little flying zebra leaped from her bandolier to flutter in front of her.

"Horsie!" Della said.

"Zee, I want you to take good care of this little girl. Do you understand? She's yours now," Hachi told Della, and the little zebra buzzed over and landed in the toddler's hands. "You take good care of her, and she'll be your best friend forever."

"Horsie!" Della said again.

Hachi's eyes watered. "You take good care of each other," she said, and turned away.

Archie walked alongside Hachi as they hauled the food back to the *Hesperus*. "I can't believe you gave her one of your toy animals."

"Della doesn't understand what's happened, but she will one day. And then she'll need a friend," Hachi told him. "Just like me. Zee and the others were the only friends I had when my father was murdered too."

11

Archie pressed his face against a porthole as Mr. Rivets swung them down close for their approach to New Rome. The sky over the biggest city in the United Nations was filled with airships—hundreds of them—taking off from public parks and docking at skyscrapers like the seven-story-tall Emartha Machine Man Corporation building. Submarines plied the choppy waters of the harbor on ferry routes to Breucklen and Queens County. Giant coal-driven machine men laid cobblestones for roads. Locomotives steamed away on elevated platforms. The city was like one great machine, all its parts working in synchronization. No matter how many times he visited, Archie loved seeing it all.

Watching over the city with him was the huge statue of mighty Hiawatha out in the harbor. Hiawatha was the legendary founder of the Iroquois Confederacy, the league of nations that had saved the European settlers' lives a hundred years ago when the Darkness fell. Cut off from the support, trade, and authority of the Old World, the colonists of New England had retreated to the cities on the coast and struggled to survive. Just when things looked their worst, a savior had come—not from the east, over the suddenly impassable waves, but from the west, from the very people the Europeans had been driving off their lands. The Iroquois Confederacy adopted the settlers as a seventh tribe—the Yankee tribe—and invited more tribes to join them, becoming the United Nations of America. The new confederacy stretched from the Atlantis Ocean to the Mississippi River, and was rivaled in power only by Acadia in the north, New Spain to the south, and the Republics of Texas and California to the west.

Archie caught Hachi watching out the window too.

"First time to New Rome?" he asked.

Hachi pulled away from the window, trying to look uninterested. "I've seen better. The wheeled city of Cheyenne. Now *that's* impressive." Hachi went back to her hammock to wait, but Archie saw her still craning her neck to look outside as they flew into the city.

That neck with the awful scar on it. She'd said her father had been killed. Did she get the scar at the same time?

Mr. Rivets took the *Hesperus* in to moor at New Rome's Central Park, the public parking green on Mannahatta Island where dozens more airships of various sizes and designs twisted in the wind. Grazing sheep scattered as they made anchor. Archie swapped Mr. Rivets' Airship Pilot talent card out for his New Rome and Surrounding Areas Visitors Guide card— his parents had bought it specially for trips to the city—and one paid parking toll later they were on their way to find John Douglas.

"I only know him as Uncle John," Archie said as they walked, making sure to go slowly enough for Fergus to keep up. "He comes by our house in Philadelphia a couple times a year, and he always sits and talks with me."

"What about?" Hachi asked.

Archie shrugged. "What I've learned in school, what I think about things. Nothing important."

"What's he do?" Fergus asked.

"He is a printer, Master Fergus," said Mr. Rivets. "Both publicly, as a profession, and privately, for the Septemberists."

"This League you told us about, it's different from the Septemberists?"

"Yes," said Archie. "A long time ago, so far back nobody really remembers when, seven heroes from different parts of the world came together to use their powers to defeat the Mangleborn."

"Powers?" Hachi asked. "What kind of powers?"

"Superhuman powers. Oh! This is what I realized back in Jersey, when I saw you putting together your knee brace, Fergus! We're like three new heroes!"

"What?" Hachi asked.

"See, the original League of Seven beat the Mangleborn and hid them away in prisons in the earth and under the sea. But then the world forgot, see? The Mangleborn were gone and the League went away, and all of it just became legends. Stories about heroes and titans and monsters. People forgot, and they discovered lektricity all over again, and the Mangleborn fed off it and broke free. So a new League of Seven had to come together to save the world!"

"Heroes with superpowers," Hachi said doubtfully.

"Yes," said Archie. "And it keeps happening over and over

again. The League beats the Mangleborn and hides them away, centuries go by and everybody forgets, and then somebody starts experimenting with lektricity again."

"Like Edison," Fergus said.

"Right. But last time, after the Medieval League of Seven defeated the Mangleborn, the Septemberist Society was founded. It's a secret society of regular people who work to keep the world safe from lektricity and the Mangleborn. That's what my parents and Uncle John do, along with a bunch of other people, I guess. Is that right, Mr. Rivets?"

"More or less, sir. The Dent family have been Septemberists for centuries, long before coming to the Americas."

"So what's this about us being three new heroes?" Fergus asked.

"Oh! Right," said Archie. "So, the seven superhuman heroes, they only come together when the Mangleborn rise, when the world needs them most. But they're always the same! I mean, not the same *people*, but the same kind of heroes. There's always a tinker—a maker—like Huang Di or Wayland Smith or Kaveh. And that's you, Fergus! There's always a warrior too, the greatest fighter of the age, and the way you fought that machine man Mr. Shinobi, Hachi, it reminded me of those champions—Gilgamesh and Brynhildr and Hippolyta. And there's always a law-bringer, a scholar, a strongman, a trickster—"

"And . . . which one are *you* supposed to be, exactly?" Hachi asked. "What's *your* superpower?"

"I'm the leader! The Theseus. The Arthur. The Rama. The one who speaks for the League."

Hachi and Fergus looked at him skeptically.

"Well, I'm the one who knows the most about the League and the Mangleborn," Archie said, pouting.

"If we're a new League of Seven, where are the other four?" Hachi asked.

Archie shrugged again. "I don't know. Maybe we just haven't found them yet."

"But, wait," said Fergus. "I thought you said this League, the seven heroes, they only show up when the beasties rise and the world comes to an end."

"They do. My parents think that's why we lost contact with the Old World. They think the Mangleborn have already risen there and taken over. And the Americas are next."

Fergus looked pale. "I think I'd rather there not be a new League for another hundred years, then. At least until I'm long gone."

"Here we are, Master Archie," said Mr. Rivets.

They stopped in front of a simple brownstone building with a sign over the door that said JOHN G. DOUGLAS, STEAM PRINTER AND TYPESETTER.

"Remember, the Septemberists are a secret," Archie told them. "Uncle John is probably the only person here who even knows they exist. Just let me do the talking."

Hachi rolled her eyes, but she said nothing.

A bell on the top of the door jangled as Archie went inside. The reception area of the print shop was small, with three wooden chairs on one side and a bookshelf of newly printed and bound editions on the other. A fair-haired woman in a blue dress sat sideways at her desk, facing a smaller desk with a typewriter on it. She turned at the sound of the doorbell, giving them a big, fake smile.

"Hello!" she said. "Welcome to the offices of John G. Douglas, steam printer, typesetter, and Septemberist."

"Some secret," Hachi muttered behind him.

The woman's big smile worried Archie. "Um, hi," he said. "We, uh—my name's Archie Dent, and I, uh, we—oh!" The Septemberist pass phrase! He should use that first. "Thirty days hath September. . . ."

"We need to see Mr. Douglas," Hachi cut in. "Septemberist business."

"Thank you for your inquiry," the receptionist said, still smiling. "Please have a seat. Someone will be with you in just a moment."

"Look here, you smiling flange," Hachi began.

"Thank you for your inquiry," the receptionist said again. "Please have a seat. Someone will be with you in just a moment."

"Thanks! We'll just wait over here," Archie said. He grabbed Hachi and Fergus and pulled them over to the chairs along the wall, and the woman at the desk turned back around and put her hands on the typewriter.

"What are you doing?" Hachi asked.

"We've seen this before. Me and Mr. Rivets, back at the Septemberist headquarters. Look at her typewriter. There's no paper in it. And the p-mail. Look at the tubes."

Archie nodded to the wall behind the woman's desk, where half a dozen glass pneumatic tubes came down from the ceiling. Just about every business and home in the city had at least one p-mail line, in which rolled-up messages could be delivered in airtight capsules either to other rooms or to other buildings around the city—even the country—via a series of tubes called the Inter-Net. The capsules were pushed along the tubes by compressed air until they popped out at their final destination. But the print shop's tubes were clogged. There were half a dozen capsules backed up in each.

John G. Douglas' inbox was full, and no one was answering the p-mails. Archie knew that wasn't a good sign.

"You've seen this before? When?" Hachi asked.

Archie told Hachi and Fergus all about the thing in the catacombs of Septemberist Society headquarters, and how its little bug babies had affected his parents and the Septemberist council.

"You knew this society of yours was being controlled by a monster and you brought us all the way back here anyway?" Hachi said.

"Not all of them! I didn't know if Uncle John was being controlled by it too! And he still might not be. We have to find him!"

Hachi gave Archie an angry look before stalking off down the hall. Archie shot a glance at the receptionist, afraid she would stop them, but she still sat with her hands on the typewriter and not typing. She was probably still smiling too.

"Hold on," Archie whispered they caught up to Hachi. "What if somebody comes for us?"

"Who?" Hachi asked. "She never told anyone we were here."

The hallway off the reception area was lined with offices, each of which had some print shop employee sitting at a desk doing nothing but smiling. They didn't react at all as Archie and the others walked past.

"This sure is one happy company," Fergus said, "but I don't think I'd want to work here."

In another room down the hall a woman ran a hand-cranked printing machine. She turned the drum as mechanically as one of those cheap, single-purpose Tik Toks the Emartha Corporation sold for cleaning dishes. *Ka-chunk-chunk. Ka-chunk-chunk. Ka-chunk-chunk.* But the woman wasn't making copies of anything. She was just running the machine.

"We've got to find Uncle John," Archie whispered, and he started off again down the hall.

Hachi grabbed his arm and pointed. *"Look at her neck."*

Beneath the tight bun of the woman's hair, just visible above her high collar, was a bug just like the ones on Archie's parents. Just like the ones on the Septemberist council members.

"I told you," Archie whispered.

Schnik. Hachi drew her dagger.

"No, don't," Archie said. He pointed to a door at the end of the hall marked "John G. Douglas, Printer." They crept down the hall, and Archie put his hand on the knob and turned it. *Don't be smiling, don't be smiling, don't be smiling—*

Uncle John sat behind his desk, smiling.

Archie wilted. Uncle John was his last, best hope for rescuing his parents. If John couldn't help them—

"Hello, Archie Dent," John said.

"Uncle John!" Archie hurried to the desk. He must have just been smiling to see him! "Uncle John, I'm so glad you're all right. All the other people here and at Septemberist headquarters, they have these bugs on the back of their necks, and—"

"Hello, Archie Dent," John said. "There's something in the basement I'd like you to see."

"We don't have time," Archie told him. "You have to help us. My parents, they're prisoners of Malacar Ahasherat, the Swarm Queen. You have to call the rest of the Septemberists."

Uncle John stood. "Hello, Archie Dent. There's something in the basement I'd like you to see."

Archie's skin grew cold as he realized what Uncle John was saying. It was the same thing the Septemberist council had told him, over and over again. He felt sick. Uncle John must have one of those bug things on him too. Archie took a step back.

"Hello, Archie Dent. There's something in the basement I'd like you to see," John said again.

"Um, no thanks," Archie said.

Hachi stepped behind Uncle John. "There's a bug on him, just like the rest."

"There can't be," Archie said. "We need him!"

Uncle John came around the desk toward Archie.

"Hello, Archie Dent. There's something in the basement I'd like you to see."

"Okay," Fergus said. "That's just creepy."

"Uncle John, please. It's me. Archie. I need your help," Archie said.

"Hello, Archie Dent. There's something in the basement I'd like you to see."

Hachi jumped onto Uncle John's back and rode him to the ground.

"Don't hurt him! Don't hurt him!" Archie told her.

"I'm not going to hurt him. I'm going to get this bug off him. Help me hold him down."

"Hello, Archie Dent. There's something in the basement

I'd like you to see," Uncle John said into the rug. Archie, Fergus, and Mr. Rivets held John still while Hachi slid her knife under the throbbing, bulbous insect on the back of his neck.

"Careful—taking it out's going to hurt him. He's going to scream and cry," Archie told her.

"Has to be better than having this thing in him," Hachi said through gritted teeth. The sucking insect *slurched* as she pried it out. Beneath her, John shuddered and screamed.

The bug wrapped its little legs around Hachi's dagger as she lifted it away, the tail sliding out inch by painful inch. Archie felt sick just looking at the thing, especially knowing there were two of them buried in his parents' necks.

The bug finally came free, and Uncle John screamed again and then went slack, sobbing into the rug. Hachi flipped the insect away and leaped on it, driving her dagger into it. *Pltttt.* It popped like a balloon, splattering everything around it with a filmy green pus.

"Uncle John?" Archie said. "Uncle John? It's me. Archie Dent. Can you understand me?"

"Archie?" John said, still blubbering. He kicked and thrashed. "No! . . . shouldn't be here. Go. Now. You have to run. Get away."

"I can't. Uncle John, my parents are in trouble. They went to Florida. To Malacar Ahasherat's prison. She has them. They have bug things in their necks, just like you. Just like everybody here."

Uncle John cried into the rug. "Run, Archie," he said through his tears. "Please. Run. The basement. Everywhere. Bugs are everywhere. Can't—can't let them have you."

Hachi hurried over to John's desk and started rifling through the drawers.

"What are you doing?" Archie asked her.

"He's useless. I'm trying to find who his other Septemberist contacts are."

Fergus got up and went to help her. Archie stayed with Uncle John.

"Please, Uncle John. You're the only Septemberist I know. You have to help us."

John shook his head, still weeping.

"Then tell me who to go to! Uncle John, my parents are in trouble!"

"Shouldn't be here . . ." John burbled. "Too soon. Not ready."

"What do you mean too soon?" Archie asked. "What's not ready?"

"There's just a bunch of pages of nursery rhymes," Hachi said, pulling papers out of a drawer.

"Wait, I've got something," Fergus said. "Um, Archie? You better take a look at this."

Fergus laid a scrapbook on the desk. It was filled with sepia-toned daguerreotypes and handwritten notes and letters.

All about Archie.

"What is this?" Archie asked.

"I found it in a hidden compartment in the bottom drawer," Fergus said. "Had a spring mechanism that activated it. Simple, really. You just put a tension rod in the . . . But, you don't care about that right now, do you?"

No, Archie didn't care about the hidden compartment. All

of his attention was focused on the book about him hidden in Uncle John's desk. Pictures of him as a baby, as a toddler. A picture of him from just last year, when John had visited. He hadn't even known a picture had been taken of him. And the papers—letters about his academic progress, graphs of his height and weight, charts plotting his reaction speeds and strength. When had all this been written? *Why* had all this been written?

"Uncle John, what is this? Why do you have a book about me in your desk?" Archie asked.

John just cried into the carpet.

"Mr. Rivets, why does Uncle John have a book about me?" Archie asked.

"I'm afraid I couldn't say, Master Archie," the machine man told him.

Archie almost didn't hear it, almost didn't make the connection, but then it hit him like a blast of steam. "What did you say?" Archie asked.

"I said, 'I'm afraid I couldn't say, Master Archie.'"

I'm afraid I couldn't say. That was what Tik Toks said when they'd been ordered to keep a secret.

What did Mr. Rivets know that he wasn't telling him? "Mr. Rivets—"

"Archie!" Hachi said. More bugs like the one she had pulled off Uncle John's neck were squeezing their way under the door.

"Twisted pistons!" Fergus said, and he tried to climb up on top of the desk.

Hachi was already moving. She grabbed a small wooden step stool from the foot of a bookcase and flipped it over, using it like a mallet to flatten the things as they came. *Splurch.*

Splurch. Splurch. Splurch. Mr. Rivets waded in among them too, stepping on as many as he could, but there were more of them than they could ever hope to kill.

"What do we do now? How do we get out?" Archie cried.

"Window!" Hachi said without turning around. Archie hadn't even noticed it, but there was one, right behind John's desk. He was as thick as clinker. He ran to it and yanked on it to open it, but the handle snapped off in his hand. He shook it, angry, like it was the handle's fault he was such a clacking klutz.

"I broke it! I can't open it!"

"Hang on, I can fix it!" Fergus said. He dug into the pouch on his belt for his tools.

Hachi gave the boys an exasperated huff and tossed the stool through the window, showering the fire escape outside with glass.

"Or we could do that," said Fergus.

Archie ran for Uncle John as Hachi climbed out the window. The door splintered and cracked, and more smiling, en thralled people from the office began to push their way inside. The bugs were coming fast and furious now too, their back ends raised like scorpion tails.

"Hello, Archie Dent. There's something in the basement I'd like you to see," the woman from the copy machine said. The people behind her started saying the same thing, over and over again.

"Archie! Leave him! We have to go!" Hachi called from the window.

"No!" he said. "He's a Septemberist!" He picked up Uncle John's arm and pulled, but bugs already covered John's feet and were scurrying up his legs.

"Everywhere. Everywhere!" he blubbered. "Shouldn't be here, Archie . . . Too soon . . . Too soon!"

"Help me!" Archie cried. The bugs were already up to Uncle John's chest.

"Mr. Rivets! Bring Archie!" Hachi called.

Archie felt Mr. Rivets' metal hands snatch him up just before the bugs got to Uncle John's hands. Uncle John jerked and screamed as the bugs covered him, and Archie saw one of them settle onto John's neck and slide its long tail down into his spine. John Douglas suddenly stopped thrashing and crying. He stood and came after Archie like the rest of the smiling people.

"Hello, Archie Dent," Uncle John said. "There's something in the basement I'd like you to see."

"No—no!" Archie said, squirming in Mr. Rivets' arms. "You're not supposed to take orders from Hachi! You're *my* machine man!"

"And I should like to remain so, Master Archie," Mr. Rivets said. "But that will require our immediate departure."

"No! Noooo!" Archie cried, but there were so many of them. Crawling up the walls, covering the floor and ceiling.

Mr. Rivets handed him through to Hachi and Fergus, and together they hurried down to the alley below where Archie ran, slag his cowardly hide. He ran as fast and as far away as he could.

12

"We need rayguns," Hachi said. "Big ones."

"Aye," said Fergus. "We'll need coffins too, we go back down to Florida to fight that beastie. I've always fancied a brass one myself. With a tartan blanket inside. Maybe a clockwork tombstone too, like those ones where the planets circle around."

"An orrery, sir," Mr. Rivets said. "That is the device to which you refer."

"Aye. An orrery. Lovely piece of mechanics. Bring a tear to me mum's eye when she comes to visit me *in my grave*," he said, emphasizing that last bit for Hachi. She voted for gearing up and going back to Florida, of course. Fergus voted for—well, Archie couldn't tell *what* he was in favor of, besides not dying.

Archie hadn't said a word since they'd dragged him out of the print shop office. To leave Uncle John there like that . . . And why did Uncle John have a scrapbook filled with pictures and graphs and notes about Archie? He flipped through the pages as they sat on a bench in Central Park, trying to figure out their next move. Every year of Archie's life was in this book, every accomplishment, every milestone. He looked back on Uncle John's regular visits now with new eyes. Tossing a lacrosse ball in the yard with Uncle John—that must have been a test of his coordination. Asking Archie to carry his luggage to his room—a test of his strength. The parlor games they played after dinner—a test of his intelligence? But why? Why did Uncle John care? And was it just he who cared, or was he watching Archie for the Septemberists?

Mr. Rivets knew. Mr. Rivets, who Archie thought had never kept a secret from Archie in his life, who was Archie's tutor, his guardian, his best friend. Mr. Rivets knew why Uncle John kept a scrapbook of Archie in his desk and visited twice a year for checkups—for Archie realized now that's what they were. "I'm afraid I couldn't say, Master Archie." That's what machine men said when someone had ordered them to keep a secret. Mr. Rivets knew what the scrapbook meant, but someone had told him not to tell.

Which meant, Archie suddenly realized, that his parents knew too. They were the only ones who could give Mr. Rivets the order not to say anything.

"What do you say, Archie?" Hachi asked.

"What?"

"What do you say to going to find this other Septemberist contact Mr. Rivets knows?" Fergus said.

"Mr. Rivets says he's got rayguns. Lots of them," said Hachi.

Archie had missed part of the conversation. "You know another Septemberist, Mr. Rivets? Here in New Rome?" Mr. Rivets suddenly seemed to know a lot of Septemberist secrets that Archie didn't.

"Not here, sir, no. He is ensconced in a hidden facility some miles north, as the airship flies. And if he has been . . .

compromised the way Mr. Douglas and your parents have been, the trip may prove a waste of time."

"Aye," Fergus said. "And get us killed to boot. Or taken over by those little clinkers."

"There is that concern too, sir," Mr. Rivets said. "Instead of flying there directly, I suggest we send a dispatch by pneumatic post. If his response is anything other than a sunny salutation and an invitation to the basement, we may assume that he has not yet been placed in the thrall of the Manglespawn in the catacombs, and thus seek his help in person with all due haste."

"And he's the only other Septemberist contact you've got?" Hachi asked.

"I'm afraid so, miss," said Mr. Rivets.

Archie knew Mr. Rivets couldn't lie, but he still found himself doubting everything his old friend said now.

"You guys should have a member directory, with addresses and everything," Fergus said.

"A written directory would not do well for a secret society, sir."

"Nae, I guess not," said Fergus.

"All right. The post office then," said Hachi. "What's the closest branch, Mr. Rivets?"

Mr. Rivets clicked and whirred as he accessed his New Rome and Surrounding Areas Visitors Guide card.

"The Pennsylvania Pneumatic Post Office should be the fastest way to send a message from here, miss. Operating hours are eight to five Monday through Friday, with service until noon on Saturday. Automated postage stamp sales are available in the lobby, as are private post office boxes, which can be rented for a dollar a month. The Pennsylvania Pneumatic Post Office is the busiest post office in the United Nations of America, posting hundreds of thousands of—"

"We don't need the whole entry," Hachi said, cutting him off. "We just need to know where it is."

"The Pennsylvania Pneumatic Post Office is located on Eighth Avenue, across the street from—"

"Better yet," Hachi said, "just show us."

The Pennsylvania Pneumatic Post Office on Eighth Avenue, across the street from the Pennsylvania Railway Station, was, as Mr. Rivets had tried to say, the busiest post office in the United Nations—if not the known world. Hundreds of thousands of pneumatic tubes of all sizes came and went every day at reported speeds of up to twenty miles per hour. If you couldn't mail it from the Penn Post Office, it couldn't be mailed by pneumatic post. In the marble above its Corinthian columns on the front of the building was written, *"Neither snow nor rain nor heat nor gloom of night stays these cylinders from the swift delivery of their anointed dispatches."*

Archie, Hachi, Fergus, and Mr. Rivets climbed the marble steps of the Penn Post Office to an open, two-story lobby filled with light. The place was packed. Some people checked post office boxes, others waited at stamp machines, still more stood in line to send or receive posts. At the far end of the room was a row of teller windows, and behind them, stretching from floor to ceiling, were the brass pneumatic tubes that connected to every other p-mail station up and down the Eastern Seaboard. One or two, Archie knew, even went as far as the Republic of

California and New Spain. *Thoomp thoomp thoomp thoomp thoomp thoomp thoomp*—the cylinders flew nonstop in and out of tubes as thin as pencils (for pneumatigrams) and as big as Mr. Rivets (for oversized parcels). They crisscrossed up and under and over each other in a maze of brass, glass, and valves. This was the Grand Central Station of pneumatic mail.

"I think I could live here," Fergus said in awe. Archie watched as the black lines on Fergus' skin shifted and changed, mimicking the maze of tubes on the far wall. Archie wondered if Fergus even knew it was happening. But Archie wasn't the only one staring.

"Get a good look, did you?" Fergus asked a particularly gawky Seneca woman with a stroller. She squeaked and hurried away.

"I suppose I've become a right monster, haven't I?" Fergus asked.

"*They're* the monsters, not you," Hachi told him. She pulled up on her scarf. "Let's go."

Mr. Rivets steered them toward the shortest line, but they still had a bit of a wait.

"So, these Mangleborn," Hachi said quietly. "There's more than one of them?"

"There's Antaeus the Unbeatable, in Cahokia In The Clouds," Archie said. "The Eater of Children, entombed in the Republic of Texas. Grumalch the Boar-Headed, buried somewhere near Cincinnatus. Yog-vorantha, Queen of the White Wastes, watched over by the Inuit tribes. Those are just a few my parents told me about."

"Bet you had a really easy time getting to sleep when you were little, eh?" Fergus said.

Hachi frowned at the news that there were more of these things, buried all over the United Nations—all over the world—but they were up to the counter before she could say anything more. Mr. Rivets dictated a brief message, which the clerk punched in on a steam-powered keyboard. He tore the paper out and rolled it into a slender pneumatigram tube.

"That'll be ten cents," he said.

"Oh, um—" Archie said, realizing he had no money.

"Not to worry, sir," Mr. Rivets said. He withdrew a dime from a pocket-drawer on his fake brass vest. Archie fumbled it, clumsy and useless as always, and bent down to get it.

Thunk. Thunk. Thunk. Three metal stars with blades for points buried themselves in the wooden counter right where Archie had been standing. He came back up with the dime and stared at them.

"What the—?" he began.

"Get down!" Hachi cried. Mr. Shinobi, Edison's meka-ninja, was running straight toward them from the lobby with a long sword in its hands.

"Circus, showtime!" Hachi said. Her four remaining animals burst out from her bandolier and hovered in front of her. "Interference!" she told them, and they hummed off to harry the Tik Tok again. "You two! Behind the counter! Go!" she told Archie and Fergus.

Hachi leaped toward the black machine man. It swung its sword—*whhht!*—but Hachi was already ducking it. She slid between the meka-ninja's legs and popped up behind it, dagger raised.

"Whoa," said Fergus.

"Yeah," said Archie.

Clink! A smaller sword popped out of Mr. Shinobi's back and deflected her blow. A third arm! The Tik Tok's head spun, and Archie saw another pair of glowing red eyes open on the back of its head. It held off Hachi while it advanced on Archie and Fergus.

"MisterRivetsMisterRivetsMisterRivets!" Archie cried, backing into the post office counter. Clerks and customers ran screaming.

Mr. Shinobi raised its sword. Archie and Fergus cowered.

Clang!

The meka-ninja's long, curved sword rang out on Mr. Rivets' back as he bent over to cover Archie and Fergus.

"Mr. Rivets! Fight! Help Hachi!" Archie said.

"Alas, sir, my Protector card is back on the *Hesperus.* If you will recall, I have in my New Rome and Surrounding Areas Visitors Guide."

"Then tell it how to get to the Union Grounds lacrosse field!"

"Ah, yes, sir." Mr. Rivets stood and turned toward the meka-ninja. "A trip to see the New Rome Knickerbockers can be one of the most pleasurable pursuits for any visitor, especially those traveling with young children. The field is serviced by pneumatic subway, elevated train, or by street car. To arrive by subway—"

"Behind the counter. Let's go!" Archie told Fergus. They scrambled behind the wooden desk and hid while Hachi attacked the meka-ninja from the back and Mr. Rivets bored it with entries from the New Rome and Surrounding Areas Visitors Guide from the front.

"I'm starting to think we ought to just leave his Protector card in," Fergus said.

Crunch. The desk behind them snapped in half. Archie looked up to see Mr. Shinobi yanking his long sword out of the wood.

"Run!" cried Archie. He pulled Fergus to his feet. There had to be a place to hide among the forest of brass pipes that hummed at the back of the room, still active but abandoned by fleeing postal workers.

Fergus limped along behind him, falling off the pace. "I can't run!" he called.

The meka-ninja leaped over the counter, landing silently on padded feet. Its head swiveled to focus on Archie and Fergus.

"I'll distract it!" Archie yelled. He veered off toward a pile of incoming packages. "Hey! Hey meka-ninja! Over here!"

Only after he said it did Archie realize what a flange he was. What was he supposed to do when the meka-ninja *did* come after him?

But it didn't. It ignored him and kept running for Fergus.

"Steambrain!" Archie said, cursing himself. "Fergus is the one Edison wants!"

Fwip-fwip-fwip. Three tiny darts shot from the meka-ninja's arm and hit Fergus square in the back. Fergus spun and fell into one of the big pneumatic tubes. He grabbed the "Send" plunger as he fell, and gaped in surprise as the cylinder slid closed around him.

There was a pneumatic whoosh of air and—*thoomp*—Fergus was gone.

Archie stared at the empty space where Fergus had been as

Hachi and Mr. Rivets ran up to him. Hachi had a long, bleeding gash down one arm.

"He—Fergus—he—" Archie started to say. *Ding!* Another capsule slid down to replace the one Fergus had left in, and the meka-ninja hopped inside. It pushed the "Send" plunger, and—*thoomp*—it was gone.

"It just—they both—" Archie started again.

Ding! Another capsule slid down into place. Hachi grabbed Archie, pulled him into the capsule with her, and slapped the "Send" plunger.

"I'll just wait here for the return post, shall I?" Mr. Rivets asked.

The capsule closed, and the world dropped away beneath Archie and Hachi's feet.

13

Archie and Hachi hit the ceiling of the capsule, then tumbled when it turned horizontal. The capsule twisted and turned in its tube, shaking them up like dice in a cup. The capsules were made for packages, not people. Archie suddenly understood why every parcel they'd ever gotten by pneumatic post was creased and dented. He had just gotten up on his elbows when the capsule spun again and he landed flat on his face. It dipped again and he hit the roof. It leveled out again, and he fell onto Hachi.

"Slag it—*oof*—this is—*ow*—"

Archie and Hachi were a tangle of arms and legs. He tried to brace himself for the next turn, but it was useless. There was nothing to hold onto inside the smooth round capsule, and he had no idea where it was going next anyway.

The capsule thumped to a stop and opened, and Archie and Hachi rolled out into a pile of crates. *This is what clothes must feel like in a washing machine,* Archie thought as he untangled himself. A woman screamed, and Archie saw Fergus in the far corner, fending off the meka-ninja with a wooden mannequin.

"Where are we?"

"Macy's Department Store. Package Delivery," said Hachi.

"How do you know that?"

Hachi pointed to a sign on the wall. It said MACY'S DEPART-MENT STORE. PACKAGE DELIVERY.

"Oh."

Customers and clerks lined the walls, trying to get as far away from the killer machine man as possible. Fergus jabbed at Mr. Shinobi with the wooden mannequin, keeping the Tik Tok at bay, while Hachi's Tik Tok animals tugged on the meka-ninja's sword arm. Mr. Shinobi used its free hand to pull a new weapon from a slot on its leg. It was two wooden sticks connected by a short length of chain. Its hand began to twirl, and the weapon whirred like a propeller blade. *Whack-whack-whack-whack!* The meka-ninja chopped the wooden mannequin to pieces.

"Crivens!" Fergus cried. The meka-ninja backed him into a corner, and Fergus threw what was left of the mannequin into the whirling weapon. "Help!"

Hachi went after the machine man, her dagger drawn, but Archie had a better idea. He grabbed a pair of scissors from the wrapping counter, tied them to a roll of twine, and tossed them into Mr. Shinobi's spinning weapon. *Fwip-fwip-fwip-fwip!* The twirling propellers sucked up the twine like a fishing rod reeling in a catch. Within seconds the meka-ninja's hand was wrapped in a big useless ball of string and the weapon hung limp.

"Brass!" said Fergus.

Mr. Shinobi stared at the mess of twine on its hand, then started to hack away at it with its sword.

"Slag! Slag! Slag!" said Fergus.

Hachi grabbed Fergus and dragged him toward the pneumatic tubes.

"Oh no," Archie said. "I'm not getting back in there. No way. Two people is bad enough. There's not room for three."

The meka-ninja cut through the last of the twine and turned on them, its red eyes glowing.

"Scootch in! Scootch in!" Archie cried, pushing his way into the capsule.

Hachi whistled her flying circus back and smacked the plunger. Archie only saw three of her four toys make it back, but he didn't have time to say anything before the door slid closed and—*thoomp*—they were gone. There was less room to be tossed around this time, but that didn't make it any less painful. Archie took an elbow to the gut, a fist to the head, and accidentally kneed Fergus in the kilt. They flew up, up, down, down, left, right, left, right.

"Ba!" Archie cried. They thumped to another stop and tumbled out onto a rooftop loading dock. An enormous skyliner airship floated above them, its long cigar-shaped gasbag painted orange and red, the colors of Apache Air. A young Yankee woman wearing a blue-and-white sailor dress was loading crates into its hold with a steam winch. When she spotted the three of them, she climbed down out of the loading crane and pushed her Apache Air sailor hat aside to scratch her head.

"You're not Mrs. Nittawosew's new mink coat," she said.

Archie helped Fergus to his feet while Hachi scouted the loading dock.

"Watch your knees in there, mate," Fergus told him.

"Sorry," said Archie.

"We're seven stories up," Hachi told them.

"Where'd you think you were headed, Coney Island?" the woman asked.

"Only way down is an elevator," Hachi told them. "And right now it's on the second floor."

Fergus peered off the edge. "I think I can see my house from here."

Archie looked back nervously at the chutes. The Tik Tok could be there any second. "Where's this ship headed?" he asked the woman.

"Brasil."

"Not far enough away," said Fergus. "Not *near* far enough. Got anything going to the moon?"

Ding! A new capsule thumped into place to replace the one they had arrived in.

"Maybe it's just Mrs. Nittawosew's new mink coat," Archie said hopefully.

The capsule slid open and the meka-ninja stepped out.

"Or not," said Archie.

Fergus backed away, and Archie and Hachi closed ranks around him. Not that Archie could do much to stop the thing.

"Locked sprockets!" the woman said. "What's that?"

"It's about to be a pancake!" Fergus said. He'd climbed up into the steam winch and was working the controls. "Sayonara, Mr. Shinobi!" He punched the claw release, and a giant crate fell and smashed down on the loading dock right where the meka-ninja was standing.

"Woohoo! Take that, you big bucket of—"

Mr. Shinobi stepped out from behind the busted crate. He'd jumped back out of the way before it could hit him.

"Oh, crivens," said Fergus.

The meka-ninja drew its long sword from its back, took a step forward—and then paused. Something inside its black metal chest rattled and tinked and sproinged, and its left arm fell off. Archie stared in disbelief. The Tik Tok took a step back and looked down at itself, trying to figure out what was going on. Something rattled inside the meka-ninja's chest and down through its stomach. A flap on its bottom swung open, and Freckles the wind-up giraffe dropped out of it onto the ground.

"Did that Tik Tok just poop a giraffe?" Fergus asked.

Hachi called Freckles back to her compartment. "My sneaky, sneaky little girl," she whispered.

The one-armed Mr. Shinobi didn't stand still for long. It picked up its sword with its good hand and took another step closer to Archie and Hachi.

Wham! The boom arm of the steam winch slammed into the meka-ninja, knocking it off its feet. It crashed into the rail at the edge of the rooftop and it tore away. Mr. Shinobi teetered, trying not to follow it over the side.

"Gotcha!" Fergus said.

"Into the capsule!" Archie cried. He wasn't going to wait around to see if Mr. Shinobi fell.

Hachi and Fergus climbed in after him.

"Sorry about the crate!" Fergus told the lady, and he smacked the plunger.

The cylinder closed and the capsule dropped. Down, down, down. Right. Up. Left. Down. Left. Up. Right. After a while, Archie stopped thinking about what direction they were flying and just focused on not throwing up. Fergus gave a little burp like he was fighting it too.

"Don't," Hachi warned them.

Fergus swallowed loudly.

"Next time, don't get out," Hachi managed to tell them. "We'll just hit the plunger and keep going. Maybe lose him."

The capsule thumped to a stop and opened onto another loading dock—this one made of wood and riveted steel. A pair of empty railroad tracks lay just beyond the platform, and the hiss and chug of train engines filled the air. High above, beyond a series of elevated tracks and platforms and stairs, sunlight filtered in through thousands of tiny windowpanes.

"Wait! I know where this is!" Archie cried. "It's—"

Hachi punched the plunger. The capsule door slid closed, and they dropped again, Archie's last meal threatening to make an unwelcome return.

"—Penn Station," Archie said. "Right across the street from the post office."

"We can't get out until we have a plan," Hachi told them. "Some way to—"

The capsule dropped sideways, which it never did, and they all cried out. The capsule slammed to a stop on its side, but the door stayed closed. Archie, Hachi, and Fergus froze.

"What's happened?" Archie whispered. "Why did we—?"

Hachi shushed him. Somebody was talking outside the capsule.

"Open her up," said a woman's voice.

Something scraped and clanked on the outside of the capsule. The door mechanism triggered and the capsule popped open. All Archie could see was the ceiling of a dark tunnel, covered with dozens of pneumatic tubes, large and small.

A lantern appeared suddenly, blinding them.

"Well? What'd we get?" asked the woman.

"We got kids."

14

"What do you mean, 'We got kids'?"

Three more heads appeared over the sides of the capsule, and the man with the lantern gestured with an aether pistol.

"See? Kids! In the dern capsule!"

"All right, all right. Get that light out of their faces and help them out. And for Pete's sake, put that aether pistol away," the woman said.

The bright light went away, and hands helped them out of the capsule. Archie's first impression had been right—they were in a tunnel. Water dripped from a crack in the brickwork, and the only light came from a few lamps hung on posts stuck in the muck on the ground. There was just enough room for a grown man to stand without hitting his head on the dozens of pneumatic tubes that ran along the ceiling overhead.

Pneumatic tubes! Any second now the meka-ninja would arrive, and—

Shung-shung. Shung-shung. Shung-shung. The big tube their capsule had dropped out of rattled over their heads as a cylinder whooshed by and was gone. Archie breathed a sigh of relief. Their capsule had been diverted, but the one carrying

Mr. Shinobi (he presumed) had just sped by. The meka-ninja would never know where they had gone.

The man raised the lantern to Archie's head. "Is your hair white, boy?"

A girl with a huge scar on her neck and a boy with black tattoo lines all over him, and he wanted to know about Archie's hair? Archie pulled away from the light.

"You kids do a lot of traveling around by pneumatic tube?" the woman asked them.

"We were . . . kind of trying to get away from something," Archie said. Hachi shook her head at him and frowned, and he realized with a pang he shouldn't have told these people they were wanted. There was no telling who they were or what they were up to.

"Well, you've disappeared nice and good," the woman told him. "Ain't nobody gonna find you down here."

"A dump well," Fergus said. He was looking at the ramp grafted onto the tube they'd been traveling in. The whole contraption was made of different kinds of scrap wood and metal, and there were more like it, all within a few yards, tapping into tubes big and small.

"You're shunting capsules off the main line, so you can—"

Archie saw the donkey cart for the first time, just beyond the circle of light from the lanterns. It was piled high with boxes and packages.

"So you can steal from them," Hachi said tiredly. She drew her dagger, ready for another fight, and the man with the aether pistol pulled it back out again and aimed it at her.

"Whoa, whoa, whoa," the woman said, stepping in between them. "Yes, we're thieves. But we're not killers, and we're not kidnappers. By the sound of it, you're looking to stay as incognito as we are. So unless you kids are gonna make trouble, we're not either."

"If you're not killers, what's the aether pistol for?" Hachi asked.

"The rats," the woman said. "Those we kill, because I think they're icky. Go on now, Hector. Put it away."

"Aw, Liv! You used my name!"

"You just used hers too," Archie told him.

"Dern it!" Hector said. He holstered the aether pistol, and Hachi put away her knife.

"This here's Hector," the woman said. "I'm Liv. That's Luis over there. And Onatah."

Archie and the others introduced themselves, and there were nods all around. The thieves wore breeches tucked into their boots—even the woman, Archie was surprised to see—and each of them had on dirty shirts and gloves and hats. They looked like they'd been down here a while. Liv, the ringleader, wore a long black duster and had her long hair tied back in a ponytail.

"I get the big capsule shunts," Fergus said. "But why all these smaller dump wells? What are you stealing from those? Money?"

"Checks sometimes, yes," said Onatah. He was shorter than the others, an Iroquois with long, dark hair. "But bank records, bills, deeds—personal information like that is even better. Then we get access to whole accounts. We hack into the line, intercept a few p-mails, and we can steal more than your new pair of shoes or your new vacuum cleaner. We can steal your identity."

"Dern it, Onatah! You gotta tell them all our business?" Hector said.

"It's all right," Archie said. "We won't tell anyone. We just need to get out of here."

"Well, that's a problem, isn't it?" said Liv. "We lead you out, you'll know where we are. Took us a little while to set up this little operation, and I'd hate to come back and find out you've led some lawman down here to catch us."

"But you can't just—!"

Liv held up a hand. "We're not going to leave you down here either. There's miles of tunnels under Mannahatta. But I think we'll have to blindfold you on the way out. You'll have to walk too—there's no room in the cart. It's been a good day. Onatah, get that capsule they came in back in the system, and then make sure all the dump wells are tied off. Luis, you about finished over there?"

Luis was the one of the four they hadn't heard from yet. He was young and very dark skinned, the deep tan of the southern tribes, but his curly black hair pegged him as New Spanish.

"Almost done," he said. He was rolling up letterpress fliers and putting them into capsules from the cart, which he fed into different lines.

Hector ripped blindfolds from a rag in the donkey cart, and Archie and the others let the hackers tie them on. Archie thought Hachi would protest, but she was relaxed and quiet. Archie figured she must be up to something. She was always thinking ahead. Had a plan. Archie had been stupid to think he was any kind of leader of a new League of Seven. Hachi might be a warrior, and Fergus might be a tinker, but Archie was nothing but a twelve-year-old kid blowing steam.

Archie's blindfold went on, and Hector led him to the side of the cart for him to hang on. The hackers finished securing their dump wells and packing up, and soon they were on their way.

"Luis, you hang back with the kids. Keep an eye on them," Liv said. "Hector, don't take us straight out. Take a roundabout way, so that girl can't find her way back. I think she's the smart one of the bunch."

Of course. That's what Hachi was doing. She was quiet because she was paying attention to the turns they made. Archie shook his head. She *was* the smart one.

"What was that you were sending out, Luis?" Fergus asked. "I thought you just stole stuff."

"Oh, no. It was Liv's idea. She hired me to write them. They're letters, fishing for people to send their account numbers to a special p-mail address we have."

"Who would just send you their account numbers?"

"Oh, no one would send them to me. But the letters don't come from me. They come from a Nigerian prince who needs a small sum of money transferred to him to free up a fortune in stolen diamonds. Which, of course, he will split with the person who sends him the money, as a reward. It's an old con, and many people fall for it."

"You guys are behind those?" Archie said. "We get those at the house all the time! All they do is clog up the Inter-Net and fill up our inbox!"

"It's not just us. We run into other hackers down here sometimes." Luis lowered his voice, like he was talking just to them. "I would rather write books. *The Adventures of Professor Torque and His Amazing Steamboy*. Do you know these novels?"

"Professor Torque's my favorite!" Archie said.

"I want to write books like these. Adventure stories. But Nigerian prince letters pay better. Perhaps one day we'll make a killing and I can quit," Luis said.

"I'm not sure 'make a killing' is a phrase I want to hear while I'm being led blindfolded by a pack of criminals down in the sewer," Fergus said.

"Oh. Yes. Sorry," Luis said.

They walked on without talking for a little while, the only sounds in the tunnel the echo of the squeaking donkey cart and the *slurch* of their shoes in the muck. Archie didn't like not being able to see where they were going. It made being lost in the tunnels underneath the city even more scary.

"*Screeeeeeee.*"

Something big and inhuman squealed deep within the underground caverns. The donkey whinnied and backed up in his tracks.

Archie's heart skipped a beat. "What was that?"

"It's just the rats," Liv told them.

"That's some rat then!" Onatah said.

"*It's just the rats,*" Liv said again, in a tone that said she didn't want to hear any more about it. "Hector, get that donkey moving. Where in Hades are we?"

"You said take a roundabout way out!"

"I didn't say get us lost."

"I know where we are. I been following the tubes. See?"

"*Screeeeeeee!*" The sound was closer now. The donkey brayed and fought to get out of its bridle, and the cart jerked under Archie's hands.

"I don't like the sound of that," Fergus said.

Archie heard the *schnik* of Hachi's dagger, and he knew she didn't much like the sound either. He still had his blindfold on and was listening as hard as he could, turning this way and that.

"Hector, give me that pistol," Liv said. "I think there's something—"

Slosh. Crunch.

Liv screamed. Archie let go of the cart and staggered back in fright. The ground shook and the donkey thrashed. Archie ducked down low and ripped off his blindfold. Hachi, Fergus, and Luis crouched with him.

"Liv! Liv!" Hector yelled. The red beam from his aether pistol lit up the dark corridor and sizzled in the damp air. *Zaaaaak. Zaaaaak.* "What in the name of Hiawatha *is* it? Liv!"

The thing screeched again, and Archie peeked over the top of the cart. The creature at the far end of the tunnel was enormous. It filled the passageway completely, its giant molelike head hitting the ceiling and walls. Tentacles wriggled from its mouth, and patchy bald spots on its hairy face oozed orange pus. Its eyes were so pale and glassy Archie thought it must be blind, but it had found Liv well enough. It swallowed the second half of her with a gulp.

"Liv!" Hector cried again. As Archie's eyes went to him, so too did the mole monster's. *Zaaaaak. Zaaaaak. Zaaaaak.* Hector fired into the thing's tentacles, severing some of them with explosions of orange pus. It squealed again and lurched forward, snatching Hector up and stuffing him in its mouth.

Archie dropped back behind the cart with Hachi, Fergus, and Luis.

"What—what is it?" Luis asked.

"Is it a Mangleborn?" Hachi asked.

"No," Archie said. "It's too small for that. A Manglespawn maybe. A child of a Mangleborn."

"*Too small?*" Fergus said. "Crivens. Do we run for it?"

"Where would we go?" Hachi asked. "I had Freckles watch all the turns, but that'll only take us back where we came from." The little giraffe's head stuck out of one of the bandolier pouches.

Luis stared at Freckles as the creature snuffled and sloshed behind them. "Who *are* you children? How do you know what's going on?"

"Do you know any other way out?" Fergus asked.

Luis shook his head, his eyes bulging.

"Wait. Where's Onatah?" Archie asked. He popped back up for another look. He scanned left and right, the creature's head turning with him. There—Onatah was crouching in the darkness at the edge of the tunnel, frozen with fear. The creature turned its head to Onatah just as Archie's eyes found him, and its tentacles snaked out for him.

"Onatah! Onatah, move!" Archie cried.

The hacker was too scared. The tentacles wrapped around him and dragged him, screaming, into the thing's sucking mouth. Archie looked away, and the monster's head moved with him.

No, Archie thought. No. *It can't be.* He glanced right, and the thing looked right. He glanced left, and the thing looked left. He looked up at the ceiling, and the thing's tentacles groped there, searching.

Archie dropped back behind the cart, thinking hard.

"Do we attack or run?" Hachi asked him.

Archie blinked. Hachi was actually asking *him* to make a decision?

"You know more about these things, White," she said. "Do we attack, or run?"

"I—I think we need to put the blindfolds back on."

"*What?*" Fergus and Luis said together. Everyone looked at him like he was crazy.

"If we do that, we'll be helpless!" Luis said. He turned and looked underneath the cart, through the snorting donkey's legs.

"No, don't look at it!" Archie told him, but it was too late. Tentacles wriggled out and snatched up the donkey, dragging it and the cart toward his mouth.

"It's blind!" Archie yelled, scrambling to put his blindfold back on. "The monster's blind, but it can see through our eyes. It sees what we see. Trust me. Put your blindfolds on and it can't see us! Hurry!"

Hachi immediately did as she was told, but Fergus still wanted to argue.

"Fergus, look at the tubes," Archie told him. "Don't look at any of us. Just the tubes. Watch what it does."

Archie had his blindfold on now and reached out to find Hachi.

"Twisted pistons!" Fergus said. "It's—it's moving wherever I look!"

"Blindfolds, everybody!" Archie said again, feeling more confident now. He was doing it. He was saving them. He was in charge.

"I don't have a blindfold!" Luis said.

"Just close your eyes, then," Archie told him. "Close your eyes and don't open them, no matter what you hear!"

The donkey brayed in panic, and then—*crunch*—it was quiet. They listened as the tentacles tore apart the cart and the packages in the back crashed to the ground.

"Freckles, I need you," Hachi whispered, and Archie heard the mad fluttering of metal wings.

"What is it? What is that?" Luis asked in a panic.

Archie shushed him.

"Freckles, I need you to be my eyes. Tell me what you see."

More fluttering, then more of the music box chittering sounds the little lion and gorilla had made at her back in the glade.

"Can you actually understand that?" Fergus asked.

"In a way," Hachi said. "Now hush." She paused. "It's getting closer, Archie. Coming this way. What do we do?"

Archie's heart raced. Hachi was the warrior. She was the one who always knew what to do. But for once Archie knew more than she did. Only he didn't *really* know anything about the thing behind them. What could they do to get away?

The thing snuffled near them, and Freckles chittered again.

"*Archie*," Hachi whispered, "*It's almost on top of us.*"

Shung-shung. Shung-shung. Shung-shung. Another capsule rumbled its way toward them in the big tube overhead, and Archie had a sudden inspiration. His heart in his throat, he yanked off his blindfold.

The thing was right next to him.

Tentacles snatched him up and lifted him out of the muck, raising Archie toward the monster's slurping mouth. Hard as it was, as scared as he was, Archie tore his eyes from the mole-creature and stared as hard as he could at the big pneumatic tube overhead.

"Come on, you ugly monster!" Archie cried. "Get it. Get it!"

"Archie?" Hachi asked. "Freckles says it's got you!"

The creature's tentacles followed Archie's eyes to the ceiling and yanked the pneumatic tube loose. *Shung-shung. Shung-shung. Shung—ptoom!* A huge capsule fired out of the broken tube and slammed into the thing's face. *Krang!* It staggered back, stunned, dropping Archie in the muck as it collapsed.

"What the—?" Fergus cried, ducking even though he couldn't see anything.

"It's all right," Archie said, panting. "You can take your blindfolds off now."

Hachi pulled hers off and quickly moved to help Archie up. When he was on his feet, she surveyed the downed monster, the crumpled capsule, and the broken tube. A hint of a smile curled at the end of her thin lips as she put it all together.

"Better," she told him.

"Is it—is it dead?" Luis asked.

"I don't know," Archie told them, "but I don't think we should hang around to find out."

Nobody argued with him. Hachi picked up one of the fallen lanterns and led them around the side of the thing. They had to squeeze flat against the wall to move past it, once even having to climb over one of its misshapen paws. The awful wet-rat smell of the thing was so powerful they could barely speak.

"That was no insect creature," Hachi said once they were clear. "Do you think it's under the control of that thing back in Florida?"

"No," Archie said. "No, I think it's something else entirely.

The spawn of some other Mangleborn. Something imprisoned here, below Mannahatta."

"A creature imprisoned beneath Mannahatta?" Luis asked.
"What are these Mangleborn? How big are they? What do
they look like?"

"I think we better worry about getting out of here," Archie said, trying to avoid the questions. "Does anything look
familiar?"

A few yards on, Luis thought he recognized some graffiti,
and they followed him through another few passageways until
they found a ladder leading up to an alleyway behind a Texian
restaurant. Night had fallen, and fatigue set in when Archie
realized they'd been going nonstop all day.

"I think I can find our way back to the ship from here,"
Archie told them.

Luis took each of their hands in his own in turn, shaking
them fervently.

"You have saved my life, my friends. You have saved my
life! And these Mangleborn of which you speak, you have
inspired me to write about them!"

Archie shared a concerned look with Hachi and Fergus.

"Look, don't say too much about them. People aren't supposed to know," Archie said.

"Oh, I will not tell anyone what I saw in the tunnels tonight. Who would believe me?" Luis said. "No—I shall write
stories about them. Novels. About the Mangleborn, and the
heroes who fight them! They will be bigger than Professor
Torque ever was."

"Um, I don't know . . ." Archie said.

"Here. Please." Luis pulled a Nigerian prince letter from

his satchel and pushed it into Archie's hands. "Please, if there is anything I can ever do for you. The address on here. Just send a p-mail to this address. My name is Luis Philip Senarens. Here." He scribbled his name on the paper.

"Okay. Sure," Archie said. It felt strange to have a grown man thanking him like this. "We'll let you know. Thank you."

Luis thanked them again profusely, and finally they were able to make their escape.

"What good is a writer going to be?" Fergus said once Luis was gone, but he stuffed the note in his pouch all the same.

Mr. Rivets was waiting for them in the *Hesperus*. He was much relieved to see they had escaped the meka-ninja, but was not at all happy to hear about their run-in with the mole monster in the tunnels.

"I concur with Master Archie: a Manglespawn, not a Mangle-born."

"And what's a Manglespawn again then?" Fergus asked.

"The monstrous offspring of a Mangleborn and some other creature. Sometimes with a human, sometimes with an animal."

"Well, in this case it was with an elephant-sized mole," Fergus said.

Mr. Rivets' worry subroutine knitted his brass eyebrows. "If Manglespawn such as these are becoming more active, we may have more than just the Swarm Queen to worry about soon. We may indeed be seeing other Mangleborn growing stronger and rising anew."

"And where exactly is this Septemberist Society of yours?" Hachi asked.

"*I don't know*," Archie said. "Mr. Rivets, did we hear back from your contact?"

"We did indeed, sir." Mr. Rivets produced a piece of paper and handed it to Archie. Hachi read it over his shoulder.

"It's nonsense," she said. "'No one here. Gas main explosion. Big fire. Outbreak of whooping cough—very contagious. Possibly also bears. Stay away.'"

"We're too late then," Fergus said. "That bug thing has already got him."

"Quite the contrary, sir," said Mr. Rivets. "Unless I am very much mistaken, this missive proves the man in charge of Atlantis Station is still very much himself."

"Did you say . . . Atlantis?" Fergus asked.

"Yes, sir. The sole occupant of Atlantis has always had . . . how shall I put it? A leaky gasket."

"Atlantis," Fergus said again skeptically.

"You've met him, Mr. Rivets?" Archie asked. "The contact?"

"I have indeed, sir, as have you, though you may have been too young to remember it. His name is Nikola Tesla."

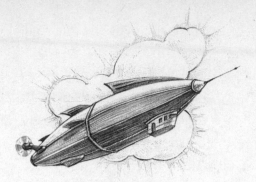

15

As they drew nearer to Atlantis Station, Archie had the vaguest memories of having been there before. He remembered water—lots and lots of water.

What he had forgotten was that Atlantis was a tourist attraction.

"Niagara Falls?" Fergus said. "*Niagara Falls* is Atlantis?"

Out the front window, the biggest waterfall in the United Nations spread out in a horseshoe of cascading water, plunging more than a hundred feet to the boulders at its base. White spray filled the air around the falls like steam.

"Niagagarega," Hachi corrected him. "The Niagagarega lived here long before the Seneca."

"Atlantis," Archie corrected them both. "An Atlantean power station, at least. Atlantis wasn't a city, like in the old stories. It was an empire, and they ruled the Old World and the New World. They were bigger than Rome."

"That is correct, Master Archie," said Mr. Rivets. "The Septemberists have uncovered traces of Atlantean civilization as far west as California and the Seattle Alliance. Some even believe Atlantis to have begun here and spread east across the

Atlantis Ocean, making this their Old World and Europe their New World. Many First Nations languages are thought to be descended from ancient Atlantean. The First Nations tribes themselves are very probably the descendants of Atlantis."

"You know, half the time I think you're making this stuff up," Fergus said.

"I assure you, sir, I am incapable of lying," Mr. Rivets told him.

But you're really good at keeping secrets, Archie thought bitterly.

Mr. Rivets steered the *Hesperus* toward a public park near a suspension bridge on the far side of the falls. "The Romans found this power station when they conquered the Americas," he explained. "They realized at once it was an artifact from a previous civilization, even though Atlantis was almost as much a mystery to them as it is to us. The Mangleborn did a most thorough job of destroying Atlantis, as they did when the Romans filled the world with lektricity. Afterward, Atlantis became a legend once more—one remembered as being underwater."

"It's like half of what I think is true is a lie," Fergus said.

"'Misremembered' might be a more charitable way of putting it, sir," Mr. Rivets said. "That is what happens when the Mangleborn rise. Civilizations, and their accumulated knowledge, are destroyed. Humanity is returned to a primitive state and made slaves to the Mangleborn. Eventually we overcome our own ignorance and regain control, but only with the help of a new League of seven heroes. By that time, however—"

"We've forgotten everything we knew and we have to start all over," Archie said.

"Except for myths about titans. And a deep-down fear of lektricity," Fergus said. "Explains why people called Edison the Wizard of Menlo Park. They thought he was working dark magic." He lowered his voice. "Turns out they were right."

"Indeed," said Mr. Rivets. "The Septemberists encourage these myths. That fear—and the Septemberists' efforts—have held science in check and kept humanity safe for hundreds of years."

Mr. Rivets settled the *Hesperus* onto a mooring, and they rode down in the elevator basket. The falls in the distance roared like a blacksmith's fire, and the air was cool and damp. All around them, families from tribes across the United Nations and Acadia piled out of airships carrying raincoats, cameras, and picnic baskets for an afternoon of sightseeing.

Mr. Rivets bought them tickets for the Cave of the Winds attraction, and they rode an incline railway down the steep slope to the bottom of the falls. A series of elaborate wooden walkways had been built helter-skelter among the rocks and boulders at the edge of the river below. Farther out in the water, the *Maid of the Mist* steamboat carried a load of gawking sightseers, its great paddle wheels keeping it steady in the churning water at the bottom of the falls.

Archie, Hachi, and Fergus donned raincoats and followed Mr. Rivets along the snaking wooden platform to where water crashed down on rocks. The roar of the falls was so loud they could barely hear themselves if they yelled, so they stayed quiet and kept moving. The winds that gave the cave at the base of the waterfall its name swirled around them, blowing them this way and that. Walking was hard for them all, but Fergus had the most trouble, his locked left leg almost useless in bal ancing himself against the shifting winds. He clung to the railing and inched his way forward.

At the top of the wooden walkway they came to the water-fall itself. Tourists pulled themselves through the pounding water on a rope line, laughing and screaming as they got drenched. Mr. Rivets strode through, and Archie and Hachi followed. Water came down on Archie like dozens of giant hands clapping him on the back, but he didn't fall. On the other side, Mr. Rivets climbed up stone steps into a small cave beyond the waterfall. Hachi followed, but Archie realized Fergus wasn't with them and went back through the pounding water to look for him. He found Fergus still clinging to the rail.

"Come on," Archie called over the roar of the falls.

Fergus shook his head.

"What's wrong?"

"My leg won't hold," Fergus yelled back. "I'll get knocked on my butt."

"Lean on me," Archie told him. Fergus looked reluctant. "We have to go through," Archie told him. "That's where the place is."

Fergus closed his eyes, then nodded. He leaned on Archie, and even though Fergus was older and bigger, Archie barely felt his weight on him. They worked their way through the waterfall together. Fergus slipped once, but Archie kept him on his feet long enough to push through.

"Never did like water," Fergus said on the other side. "Thanks."

Archie helped Fergus up into the cave where Hachi and Mr. Rivets had disappeared. At the back of the small space was a metal door marked with a pyramid eye inside a seven-pointed star—the symbol of the Septemberist Society.

The four of them stepped inside, and Archie and Hachi pushed the door closed against the thundering winds. It clicked shut, and the world went mercifully quiet again but for the dripping of their raincoats and the soft clicking of Mr. Rivets' clockworks. Archie hadn't realized just how loud the falls were until they weren't trumpeting in his ears anymore.

Fergus slumped wearily against the wall while Archie and Hachi had a look around. They were in a small room, perhaps ten feet by ten feet, made entirely of a dull gray metal. A gramophone horn was attached to the wall up high in one of the corners, and another door like the first stood at the opposite end of the small space.

"The power station is just through here," Mr. Rivets said. But as he approached the other door, it *ka-chunked*, followed by a similar *ka-chunk* from the outside door—the unmistakable sounds of doors locking.

Hachi drew her dagger.

Something started to hum within the walls, like the sound of a distant steam engine. But different somehow. Archie didn't recognize the sound, but it meant something to Fergus. He pushed himself up off the wall and frowned, listening to it.

"I know you've come for me like the rest!" a man's voice cried through the gramophone horn on the wall, making them all jump. "You won't get out of this room alive. I'll leave you in there until you die, then go out at night and slip your dead bodies into the water, where you'll be washed miles downstream before anyone finds you!"

"Well, that's some welcome," Fergus said.

"I thought you knew this person," Hachi said to Archie and Mr. Rivets.

Archie shrugged. He barely remembered anything about this place.

"Mr. Tesla, I am Mr. Rivets, Tik Tok valet to Dalton and Agatha Dent, and personal tutor for their son, Archibald."

Fergus and Hachi raised their eyebrows at him.

"Well? What did you *think* Archie stood for?" Archie said.

"If you will remember, sir," Mr. Rivets continued, "we came here eight years ago when Mr. and Mrs. Dent used the Septemberist archives to identify an odd specimen that had washed up near Charles Town."

"You could be impostors!" Tesla said through the speaker. "Yes. That's it. Impostors!"

"Thirty days hath September," Archie said, using the Society's secret pass phrase. "Seven heroes we remember."

"You'd still know the Septemberist code words if you were brainwashed!"

"If you'd just open the door, we could show you we're not brainwashed," Fergus said.

"Oh, very clever! Yes! I open the door, and you put one of those bug things on me and brainwash me like all the others," Tesla said. "No thank you!"

"Wait, I think I remember you now," Archie said. "You had these shiny silver discs with holes in the middle of them. From Atlantis, you said. You put them in a machine with lektric coils that glowed orange, but it melted them. So you just used the machine to make toast instead. I was little, but you showed me. We had strawberry jam on toast."

The speaker was quiet for a moment.

"Of course you would know that," Tesla said finally. "Just like you know the Septemberist pass phrase. You're the boy who was here before, but you and your friends have those little bug things in your necks!"

"No, that's why we're here," Archie said. "My parents, they have those bugs on them, and—"

"I'm not letting you in!" Tesla interrupted. "And you're not getting out. Not without frying yourselves. I may be the last Septemberist left, but I'm not going down without a fight!"

"He's lost his mind," Hachi said.

"Fried? What does he mean by that? Is he going to heat up the room?" Archie asked.

"Nae. Listen," Fergus said. He was listening to that hum again. "We're in a Franklin cage."

"A what?" Archie asked.

"A who?" Hachi asked.

"Did someone just say 'Franklin cage'?" Tesla said over the speaker.

Fergus put a hand out to the wall and touched it, but nothing happened. He nodded.

"Franklin was a Yankee inventor. He experimented with lektricity," Fergus said. "Edison had some of his old papers. I saw them. Franklin was a genius."

"You'll remember Benjamin Franklin, sir," Mr. Rivets told Archie. "A local printer and diplomat from Philadelphia who was instrumental in convincing the Iroquois to accept the Yankees into their confederacy after the Darkness fell. He was eventually recruited by the Septemberists, and worked in secret for them for decades."

"He had this idea, Franklin did," Fergus said. "You take a metal box, or a cage, or a can, doesn't matter, long as it's metal on the outside. You run lektricity to it, and the lektricity stays on the *outside*. Spreads around it, but not inside it, see?" He put his hand to the wall again. "No charge on the inside, but all around the outside is lektrified." Fergus frowned as he thought. "But to generate the kind of lektricity that would fry us, that would take—"

"Who is that?" Tesla asked. "Who's talking? How do you know so much about lektricity?"

"Let us in and we'll tell you," Hachi said.

"No. No tricks!" Tesla said. "I don't care. I don't. I'm going away now. I'm not listening to you anymore. *La la la la la la la la.*"

"He probably has his fingers in his ears," Hachi said.

"I heard that!" Tesla said.

"I thought you said you weren't listening anymore," Hachi told him.

"*La la la la la la la la,*" Tesla said again.

Hachi flung her dagger at the door in frustration, and it lodged there with a twang.

"That's helpful," Archie said.

"Just letting off steam," she told him, and she went to retrieve her knife.

"Nae, wait!" Fergus said, reaching for her. "Don't touch that! If it penetrated the outer wall, it could—"

A white-hot bolt of lektricity leaped from the dagger to Fergus' outstretched hand. *Kazaaak!* But Fergus wasn't jolted or thrown across the room. Archie and Hachi stepped back in fear as lightning arced from the dagger to his hand in a constant stream. All over Fergus' skin, the black lines danced and rearranged themselves.

"Fergus, what—?" Archie asked.

"I—I don't know," Fergus said. His startled face glowed in the lektric light. "But keep back. I should be dead. This should be killing me, but I don't even feel it."

Lektricity surged between the dagger and Fergus' outstretched hand, more and more of it, until the humming sound outside the room died and the sparks stopped coming. Fergus staggered back and stared at his hand. The black lines on his skin were moving again, rearranging themselves.

"Your face and arms," Archie told him. "The lines are moving there too."

The door to the inside of the facility *kachunked*, and a tall, thin man with a metal cage on his head ran out. He wore oversized rubber gloves and rubber boots, and metal foil stuck out of his sleeves and pant legs like he was wearing tin long johns.

"How did you do that?" Tesla demanded, his curiosity apparently overcoming his paranoia. "That was one hundred milliamperes! Where did it go? You should be dead!"

"I know. I think I—I think I absorbed it," Fergus said. He tapped the ends of his thumb and forefinger together, and lektricity sparked between them.

"O Bozye!" Tesla muttered. He took a screwdriver out of his pocket and touched it to Fergus' skin, but nothing happened. "No discharge! You're nonconductive now. Come with me."

Before any of them could protest, Tesla grabbed Fergus and pulled him inside. Tesla forgot he was wearing a cage on his head and banged into the door frame. He cursed in some Old World language and turned to them, embarrassed. "To keep the voices out of my head," he whispered, tapping the cage. "So they can't *control* me."

Archie might have thought Tesla was crazy if he hadn't heard voices in his head himself. The voice of a Mangleborn. *JANDAL A HAAD*, the Swarm Queen had said. Like she was speaking just to him. Like she was . . . calling his name.

Archie shook off the memory. Hachi was tapping at her dagger, seeing if it was going erupt in lightning again. It didn't, and she plucked it from the wall and followed Archie into Atlantis.

16

Archie, Hachi, and Mr. Rivets followed Tesla and Fergus through a short concrete corridor into a chamber so vast they slowed down to marvel at it. The curved ceiling must have been eight stories tall—nearly as high as the river above. Catwalks circled the walls, leading off to smaller corridors cut into the bedrock. Suspended from a spider's web of steel frames three stories up was a series of chains and pulleys, meant, no doubt, to service the seven massive machines scattered around the cavern floor. They were giant, humpbacked things, like ten-foot-tall metal turtle shells, connected by a jumble of tubes, wires, and conduits.

"Hydro-lektrics," Fergus said.

Tesla stopped when he realized Fergus wasn't following him. "What? Oh, yes. Built by the Atlanteans to run off the water from the falls. You know all about the Atlanteans, I take it? Geniuses. The marvels they created! By my conservative calculations, this facility can generate close to two thousand megawatts. Now, if you'll follow me. Just down here," he said, climbing down a ladder.

"Two thousand megawatts," Fergus said reverently.

"What does that mean?" Hachi asked.

"With Edison's lektric lights, two thousand megawatts could light up an entire city. Maybe the whole Eastern Seaboard."

"Or raise a Mangleborn," Archie said.

They followed Tesla down the ladder into a room set into the floor. It was filled with workbenches and shelves covered with metal parts, wires, and tools, but the rounded walls and the drain in the floor reminded Archie of a big, empty pool—which, it turns out, was exactly what it was.

"A repurposed water tank," explained a machine man who helped them down off the ladder. He was a silver-gray color, not brass like Mr. Rivets, and white smoke puffed from his stovepipe hat. The nameplate welded to his chest said his name was Mr. Piston. He was one of a small army of silver-gray Tik Toks working at various tasks around the facility.

"The pools were previously used in the operation of the hydro-lektric generators," Mr. Piston said, "but Mr. Tesla drained a few to use as extra workshop space, as most of the generators are not online."

"*Most of them* aren't online?" Archie asked. "Does that mean some of them are?"

"He had to lektric that Franklin cage somehow," Fergus said.

Tesla looked up from a shelf of equipment like a child caught with his hand in the licorice jar. "Oh. Well. I do keep *one* of them online. For security reasons, you understand. And perhaps the odd experiment . . ."

"Mr. Tesla!" Archie scolded.

Tesla waved a hand. "It's all right, it's all right. I know what

I'm doing." A metal box with wires sticking out of it fell off a shelf and crashed to the floor. Tesla kicked it aside and kept digging through the machinery.

"Does anybody else hear that?" Fergus said, frowning. He looked around the room.

"Hear what?" Archie asked.

"A . . . beeping. A lektrical sound. Beep beep beep beep. It won't stop."

Hachi shook her head. She couldn't hear anything strange either.

A cockroach scurried out of the drain and stopped like it was spying on them. Archie stepped on it, just in case it really was.

"I must say, it's nice to have you back at Atlantis Station, Master Archie," Mr. Piston said.

"You remember me?" Archie asked

"Of course, sir. You were very young then, but machine men never forget. Have your parents come to do research in the archives again?"

"No. My parents have been captured. By a Mangleborn. That's what we're here for, Mr. Tesla. We need your help!"

"And rayguns," Hachi said. "Big ones."

"Yes!" Tesla said. He thumped something big and heavy down on a workbench and put Fergus' hands on the two poles sticking out of the top.

"What is it?" Fergus asked.

"A hundred-volt battery," Tesla said.

Fergus jumped back, lektricity arcing between his hands and the battery poles.

"Crivens! That could have shocked the clinker out of me!"

"But it didn't," Tesla said, his eyes alight with excitement. He took Fergus' hands in his own and turned them over. "Yes! Circuits, I think."

"What?" Fergus asked.

"These marks on your skin. They are forming circuits. Circuits that change and adapt as needed."

"Of course," Fergus said. He gaped at his hands while Tesla sifted through another box, looking for something.

"What does that mean?" Archie asked. "What's a circuit?"

"Circuits are what made the Archimedes Engine work. It's like little paths that make lektric current do what you want it to do," Fergus said.

"Unlike aether, we know quite a lot about lektricity," Tesla explained. "The aether operates with a strange geometry that no human mind has been able to comprehend. All we've been able to do with it for the last two millennia is make crude weapons that collect it and discharge it through crystals. But lektricity—lektricity is measurable. Serviceable. Understandable! Lektricity conforms to quantifiable mathematics! The Romans, the Atlanteans, the Lemurians, the Mu—perhaps even the First Men—they all discovered the secrets of advanced circuitry, building fantastic computational engines that could fit in the palm of your hand!"

"That's what Edison did," Fergus said. "He turned me into a lektrical computational engine. I'm a human computer."

"Edison?" Tesla said. "I worked for that madman once." Tesla grabbed Fergus' arms, the metal foil under his suit crinkling. "Now, we are sworn enemies! Tesla and Edison! I am his nemesis, and he is mine! Although I'm not actually sure he knows I exist. Do you work for him?"

"I—I did. But not anymore. He did this to me," Fergus said.

Tesla nodded and calmed down, watching Fergus' tattoos shift and change. "How do you do it? How do you change the circuits?"

"I don't. I mean, I don't think about it at all. It just happens."

"Can you reverse the flow, I wonder? Discharge lektricity at the rate you absorb it? Here—" Tesla went rummaging again.

Fergus put his hands to his head. "Ach. Are you sure none of the rest of you can hear that infernal beeping? It doesn't stop."

Hachi gave Archie a "get on with it" look.

"Mr. Tesla, I'm sure Fergus wants to know everything that's happened to him," Archie said, "but there is a Mangleborn rising in Florida. Malacar Ahasherat. The Swarm Queen. There may be more of them rising in other places too. We fought a Manglespawn in the tunnels beneath New Rome."

"Aha!" Tesla said. He came up from a box with a glass bulb with wires coiled inside it. "You know what this is?" he asked Fergus.

"One of Edison's lektric lightbulbs!"

"Well, no. This is Atlantean. But I'm sure it's the same principle." He handed it to Fergus. "Make it glow."

"How?"

Tesla shrugged. "Think it. You know the principles. Imagine it working."

Fergus closed his eyes and concentrated. The lines on his skin reconfigured, and in moments the glass bulb began to glow. Archie gasped, and Fergus opened his eyes.

"I did it!" Fergus said.

The lightbulb glowed brighter and brighter until it exploded in a shower of glass, making them all duck.

"Yes. Well, I think it will take some measure of control," Tesla said. "But we can test your capacity."

"Archie," Fergus said. "The Archimedes Engine. The tower you destroyed. Edison made me *into* one. That's why he's after me. He wants to use me to raise that Mangleborn."

Tesla looked up from a crate. "Edison is trying to raise a Mangleborn? Which one?"

"That's what I've been trying to *tell* you," Archie said. He was losing his patience. "Malacar Ahasherat. The Swarm Queen. She has my parents!"

As Archie said it, he had another vision of them. A waking dream. He was standing in the middle of a great machine. Gears the size of boulders rotated and clinked around him. And there were his parents, slipping down between two of the gears. They would be crushed! He ran for them, screaming their names, when suddenly the vision disappeared and he was jerked back into Atlantis Station. Tesla was staring at him up close through the wire cage around his head.

"You heard something, didn't you? Saw something?" Tesla said.

There was something on Archie's head. He put a hand up to it, but Tesla stopped him.

"Ah ah ah. Don't take that off. It's to keep the voices out."

Archie looked around. Fergus was wearing a metal hat like a big bowl with wires coming out of it, and blinking like he'd just woken up. So was Hachi. Archie assumed he was wearing the same thing.

"You all went quiet for a time," Mr. Rivets said. "You couldn't hear us or see us either. Not until Mr. Tesla put those devices on your heads."

"Wait, you saw it too?" Archie asked Hachi. "Have you been seeing the same things we have this whole time?"

Hachi nodded reluctantly.

"You didn't say anything. You said you didn't believe me when I told you my parents were still alive, but you *saw* them."

"But how?" Mr. Rivets asked. "Miss Hachi did not touch the green flame."

Hachi looked away. Either she couldn't explain it, or didn't want to.

More secrets, Archie thought. He was getting slagging tired of all the secrets.

"Crivens. I wish these tinfoil hats blocked that beeping noise," said Fergus. "You sure none of you lot can hear it?"

Tesla tutted. "This is more serious than I thought. Edison raising a Mangleborn. Why didn't you say so? If he does, he could remake the world with lektricity. Which, frankly, would be fascinating."

"And kill us all," Archie said.

"Yes. That too," Tesla said. "Mr. Piston—show them to the archives on the fifth floor. That's where you'll find anything the Septemberists have on this Mangleborn." He waved a hand. "I don't know anything about that. The Society just stores the books here for safekeeping."

Mr. Piston nodded and invited them to climb the ladder with him.

"We need weapons too," Hachi said. "Big ones."

"That I *can* do," Tesla said. "Run along, and I'll have something for you when you come back. Ah ah ah. Not you," he told Fergus. "You can stay and help. And if we have a bit of extra time, I want to try hooking you up to a few things."

"Fine," Fergus told him. "As long as you do something about that bloody beeping."

17

Archie stared at Hachi as they rode the elevator to the fifth-floor archives. Why hadn't she said something about having the same dream he and Fergus had on the *Hesperus*? That must have been why she was awake—not because they were talking, but because she'd had the same nightmare. She had seen his parents. And back in the glade too, she must have had the same vision of his parents in the brass room with the empty picture frames. Why had she told him his parents were dead if she'd seen them alive? And where had she made her connection with the Swarm Queen, if it wasn't through the green flame that had connected Fergus to the Mangleborn?

And for that matter, where had Archie gotten *his* connection?

"Would you care for some music while you wait?" Mr. Piston asked. A gentle music-box version of "Mr. Twister, the Melancholy Machine Man" tinkled mechanically from somewhere inside his body.

"You can play music without a Concert card?" Archie asked.

"It is just one of the many standard features of the new and improved Emartha Mark IV Machine Man, sir. Each of us comes standard with aluminum memory cards, titanium alloy bodies, and a compact coal stove and boiler which provide a great deal more torque and a longer run-time than the clockwork mainspring which powers the Mark II."

Mr. Rivets straightened and whirred almost indignantly. He was a Mark II Machine Man.

"We're very happy with our Mark II," said Archie.

"Thank you, sir," Mr. Rivets said.

"Customer loyalty is a hallmark of the Emartha Locomotive and Machine Man Company," Mr. Piston said. The elevator came to a stop, and he slid open its cage. "That is why so many owners choose to replace their obsolete machine men with newer models from the same foundry."

Mr. Rivets waited for everyone else to leave the elevator before following a few steps behind.

The League's archives were in another long, tall corridor, though not nearly as long and as tall as the one below with the lektric generators. The room had been converted to a library decades ago, but despite the dedicated upkeep from half a dozen machine men—all Mark IVs, Archie noted with disappointment on Mr. Rivets' behalf—the place still smelled ancient and dusty.

"I think I remember this place," Archie said. "I remember playing hide-and-seek with Mr. Rivets in the shelves while Mom and Dad looked things up in books."

"Just so, sir," Mr. Piston said.

Archie had never shared his parents' love of libraries. Just the sight of the stacks and the thousands of books cataloged here made him sag. If this was anything like the library back in Philadelphia, there would be books in here as old as Ancient Greece. A few might even hold secrets from old Atlantis. All they needed was for one or two to be about Malacar Ahasherat—to tell them how to stop her and get his parents back. But the thought of wading through all these books looking for answers made him tired already.

Mr. Piston brought them a stack of decomposing old tomes, and Archie and Hachi got to work, skimming through them for any reference they could find to the Swarm Queen. There were accounts of all manner of Mangleborn and Mangle-spawn, from giants with antlers the size of trees to lesser creatures with feathered arms and bodies like snakes.

"I can't believe all these things are real," Hachi said, shutting a book.

Archie turned the next page of his book and froze. There in an illustration was Malacar Ahasherat, the Swarm Queen, fighting a hulking First Nations man wrapped in a bearskin.

"I found her," Archie said, and Hachi came around to read with him.

The man in the picture was the Great Bear, a member of some former League of Seven, one of the superheroes who had come together to save their world from the Mangleborn once again. He had been a mighty champion of the Mi'kmaq, a First Nations tribe in Acadia.

"'After six did fall in battle, only the Great Bear, his pelt impervious to every weapon, remained,'" Hachi read aloud. "'Thence it was that the Great Bear alone, he with the strength of a hundred men, came to defeat the Queen of Swarms, the last of the ancient monsters called the Mangleborn.' But it doesn't say *how*," Hachi said. She flipped forward and back in the book, looking for answers.

"'His pelt impervious to every weapon,'" Archie said. "That bearskin he's wearing. It must have protected him. If we had that pelt, we would be protected too."

Hachi pulled another book to her. "I saw something else about the Great Bear in this one."

Archie read the rest of the entry about Malacar Ahasherat in Plutarch's *Seven Lives of the Mangleborn* while Hachi flipped back through her book. There wasn't much more except descriptions of all the plagues and disasters the Swarm Queen had caused. "'The monster, like its cousins the insects, is attracted to the light of the full moon and draws strength from its pull,'" Archie read aloud. "Mr. Rivets, when is the next full moon?"

"I'm afraid I don't have that information, sir," Mr. Rivets said. "Perhaps one of the Mark IVs will have the answer encoded on his shiny new aluminum memory cards."

If Archie didn't know it was beyond his programming, he would have thought Mr. Rivets was being a little snippy.

"Here," Hachi said. "It says the pelt was buried with him. The bearskin and his club. 'In the mouth of the great bear.'" She looked up. "The Great Bear was buried in the mouth of the Great Bear? How does that work?"

"I don't know. Does it say where he's buried?"

"What, now we're going to rob a grave?"

"If that's what it takes to beat this Mangleborn and get my parents back, yes!"

"Archie, it's just a story," Hachi told him. "One of your half-truths, like Atlantis. There's no such thing as bearskins that weapons can't pierce, or people with the strength of a hundred men. It's just mythology. Tall tales. Some guy was strong, and a thousand years later people remember him being some kind of superman."

"You mean like mole monsters that can see through other people's eyes? Or ichor of lektric squid turning Fergus into a computing machine?" Archie stood. "Why do you have to be like that? Why do you have to deny everything, even when you can see it with your own eyes? You told me my parents were dead when you knew they weren't. You saw them, didn't you? In a dream, just like I did! Just like Fergus did!"

"All right," Hachi said, standing to face him. "Your parents might not be dead. *Yet*. But they will be. You can't go down there with that thing and live. Nothing can. You heard it beating on the seal. It's going to get out. Nobody's safe. Not even aboveground. They're dead, we're dead—everybody's *dead*."

"Then what were you doing there? In Florida?"

"I was going to kill Edison. And then I was going to kill that thing that lives underground."

"How, exactly?"

"I had a plan, okay? A plan you ruined."

"Then why don't you just go do it yourself then, if you have all the answers?"

"Maybe I will!"

Hachi crossed her arms and turned away. Archie slapped his book closed. Behind him, Mr. Piston emerged from a row of bookshelves, his stovepipe hat puffing.

"Mr. Piston, I need more books about the Mi'kmaq hero called the Great Bear," Archie said. That pelt had protected the Great Bear from Malacar Ahasherat once, and Archie wanted it.

Mr. Piston didn't answer. Instead he played "Mister Twister, the Melancholy Machine Man" as he had in the elevator. Hachi turned to look at him.

"Mr. Piston?" Archie said.

The machine man kept walking toward them without a word. Archie heard Hachi draw her dagger.

"Hachi, what're you—?" Archie began. Then he saw Mr. Piston's eyes.

The machine man's eyes were red.

"Run!" Hachi said. She threw her chair at Mr. Piston's legs, but the Tik Tok stomped it to splinters under his steam-driven feet. Archie was barely up out of his chair before Hachi slipped under the table and overturned it, scattering the tomes they had just been reading. The researcher's son in Archie flinched at the books being tossed about, but when Mr. Piston's whirling arms smashed right through the table he decided he didn't care so much and ran.

"I don't understand what's happened to them! They're not allowed to hurt humans. It's the first law of Tik Toks," he cried.

"That meka-ninja didn't seem to be too worried about any laws," Hachi yelled as they ran.

"But these are different! They're Emartha Machine Man Tik Toks!"

"Yes, the irony hadn't escaped me," Hachi said. Archie didn't understand what she meant by that, but there was no time to ask. Another machine man with red eyes came out of the stacks ahead of them and turned, his arms windmilling. He too was playing "Mister Twister, the Melancholy Machine Man"—DING-*ding*-DING-*ding*-DING-*ding*-DING-*ding*.

Hachi ducked and slid along the floor, just missing the arms of death spinning above her. *Shink. Pfft!* She snipped a pressurized rubber hose at the back of the Tik Tok's leg and it toppled, unable to stand. *Clang! Clang! Clang! Clang! Clang!* The machine man's arms kept spinning, pounding the stone floor like a paddle wheel.

"I'm glad Fergus wasn't here to see that," Archie said.

Their path to the exit was blocked by the thrashing Tik Tok. Hachi pushed Archie down one of the rows of books instead.

"Not you, Mr. Rivets," she told their machine man. "You take the next aisle."

"As you say, miss," Mr. Rivets said.

Archie didn't see the point in running this way—they were headed *away* from the door. Things only got worse when a red-eyed machine man playing "Mister Twister, the Melancholy Machine Man" turned down the far end of their row and Mr. Piston appeared at the other end, playing the tune in stereo.

DING-*ding*-DING-*ding*-DING-*ding*-DING-*ding*.

"We're trapped!" Archie said.

"No we're not," Hachi told him.

Archie didn't see how both exits being blocked wasn't trapped. And all Hachi was doing was standing there, watching the Tik Toks get closer.

"Now—climb!" she told him. She jumped onto the shelves and started up. Books rained down as she climbed, making Archie wince again. His parents would be distraught.

"Climb!" Hachi called down. She was already halfway to the top. Archie grabbed a shelf and hauled himself up unsteadily as the machine men drew nearer. Mr. Piston's arms sliced the air near him—*whht-whht-whht-whht*—and Archie slipped, his foot breaking a shelf in half. Books slid off it and exploded in Mr. Piston's whirling arms.

Hachi grabbed the back of Archie's jacket and helped pull him the rest of the way up. Below, the spinning arms of the evil machine men chewed up the shelves.

"Mr. Rivets!" Hachi called. "Push it over!"

The next aisle over, Mr. Rivets put his metal shoulder into the shelf they were on and pushed. The bookshelf swayed under Archie.

"Jump!" Hachi told him. She leaped to the bookcase across the aisle as Mr. Rivets tipped theirs over. Archie stood shakily, tried to steady himself, and jumped. He hit the other bookcase stomach first with an *oof.* Hachi grabbed his jacket and held on as the bookcase behind him slammed down—*boom!* burying the red-eyed Tik Toks under an avalanche of books and shelves. A decades-old cloud of dust poofed up from the wreckage as Archie scrambled the rest of the way up onto the top of the bookshelf.

"A little warning next time," Archie told Hachi.

In the silence that followed the boom, "Mister Twister, the Melancholy Machine Man" still played faintly from beneath the debris of the wrecked bookshelves.

"I believe my obsolete mainspring proved to have sufficient torque, wouldn't you say, Master Archie?" Mr. Rivets said from the next aisle over.

"Without a doubt, Mr. Rivets," Archie told him.

Hachi started off down the top of the shelves toward the exit, but Archie called to her to wait. He climbed down onto the mountain of debris below and yanked Mr. Piston's talent card from his back. The machine man stopped thrashing and playing music.

"Someone's tampered with it," Archie said, holding the talent card up for Mr. Rivets to see. There were new holes punched into the metal—crudely done, but clever enough to override the Tik Toks' fail-safes and make them act out their sinister new orders.

"Who would know how to do this?" Archie asked.

"I think the question is, who's the only other person here with us?" said Hachi.

"You don't mean Tesla!" Archie said.

Another machine man turned down the aisle, "Mister Twister, the Melancholy Machine Man" tinkling merrily from his internal speaking trumpets.

Hachi drew her knife again. "Let's go ask him," she said.

18

"Come on come on come on," Archie said to the elevator. Fergus was down there, alone, with Tesla. There was no telling what the man was doing to him.

"Would it help if I hummed 'Mister Twister, the Melancholy Machine Man' while we wait?" Mr. Rivets asked.

"No," Archie and Hachi said together.

"Very good," said Mr. Rivets.

The elevator hit the bottom floor, and Archie and Hachi rushed out. Down below, in the water tank Tesla had turned into a workspace, Fergus lay flat on a table. His shirt was off and wires stuck out of him all over his body. Tesla and one of the Mark IV machine men stood over him with pliers and screwdrivers in their hands.

"Fergus!" Archie cried.

Hachi slid down the ladder like a sailor, her feet wrapped around the sides. Afraid he would kill himself if he tried the same thing, Archie hurried down the usual way, one rung at a time. Mr. Rivets followed.

"Get away from him," Hachi told Tesla, her voice raspy and hard at the same time.

Tesla looked up, blinking behind the metal cage he wore on his head. "What? Why?"

Fergus sat up too, making Archie jump. Fergus' bare chest was a maze of black lines, just like his face and arms.

"What's all this about then?" Fergus asked.

"Has he hurt you?" Hachi said. She rounded on Tesla, her clockwork menagerie already hovering in the air around her. Tesla stumbled backward into a workbench.

"What? No. Why would he? We were just mapping out one of the configurations of my tattoos. We think this one might be a difference engine. You know, something that can calculate logarithms and trigonometric functions by approximating polynomials. We still can't figure out why I hear beeping, though. We think—"

"Fergus, we were attacked," Archie interrupted. "By reprogrammed machine men."

"Impossible," said the Mark IV at Tesla's side. His nameplate said he was Mr. Stoker.

"I'm afraid not," said Mr. Rivets. "Their human interaction fail-safes were overridden."

"By who?" Fergus asked.

"Oh, I don't know," Hachi said, cornering Tesla. "Who else is here with us?"

"These wind-up animals of yours really are quite astounding," he said, watching the flying circus buzzing around his head. "Wait. I'm sorry. You think *I* overrode the fail-safes on those Tik Toks? I didn't—*Aaah!* What's that?" Tesla pointed over her shoulder.

"Right," Hachi said. "Like I'm falling for that one."

Clang! A one armed black Tik Tok leaped from the balcony onto Mr. Stoker's back, startling them all.

"Crivens!" Fergus said. He fell off the table in fright.

"The meka-ninja!" Archie cried.

"The what?" said Tesla.

The titanium Mr. Stoker staggered under the weight of the assassinbot on his shoulders. As they watched, Mr. Shinobi disengaged the Mark IV Machine Man's talent card, punched a series of quick holes into it, and jammed it back home. Mr. Stoker's eyes turned red, and he began to play "Mister Twister, the Melancholy Machine Man."

"What is it? What's it done?" Tesla cried, cowering behind Hachi.

"You don't know?" she asked.

"No! I've never seen that Tik Tok before in my life!"

Archie expected the meka-ninja to jump at Fergus, weapons flailing, but instead it leaped from Mr. Stoker's shoulders onto one of the ladders and scurried back up to the top of the empty pool. It stood there and watched as Mr. Stoker's arms began to spin, chewing up the table where Fergus had been lying just a few seconds before. Above them, more reprogrammed Tik Toks with red eyes started climbing down into the empty pool.

Hachi pushed another table into the path of Mr. Stoker, whose new and improved steam-powered arms smashed it to pieces. "Tesla! I don't suppose you got those weapons you promised us before you started tinkering with Fergus," Hachi said.

"Oh. Um. Well, you see, we got carried away with our experiments, and—"

Hachi huffed. "That's what I thought."

Mr. Stoker's spinning arms backed them into the middle of the room as the other reprogrammed Tik Toks reached the floor.

"If I might be so bold, sir," Mr. Rivets said, "perhaps we could employ the same exit strategy Miss Hachi used in the library."

"I don't see any bookshelves to climb here, Mr. Rivets," Archie told him.

"No, sir. But Mr. Tesla does have a winch to raise and lower equipment out of the tank."

"But someone has to stay here to operate it," Tesla said. Clearly, that wasn't going to be him.

"I will stay, sir," Mr. Rivets said. "The other Tik Toks have proven disinterested in me, and I daresay I can survive their attacks better than any of you."

"Go. Go, then," Hachi said, shooing everyone onto the platform. The zombielike machine men were almost on top of them.

Mr. Rivets activated the lektric winch. The platform lurched and lifted off the ground. The spinning arms of the reprogrammed Tik Toks clanged against the sides of it as they rose, but soon Archie, Fergus, Hachi, and Tesla were safely away and headed for the top of the empty tank.

The Tik Toks turned and went back for the ladders.

"They're just going to climb back up after us!" Tesla cried.

"If I might make another suggestion, sir," Mr. Rivets called out. "If this tank is still functional, it could be refilled." He nodded to an enormous spigot that curled out over the tank.

"Yes, yes!" Tesla cried. "Swing us over to the balcony."

Mr. Rivets guided the hanging platform to the railing and

they climbed over. The red-eyed machine men were halfway up the ladders. The black meka-ninja stood at the railing on the other side of the empty pool, still just watching them.

Tesla ran to a big round wheel attached to the spigot. "I don't know how we're going to—*unh*—turn this thing. I had to—*unh*—had to have the steam-powered Tik Toks do it!"

Hachi ran over and hung onto the wheel. Fergus put what weight he could into it too. It still wouldn't budge. Archie found a place to put in a hand and tugged too. *Squeak!* The wheel came loose, and Tesla spun it. Gallons of water gushed from the pipe, pouring into the empty tank below. Tesla's equipment sparked and shorted out as the waves caught it, but he didn't seem to care. The water rose, swirling the wooden tables and chairs around and swallowing the thousand-pound Mr. Rivets. It filled the room quickly, catching the climbing Tik Toks on their ladders too. They fell off one by one and sank motionless to the bottom.

"Mr. Rivets!" Archie cried.

Tesla cranked the valve shut, and the flow slowed to a trickle. The water was clear, but pieces of furniture and bits of equipment swirled on the surface. Archie leaned out over the railing, but he couldn't see the bottom.

"We have to drain the pool!" he said. "We have to get Mr. Rivets out of there!" All his anger at Mr. Rivets' keeping secrets from him was gone in an instant. The machine man had been his constant companion since the day he was born—his nursemaid, his teacher, his guardian, his best friend. He couldn't lose him here, now. Not like this.

Fergus put a hand on Archie's shoulder. "He saved us,

mate. He made the ultimate sacrifice for any Tik Tok: He gave himself to save his owner."

"No! No, we have to drain the pool," Archie said. "We have to—"

Archie stopped. A brass hand grabbed the top rung of the ladder, and Mr. Rivets pulled himself up out of the water.

"Mr. Rivets!" Archie ran to the machine man and threw his arms around him. Archie knew the hug Mr. Rivets gave him back was just the automatic response of the Tik Tok's compassion subroutine, but he didn't care. "I thought I'd lost you!" Archie said.

"You forget, Master Archie, my 'obsolete' clockworks do not run on steam power, but the Emartha Mark IV Machine Man does. While steam power makes the Mark IV significantly stronger than the Mark II, it also requires a fire to boil water to create steam. Too much water, though, and the fire is extinguished, rendering the Mark IV just so much titanium scrap metal. With all due respect to the Emartha Locomotive and Machine Man Company, I believe you may call the Mark IV Machine Man 'defective by design.'"

"You know, what we need is a hybrid Tik Tok," Fergus said. "A machine man that runs on steam power, but has clockwork backups when its fire goes out."

"Oh, that's a rather good idea," Tesla said. "In fact, the steam engine could keep the backup clockwork engine wound. All you'd have to do is—"

"I hate to break up this fascinating discussion," Hachi said, "but we still have the meka-ninja to worry about." She nodded at the mysterious Tik Tok across the room, its red eyes staring at them from the shadows.

Before any of them could say anything more, Mr. Shinobi backed away and disappeared among the machinery.

"What's the clacking thing up to?" Fergus asked.

"It's playing with us," Hachi said.

"It's waiting for something," Archie said. Then it hit him. "Or some*one*."

"Edison, you mean?" Hachi asked. "But how would Edison know where it is?"

"Oh!" Tesla cried. "Oh! Oh oh oh! How could I be so stupid?" He rapped his fist against the metal cage around his head, then pointed at Fergus.

"What? You don't think I'm still working for that madman, do you?" Fergus asked.

"No, no. That beeping noise you've been hearing!" Tesla ran to a cart of lektric machines and rifled through them. He found what he was looking for, hooked wires to it, and clicked it on.

Beep. Beep. Beep. Beep. Beep. Beep. Beep. The sound came out of a little round mesh screen.

"Aye, that's it! That's what I keep hearing," said Fergus. "Is that what's doing it? Crivens, it's annoying."

"No, no. This is just a receiver. Your tattoos turned you into one too when they detected the signal. I suspect that's what that configuration was at the small of your back. The one we couldn't identify. Just above your—"

"Where's it coming from then?" Hachi asked.

"What? Oh. That black Tik Tok, I suspect," Tesla said. "It's a sort of an auditory . . . beacon. A homing beacon. With a device like this, Edison can follow it right to its source."

"And it's just going to hide out from us until Edison gets

here," Hachi said, looking up into the maze of walkways and corridors and caverns inside the enormous power station. "The reprogrammed Tik Toks were just to keep us busy."

"We can*not* let Edison find this place," Archie said. "Can you imagine what he could do with all this lektricity?"

From the looks on their faces, each of them had different ideas of what that would mean, and none of them were pleasant.

"How did it get in here?" asked Hachi. "What happened to that lightning room back at the entrance? Shouldn't that have kept it out?"

Tesla's dark eyebrows went up. "Oh. Oh dear. I suppose in all the excitement I . . . I left the door unlocked."

Fergus snapped his fingers, making a little spark. "The Franklin Cage! Mr. Tesla, if we trap the meka-ninja in the Franklin Cage, would the lektrical current block the signal?"

"It's possible. Yes. Yes, I think it would! In theory, it will reduce the radio frequency's lektromagnetic radiation, which—"

"Great," Archie interrupted. "But how do we get it in there?"

"It's following Fergus," Hachi said. "We get *the rayguns*," she said pointedly, "then we leave, and Tesla locks Mr. Shinobi in the room on the way out."

"Yes. Yes!" Tesla said, running for a large metal door set into the rock wall. "Here." Tesla tapped a series of numbers on a flat, glowing keypad, and the door rolled open with a clink and a hiss. Inside were racks and racks filled with oscillators, aether pistols, wave cannons, and more weapons Archie had never seen before. Hachi's eyes went wide.

"Mr. Tesla, come with us," Archie said. "Help us."

"What? Leave Atlantis Station? Oh, no. I haven't been outside since . . . um, what year is it?"

"Eighteen seventy-five," Fergus told him.

"Oh. Oh dear. No, really? That long?" Tesla shook his head. "No. If I go out there, I'll hear them. They'll whisper to me. I've been touched, you see. By the Mangleborn. Just like you. No. Too easy for me to be lost. I'm safer in here." He looked around at the walls as though frightened of what might lie beyond. Archie wasn't thrilled to know that the thing that scared Tesla most was the same kind of connection each of them shared with the Swarm Queen.

Hachi pushed oscillating rifles and aether pistols into the boys' hands. "We need someone to shut that Tik Tok in the lektric room behind us anyway," she said. "Somebody has to stay behind."

"Are there any more Septemberists who can help us?" Archie asked Tesla. "You have to know lots."

Tesla shook his head. "All enthralled with those bug things. Every last one of them."

Archie's heart sank. How could three kids and a Mark II Machine Man ever hope to defeat a Mangleborn?

Hachi came out of the weapons vault with a Chenault-Duffier personal wave cannon on her hip. "Let's do this."

They hurried toward the corridor that led back outside. Archie glanced over his shoulder and saw the meka-ninja's red eyes glowing in the shadows.

"It sees us!" Archie said. "It's coming!" They had to move more slowly to stay with Fergus, and the meka-ninja gained on them quickly.

"Go, go, go, go!" Hachi cried. She turned and fired the

wave cannon—*wom-wom-wom-wom-wom.* The walls shuddered and floor tiles shattered, but Mr. Shinobi jumped acrobatically out of the way of the wave pulse.

Archie burst through the outer door into the misty Cave of the Winds. Mr. Rivets came next, and Fergus hopped through after him. Hachi backed through, her Chenault-Duffier personal wave cannon at the ready, but Archie and Fergus slammed the door on the meka-ninja before it could slip out. *Clang!* The hinges rattled as Mr. Shinobi slammed into the door, but it held.

Ka-chunk. Ka-chunk. Archie recognized the sounds of the automatic locks clicking into place.

"Tesla got it!"

The door began to hum, and Fergus grabbed Archie and Hachi and pulled them away. "Um, I think you guys better step back from the door."

Spray from the waterfall sizzled as it hit the lektrified surface. Inside, the meka-ninja beat against the walls of its cage.

"If that thing's trapped in there, how's Tesla ever going to get out?" Archie asked.

"Don't know. It's clockworks, yeah? It'll run down eventually, won't it?" Fergus asked.

"Perhaps not, sir," Mr. Rivets told him. "From the placement of the imported machine man's mainspring key, I believe it to be capable of winding itself."

"A *self-winding* machine man?"

"Yes, sir. A feature wished for among many Self-Determinalists, some of whom have set up FreeTok communities among the western tribes and in Brasil. But the notion is still rather uncommon here in the United Nations."

"We're wasting time," Hachi said. "We have to go back to Florida. Now."

"No," Archie said. "We have to find the Great Bear's tomb. The bearskin, remember?"

"Archie, we have *very big guns*," Hachi said. "We don't need to go on a snipe hunt for this magical pelt."

"Look, it's *my* parents who are down there doing whatever the Swarm Queen tells them to, and I know that we've only got until the next full moon before Malacar Ahasherat is strong enough to get out. I want to get back down there faster than anybody. But we *need* that pelt. I know it. We can't beat the Mangleborn without it!"

"How are you so sure?"

Archie didn't want to say *because I'm the only one of us who's useless and I need it*, but that's the way he felt. "I just—I just am," he told them.

Hachi scowled, then let out a heavy sigh. "It's your parents."

She climbed down the rocks toward the waterfall, and Fergus gave Archie a supportive nod before following her down. Archie was glad for the vote of confidence.

He just wished he could give himself one as well.

19

The leaves were just beginning to change in Nova Scotia. A sea of red and yellow and orange stretched out beneath the *Hesperus* as it skimmed the treetops, the real ocean a misty blue line on the horizon. If he had been outside on the airship's gangplanks, Archie could have reached out and plucked a handful of maple leaves from a branch, could have smelled the salt in the air and soared like a hawk on the wind. He'd watched the airship sail over plenty of impressive vistas before, from cities to mountains to swamps, but he had never thought before how beautiful the world was in all its varied colors and shapes. It was almost inconceivable that the Mangleborn—hideous, monstrous things so different, so alien—lay just under the surface. He could see why the world above would believe the Mangleborn were just myths. Scary stories told to keep children in their beds. How could there be such awful monsters in a beautiful place like this?

But Archie knew better.

He caught sight of himself in the reflection of the airship's window—a white-haired, serious boy he barely recognized—and looked back at the scrapbook from Uncle John's office.

Why did John have it? What did it mean? What were Archie's parents and Mr. Rivets not telling him?

Archie remembered the last time his family had taken the *Hesperus* on a trip. A family vacation last year to the Jersey Shore. He'd loved running along the boardwalk, eating iced cream, riding the steamcoasters, playing the carnival games and the penny arcade. Had his parents been studying him then, the way Uncle John had? Making little notes about his taste in desserts, his aim in skeeball, the number of prizes he won in the ring toss? Had Mr. Rivets secretly snapped a photo of him swinging the hammer on that faulty strength-testing machine, the one so rigged one hit sent the bell on the top flying into the surf? Was there another scrapbook hidden somewhere in his own home, filled not with his parents' happy memories of their son, but instead with clinical, dispassionate observations about his behavior?

And yet all Archie could remember was his father rolling up his sleeves to play the pneumatic Whack a Mole, his mother's delight at the puppet show, her laughter carrying on the wind above the dull growl of the waves. His parents trailing behind him, arm in arm, smiling at him as he ran ahead. Try as he might, he couldn't see them any other way.

And yet they knew some secret about him. Some secret they had ordered Mr. Rivets not to tell him.

Across the cabin, Fergus slept, and Hachi muttered her list of names over and over again in her hammock.

Archie turned back to page one and read the scrapbook about himself all over again.

Mr. Rivets anchored the *Hesperus* in a clearing in Kejimkujik National Park in Nova Scotia, and Archie switched out the machine man's Airship Pilot talent card for an Explorer card.

The Great Bear Monument in Kejimkujik National Park, according to Mr. Rivets' internal copy of *Avery's Library of Universal Knowledge* (seventh edition), was considered by the Mi'kmaq tribe of the Wabanaki Confederacy to be the Great Bear's final resting place. The monument itself was a group of seven large stelae surrounded by a scattering of smaller stones, spread out over a clearing the size of a city block. Legend had it that the Great Bear had pulled trees from the ground to make the clearing, and arranged the massive standing stones himself before he died.

"He built his own mausoleum?" Fergus asked. "That's morbid."

"It was probably built later, using steam-powered wagons to move the stones from the quarry and pneumatic cranes to lift them into place," Hachi said. She glanced at Archie. "If there really *was* a Great Bear to begin with at all."

"He was real," Archie told her. "He was a Leaguer. The book said so. And this is where he's buried."

The stones lay beyond a small wooden building with a sign that said GREAT BEAR MONUMENT INFORMATION CENTER AND GIFT SHOP.

"Oh, a gift shop!" Fergus said. "I love gift shops."

The Information Center and Gift Shop was light on the information and heavy on the gifts. Hachi picked up a plush stuffed polar bear from a table full of them while Fergus tried on a fake white bearskin cape.

"Get me—I'm the Great Bear," he said. "Raaaaaaaaaar."

Hachi tossed the stuffed bear back on the pile. "I don't suppose anyone cares that there isn't a polar bear around for a thousand miles."

Archie spun a rack of airship key chains meant to look like little Great Bear clubs.

A woman in a brown Acadia Park Service uniform with ranger badges sewn onto it came out of the back room to greet them. Her skin was brown like most First Nations people, but her light hair and thin face said she had Acadian blood in her too.

"*Comment pouvoir je vous aide?*" she asked.

Archie looked helplessly at the others. He couldn't speak Acadian. "Um, we'd like to see where the Great Bear is buried," he said loudly.

The woman smiled at him. "Ah. Yankees, yes?" she said in heavily accented Anglish.

"I'm Seminole," Hachi said.

"You are a long way from home, yes?"

"Yes," Archie said. "Is the Great Bear buried here? We'd like to see his tomb."

"Ah, well, zer is no tomb, I am afraid. Just ze monument. We are not sure ze Great Bear really exzisted at all. But it is a wonderful legend, and very important to ze Mi'kmaq."

Archie tried to ignore Hachi's *I told you so* look.

"Well, I suppose we'd still like to have a look around anyway. While we're here," he said. The woman had to be wrong. The Great Bear *had* to be buried here. And his pelt had to be with him.

"Zertainly. Are your parents wiz you?"

"Their care has been entrusted to me, madam," Mr. Rivets said. "I am their tutor, Mr. Rivets."

"Well, we have a brochure here, if you like, or zere is an audio tour on wax cylinder for fifteen cents, with a ten-cent depozit."

Archie glanced at Mr. Rivets, but the machine man shook his head. "I apologize, Master Archie. My meager financial reserves have been depleted. If you would like, I could go back to the airship and see if any more money can be found."

Hachi grumbled something in Seminole and pulled a dollar coin out of her bandolier. "*Trois, s'il vous plaît,*" she told the ranger.

"Oh! And a postcard," Fergus said. He grabbed one with an aerial photo of the monument and slipped it onto the counter.

Hachi gave him a tired look.

"What? I promised Mrs. Henhawk I'd write," Fergus told her.

The ranger laid three portable personal gramophones on the counter. They were small brass tubes with grooved wax cylinders around the outside. Rubber hoses connected the gramophones' needles to amplification trumpets that fit over the listeners' ears.

"Just fit ze earphones on your head, like zis," the ranger told them, "crank ze handle, set the needle, and off you go."

"Very fancy," Fergus said as they took the high-tech gadgets outside. "You could sell music cylinders for these. Let you listen to your favorite songs while you walk around."

"Like 'Mister Twister, the Melancholy Machine Man,'" Archie said.

"No," Hachi told him.

The audio tour took them along a gravel path past each of the stelae. The first of the giant standing stones had a series of carved faces running down it. It was a totem pole, chronicling the Great Bear's ancestors all the way back to an actual bear, which snarled at them from the top of the stone.

Archie glanced back at the Information Center to see if they were being watched, then stepped over the low ropes that separated the path from the standing stones.

"What are you *doing?*" Hachi whispered.

Archie put a foot on the nose of the face at the bottom and tried to climb. "The book said the entrance to the Great Bear's tomb was through the mouth of the Great Bear. There's a big bear with a mouth on top of this stone."

Archie struggled to get past the third head. He tried to haul himself up on a woman's ear and slipped, tearing his pants on the rough stone.

"Get down here before you hurt yourself," Hachi told him.

Archie slid back down reluctantly, knowing he would never make it to the top. Hachi handed her portable record player to Fergus and scurried to the top of the totem pole in half the time it had taken Archie to get a third of the way there.

"There's nothing here," Hachi reported. She stuck her hand in the bear's mouth, showing them that it wouldn't go in any farther than her wrist. "The inside of his mouth is solid. And we wouldn't be able to fit inside even if it wasn't."

"It has to be somewhere else then," Archie said.

Hachi *humph*ed and scrambled down again, and they continued with the audio tour.

The voice on the audio recording told them the Great Bear was the son of a human chieftain's wife and the chief of all bears, who had kidnapped her. By the age of four the boy could wrestle his bear father to the floor; when he was twelve, he bashed his father's head in with a club and escaped with his mother, wearing his father's bearskin as a trophy.

"I guess you could say he'll always carry a part of his father around with him wherever he goes," Fergus joked.

The next few stelae recorded the Great Bear's further adventures in crudely drawn pictures. In one, he called down lightning on the Mi'kmaq chief who had married a servant girl while his first wife, the Great Bear's mother, had been held prisoner by the Bear Chief. On another, the Great Bear fought a giant snake, his father's bearskin pelt protecting him from harm.

Archie pointed to it, knowing Hachi was hearing the same description of it.

"Fiction," she told him.

As they made their way around to the last of the standing stones, Archie had to admit that it was looking less and less likely that there was anything here that could help them. His parents were slavishly doing the bidding of Malacar Ahasherat while he was listening to a boring old historian on an audio tour drone on about stone-carving techniques. What had he been thinking? His parents needed him in Florida, not here in Nova Scotia.

The truth was, he was scared. What could the three of them really hope to accomplish, big rayguns or not? Malacar Ahasherat was a Mangleborn. An ancient being who had terrorized the world over and over and over again, who had fought the greatest heroes in human history. What chance did they really have? What chance did *Archie* have?

On the last stela, the Great Bear's wife rescued him after a magical dog made him forget himself and wander the Earth half-crazy and alone, and together they rode off into the clouds on the back of a giant bird, never to be seen again. Hachi was right. This was fiction. All of it. And so was the Great Bear's pelt.

The needle on Archie's portable record player scratched to the end of the cylinder and lifted, the audio tour finished.

"All right," Fergus said. "I'm ready to take the test."

Archie pulled off his headphones and stared at the giant standing stones around them.

"It's not here," Hachi said. She said it quietly, like she was actually making an effort to be nice this time, but she still wasn't brass-plating it. She was right. Archie knew it now. He'd wasted their time, and put his parents in even more danger.

"Huh. It looks like a constellation," Fergus said.

"What?" Archie and Hachi said at the same time.

Fergus showed them his postcard of the monument. It was a picture taken from an airship high above the monument grounds, showing the standing stones not as tall spires but as dots seen from above. Dots that formed a familiar pattern.

"The stones are laid out like the stars in the Ursa Major constellation!" Hachi said.

"*The Great Bear*," Archie and Hachi said together.

"You two gotta quit doing that," Fergus said.

"All we have to do is find the one that's the mouth," Archie said. "That's where we'll find the Great Bear's tomb!"

"Well, it's more like his nose, but I'd have to say the best bet is this one, here, on the end of his head," Fergus said.

Archie turned the postcard to orient himself and set off for the stone at a run. The stela stood at the end of a long plaza cut from quartz. Just like the rest of the stones, this one had images of the Great Bear's adventures carved into it, but these had nothing to do with the Great Bear's pelt or his death. If Archie remembered correctly from the audio tour, this was a story about the Great Bear defeating and then befriending another man who was almost as strong as he was.

"I don't understand," he said. It was a standing stone just like the rest. "Where's the entrance? How are we supposed to get in?"

"Hoist me up," Hachi told them, and together Archie and Fergus helped her scale the standing stone. "There's nothing up top," she told them. "No way in."

"Maybe there's a hidden panel," Archie said. He pushed on the stone's surface. "You know, like a button or a lever you push."

Hachi frowned down at him. "And nobody's accidentally pushed it in all the years this rock was—whoa!"

The stone moved under Archie's hands. It clicked back a few inches like something mechanical was moving it, then lowered slowly into the ground with a grating sound of rock on rock. Hachi leaped off, and together they watched as the ten-foot-tall standing stone disappeared into the ground, leaving a hole large enough for them to climb into.

"Well *that* wasn't on the audio tour," Fergus said. "I think I'm going to ask for my money back."

"It wasn't your money to begin with," Hachi told him. She drew her dagger and hopped down into the hole, disappearing into a dark cave.

Archie helped Fergus climb down and shot one last look back at the Information Center to see if the park ranger had noticed the sudden disappearance of one of the monument's seemingly immovable giant stones. She hadn't come running, so Archie figured they were okay. For now.

"Mr. Rivets, I think you'd better stay here. I don't know if we could get you back out of there once we got you in."

"Indeed. I have no wish to be buried with the Great Bear, Master Archie. If the park ranger comes outside, I shall do what I can to distract her. But do be careful, sir."

Archie had expected the cavern to be dark, but it was suffused with a bright, sparkling glow. The quartz plaza above formed the cave's roof, and the light of the sun filtered through, giving the place an almost mystical shimmer. He found Hachi and Fergus near the opening of the cave, staring at something on one of the walls.

"It's more pictures," Fergus told him. "Images of the life of the Great Bear, looks like. But different from the ones above."

"Very different," Hachi added.

The images were crude drawings, ancient cave paintings done with ochre and red clay and charcoal. In the first one, the Great Bear was being born to a human woman, but her husband was not a bear. It was a monster. Not a Mangleborn, Archie guessed, but a Manglespawn—something like the thing in the basement of the Septemberist Society, or the creature they'd fought in the sewers. This one was bearlike. Sort of. It had white, shaggy fur like a polar bear, but it stood on two legs and had four arms, with claws like tusks and a long laughing mouth full of teeth like a shark. In the half-light of the dark cave, the primitive painting gave Archie shivers.

In the next picture, the Great Bear, now a boy, was twisting the bear-thing's tusklike claws back on itself to kill it. Blood, still as green as the day it had been painted on the rock, gushed from the Manglespawn where its own claws pierced it.

"Okay, if my dad was that thing, I'd kill it too," Fergus said.

"And look here. It looks like he fought beasties all his life, even though he was the son of one himself."

In the rest of the images, the Great Bear grew to be a man and had all manner of adventures—but unlike the exploits carved on the stones aboveground, these were darker. In one, he slew an entire village of half men, half ravens. In another, he defeated a seven-headed devil and earned an oversized club, which he wielded in every picture from then on. In yet another, he journeyed into a deep cave in the earth to wrestle a wormlike thing the size of a locomotive.

And in every picture, the invincible white pelt of his demon father protected him from harm.

"I wish there was an audio tour for these," Archie said.

But nobody would ever hear these stories, Archie knew. Nobody but the League of Seven. On these walls were dark horrors not meant for the people who lived in the bright, beautiful world above to see. The gentle myths of the Great Bear—the half-truths and misremembered events carved into the standing stones above—were enough for them. There could be no gift shop for the deeds memorialized here in this cave.

In the pictures toward the end of the cavern, six other figures joined the Great Bear in his battles.

"The League of Seven," Archie whispered. Was this the Atlantean League, or an earlier incarnation? He had no idea. But there in the paintings were crude representations of heroes lost to time: a black man with a book, a tan-skinned man in yellow robes pulling a chariot with a pointing figure on top, a smiling brown man with a hat that was black on one side and red on the other, a blindfolded white man with a raygun, a dark-skinned man with a longbow, and a yellow-haired woman in white with a sword, a shield, and a winged helmet. Together they fought giants the size of mountains.

The Mangleborn.

"This Great Bear of yours seems to have quite a temper," Fergus said. "I thought these people were his mates." Fergus pointed to a painting where the Great Bear fought the other six members of the League.

"After six did die in battle, only the Great Bear remained," Hachi said, quoting the book she and Archie had read in the Atlantis Station archives. "Maybe he was the last one left because he killed all his friends."

"No," Archie said. "He had to be under the control of a Mangleborn. Like with the bugs. And he had to have overcome it. He couldn't have killed them all. Could he?"

"It's a classic myth," Hachi said. "The strongman driven mad by a god until he hurts the ones he loves. In Greek mythology, Heracles killed his own children when Hera drove him mad."

"Aye," said Fergus. "And my father used to tell me and my brothers stories about Cú Chulainn, an ancient Hibernian warrior. He would go into a berserker rage for nae reason and kill anyone who came near him, friend or foe. Killed his own son too."

Archie wasn't listening anymore. His eyes had found an enormous stone coffin at the end of the chamber big enough for two grown men to lie down inside. The outside of it was decorated with crude drawings of bears.

Laid over the top, under a club as big as a tree stump, was a white fur pelt with a monstrous head and six shaggy limbs.

"I don't believe it," Hachi whispered.

Archie did. He clutched one end of the pelt, almost afraid

to disturb this place that hadn't been entered since the Great Bear was laid to rest. But he had to have it to save his parents from the Mangleborn in the swamp.

"I'm sorry," he whispered. "I really need it."

Archie tugged on the white pelt, and the massive club on top of it thumped to the stone floor with a great crash, making them all jump. Archie was sure the park ranger would come running at any moment.

He didn't care. He had it. *He had the Great Bear's invulnerable pelt.*

Suddenly he was scared of the thing. Something about it, something about just *holding* it, made his skin crawl. He held it out to Hachi. "Here."

Hachi looked as scared to touch the thing as Archie was.

"No way," she said.

"It'll make you invincible!" Archie said. "You can't be hurt if you're wearing this."

Hachi shook her head. "I couldn't fight with that thing tied around me. It would just slow me down," she told him.

Archie offered it to Fergus instead. "Here then. You use it."

"Ah, nae, Archie. While I'm happy not to be dying anytime soon, I think it's wasted on me. It's not like I'll be wading into too many battles with this leg. You wear it."

Not sure why he was so scared of it, Archie pulled the white pelt up over his back and tied two of the long arms around his shoulders. It made it look like the thing was eating him.

"Aye, see?" Fergus said. "It even matches your hair."

20

Archie was dreaming again.

He was in the chamber with the big round well again. The one with the stone doors in the floor that said XX. His parents were here too, staring at the covered pit.

THOOM. THOOM. THOOM. Malacar Ahasherat pounded on the door of her prison.

At a silent signal, Archie's parents turned together and walked to the wall. Archie's father pushed on a stone, and it slid into the wall and clicked. Gears ground and the stone wall dragged away, revealing an enormous machine built into the rock. Its huge brass gears and chains were still.

THOOM. THOOM. THOOM. Rock dust rained down from the ceiling.

Archie's mother walked slowly and deliberately to a control panel filled with dials and levers and gauges. She stared at them for a moment, then started turning and pulling and flipping them.

The machine's gears began to turn. Weights lowered. Wheels spun.

Behind them, the great stone doors that sealed the Swarm Queen in her tomb rumbled and parted.

"No!" Archie cried as he woke. He looked around, disoriented. He wasn't underground with his parents. He was in the *Hesperus*, on his way to Florida with Hachi and Fergus and Mr. Rivets. The Great Bear's white fur pelt lay on top of him like a blanket, and he was covered in sweat.

Hachi stared at him from her hammock across the cabin, looking like she too had just woken up.

"Did you just see my parents in a dream?" Archie asked.

Hachi nodded. "Now we know why that monster kept them alive."

"It brought them there to open its seal."

"I don't think they know how to operate that machine though," Hachi said. "The seal opened, but just a crack."

"They got through because they're librarians—they've studied the puzzle traps. They know how to navigate them. But they're not machinists. They don't know how to work the mechanism that opens the seal."

"That's the only thing buying us time," Hachi said. "But they'll figure it out eventually, just through sheer dumb luck."

"Fergus?" Archie called. "Fergus, did you see that machine?"

Something metal clanged to the floor, and Archie and Hachi stuck their heads out of their hammocks. Fergus lay on his back at the front of the cabin, under the steering console. Half the ship's tools lay scattered on the floor around him. Mr. Rivets stood watch nearby.

"Fergus, what are you doing?" Archie asked.

"Sorry. Did I wake you?"

Archie and Hachi climbed down to join him. "No, we had another dream. What's wrong? Is the *Hesperus* broken?"

"No, sir," said Mr. Rivets. "Master Fergus is not fixing anything. He is instead taking the airship apart piece by piece."

"I hear it again," Fergus said, his head still hidden inside the helm. "The beeping. Very faintly."

Archie was suddenly very much awake. "The meka-ninja, you mean? It's back?"

"No. I don't think so. But I think it must have planted another homing device on the *Hesperus* before it came into that Atlantis power station looking for us. I picked it up while I was sleeping." Fergus tossed a wrench into the ship's toolbox. "That's it. I've looked everywhere it could be. It's not inside."

"You mean—?"

Fergus tried to sit up and banged his head on the underside of the console. "*Ow.*"

"He means it's outside," Hachi said. She opened the coat closet and pulled out a duster and goggles.

"You can't go out there," Archie told her. "We're ten thousand feet up!"

"Twelve thousand, four hundred and seven feet up, to be exact," Mr. Rivets said. "The sensible thing would be for us to land and then search the ship."

Hachi slid into the coat and pulled the goggles over her head. "We haven't got time. If Edison homes in on that signal—"

"Too late," Fergus said. He had climbed out from under the console and was pointing at something through the *Hesperus'* big front window.

Up through the pink clouds it came: a massive black dirigible. Two big propellers flanked its tail fins, and a passenger cabin twenty times as big as the *Hesperus* hung beneath its rigid, cigar-shaped gas envelope. The airship broke the surface of the sea of clouds like a whale coming up for air and kept coming, turning its needle nose into the wind. Along its side, Archie could see a large letter "E" crossed by a lightning bolt: the logo of Edison Labs.

"The *Black Maria*," Fergus told them. "I've been on it before, when we flew to Florida and back. It's bigger and badder than the *Hesperus*. Much badder," he told them.

"Maybe we can outrun them," Hachi said.

"Nae," Fergus told them. "The *Black Maria*'s got twin lektric generators hooked up to a pair of Tecumseh aeroprops. He doesn't even have them up to full spin, from the looks of it. But that's not the worst of it. That thing's got a lektric cannon. He can shoot lightning."

"What's its range?" Hachi asked.

"I dunno, but it's not going to matter in a minute." The *Black Maria* was already bearing down on them. Archie and Fergus looked to Hachi for ideas. As much as Archie wanted to be the leader of their little League, Hachi was clearly the war chief of their misfit tribe.

"Where are we?" Hachi asked Mr. Rivets.

"We just crossed into the old Georgia colony, miss," the machine man told her. "Cherokee territory."

"Head for Standing Peachtree. If we can make it there, we can hide out at Lady Josephine's."

"Where?" Archie asked.

"Lady Josephine's Academy. I went to school there."

"What is it, a school to teach girls how to kick brass?" Fergus asked.

"Something like that," Hachi said. She didn't look like she wanted to explain. "Mr. Rivets, drop us low where the winds are lighter and make for Standing Peachtree, best possible speed. That should give us a little advantage over that big airship out there."

"Very good, miss."

CHUNK. CHUNK. CHUNK. The *Hesperus* rocked and the floor tilted. Archie glanced out a porthole.

"Grappling hooks!" he said. "Three lines. They're sending people over!"

"Prepare to repel boarders!" Hachi said. She tossed an oscillating rifle to Fergus and gave Archie an aether pistol, making sure to activate the aggregators on each so they'd be ready to fire. She kept the personal wave cannon for herself. She was up the ladder and out the hatch to the conning tower before Archie and Fergus knew what was going on.

"I'm glad you brought her along," Fergus told Archie.

"Yeah," said Archie. "Do you think I should put Mr. Rivets' Protector card back in?"

"If he's going to keep us flying, you'd better leave his Airship Pilot card in."

"I concur, sir. But do be careful," said Mr. Rivets.

Archie tied the white bearskin pelt around his shoulders. "Careful is my middle name," he muttered.

Fergus laughed. "That's all right. Mine's 'Coward.'"

Wom-wom-wom-wom-wom. They could already hear Hachi's

wave cannon outside. Archie and Fergus followed as quickly as they could up the ladder. One of Edison's three attackers was already gone, blasted over the side by Hachi. Now she was tangled up with another man wielding a lektric prod. The tip of it crackled and sparked. Hachi dodged back and forth on the sloped airship hull, held on only by a safety line clipped to the conning tower.

"She's insane, that one!" Fergus called over the wind.

The third Edison goon appeared at the conning tower rail. Archie raised his aether pistol and squeezed the trigger. *Bwaaat!* He missed wildly. Worse, the recoil knocked him back into the rail. He tipped over, lost his balance, and fell, sliding backward down the hull toward the ten-thousand-foot drop. He reached out helplessly for Fergus in the conning tower, slipping away too fast to even scream.

But there was Hachi again. She sprinted around the hull of the ship and grabbed him, her safety line saving them both. She had already taken care of the second Edison goon.

"Hook your safety line," she told Archie over the wind. "Don't fall off."

"Right," he said, his heart still racing from his near-death experience. "Don't fall off. I'll remember that. Look out! Fergus!"

Archie pointed to the conning tower. Fergus was watching them and not the third Edison goon who had climbed up behind him. Fergus turned in time to watch the man jab a crackling lektric prod right into his stomach.

Nothing happened.

The man frowned and pushed it into Fergus' body again, and suddenly Archie understood. Fergus was absorbing the lektricity from the prod. Three more pokes and it flickered dead, drained of its dark, forbidden energy.

Fergus and the goon stared at the spent lektric prod, then looked up at each other. Fergus put a hand to the man's chest and—*Kazaaack!*—lightning blasted the goon over the rail and off the side of the *Hesperus*.

Fergus was still staring at the inky lines on his hand when Archie and Hachi climbed back into the conning tower.

"I barely had to think about it, and I just—*boom*." he said.

Across the gulf between the airships, Archie saw Edison ordering more men over to the *Hesperus*. Fergus' old boss stood on the top deck of his airship, just below the great rigid envelope of the *Black Maria*, his black hair and black suit whipping in the wind. Goons hurried around the deck putting on harnesses, handing out oscillating rifles and lektric prods, and cranking up the platform with the lektric cannon. Edison stood still and calm among them, his eyes focused completely on Fergus.

"Oh, crivens," Fergus said. "He's seen what I can do now."

"There's more coming!" Archie said. Three more of Edison's men were zipping down the lines that connected the *Black Maria* to the *Hesperus*. He clipped his safety line to the rail, braced his feet, and took aim at the grappling hooks with his aether pistol. *Bwaaat. Bwaat. Bwaat.* He didn't go flying this time, but he didn't come close to hitting the ropes either. Two of his shots went beaming harmlessly into the sky. The third hit the *Hesperus*, knocking off a piece of the outer hull.

Hachi pulled Archie's raygun away. "Stop," she told him. She hefted her wave cannon into Fergus' arms and jumped over the rail. Hachi slid down to where the grappling hooks had punched into the *Hesperus'* hull and pulled out her dagger. *Snik-snik-snik*—she cut the ropes that linked the two airships, and the men on the lines fell screaming and flailing into the clouds.

"Maybe we should just make some popcorn and watch," Fergus said.

Poom. One of the gas airbags above them exploded in a fireball. The floor beneath Archie and Fergus dropped, and the *Hesperus* lurched. Edison's men were shooting at the airbags that kept the *Hesperus* aloft.

"I thought they wanted me alive!" Fergus yelled.

Hachi climbed back into the conning tower and took the wave cannon from Fergus. "They're just trying to bring us down. They won't shoot all of them."

Poom. Another gasbag exploded, and Archie felt the searing heat on his skin. He grabbed the railing of the *Hesperus* as they listed and dropped again.

"*Give us the lektric boy,*" Edison called through a speaking trumpet, "*and we will let the rest of you go in peace.*"

Hachi put a hand to Fergus' chest. "We won't let you turn yourself in to save us."

"I wasn't offering!" said Fergus.

Another oscillator ray crackled past the gasbags above.

"The pelt!" Archie said. "The Great Bear's pelt! We can use it protect the gasbags!"

"Go," Hachi told him. "I'll cover you." She leveled her massive wave cannon at the deck of the *Black Maria*. *Wom-wom-wom-wom-wom.* The wave pulse rippled the deck, popping rivets and tearing the metal sheathing away. Goons went spilling over the sides of the airship.

Archie climbed into the *Hesperus'* rigging and tried to fluff the pelt out to cover as many of the gasbags as he could. The wind kept catching it and making the end flutter.

On the prow of the *Black Maria*, a goon brought Edison's lektric cannon to bear on the *Hesperus*.

"If he shoots that thing, it's all over!" Fergus yelled. She nodded and shifted her aim to the man in the cannon's command chair. *Wom-wom-wom-wom-wom.* When the debris cleared there was an empty spot where the operator and his chair used to be.

"Remind me never to get on your bad side," Fergus said.

A goon on Edison's ship leveled his raygun at the *Hesperus'* balloons and fired. *Poom.* Another gasbag exploded beside Archie, and he and the pelt went flying.

"*Archie!*" Hachi cried.

The safety rope connecting Archie to the conning tower rail caught him, and he slammed into the hull of the *Hesperus*. Dazed, Archie looked back up the length of the rope and saw a tear in it popping and uncoiling. If the rope split, he would slide off the edge. He grabbed frantically at the smooth, sloped surface of the airship with one hand, his other hand clutching the white pelt that flapped in the emptiness below the airship.

Don't fall off, he told himself. *Don't fall don't fall don't fall—*

Hachi jumped over the rail of the conning tower headfirst and slid toward him. Her safety rope jerked tight just close enough for her to grab Archie's hand.

"Circus! Showtime!" she cried. Her clockwork menagerie scuttled out from under her and took flight, fighting the wind. "Grab him! Don't let go!"

Four little brass creatures grabbed Archie—his shirt, his arm, his hair, anywhere they could—and pulled for all they were worth.

Archie's legs swung like pendulums over the side. "If I can just get my feet up. Just—" His free hand squelched on the slick metal hull as he tried to gain purchase.

"Let go of the pelt!" Hachi said. "Use both hands!"

"No! I've almost got it. Almost—" His foot caught the edge. Yes! Now if he could just get his other leg up over the side—

Archie felt it more than heard it. *Pop!* The safety line snapped. His foot swung off the edge, and his hand slipped from Hachi's fingers. Archie's stomach leaped into his throat, and he dropped over the side.

"Hachiiiii!" Archie cried, and he was gone.

21

Fergus couldn't believe his eyes. Archie had just fallen over the side of the *Hesperus*.

"*Archieeeeeee!*" Hachi cried. Her clockwork animals fluttered up around her, but Archie was well and truly gone.

When the shock wore off, Fergus hurried to the other side of the conning tower rail to look down. Archie had to be okay. He had to have grabbed onto the mooring anchor. A landing strut. An open porthole. *Anything.*

But no. Fergus felt his good leg go weak as he watched Archie and the white pelt tumble through the air, down and down and down, five thousand feet or more. He hit the ground with a poof of dust and was still.

Fergus slumped against the rail. *He* had done this. Fergus was the reason Edison had come after them, and now Archie was—Archie was—

Hachi climbed over the conn tower rail, looking frantic.

"A longer rope!" she yelled. "I need a longer rope. I have to go underneath and see if—"

Fergus shook his head. "I saw him fall. He's gone."

Hachi slumped to her knees.

KSSSSH-KSSSSH-KSSSSH-KISSSH. Edison's repaired lightning cannon shot lektricity across the sky at them. It arced to the metal *Hesperus*, blasting hull panels away and lektrifying everything metal. Fergus didn't feel a thing, but Hachi arched and lurched as the volts coursed through her.

"Nae. Nae!" Fergus screamed. With every drop of black blood in his body he willed the lektricity away from the ship and into him, turning himself into a human lightning rod. Light as bright as the sun lit him up as the lektric arc shifted from the hull to his body, lashing like a snake with its fangs dug into his skin. Hachi, released from the lektricity's grip but now unconscious, slid down through the hatch into the *Hesperus*.

Edison switched off the lektric cannon, and Fergus slumped against the rail, exhausted. Lektricity crackled in his hair and between his fingers like the physical manifestation of his anger. He hauled himself to his feet and thrust his hands out at the *Black Maria*, channeling all the fury inside him. Lightning leaped from his fingers and arced back to Edison's ship. The blast wrenched aluminum hull plates off the ship, ripping it like a can opener. The lektricity bucked and kicked, but Fergus wrestled it under control, roaring like thunder. The *Black Maria* tore along its seams, and the lightning jumped to the rigid metal envelope, touching off the gasbags inside. *Boom!* The *Black Maria* burst into flames and careened toward the *Hesperus*.

Once he was going it was hard to stop, but Fergus pulled the lightning back inside as the ships collided. *Crash!* The flaming *Black Maria* struck the *Hesperus*, knocking Fergus off his feet. He tumbled down the side of the *Hesperus* just like

Archie had before, but Fergus caught a towrope on the *Black Maria* and saved himself. The ships ground against each other, dragging each other down, then pulled away. Fergus tried to hook his good leg into the rail of the *Hesperus* as the ships separated, but he couldn't reach it. Clinging to the towrope, he watched in dismay as the *Hesperus* drifted away and the flaming *Black Maria* above him plummeted toward the earth.

Whoever was at the helm of Edison's doomed ship stayed there long enough to steer the *Black Maria* for a broad lake surrounded by a forest, but soon escape gliders dropped from the sides of the dirigible. Was Edison on one of those gliders, or had Fergus taken him out with his lektric blast? With Fergus' luck, Edison had already escaped and would be waiting for him on the ground.

If he made it to the ground. His arms were already aching from hanging on. Fergus wrapped his wrist up in the rope. It burned and ripped his skin, but at least he wouldn't fall.

Not like Archie.

Another explosion rocked the *Black Maria's* gas envelope and the airship broke in half. Fergus fell, slamming into the lake and inhaling a lungful of water. The flaming airship hit just after him, pushing him farther down into the murky depths. He spun end over end, half-drowned and disoriented. He didn't even know which way was up. Fergus thrashed around, instinctively holding on to what little breath he had left, and wriggled himself away from the sinking airship.

Fergus kicked with his one good leg, fighting against the weight of the brace on his bad leg. At last he broke the surface, coughing and spluttering. The *Black Maria*'s cracked envelope sat half-in, half-out of the water nearby, smoking and gurgling as it sank. Debris bobbed to the surface all around Fergus: cushions, pieces of furniture, bottles, clothes, lab equipment. People too—some alive and gasping like him, others already dead, floating up like driftwood.

A large glass jar bobbed to the surface, and Fergus grabbed hold of it to help him stay afloat. But there was something thumping around inside it. Something pinkish gray and squishy.

It was a human brain.

"Gah!" Fergus cried, letting the jar go. He immediately sank, his metal leg brace dragging him down, and had to grab the jar again not to drown. He held the jar as far away from himself as he could and kicked his way toward the shore.

Fergus dragged himself up onto a dock, letting the brain in the jar float away. He was waterlogged and sore, and he took a few minutes to catch his breath and watch the *Black Maria* sink into the blue depths of the lake. As tired as he was, he knew he couldn't stay put for long. There were railroad tracks in the distance, which meant there would be a train eventually. That was his best chance at escape.

"Hey—hey you!" someone called from the water. "Help!"

It was one of Edison's lackeys. Fergus didn't know him, but he knew the type—hired muscle Edison kept around to do his dirty work. The man clung to a piece of lumber and looked to be as bad a swimmer as Fergus was, splashing around and breathing in big gulps of lake water. Fergus ratcheted his leg to a kneeling position and bent down to help drag the man up out of the water.

They flopped beside each other on the dock, panting and dripping.

"Thanks," the man said.

"Don't mention it," Fergus said.

The man nodded at Fergus' kilt. "You . . . you that boy Edison's after?"

"Me? Nae," Fergus lied. "I—"

The man pulled an aether pistol from his pocket aimed it at him.

"Seriously?" Fergus said. "*Seriously?* I pull you out of the water, save you from drowning, and this is the thanks I get?" Fergus sat up. The man squeezed his trigger.

Fizzt. The raygun shorted out, either from the water or the fall. The dark lines on Fergus' face rearranged to match his scowl. He raised a hand at the goon and thought *boom.*

Fizzt. Tiny sparks fizzled from Fergus' hand, but that was it. No lightning. No arcing lektricity. He had shorted out too. Lektricity and water was never a good combination.

The man hurried to get up, but Fergus was quicker. He grabbed the board the man had clung to in the water and smacked him upside the head with it. *Thwack!* The goon went flailing back into the lake.

Fergus threw the board at him, mostly for the satisfying *thunk* it made on his head when it hit him. "You can get out of there yourself this time, ingrate."

A steam whistle blew in the distance. A train! Fergus limped toward the tracks as fast as he could. If there *was* a train coming, he wanted to be on it.

White clouds of steam and smoke puffed over the tops of the trees, and an engine appeared. A passenger locomotive!

Fergus was in luck. If he could just make it to the tracks in time, position himself just right, and then find a way to grab on to a speeding locomotive without ripping off one of his remaining good limbs . . .

Fergus was liking this plan less and less the closer he got, but he didn't have any other ideas.

The train broke from the trees at what had to be forty-five, maybe fifty miles per hour, a Cheyenne-built *Iron Chief*, from the look of it. Fergus got ready to hop-skip as fast as he could alongside the train to try to grab on, but suddenly the air was filled with the squeal of the locomotive's brakes. It was slowing! But of course: The engineer had just seen the fiery crash of the *Black Maria*, and was slowing down to see what had happened.

Fergus hopped along with the train until it slowed enough for him to grab a handrail and climb aboard. None of the passengers noticed Fergus come in. They all had their noses pressed to the windows on the other side of the train, straining to see the wrecked airship in the lake. Fergus made his way to an empty seat and plopped down wearily.

Would the train take on survivors from the crash? What if Edison and his men were brought to the same train and found him here? Fergus looked around for a place to hide, even briefly debating getting back off the train. But the *Iron Chief* never truly stopped. It picked up speed again and moved on, its engineers apparently deciding that their schedule was more important than stopping to help.

More kind souls, Fergus thought cheerlessly. He'd had his fill of unhelpful people.

Passengers returned to their seats as the show out the window slid past, and Fergus found he was sitting in the empty fourth seat with a Cherokee family of three— a mother, a father, and a small boy. All three of them eyed him warily, this new Yankee stranger who had magically appeared mid-journey while their backs were turned.

The boy clutched a little wind-up toy machine man, watching Fergus with wide eyes. The mother pretended to go back to reading *The Adventures of Tom Sawyer,* but without her reading glasses on, Fergus noticed. Her husband was more blatant, giving Fergus the obvious once-over. Fergus realized he must be quite a sight: black lines like tattoos on every inch of his face and arms and legs, a mechanical contraption on his bandaged left knee, a frazzled and torn kilt, and sopping wet from his dip in the lake.

"Um, accident in the dining car," Fergus improvised. "And the tattoos are tribal. Ancient Keltic knots and all that."

Neither parent was buying it. Fergus tried friendly instead. "That's a nice machine-man toy you've got there," he said to the boy.

The kid buried his face in his mother's side.

Charming, Fergus thought. It didn't matter. As long as he was headed away from Edison and his men, he could manage. Still, it would be nice to know where he was going.

"So, um, where are you from?" he asked.

The adults said nothing for a long time. Fergus waited.

"Chota," the father said at last.

Fergus had been to the Cherokee capital once, to take an airship north to Jersey to live with Mr. and Mrs. Henhawk. Carolina was Cherokee territory. He nodded appreciatively. "And . . . where are we headed? I mean, where are *you* headed. I know where *I'm* going, of course."

The father narrowed his eyes at him. "Standing Peachtree."

"Ah! Same as me! Same as me," Fergus said. He settled back in his chair and smiled, his hair still dripping down his back. That was about all he was going to get out of these folks, he figured, and it was all he really needed. Sometime soon he would be in Standing Peachtree, and then—

And then what? Hachi had said something about a school, someplace they could hide out, but would she even make it? He peered out the window, searching the skies. Had Mr. Rivets been able to bring the *Hesperus* down safely? Was Hachi even still alive? Just asking the question weighed on him more than his cold, sodden clothes. All he could hope, he decided, was that Hachi and Mr. Rivets had survived and would meet up with him in Standing Peachtree. As for Archie—

Fergus sagged. Archie wouldn't be joining them in Standing Peachtree, or anywhere else. Archie was dead.

Archie was dead, Fergus' old friend Kano Henhawk was dead, and who knew how many more people had died in the wreck of the *Black Maria* after he blasted it. Or back in the swamps while Fergus had his head down working on the Archimedes Engine. People seemed to get hurt no matter what Fergus did.

Boom! The train lurched like it had hit something, tossing passengers out of their seats. The Cherokee mother flew into Fergus' arms, and passengers cried out as luggage rained down on them from the storage compartments above. Fergus helped the woman back to her feet amid whoops and yells and raygun blasts from outside, and the passengers rushed again to the other side of the train to see what was happening.

Fergus didn't have to hurry over to know what was going on. He needed the time to get ready. Crivens! Couldn't Edison give him a moment's peace?

Fergus cast around for something to help him defend himself, but it wasn't like there were any oscillating rifles lying about. He searched frantically through the luggage that had fallen on him. Clothes, books, toys . . . nothing here that could make a weapon. Static crackled as he slid clothes around inside one of the suitcases, and it was like it had sparked his brain. Lektricity! He could try to get a static charge from the clothing.

Fergus pulled out the silky piece of clothing and held it up. It was an enormous pair of ladies' underpants.

Fergus blushed, but desperate times called for desperate measures. He took the bloomers in both hands and rubbed them together, absorbing the static lektricity they gave off.

There were screams in the train car. A raygun blast. Footsteps. Fergus rubbed the underwear faster. He would be lucky to get one good jolt from the static. Maybe enough to stun someone and make a getaway—

The Cherokee family backed into the space between their seats, their son tucked protectively behind them. The woman saw him with her underpants and blinked.

"Ah-heh," Fergus said, trying to laugh. He handed the bloomers to the woman. "They, ah, fell out of your bag."

The mother and father stared at him like he was some kind of pervert.

"You there!" a voice said. "Come with us."

Fergus focused on what he wanted to do. *A hand to the*

chest, then zap! *and I make a run for it.* He was all set when a Muskogee warrior with war paint on his face grabbed the family and dragged them out into the aisle.

"What do you want with us?" the father asked.

"Shut up, Cherokee!" The Muskogee cuffed the father with the butt of his oscillating rifle. The mother cried out, and her son buried his face in her side again.

Another Muskogee appeared and spared Fergus a glance, then moved on. Fergus sat up, surprised. It *wasn't* Edison's men who had stopped the train. It was a Muskogee raiding party.

The two Muskogee tribesmen moved up and down the aisles, pulling more Cherokee from their seats at raygunpoint. Were the Muskogee and Cherokee at war? No, they couldn't be—there had been peace between the two tribes for a hundred years, ever since they had joined the Iroquois Confederacy and formed the United Nations.

But these Muskogee certainly didn't look like they were escorting the Cherokee to the dining car to buy them a sandwich. There were only two of them and more than half a dozen Cherokee, but the Muskogee had oscillators, and nobody seemed to want to challenge them.

Fergus slumped in his seat, relieved. Edison's people hadn't found him, and the Muskogee didn't care about a Yankee. He was safe. All he had to do was lie low until whatever this was blew over, then get on to the rendezvous point in Standing Peachtree. He closed his eyes and waited.

Someone sobbed at the far end of the train car. There was another resounding *crack* from the butt of an oscillating rifle, and another scream.

Fergus opened his eyes. The last time he had kept his head down and ignored trouble, Kano had been killed.

You can't close your eyes to the rest of the world, Fergus, Mrs. Henhawk had told him. *You can't ignore what's right for anything.*

Fergus groaned. Being a coward was so much easier, but he had to do something. He stood and went down the aisle toward the Muskogee raiders, his good leg shaking.

"Oy," Fergus called to one of the Muskogee warriors. "Sorry, but you mind letting me through to the bathroom? My eyeballs are swimming."

The Muskogee turned, and Fergus put his hand to the man's chest. *Zap!* The Muskogee jerked and fell to the floor, unconscious. His aether pistol dropped and skittered across the floor.

"Whoa," Fergus said. "Those were some serious underpants."

The Muskogee's partner pushed through the Cherokee prisoners. He took one look at his friend and raised his oscillating rifle at Fergus.

Zap! Fergus thought. *Zap! Zap! Zap!* But nothing happened. He was spent. He closed his eyes and waited for the shot to come, but it didn't. The Cherokee father he'd been sitting with jumped the Muskogee from behind and rode him to the ground. Fergus dove for the loose oscillating rifle and aimed it at the fighting men.

"That's enough now," Fergus said. "I said that's enough!"

Fergus fired the rifle at the roof to prove his point. *Bwaaaaat.* The other passengers cried out and ducked, but none of them tried to help. *Jump in anytime, people,* Fergus thought.

The Muskogee man ignored Fergus and kept fighting. The train lurched, and Fergus felt the great wheels of the *Iron Chief* grip the tracks. They were moving again. The engineers had regained control and were trying to get them out of there. The next car down, the train's private security men were restoring the peace, but the Muskogee raider in their car was still fighting like a bobcat.

"It's over," Fergus told him, but the Muskogee wasn't finished. He kneed the Cherokee man beneath the belt and rolled out from under him to come for Fergus.

Fergus hobbled backward. "Stand down now," he told the Muskogee. "Security's on the way. Let's be sensible about this then. . . ."

The Muskogee didn't appear to have much sense left. His eyes were empty, almost distant—a look Fergus had seen before in Edison. Fergus raised the oscillating rifle.

"Listen to me," Fergus told him. "You've got to snap out of whatever this is. Be sensible."

The Muskogee charged.

Bwaaaat. Fergus shot him in the chest, and the Muskogee fell.

Fergus slumped against one of the seats, the train wobbling as it picked up speed. He felt more tired than he had ever felt in his life: tired of standing, tired of fighting, tired of keeping his eyes open.

He had killed a man. Shot him in cold blood.

An arm went around him, helping him stand. It was the Cherokee father who'd sat next to him and fought alongside him.

"My name is Degotoga," he told Fergus, "and I would be honored to show you back to your seat."

"Name's Fergus. And thanks. I'd be grateful for the hand."

When the *Iron Chief* finally arrived in Standing Peachtree, the passengers were held behind to talk to the sheriff and his deputies. Fergus sat on a bench in the city's Union Station away from the others, watching them being interviewed. More than a few of them pointed over in his direction before being released. At last he was joined by an officer, a dark-skinned First Nations man with a star on his black uniform and an ivory-handled aether pistol in a holster at his side. Fergus started to get up, but the man motioned for him to stay where he was.

"Sit, sit," the man said. "You look like a man who needs ten nights' sleep. I'm Sheriff Sikwai. I understand you had a bit of an adventure getting here."

Fergus didn't want to talk about it, but there was no way he could have avoided it. He was a Yankee in a kilt with black lines all over his skin. He didn't exactly blend in in a city of Muskogee and Cherokee. He very carefully went back over the details of what had happened on the train, leaving out everything before he had sat down, wet and exhausted, next to the Cherokee family. All the sheriff was interested in was the Muskogee attack anyway, writing things in a notebook and nodding as Fergus told his story. Fergus left out the lektric shock too, substituting a punch to the Muskogee's face. It was easier to explain, and it sounded more heroic anyway.

"Pretty brave," the sheriff told him. "Those Muskogee didn't want anything with Yankees, or any of the other tribes on the train. You could have let them be. Not gotten involved."

"No," Fergus told him. "I couldn't."

The sheriff nodded. "I wish more people felt that way."

"What did those Muskogee want? Are the Cherokee and Muskogee at war? I haven't heard anything about that."

"Not at war, no. But the tribes are restless." The sheriff closed his notebook. "This town is half Cherokee, half Muskogee— Great Selu, *I'm* half Cherokee and half Muskogee—and after generations of peace, suddenly there's trouble again. Arguments, fires, fights in the streets. And now this. I would blame it on the full moon, but that isn't for a week yet."

"Are the Cherokee and Muskogee halves of *you* fighting?" Fergus asked.

The sheriff laughed. "No. But maybe my wolves are."

"Your wolves?" Fergus said.

"I have two of them inside me, just like everyone else. One good, one bad," Sheriff Sikwai told him. "One is angry. Cruel. Heartless. The other is gentle, kind, and caring. Always the two wolves are fighting each other for control. And do you know which one will win?"

"No."

"Whichever one we feed," the sheriff said. "You have someone coming to the station to meet you? Someplace to go? It's almost curfew."

Curfew? The bad wolf must have been eating well in Standing Peachtree. "Yeah, um, maybe you could give me directions. I'm looking for Lady Jennifer's Academy? No. Um, Lady Joanna, maybe?"

"Lady Josephine's Academy?" Sheriff Sikwai asked.

"That's the one," Fergus told him.

The sheriff looked surprised, but he gave him directions anyway.

Fifteen minutes later, Fergus turned down a cobblestone street past a tavern with a stuffed buck's head over the door. A Muskogee man lit the gas lamps that lined the avenue, and a steam-powered streetcar clanged past full of First Nations tribesmen and a couple of Yankees, all wearing black suits and bowler hats. A gaggle of Cherokee women hurried down the other side of the street wearing hoop skirts and matching bonnets and carrying parcels. Overhead, a sky liner droned toward the Piedmont Public Airship Park, reminding Fergus unhappily of the pneumatic post capsule that had deposited him, Hachi, and Archie underneath a similar airship in Mannahatta.

Maybe he would see Hachi again, at least. A small sign just off the sidewalk, written in Cherokee, Muskogee, and Anglish, gave the name of the school where Hachi had said they could lie low. Fergus went through the school's metal gate and up the tree-lined walk to its door. It didn't *look* much like a training ground for warriors. It was built in a neoclassical style like some Yankee buildings—white marble and square-shaped, with tall Doric columns supporting a triangular roof. The only nods to the local Muskogee and Cherokee architecture were the small round buildings that dotted the grounds beyond it.

Fergus limped up to the massive wooden front doors and knocked, happy to finally be someplace warm, safe, and friendly where he could rest. He looked around at the school grounds while he waited, spying a lacrosse field and archery targets. If this was the school Hachi had gone to, he wouldn't have been surprised see a rifle range too.

The deadbolts on the door unlatched behind him and he turned, smiling, to find an oscillating rifle pointed right in his face.

22

Hachi woke in one of the hammocks on the *Hesperus*. Or what was left of the *Hesperus*. Steam hissed from cracked and broken pipes, and the ceiling bent down to the floor, crushed like a giant had stepped on it. And the airship wasn't rocking, which meant it was on the ground. Clearly the *Hesperus* had crashed, but she didn't remember a moment of it.

"Circus," she said wearily. "Showtime."

Only three of her little clockwork friends came out this time. Zee was gone, given to little Della Henhawk in a moment of weakness. No—she couldn't beat herself up for that one. Hachi knew what it was to lose a father and to need a friend. But Tusker . . . the little elephant had gone over the side with Archie. Fallen with him, or been lost on the winds.

Now only three of her circus remained: Jo-Jo, Freckles, and Mr. Lion. But that was all right too. Soon she wouldn't need their help ever again. But first things first.

"I need a way out," she told them.

The three clockwork animals fluttered away, darting here and there around the odd angles of the crushed cabin. She closed her eyes while they were gone but tried not to go back to sleep. She had to stay awake. Stay focused. She repeated her mantra:

Talisse Fixico, the potter.

Chelokee Yoholo, father of Ficka.

Hathlun Harjo, the surgeon.

Odis Harjo, the poet.

Iskote Te, the gray haired.

Soon her little friends were back, chirping and chattering in their infant language.

"All right," Hachi said. "Looks like the only way out is through the conning tower hatch." It was just beyond her on the bent ceiling, but to get there she'd have to slide through the tight space between the bent roof and the twisted floor. Hachi shifted in the netting, and her ankle flashed hot with pain. She sucked in a gasp, willing herself not to cry out.

"*Roar-roar-roar-roar,*" Mr. Lion said.

"I know, I know," she said. But she had to get out of the airship. Mixed in with the steam she could smell smoke, and she heard the boiler popping and hissing. It was still building pressure.

But that, she knew, wasn't the worst of the danger.

Hachi grunted her way along the floor until she could reach the wheel on the hatch. She tugged on it, her circus pulling with her, but it wouldn't budge. It was bent beyond use. That just left the front window, which was on the other side of the bent ceiling. It would be a tight squeeze, but *maybe* she could wiggle her way through the twisted metal—

CRUNK. The hatch suddenly lifted away, and Mr. Rivets' brass face appeared in the crooked round hole.

"Miss Hachi—I'm so very relieved to find you conscious

and intact," he told her. The machine man set the broken hatch aside and helped her out while her circus flew around the Tik Tok's head, chittering at him.

"Are you seriously injured, miss?"

"A few cuts and bruises. Twisted ankle is the worst of it, I think. I'll be all right. What about you?"

"Dented, miss, but undaunted." Mr. Rivets turned to show her a large depression in his backside.

"Where's Fergus?" she asked. "Is he still inside?"

"No, miss. He was not on board when we crashed. I fear he gave his life saving us from Mr. Edison's lektric weapon."

Hachi felt a pang of grief at the news, but she didn't have time to dwell on it. Neither of them did.

"We've got to get as far away from the airship as we can," Hachi told the Tik Tok. "Circus, return!" She hopped-limped as fast as she could toward a nearby line of trees, and within moments Mr. Rivets was there with an arm under hers, helping her run.

"There is no need for alacrity, miss. The firebox has been compromised and flames have spread to the cabin, but there is no immediate danger of the boiler exploding. Once you are a safe distance away, I will go back and retrieve anything I can in the way of weapons and supplies."

Hachi kept hopping away furiously. "No, Mr. Rivets, you don't understand. We've got to—"

BOOM. The *Hesperus* exploded behind them, knocking Hachi to the dirt. The big machine man fell with a *thud* next to her, and Hachi covered her head. Smoking fragments of the airship rained down on them, a chunk of the helm missing her by inches.

When the last of the debris had fallen, Hachi looked back over her shoulder. Where the airship had been was a scarred, black crater.

"By the Maker," Mr. Rivets said. "The boiler shouldn't have caused *that* much destruction."

"It didn't," Hachi told him. "There were ten sticks of dynamite in there. I had them on under my clothes when I came aboard that first day in the swamp."

Mr. Rivets' surprise subroutine raised his eyebrow. "You stored ten sticks of dynamite on board the *Hesperus*, miss?"

"They were for that thing in the swamp. I thought I was going to get to try and use them again, but not now."

Mr. Rivets helped her up. "And I'm afraid all the weapons Mr. Tesla gave us are gone too."

"What about your talent cards?"

They found Mr. Rivets' talent card chest in a nearby tree. The cards themselves lay like crumpled brass leaves among the real red and yellow leaves scattered on the ground.

Mr. Rivets held up the only one undamaged enough to use. "My Chef talent card."

"Great. Very useful. What have you got in right now?"

"My Airship Pilot card, miss."

"Well, we haven't got one of those anymore," Hachi said. "Chef it is then." She disengaged the Airship Pilot card from Mr. Rivets' slot and replaced it with the culinary card. "You can cook me up a soufflé when we stop to camp for the night."

Mr. Rivets looked around at where they had crashed. They stood at the edge of a dense wood filled with half-bare trees. A crow cawed at them, and something small scurried under the bed of leaves.

"Or perhaps, given our surroundings, miss would settle for 'Squirrel Surprise'?" Mr. Rivets said.

Hachi smiled in spite of herself, then gasped as she tried to take a step and collapsed. Mr. Rivets hurried to help her back up.

"Just before the *Hesperus* went down, miss, we were approximately twenty miles from Standing Peachtree, as the airship flies. Given your present condition, I think it would be better if you allowed me to carry you."

"I don't like being carried."

"Master Archie never liked to take baths, miss, but that didn't mean I allowed him to refuse."

Hachi wanted to argue, but she couldn't. There was no way she could walk any real distance with her ankle like this, and it would heal faster if she stayed off it. They couldn't do anything until they reached Standing Peachtree anyway, and it would take them a day of travel to get there—more if they stopped for the night. Reluctantly, she climbed into Mr. Rivets' arms.

"There we are, miss," Mr. Rivets said, immediately setting off to the southwest. "I promise not to tell anyone you allowed yourself to be carried."

As though there was anyone to tell, Hachi thought. Archie was dead—there was no denying that. She and Fergus had watched him fall. Fergus had seen him hit the ground. And Fergus, he was probably dead now too, doing something stupidly heroic like absorbing too much lektricity from Edison's cannon to buy Mr. Rivets time to pilot her to safety. Fergus had just started to grow on her too. Both of them had.

That familiar pang of grief came back again, and she fought it. *It's what I deserve. I can't have friends. I can't have friends and still do what I have to do.* She put a hand to the long scar on her throat without thinking. *I should never have let them take me away from Florida. I should never have let them become my friends.*

Hachi slipped her bracelet off and thumbed through the beads one by one.

Talisse Fixico, the potter.

Chelokee Yoholo, father of Ficka.

Hathlun Harjo, the surgeon.

Once again, she had been the only one to survive. Why her? Why did fate hate her?

Odis Harjo, the poet.

Iskote Te, the gray haired.

Oak Mulgee, the machinist.

The first time, there had been nothing she could do. But since then she had trained every summer. Spent her parents' fortune. Dedicated her life to becoming the perfect fighting machine.

John Wise, the politician.

Emartha Hadka, the hero of Hickory Ground.

Harmer Thlah, the wicked.

All that time, all that money, all that *training*, and she hadn't been able to save her friends. Still hadn't destroyed her enemies.

Hahyah Yechee, the sheriff.

Thomas Stidham, the horse breeder.

Arkon Nichee, friend to many.

She was a failure. That's all there was to it. She had failed to kill Edison. Failed to kill the thing imprisoned under the swamp. Failed to save her friends.

Claiborne Lowe, twelve times a grandfather.
Pompey Yoholo, seventh son of a seventh son.
Woxe Holatha, the banker.

This was her punishment: to live while everyone else around her died. Unless she could break the cycle. Go back to Florida, to the land of her parents and her parents' parents, the home of her people, and do what she should have done that night twelve years ago:

Die.

Ficka Likee. Petolke Likee. Ockchan Harjo. Micco Chee. Sower Sullivan. Cosa Yoholo. Artus Harjo. Abraham Emathlau. Tuscooner Thlah. Noble Kinnard. Chofolop Fixico. Stana Haley. On and on she recited their names, counting them off on her beaded bracelet as Mr. Rivets trudged on through the woods. *Nocose Stidham. Gristy Perryman. Nehar Larne. Tall Pot Yoholo. Konip—*

"Miss Hachi. *Miss Hachi*," she finally heard Mr. Rivets saying. "My mainspring has run down. Miss Hachi, do you hear me? I have wound down. Miss Hachi—"

Hachi blinked and realized they had stopped. Night had fallen, and she was shivering. How long had she been counting out the names?

"Yes. I'm sorry. Of course," she said. She slipped from Mr. Rivets' arms and limped around behind him to turn his key.

"Many thanks," Mr. Rivets said, straightening. "I worried I might run down completely before you heard me."

Hachi was still disoriented. She'd been so focused on her mantra she had neglected the here and now—a dangerous thing to do. She needed to rest. To regroup. To pull herself together.

"Why don't we stop here for the night?" she suggested. "There's an outcropping of rocks over there that should give us some shelter if it rains. I'll need a fire to keep warm though."

"Very good, miss. I'll just see to some firewood," Mr. Rivets told her. "And then, perhaps, a dinner of roasted mushrooms stuffed with onions and chopped pecans? I saw everything I need as we walked. It would be no trouble at all to—"

"No, don't go," Hachi interrupted, surprising herself as much as the machine man. "I—I'd like you to stay close, if that's all right. I'm not very hungry anyway."

"As you wish, Miss Hachi," the Tik Tok said, and he moved off to gather wood nearby.

Hachi hated admitting she needed company right now, and she cursed her own weakness. But the feeling of loneliness and failure was just too overwhelming. Her family, her friends, her relatives, her clan—just about everyone she had ever known and loved was dead and she had failed to help them. Right now, even a machine man was welcome company. She called what was left of her circus out, and they did tricks for her in the air while he was gone.

Mr. Rivets soon had a fire crackling, and Hachi warmed herself by it, declining again his offer to cook her a feast from the forest. With his Chef card in, Mr. Rivets seemed to view the world as though it were one great pantry with which to cross-reference the recipes in his database.

"I'm sure I saw some kale nearby, miss," he tried again. "I could sauté a little with some garlic . . ."

"No thank you, Mr. Rivets."

Hachi thumbed through the beads on her wrist, picking up where she had left off as she stared into the flames.

Konip Fixico. Chular Fixico. Tallassee Tustunnugee. Long John Gibson. Talkis Yoholo.

"Pardon the interruption, miss," Mr. Rivets said.

"I'm really not hungry, Mr. Rivets. I'll be fine."

"Yes, miss. I was just going to inquire as to the names you've been repeating. Is it a poem? A cypher? A mnemonic device of some kind?"

"I—how did you—can you read my mind?" Hachi asked.

"No, miss. You said them out loud all afternoon as we walked. And you muttered them before, on the *Hesperus*."

Hachi hadn't realized anyone else could hear her. How many times had others heard her saying her mantra when she thought she was thinking it to herself?

"I thought I was just saying them in my head," she said.

"If I may, miss, that is not surprising. I spoke to you a number of times while we traveled, pointing out a variety of fruits and berries I could use in recipes, but you were unresponsive— except for the continuation of your list of names and their associations."

"I'm sorry. I didn't realize."

"It's quite all right, miss. But I am curious—unless it is a personal matter, of course."

It *was* personal, more personal than anyone could know. Hachi's natural instinct was to tell Mr. Rivets it was none of his business—or anyone else's, for that matter. But suddenly she saw that she was only keeping the names a secret because it was easier for her. Because it hurt to talk about them. If she really wanted to honor these people, if their memory was worth dying for, wasn't it worth sharing with as many other people as she could before she too was gone?

Mr. Rivets sat clicking and whirring across the fire from her, watching her with a little tilt to his head. Could she tell him what she had never been able to tell Ms. Ambrose back at school? What she'd never even told Tooantuh in their quietest moments?

"They're the names of all the men from my mother's tribe," she told him. "I—they—" She hardly knew where to begin. Her mother had told her the story many times, but Hachi had never told it herself. "All I remember is the lightning, and the green flame, like the fire Edison conjured the other night in the glade. But my mother told me the rest. When I was a year old we went to Chuluota, near the glade where you found me. While we were there, a group of strangers came to town. Some of them were Yankees and some were First Nations, but all of them were servants of the Swarm Queen. That was the name my mother's tribe had for it. The darkness that lived beneath the swamps."

"Malacar Ahasherat," Mr. Rivets said. "The Mangleborn that took Archie's parents."

Hachi nodded. "No one knew the names of these outsiders, or why they had come to Chuluota, but they—they killed every man in the town. One hundred of them. Every man over the age of seventeen." She paused, looking into the fire. "They killed women too, but my mother says the strangers didn't really care about them. The women of my clan were shot or slashed to drive them away so the strangers could deal with the men. One of them picked me up and dragged a knife across my neck." Hachi put a hand to the long scar beneath her face, her eyes still on the fire.

"How did you survive?" Mr. Rivets asked.

"My mother. She took me up in her arms and held a hand

to my bleeding neck and ran—ran through the night to the next town, where a surgeon sewed me back together."

Mr. Rivets let her sit in silence for a few moments, then asked, "What did they want with the men? The servants of Malacar Ahasherat who attacked your town?"

"When the warriors from the next town went to Chuluota the next day, they found the bodies. Every man of my mother's tribe had been killed. From what the warriors could tell, the strangers had laid the men of Chuluota on an ancient stone altar, one by one, and slit their throats. That same stone altar Fergus was on, in the glade. The strangers drained their blood, then threw the empty bodies off into the swamp. One hundred of them. They worked some kind of magic like Edison did the other night, with lightning and machines and green flame and blood. That's why I share a connection to the monster. I was there. I've had dreams of her since I was twelve months old."

Freckles the giraffe laid her long neck on Hachi's arm.

"After that, no one returned to Chuluota," she said. "There were too many ghosts. My mother took me back to Standing Peachtree, but she died soon after of a broken heart. But not before she taught me the names of every last man who had died, and something to remember him by. Including the last one: Hololkee Emartha, my father."

"Hololkee Emartha? *The* Hololkee Emartha?" Mr. Rivets asked. "Former chairman of the Emartha Locomotive and Machine Man Company? The richest man in the United Nations?"

Hachi nodded.

"Hololkee Emartha," Mr. Rivets said reverently. "*The Maker.*"

"He inherited the family genius for engineering. He made these for me," she said, meaning the clockwork animals in her lap. "My circus. When I was born." A tear rolled down her cheek. "He made them for my crib. To sing and dance in the air above me. Now they're all I have left of him."

"Hololkee Emartha lived in Standing Peachtree, where the corporate headquarters are for the Emartha Locomotive and Machine Man Company," Mr. Rivets said. "What were you doing in Florida?"

"Visiting my grandmother," Hachi said. "My mother was born in Chuluota. The town that once existed there. We shouldn't even have been there that night."

"And they never caught the people who murdered your mother's tribe?"

"No. I spent every spare minute—every night and weekend and summer I had away from school—teaching myself to fight, to be the best warrior anyone had ever known, so that one day I could punish the men and women who destroyed my family. And all the time I searched for the people who had been there that night. Last month, I finally found one. One of the people who killed my father. My mother. Her tribe. One of the people who ruined my life. *Edison.*"

"You were there to kill Mr. Edison," Mr. Rivets said. "And then . . . to attempt to destroy the Mangleborn? With the dynamite?"

"Yes."

"Killing yourself as well, I must point out."

Hachi looked away into the darkness. "I should be dead already, Mr. Rivets. I should have died that night, with the rest of my people. With my family."

"You'll forgive me, miss, if I fail to see the logic in that."

"Why me, Mr. Rivets? Why did my mother and my father and my grandmother and my whole tribe die, but I didn't?"

"Why should some not survive?" Mr. Rivets asked. "If Master Archie's ancestors had all died out when the first among them died, I would not have been able to serve many more generations of Dents. It is undoubtedly a tragedy your parents died as they did. When viewed another way, however, it is a miracle that you survived. And if you will permit the observation, miss, you have not just survived, you have flourished. Like a tempered steel blade hardened in the blacksmith's forge, you have come out stronger and sharper than before. You are, in short, the most extraordinary thirteen-year-old I have known in more than one hundred years of service."

"Slag it all, I don't want to be tempered steel! I don't want to be the greatest warrior who ever lived!" Hachi told him. "I want to go to school, and worry about homework, and clothes, and boys. I want to laugh and play and live like other kids." Tears streamed down her face now. *I want my parents back, Mr. Rivets.*

"Of course, miss. But choices like that are not ours to make. I too feel responsible for the loss of my family. Ever since our encounter with Mr. Edison and Mr. Shinobi in the glade, I have continually played out the variables in my clockworks to determine if another course of action might have saved them."

Hachi sniffled, trying to regain control. "I'm so sorry. You've lost everyone too, haven't you? Mr. and Mrs. Dent, and now Archie. What happens to machine men when their owners die?"

"Tik Toks are property, miss. Like the rest of the Dent

estate, I will most likely be put up for auction to pay off their creditors—but I am not convinced Mr. and Mrs. Dent are dead. Master Archie assured me he had seen them in his dreams, and I trust his intuition, as I have none."

"They are," Hachi told him. "They're alive. I've seen them in my dreams too."

"Then I shall go back to Florida," Mr. Rivets said. "I will go back to where I lost them, and I will do whatever I can to rescue them—or wind down trying."

"It's hopeless," Hachi told him.

"Hope—and its antithesis—are not part of my programming, miss."

Hachi nodded through her tears. They weren't part of her programming either. Not anymore.

"If I told you about the men of my tribe who died, Mr. Rivets, if I recited the hundred names," Hachi asked, "would you record them on your memory cards?"

"It would be my honor, miss," said Mr. Rivets.

23

Archie roared. His club rang out on Brynhildr's shield, knocking her back into the shallow water. The Yellow Emperor lit a rocket that screamed at him and exploded, setting the pelt on his back on fire. A ruby raygun blast cut through the darkness, searing him. He felt the pain and screamed, but it didn't kill him. It didn't even hurt him.

Nothing could hurt him.

He was the Great Bear.

This is your birthright, Malacar Ahasherat whispered in his head as he destroyed the Yellow Emperor's South-Facing Chariot. *You are Mangleborn*, she told him as he swiped his club at one of Eshu's ghost-images of himself. *You are the Jandal a Haad*, she sang as Archie kicked the Atlantean hero Cadmus before he could sow the teeth of Yog-Lerna and summon his Spartoi warriors.

The Yellow Emperor's chemicals burned on his hunched, heaving back, making him look like a crackling orange demon glowing in the night. He howled at the red moon as his friends fell beneath his club.

He was the Great Bear. He was unbeatable. He was the Jandal a Haad.

He was a monster.

"I'm not a monster!" Archie cried out, sitting up straight.

"I am glad to hear it," an old Cherokee man said, sitting cross-legged beside him. He wore a white shirt under a black vest, with a bright red scarf tied around his head to hold back his stringy black hair. Wrinkles lined his brown face, but his eyes were young and alight with mischief.

Archie panted, bathed in sweat. He had been dreaming. He had dreamed he was the Great Bear, fighting his friends. Fighting the League. He was the Great Bear, but Malacar Ahasherat had called him Jandal a Haad. Was she talking to him, Archie the dreamer, or to the Great Bear in the dream? Or both?

Archie tried to focus on the here and now. He was naked underneath a woven blanket, in a hot, smoky room filled with jars and medical equipment and books. The air smelled like herbs and dirt. A fire smoldered in the center of the room, and here and there cots were lined with animal skins. He recognized one of them right away: the Great Bear's pelt.

The pelt—the pelt was the last thing he remembered about falling from the *Hesperus*. He had lost his grip on it and it ripped from his fingers, fluttering up and away as the airship grew smaller and the world below him got closer and closer.

Archie put his hands to his head, his chest, his legs.

"Looking for injuries?" the Cherokee man asked him. "Your little friend hasn't let me get too close, but from what I can see, you haven't any."

"My little friend?"

A tiny clockwork elephant with wings fluttered up in front of Archie and trumpeted.

"Tusker!"

The elephant landed on top of Archie's blanket protectively, guarding him from the old man across the room as if the little wind-up toy were a full-sized elephant. Tusker had survived the fall! But that made sense. Tusker had wings.

Archie didn't. So how was he still in one piece?

Archie looked around again at the cots and the books and the jars. "Are you a doctor?" he asked.

"Yes," the man told him. "Not that you need one. I daresay you've never needed a doctor in your entire life, have you?"

Archie frowned. He'd never been to the doctor, no, but that wasn't so unusual, was it? Not every boy got broken arms and legs or cuts that needed sewing up. But now that he thought about it, he couldn't remember the last time he'd even been sick.

The old man smiled. "My name is Hul-lih, but you may call me John Otter."

"How did I—the last thing I remember was—but that's impossible," Archie whispered.

"Two young lovers away in the woods saw you fall from the sky." John Otter clapped his hands. "*Smack!* You left a boy-sized hole."

The old man crossed the room toward him. Tusker tensed, raising his little tusks defiantly. "Your clothes were ripped and shredded," John Otter said. "All that survived intact were this overly protective clockwork marvel, that curious white animal skin, and you. Three wonders, each more incredible than the last."

The pelt must have protected me, Archie thought. *That's what saved me. I was wrapped up in it, and it absorbed the impact. Broke my fall.* But Archie distinctly remembered losing it in midair. Watching it slip away. Somehow he must have gotten it back . . . or lucked into falling on it?

John Otter bent over to pick up a kettle, and Archie caught a glimpse of a black tattoo on his arm: a pyramid eye inside a seven-pointed star.

"That tattoo," Archie said. "You're a Septemberist!"

"Oh, do you know it?" John Otter said casually. He hung the kettle over the fire and pulled two pottery cups from a cabinet. "Yes. My family have fought the Mangleborn for many generations. As the medicine men of my clan, it is our duty to watch the Earth for signs of their return, and to do what we can to prevent it. As have your family in their way, I take it? Your adopted family, I mean."

"Adopted? What? I—no." What a strange old man! "I mean, yes, my family have been Septemberists for centuries. When I grow up I'm going to be a member too. But I'm not adopted."

"Ah, I see," he said lightly. "So, tell me how you and your little friend came to fall from the sky."

Archie was glad to finally have an adult who was interested in hearing his story. Someone who knew what the Mangleborn were capable of, who could help him get his parents back. He started with the thing in the basement of Septemberist headquarters and brought John Otter with him up to the present, leaving nothing out. John Otter was quiet until Archie was done, moving only to pour them tea when the water boiled.

"It is quite a story already, even though it is not yet finished," John Otter said. He rubbed the white pelt of the Great Bear between his fingers, thinking. "What you have told me about the Mangleborn rising does not surprise me. There have been signs. Weaker men feel their stirrings and become monsters themselves, though they know not why. Cherokee warriors have made raids on Muskogee villages, and Muskogee warriors have responded in kind," John Otter told him. "So far they have been isolated incidents, but now there are rumblings of war. A war between the tribes."

"A war between the Muskogee and the Cherokee?"

"And the Shawnee, and the Choctaw, and the Illini, and the Powhatan. And the Yankees. A war between the nations. A civil war that will undo all that the Iroquois did to bring peace to this land. That is, if the Mangleborn are allowed to escape their bonds."

"We have to do something. The *Septemberists* have to do something," Archie said. "A new League maybe, like the seven heroes of old. A new League of Seven."

"If I am not much mistaken, a new League is already forming," John Otter said.

"Where? Who? Do you mean me and Fergus and Hachi? That's what I told them! It's us, isn't it! I knew it! Fergus is the tinker, Hachi is the warrior, and I'm the leader! Who else is there? Where do we find them?"

"Come," John Otter said, slapping Archie on the knee. Tusker fluttered up from the blanket and trumpeted angrily. "Get dressed and join us for our circle dance. I think you will enjoy it. It's dark yet besides. We shall return you to your extraordinary friends in Standing Peachtree by daylight tomorrow. From the sound of it, they will be as surprised to find you alive as *you* were."

Archie wanted to keep talking about the League, but John Otter ignored his questions and instead urged him to get dressed in the Cherokee-style pants and shirt he'd given him. Why was it so hard to get adults to tell him anything? To trust him? Archie wanted to scream: *The Mangleborn are waking, and we need an army to stop them!* But all John Otter wanted to talk about was a woman named Sally Wah-yeh he hoped to see at the circle dance.

The entire village assembled for the dance around an unlit fire pit. The trunk of a tree that looked like it had been split apart by lightning was carried ceremoniously to the fire pit and was lit, its flickering orange flame fighting off the darkness that fell around them. Men and women in costumes decorated with beads and feathers and animal skins danced around it in a circle, while the spectators beat drums and chanted in Cherokee.

"They dance to celebrate Selu, the Corn Mother," John Otter told him, leaning in close to be heard over the singing. An old woman bowed in front of them, offering Archie and John Otter bowls of what smelled like beef stew. Archie thanked her and took the bowl hungrily. It felt like weeks since he had eaten anything. The woman winked at John Otter, and went to serve more food.

John Otter nudged Archie with his elbow. "Sally Wah-yeh," he said. "I think she is sweet on me."

Archie had seconds—and then thirds—of the stew while he watched the dancing. When the food was gone he was handed a dry, hollow gourd with small rocks inside it, which he shook in time with the dance like others around the circle. John Otter took a drum made from a hollow log and a deerskin and beat on it with his palms. Archie didn't know what most of the dances meant or what they were for, but it was easy to get caught up in the thumping energy, the push and pull of the ceremony, like the rhythmic sway of a train ride or a submarine voyage.

Or a Mangleborn vision.

John Otter nudged him again. "Pay attention now," he told Archie. "I think you'll like this next part especially."

Archie tried to recapture the thrill of the dance, to lose himself again in the hypnotic stomping and singing, but the thought of the Swarm Queen's dreamsongs had chilled him. Now he watched, distantly, as a man on stilts wearing a shaggy shirt and a buffalo mask danced into the circle. Archie didn't see what this had to do with him until the buffalo man was joined by seven others: a blindfolded man with a "seeing stick" to help him find his way; a handsome warrior wearing armor and wielding a sword; a laughing woman with the head and wings of a raven; a limping man with a hammer; a woman with war paint on her face, carrying a bow and arrow; another woman wearing big goggles and carrying a book; and, hidden among them and hard to see, a huge man in black carrying a club.

"It's—it's the League of Seven!" Archie told John Otter over the beating of the drums and the shaking of the gourds. "It's the League, and they're fighting a Mangleborn! But—" Archie looked around at all the spectators. The entire village was watching. "Does *everyone* know about the League here? It's supposed to be a secret!"

"You recognize the League, do you?" John Otter asked, the firelight glinting in his smiling eyes. "Ah, but where you and I see the League of Seven, these good people see a myth. 'The Seven Strangers and the Thunder Giant.' A story told for so long and by so many that its true meaning has been lost. A hundred years from now, will anyone remember you fought a Mangleborn in the swamps in Florida? No. They will say that a crazy scientist blew himself up trying to bring down the lightning. This Thunder Giant—even now its true name and powers are lost to us. It might be the very same creature that controls your parents. Or perhaps it is the abomination that lies beneath New Rome. Or maybe it is some other Mangleborn entirely."

Archie watched as the heroes danced around the Mangleborn, each bringing his or her unique talents to bear. The woman with the book read and pointed. The blind man listened to his seeing stick and danced out of the monster's way. The tinker built a trap. The raven woman flitted about, playing tricks on friends and foe. The handsome warrior orchestrated their movements and struck the Mangleborn again and again.

Archie saw again the team of his dream. The same number of heroes, the same collection of talents. Only the details were different.

"Which League is this?" he asked.

John Otter shrugged. "The Roman League? The Atlantean League? A League even older than that? How many Leagues have there been? How many times have the people of the world built civilizations, only to have them torn down again by the Mangleborn? What has happened before will happen again, and again, and again. And just as always," he said, giving Archie a mischievous glance, "a new group of seven heroes will arise when the world needs them most."

Archie was only half-listening. All his attention was focused now on the strongman—the Great Bear of the group. The others avoided him, almost as though they were as afraid of him as they were of the Mangleborn.

"Why is that one dressed all in black?" he asked.

"He is the Jandal a Haad," John Otter said.

Archie's skin prickled. "The Jandal a Haad," he whispered. "What the Septemberist Council and the Swarm Queen called me."

"Yes," John Otter said. "His Cherokee name is Nunyanuwi. He is the Stone Man. He is the strongest among them, yet the weakest. He is anger and darkness. The sinister part of ourselves. He wears black because he is the bad wolf, given form." John Otter turned to Archie, his eyes no longer smiling. "The others fear him because at any moment he can forget that small part of him that is human. Should that happen, should he forget himself and embrace the shadow within, he will become a monster more powerful than the rest of them combined."

Archie's heart hammered. *Jandal a Haad.* Malacar Ahasherat had called him that. But how was he a stone man? A shadow?

No. He was the leader. The one out front. Cadmus. Theseus. Arthur. He was a hero, not a monster.

And yet the Mangleborn's words echoed in his head. *Jandal a Haad.*

Archie shuddered. "If the Stone Man is so scary, why do they keep him around?"

"Because he is the only one who understands the darkness well enough to defeat it," John Otter said. "And, because he is their friend."

24

A trio of young Cherokee warriors on steam horses escorted Archie to Standing Peachtree the next day to help him find his friends. John Otter had told him he couldn't come—something evil was stirring along the border of Cherokee and Muskogee territory, and he and his tribe had to make sure it didn't rise. Instead he sent Archie off with a bear hug and made him promise to come back one day and tell him how the story ended. Archie wasn't convinced he'd be around after the story ended, but he had promised anyway.

Standing Peachtree had a long and complicated past, Archie knew. The farthest back anyone remembered, the site was a Roman garrison town called Persicorum, a tiny fort on the frontier of an empire ruled from a city across the sea. After Rome had fallen to the Mangleborn, the fort beside the Chattahoochee River had become a meeting place for the Muskogee and the Cherokee, a border station between two territories. Then the Yankees had come—more invaders from the Old World—calling the place Georgia after some now-forgotten king and turning Standing Peachtree into a trading outpost they called Atalanta. But then the Darkness had fallen and the frightened Yankees had retreated to their cities on the coast, leaving Standing Peachtree to the Muskogee and Cherokee once more.

The Romans had founded it, the Muskogee and Cherokee had made it a meeting place, and the Yankees had made it a town, but it was the railroad that had made Standing Peachtree a city. As Archie and his Cherokee escorts rode into town, they crossed the tracks that connected the metropolis to the rest of the United Nations, making Standing Peachtree the business hub of the southern tribes. Steamwagons filled with pumpkins and squash and apples clattered past. Airships big and small took off and landed. Muskogee and Cherokee children played lacrosse in the streets—the streets that weren't being torn up and widened, at least. Everywhere the city was being knocked down and rebuilt to be bigger, taller, and more modern, highlighted by the ten-story-tall Emartha Locomotive and Machine Man headquarters and its huge foundries at the heart of the city.

Archie was never more glad of his escort than when they led him through the city's winding, forking streets, fully half of which seemed to be called "Peachtree Street" or some variant. The warriors knew where they were going though, and just as dusk began to fall they stopped and pointed to a large white building on a gaslit street on the north side of town. The sign outside said LADY JOSEPHINE'S ACADEMY FOR SPIRITED GIRLS.

Spirited girls?

"Are you sure this is where you want to go?" one of the Cherokee asked him.

"Unless there's some other 'Lady Josephine' school in the city . . ."

The warrior shook his head. Archie dismounted his steam horse and thanked them, and his escorts headed off for dinner at the Buck Head Tavern up the street. Tusker flitted about watching for trouble as Archie walked up the lane to the front door of Lady Josephine's. Just as he got to the door he realized he was still wearing the Great Bear's pelt around his shoulders, and he self-consciously pulled it off before knocking.

A few moments later, a thin young woman in a blue bustle dress opened the door. Her long, delicate arms were pale, but the round face under her pinned-up brown hair was flushed pink, as though she had hurried a long way.

She did a double take when she saw Archie, like she had been expecting someone else.

"Hi," said Archie, suddenly wishing he had rehearsed what he was going to say. "I'm Archie Dent. I'm a friend of Hachi," he told her, realizing he didn't know Hachi's last name—or if she even had one. "She, um, well, we were heading south, to Florida, and she said that if we needed to hide out someplace, we should come here. To meet up. Is Hachi here?"

"Athena's owl! You can't be. But that hair, and that raggedy old thing," she said, meaning the Great Bear's pelt. She glanced over his head, looking this way and that, as though there might be someone right behind him. "Hurry!" she said, practically dragging him inside. "Quickly! Before you're seen."

Archie stumbled over the sill as he entered. The entrance hall to Lady Josephine's Academy for Spirited Girls was magnificent. The floor was made of shining blue-green marble, and two great curved staircases at the far end of the room swept up to a second-floor gallery. Between the staircases stood an enormous bronze statue of a robed woman holding a book in one hand and a sword in the other. Carved into the pedestal below her were the words *"Flectere si nequeo superos, Achaeronta movebo."*

"Is Hachi here? Did she and Fergus—?" Archie began, but the woman was already pulling him by the sleeve through the great hall and up the stairs.

"Just through here," she said. She pushed him into a smaller room filled with rows of seats, all pointed toward a wooden stage at the front with a painted backdrop of castle turrets and trees. "I think we have something that might fit you," she said, working her way quickly through the costumes on a rack. "Yes, here." The woman handed him a black suit coat and trousers. Archie stared at them uncomprehendingly. He hadn't the faintest idea what was going on.

"Hurry now! Put them on," she told him. "Here, there's a changing screen over here. And give me this," she said, taking the Great Bear's pelt from him.

"Wait, that's—"

"I know perfectly well what it is," the woman told him. She held it out from her as though it stank and needed washing. "Or what it's supposed to be. But it will hardly help us hide you and your friends from Edison's agents. We expect them back in force any time now, and we *don't* expect them to take no for an answer this time. This will be returned to you later. Quickly now."

The mention of his friends—and Edison—lit a fire under Archie's boiler. He hurried behind the changing screen and stripped out of his Cherokee clothes.

"Are you a Septemberist?" Archie asked.

"Since I do not know what that means, I will have to

answer in the negative," the woman said. "I am Ms. Ambrose. I run this school. Now hurry."

The black suit Ms. Ambrose had given him was too big, but he put it on anyway.

"Tusker, you better hide in here for now," Archie said. He held one of the jacket pockets open so the little elephant could fly down inside, but it kept sticking its head out to see.

Archie stepped out from behind the screen to show off the poor fit, and Ms. Ambrose tutted as she stuffed his cuffs up inside his sleeves a few inches to shorten them.

"You're rather small for your age, aren't you?" she said. Archie opened his mouth to argue, but she was too fast for him. "Oh! And that white hair. You'll stand out like a Hyperborean in Afrika. Here." She thrust a short black wig at him, and Archie put it on reluctantly. With his baggy clothes and his black bowl-cut wig, he looked like a down-on-his-luck vaudevillian.

"Not ideal, but it will have to do," Ms. Ambrose told him. "Come along, come along."

Archie let her drag him away again, leaving the Great Bear's pelt in among the costumes on the rack. It was as good a place to hide it as any, Archie realized—right in plain sight with lots of other strange clothes and costumes.

Back down the staircase they went, Archie doing his best to keep up and not ask any more questions. If Hachi and Fergus were here and Edison's men were due any moment, Ms. Ambrose was no doubt taking him to wherever she had hidden the others. A concealed room somewhere. Maybe a secret corridor. But as they hurried across the great hall to another set of double doors, Archie heard music. A string orchestra.

The woman swept the doors open and pulled Archie into a dance hall?

Boys and girls of all tribes and colors twirled around a glittering gold ballroom hung with mirrors and chandeliers. More young people, all in sharp dress suits and colorful hoop skirts, stood laughing and talking with one another on the edges of the dance. At the back of the room an orchestra played a dignified waltz, and along the sides of the room Tik Tok waiters laid out food on an extravagant buffet.

Curious groups of boys and giggling groups of girls stared at Archie as Ms. Ambrose led him into the room. One waggle of the headmistress' finger turned them away again, and they talked animatedly among themselves.

"We'll wait until the song ends," she told Archie. "That way we'll cause less of a scene."

Archie didn't understand what she meant until he recognized two of the dancers spinning past them. One was a beautiful dark-skinned girl with her black hair done up prettily, wearing a fancy wine-colored dress. The other was a tall, handsome Yankee boy in a black suit and tails who stumped along awkwardly.

Hachi and Fergus!

Archie stared as they wheeled slowly around the dance floor arm in arm, Hachi gracefully compensating for Fergus' limp. Hachi wore a pearl necklace and earrings, her scar plainly visible but hidden in her beauty, and Fergus—Fergus had no black lines on his skin! It was like seeing the heads of his friends on two new and different bodies. But Archie's wonder was quickly replaced by anger. If these two had thought him dead—and why not? he had thought himself dead too—they didn't appear to be too broken up over it. In fact, they looked like they were glad he was out of the way.

The music ended and Fergus led Hachi off the dance floor, his arm still tight around her. Hachi leaned her head on his shoulder, and Archie went red with embarrassment. It was like they were on a date!

Tusker poked his head out of Archie's pocket. When he saw Hachi, he trumpeted happily.

"Might as well go see her," Archie said. "At least she'll be happy to see *one* of us."

Tusker burst from his pocket and flew across the dance floor to Hachi, who looked up in surprise. "*Tusker?*" she said. From somewhere underneath her skirts the other three clockwork animals flew out, chittering with Tusker in their baby language. But Hachi's tear-stained face wasn't watching her elephant, it was searching for—

"Archie!" she cried. She broke away from Fergus and ran at him, catching him up in a hug that was as fierce as it was unexpected.

"Archie! Archie! Oh, we were sure you were dead." She stepped back to make sure it was really him under the suit and wig, then hugged him again. Over her shoulder, Fergus smiled at him.

"I don't ken how you did it, White, but we're glad to have you back."

"There's not a scratch on you!" Hachi said, finally letting him go to have another look. "How did you survive the fall? And how did you get here? When did you arrive?"

"He showed up at the door wearing a filthy old bearskin rug," Ms. Ambrose told them. "If you want to know more, I suggest you take to the dance floor. We're beginning to draw stares."

"Ms. Ambrose is right," Hachi told them. The music had just begun to play again, another waltz, and couples were heading out onto the dance floor.

"Aye, you two go," Fergus said. "My leg is sore enough. Besides, my shoulder's soaked through from her crying over you." Hachi punched him playfully on the arm, and he winced. They *had* grown closer, Archie saw, but they were both clearly elated that he was safe and back together with them. He felt awful for thinking they hadn't missed him. "I'll be at the buffet table," Fergus said, bowing away. "I'll let our other friend know you're back and safe."

"Our other friend? Mr. Rivets! He's here?" Archie twisted to look around for him as Hachi led him out among the dancers.

"Yes. I'll tell you all about it after you tell me *your* story," Hachi promised. Her flying circus was starting to draw attention, and she shooed them back under her skirts.

"Where exactly are they going under there?" Archie asked.

"A lady never tells," she said. To Archie's surprise, she took his hand in one of hers and put his other hand on her hip. The waltz! He was supposed to dance with her.

"Um, I don't know how to dance," Archie confessed.

"Oh. All right." Hachi switched hands, putting hers around him instead. "Just follow my lead."

The music started, and Archie stumbled along with her, stepping on her feet every other beat. She grimaced more than once, jumping back out of the way as best she could while Archie told her about waking up in John Otter's hospital, about his guess that the pelt must have saved him, about John Otter's worries that more Mangleborn were rising, and about how coy he had been when Archie suggested that he and Hachi and Fergus were the beginnings of a new League. Archie skipped the part about the circle dance and the Stone Man—he was still trying to figure that out himself—and pressed Hachi to tell him how she and the others had made it. His stomach lurched to hear that his parents' airship had crashed, but he was relieved that she and Mr. Rivets had survived.

"Mr. Rivets and I walked all the way to Standing Peachtree," Hachi said. "Fergus was already here. And of course we thought you—we thought you were dead. Ow! That's my foot that got twisted!"

"Sorry! I'm sorry. I never learned to dance." Archie's natural clumsiness and lack of dancing lessons weren't helped by his oversized clothes.

"It's—ow!—it's all right. This is just for cover anyway, hiding us in plain sight."

Like hiding the Great Bear's pelt in with the costumes, Archie thought. He looked around at all the other boys and girls as they twirled and realized it would be harder to find the three of them here than in a secret room somewhere.

"Pretty hard to hide a boy in an all-girls' school," Hachi told him, "so Ms. Ambrose put together an impromptu social until we can shake Edison's men. The other boys are from Dragging Canoe Academy across town."

"She did all this in a day?"

"Ms. Ambrose is nothing if not resourceful. Ow! What are you wearing, lead shoes? Your feet are like anvils!"

"Sorry. But why would she do all this for you? Ms. Ambrose?"

"I used to be a student here," Hachi told him.

"*You* went to school *here*? Where they wear frilly dresses and teach you to dance?"

"Do you know how coordinated you have to be to dance a minuet?" she asked him. "Ouch. I guess not."

"So this isn't some kind of secret warrior school in disguise?"

"No. Lady Josephine wanted her students to be strong, smart, and independent, but—*ow*—the curriculum is heavy on trigonometry and Latin, not target practice and hand-to-hand combat. I did those as what you might call . . . independent study. Ms. Ambrose knew though."

"You speak Latin?"

Hachi gave him a tired look and danced out of the way of his feet.

"What happened to Fergus' tattoos?" Archie asked.

"We had to cover them up with makeup."

Archie laughed, and Hachi smiled again. "I think he hates the pants worse. Ms. Ambrose wouldn't let him wear his kilt on account of—"

The double doors to the ballroom banged open, and a group of grown men in dark suits and bowler hats—First Nations and Yankees both—came inside. The music died away, and the dancing and talking stopped.

"On account of them," Hachi whispered.

"I must protest!" Ms. Ambrose said, intercepting them. "This is a private school. You have no right—"

One of the men produced an aether pistol from under his jacket, and the students gasped as one. Ms. Ambrose was brought up short.

"And as I told you before, miss, we don't care much for what you think is right. We're looking for a boy, and we know he came here. Just turn him over to us, and we'll let you be on about your business." The men fanned out among the crowd, each with his own raypistol, examining the faces of all the boys. "He's about five feet eight inches tall," the man went on, "with black lines on his hands and face, and wearing a skirt."

"*Kilt*," Fergus whispered, coming up behind Archie and Hachi.

Mr. Rivets came with him, carrying a tray of hors d'oeuvres. "It is most gratifying to see you again, Master Archie. Would you care for a canapé? They are stuffed with chicken and asparagus, with just a hint of—"

"Not just now, Mr. Rivets," Archie whispered. "These men, they can't be Edison's. Not if his airship went down in a lake."

"Pinkertons," Hachi told him. "Hired detectives."

"Which means that even though Edison isn't here, he survived the crash," Fergus said. "Crivens."

"What does that mean? Crivens?" Hachi asked.

"I don't know. It's just something my da always said. It's like saying 'twisted pistons.' Only different."

"It's stupid," Hachi told him.

"Crivens to you, then," Fergus said.

"Shhh," Archie whispered.

The Pinkerton agents drew closer. Would their disguises work? Archie tugged on his wig, hoping it was straight.

"We should split up," Hachi whispered. "They may have

been told to look for Fergus with another boy, a girl, and a Tik Tok. We're—"

Before she could finish, a Cherokee boy from Dragging Canoe Academy stepped in front of the Pinkertons. "You looking for two Yankee boys and a Seminole girl, one of them with black tattoos all over him? I can tell you all about them. Starting with where they are right now."

25

Archie held his breath with the rest of the room as the Pinkertons converged on the Cherokee boy. He was a fierce-looking teenager, even in a suit. He wore his black hair swept up and back to a point like a woodpecker's crown, and his thin, sharp face was covered with pockmarks.

"You know where the boy with the black lines on him is?" the Pinkerton asked.

Ms. Ambrose hurried over, trying not to look like she was hurrying. "That's quite enough of that, young man. He doesn't know what he's talking about," she told the Pinkerton agent.

"I'll be the judge of that," the detective said. He didn't raise his raygun at her, but he held it where everyone could see it. "What do you know about it?" he asked the boy.

"She hid them right here," the boy told him. Archie looked for the nearest door, but Hachi put a hand on his arm, and her eyes told him to wait.

"But they're gone," the boy said. "She gave them money and a change of clothes, and they left for the train station. She threw together this dance tonight to keep you busy while they got away."

"We had men stationed outside," the Pinkerton agent said. "Nobody left after the small boy with the fur coat arrived."

Archie blanched. They'd watched him walk right up to the front door.

"There's a secret passage in the basement," the boy said. "An underground street from where the road was raised a few years back." He looked defiantly at Ms. Ambrose. "It leads to the basement of the Buck Head Tavern."

"And why should we believe you?"

The boy sneered. "I don't care anything about any Yankees on the run, but I wouldn't mind seeing that dirty Seminole girl get what's coming to her."

Ms. Ambrose slapped the boy across the face with venom.

"Go, go," a Pinkerton agent commanded. "You three, Union Station. You three, Piedmont Park. And someone will have to check the steam horse stables, just in case." The Pinkerton agents hurried from the room, and Ms. Ambrose followed them to the door and closed it.

The boy came over to Hachi and kissed her on the cheek. Archie and Fergus stared at her.

"What?" she said. "I am a *girl*, you know."

"So I've noticed," Fergus told her.

"This is Tooantuh," Hachi told them. The boy nodded hello. "He's . . . a friend."

"So I've noticed," Fergus said again.

"I miss you," Tooantuh told Hachi.

"I know," she said. "But I have to do what I have to do."

"Whatever that is," Tooantuh said like he was trying to get her to say more, but Hachi didn't bite.

"They're gone, though I don't doubt they've left someone

posted outside," Ms. Ambrose said, rejoining them. "Tooan-tuh, I'm *so* sorry I struck you so hard."

"It's all right, Ms. Ambrose." He rubbed his rugged jaw. "It helped sell it."

"Where's the music?" Ms. Ambrose called. "Is this a dance or isn't it? And none of that slow, stodgy stuff. Let's have a contra dance, maestro!"

The orchestra began playing something lively and the students cheered, running out onto the dance floor at the invitation of a caller who told them what steps they were going to do. Archie and Fergus watched Tooantuh pull Hachi out onto the dance floor and whirl her around like the spinning governor on a steam engine.

"I think there's a lot about Hachi we don't know," Archie said.

"So I've noticed," said Fergus.

Later that night, Archie and Fergus sat on facing beds in the small dorm room that two of the academy's students had let them borrow for the night. The bedclothes didn't have ruffles and there were no dolls or stuffed animals on the beds, but the room still felt like a girl's room to Archie. It was neat, for one thing, and there was a funny smell like flowers.

"So I come up to the door having been half-drowned, beat-up, interrogated, and shot at, looking as bedraggled as a cat that's just fallen into a bathtub, and what kind of greeting do I get?" Fergus said. The makeup was gone from his face and arms, and he was back in his kilt. "A raygun in my face. I tell you, I just about told her to shoot me then and there. At least it would have gotten me off my feet. It was all a misunderstanding though. With all the quarrels they been having around here lately between the tribes, she thought I was someone come to make trouble. When she kenned I was a friend of Hachi's, she pulled me inside. And I must say, hiding out in a school full of beautiful girls is not the worst idea we've ever had."

"Blech," said Archie.

Mr. Rivets came in with a black suit draped over his arm and shut the door. "Ms. Ambrose and I were able to procure something a little closer to your size, Master Archie."

"You don't have to say 'little,'" Archie muttered, but he took the suit from Mr. Rivets and began to pull off the oversized suit he'd been wearing all night. He'd long since taken off the itchy wig.

"Hachi wouldn't tell me much about her coming here, besides waking in the smashed-up airship," Fergus said. "She seems different somehow though. Looser."

"I actually saw her smile," said Archie. "It was weird."

"You were with her, Mr. Rivets. What happened?" Fergus asked.

"I'm afraid I couldn't say, sir," Mr. Rivets said.

Archie tensed. The repetition of the stock phrase Tik Toks used when they were forced to keep a secret made him think about his parents and John Douglas' scrapbook all over again.

Fergus laughed. "Share a candlelit dinner under the stars, did you?"

"I'm afraid what transpired on our sojourn to Standing Peachtree must remain between myself and Miss Hachi, sir," Mr. Rivets told him. "But you are welcome to ask her yourself."

Mr. Rivets nodded at the window, where Hachi was climbing inside.

"Hey! I'm getting dressed here!" Archie said, quickly hiding behind Mr. Rivets.

"Please," Hachi said. "You're like a little brother to me, Archie."

Fergus guffawed while Archie pulled up his pants.

"Do a lot of climbing in and out of windows while you were here, did you?" Fergus asked, grinning.

"Not to meet boys, if that's what you mean," Hachi told him. "It's a *girls'* school. With a very early curfew. If we wanted to meet boys, we had to sneak down to the secret passageway in the basement that led to the tavern."

That shut Fergus up. He had apparently assumed the secret passageway was a lie told by Tooantuh to mislead the Pinkertons. Now, clearly, he was picturing it as real—and picturing Hachi and Tooantuh meeting up down there. Hachi gave Archie a sly smile, enjoying Fergus' confusion. Whatever *had* happened on that walk with Mr. Rivets, Hachi did seem like a new person. Or at least a softer version of herself.

"We need to talk about what we're doing next. Where we're going," she said.

"We keep going to Florida," Archie said.

"Florida," Fergus agreed.

Hachi nodded. "But we lost everything in the crash."

"Not everything," Archie said. "I still have the Great Bear's pelt."

"But we have no rayguns," Hachi told him. "Nothing to fight with. And I really liked that wave cannon."

"Aye," Fergus said. "And we even lost them kooky metal

hats Tesla gave us, the ones to keep the beastie from driving us mad."

Archie shifted uncomfortably. He hadn't said anything about it, but the loss of the hats was the most worrisome for him. The new vision he'd had, the one with the Great Bear, was different. The Swarm Queen wasn't showing him his parents anymore. She was showing him other things. Memories. Visions.

She was talking to him.

"We don't need the hats," Hachi told them.

"No?" said Archie. "But how are we going to keep Malacar Ahasherat out of our heads? She could make us crazy." He saw the Great Bear again, fighting his friends. "She could make us turn on each other."

"Come with me," Hachi said, and she climbed out the window again onto the roof.

Fergus shrugged and followed as best he could with his one good leg. Archie grabbed the Great Bear's pelt and joined them. If he fell again, he wanted to have handy what had saved him last time.

"I'll just wait here then, shall I?" Mr. Rivets asked.

Hachi was already halfway along the roofline. She took a turn along another roof and skirted around a chimney like she was walking along a sidewalk. Fergus limped along, putting his weight on his straight leg as he balanced on the high roof. Archie tried walking, then slipped and fell, straddling the roofline. If he could have hugged the roof he would have, despite the sandpaper-like shingles. Instead he crawled along on his hands and knees. He was going to be a bloody mess when he got to wherever they were going, he was sure.

Archie got to the chimney and stood and hugged it, even though his arms weren't wide enough to go all the way around. A moth fluttered away from the bricks right into Archie's face, and he spat and coughed, almost losing his balance again. A hand caught him—Hachi—and pulled him around the chimney to the other side, where there was a commanding view of the city over the treetops. High overhead, a bloodred waxing gibbous moon hid among the thin gray clouds.

"We couldn't have kept talking in the room?" Archie asked. He had little bits of gravel stuck to his hands and knees, but, miraculously, none of it seemed to have gone deep enough to cut him.

Hachi settled in beside Archie and Fergus on the rooftop. "I used to climb out here almost every night," she told them. "To practice my mantra."

"Your what?" Fergus asked.

"My mantra. It's an Old World word. It's something you say or repeat over and over again to focus your mind. We don't need Tesla's tin hats. We just need mantras."

"That thing you say all the time," Archie said. "Those names."

"Yes," Hachi said. "They . . . they remind me why I fight, and give me the strength to do what must be done."

"But surely that's not enough to keep the beasties out of our heads."

"You know I share a connection with that monster in the swamp," Hachi told them. "I have . . . I have ever since I was very little." Then, haltingly, she told them the story she had told Mr. Rivets by the fire. She told them about the strangers, about her father and mother, about her mother's town. Afterward they were all quiet for a long time.

"I've had dreams and visions of the monster since I was little," Hachi told them. "I had to learn to block them. Push them out. My mantra does that. And it helps me remember."

"What do we do?" Archie asked quietly. "Memorize yours?"

"No. What matters is that you believe in something, *want* something so strongly that it overrides everything else. It has to be something personal. What is it you most want? Why do you seek the Mangleborn's destruction?"

"That's easy," Fergus said. "It's my fault Kano and lots of other people have died. If I hadn't had blinders on, I might have seen what we were doing was wicked. I put science before conscience, and I'm not going to do that again. Ever."

"Make it simple. Something you can remember easily."

"Yours isn't simple!" Fergus said.

"No, but I spent years learning it. You two don't have that kind of time. Think of something you can tell yourself over and over again to keep your mind on what you have to do. Something you don't have to think too much about. It should be easy for you, Archie."

Archie knew what she meant—the whole reason he wanted to go back to Florida, needed to confront the Swarm Queen again, was to free his parents. That's all he had to tell himself: Save Mom and Dad. Save Mom and Dad. Save Mom and Dad.

But so many things were eating at him. Distracting him. Why was Malacar Ahasherat singing to him of past Leagues? Why did the Shadow in the Cherokee circle dance scare him so much? How had he fallen ten thousand feet from an airship and survived? And the biggest question of all, the one he thought of now whenever he thought of his mom and dad: What secret about John Douglas' scrapbook had they ordered Mr. Rivets not to tell him?

"You can't ignore what's right for anything," Fergus said to himself. "That's mine. You can't ignore what's right for anything." Beside him, Hachi closed her eyes and whispered the names of the hundred slaughtered men of her mother's tribe again.

Archie took a deep breath and tried to clear his mind. *I have to save Mom and Dad*, he told himself. *It doesn't matter what the secret is.* "Save Mom and Dad. Save Mom and Dad. Save Mom and Dad." Instead of wondering what they did and didn't know, what they were and weren't telling him, he focused on the things that connected them, the things he loved about them: the picnics on blankets on the floor of the family observatory, the vaudeville shows and Philadelphia Athletics lacrosse games they'd seen together in the city, the winter nights reading *The Adventures of Professor Torque and His Amazing Steamboy* aloud by the fire. This was the mom and dad he wanted to save. The mom and dad he needed to save. They were his entire life. If he could just keep those images in his head, he could stand up to Malacar Ahasherat—in the real world, and in his head.

"Save Mom and Dad," he whispered. "Save Mom and Dad. Save Mom and Dad."

Other voices joined their whispered mantras—jeering, yelling voices from far down the street. A mob with torches and oscillators and axes was headed their way.

Fergus nudged Hachi, and she broke from her trance. "The Pinkertons are back!" he told her.

Hachi stood. "Some of them, yes. But it looks like they've brought friends. We've got to get inside and warn Ms. Ambrose."

"What? Why? Who is it?" Archie asked.

"The Pinkertons have whipped up a mob of Cherokee," Hachi told them, "and they're coming to attack the school."

26

The door to the room flew open as Archie, Hachi, and Fergus climbed back inside. It was Ms. Ambrose, looking pink and flushed again.

"Ms. Ambrose! There's a mob outside!" Hachi said. "They're coming for the school!"

"I know, dear. We've already been targeted for letting in anyone from any tribe, and I'm afraid the ball tonight brought us too much attention."

"It's the Pinkertons," Hachi said. "They've stirred them up."

"They must have figured out your friend sent them on a snipe hunt," said Fergus.

"We're barricading the front door to hold them off," Ms. Ambrose said. "We'll send you along through the tunnel to the Buck Head Tavern. They may have men there, but you'll stand a better chance of escaping if—"

"No!" Hachi said. She dashed out the door, leaving the headmistress spinning in her wake.

"Where is she going? What's she—we have to get you to the tunnel," Ms. Ambrose said.

"You don't really think we'd leave you in the lurch, do you?" Fergus said, hurrying to join Hachi.

"It's our fault they're coming here!" Archie said, following close behind.

From the balcony overlooking the great hall, they saw Hachi undoing all of Ms. Ambrose's orders. She had the girls moving the furniture away from the front door and piling it against the interior doors instead.

"What are you doing?" Ms. Ambrose cried, hurrying down the stairs. "You're going to let them in!"

"They're going to get in anyway," Hachi told her. "This way we can control where they go."

Ms. Ambrose nodded for the girls to do as Hachi said, and they went back to moving tables and chairs.

"You have rayguns?" Hachi asked Ms. Ambrose. The head-mistress, usually so in control, stammered and spun about as though trying to think what to do.

"Ms. Ambrose! Rayguns? Aether pistols? Oscillators? Anything?" Hachi asked.

"Yes. Two. In the safe upstairs. The combination is—"

"I know the combination!" Hachi said, already on the run. "I cracked the safe in my second year!"

Archie met Hachi on the stairs running down as she was running up.

"Archie, archery."

"What?"

"Archery! The school teaches archery!" she yelled before she disappeared down the hall.

Archie found a bewildered girl in a nightshirt on the landing. "Are you in the archery club?" he asked her. She shook her head, a little lost. "Do you know someone who is?" Archie pressed her. She nodded. "Find them. Tell them to bring bows and arrows. Do you understand? It's important!"

The girl seemed to wake up and she nodded, hurrying off.

"I need some ladies' underpants," Fergus said. Two or three of the girls nearby stopped and stared at him. "For the static! The charge!" he said, his face burning red. "Seriously."

A tall, pretty Cherokee girl in a white nightshirt took Fergus' hand and pulled him off toward the dorm rooms.

The room around Archie was busier than the Pennsylvania Pneumatic Post Office. Girls in various stages of dress ran here and there, but Archie didn't know what to do. Finally Hachi came sprinting back down the hall with two rayguns in hand: an aether pistol and an old oscillating rifle.

"Hey! Should I have one of those?" Archie asked.

"Not if we actually want to hit anything with them," Hachi told him. "Meghan!" she called. A girl a few years older than Hachi glided over, her nightdress flowing like a cape. Her brown hair was pulled back in a ponytail behind her heart-shaped face.

Hachi tossed her the aether pistol. "You're in charge of the other side of the balcony. Don't shoot until they're all the way inside."

Meghan activated the aether pistol's aggregator, and the raygun hummed. "*In cauda venenum,*" she said with a little giggle.

"Go, go," Hachi told her, and Meghan was off.

"Friend of yours?" Archie asked.

"She was my Latin tutor."

Ms. Ambrose hurried up to them. "We're ready downstairs."

"And I think we're ready upstairs. I've told everyone what to do," Hachi said.

"Not me!" Archie said. "What do you want me to do?"

Hachi looked like a parent whose five-year-old asks to help fix the family airship. "You can . . ." She looked him up and down, and Archie knew she was struggling to find any job for him that would be in the least bit useful. "You've got the pelt. You can go in and drag people to safety who've been hurt."

Crash! The big double doors downstairs lurched with the force of the mob, but held. For the moment.

"Hannibal is at the gates!" Ms. Ambrose announced, her authoritative tone restored. "Prepare yourselves, girls!"

The room cleared, girls disappearing into whatever places Hachi had told them to hide. The doors rattled again, and the bar across them cracked. Archie slumped at the top of the stairs. The battle of Lady Josephine's Academy for Spirited Girls was about to be fought, and he was relegated to field nurse. Some hero he was turning out to be.

The doors surged and cracked. One more push and the mob would be through. Ms. Ambrose came to the rail to address her charges.

"Remember the motto of our immortal founder Lady Josephine, girls! *Flectere si nequeo superos, Achaeronta movebo.* 'If I cannot move heaven, I shall raise hell.'"

The doors shattered to pieces, and the mob of Pinkerton agents and Cherokee stormed into the great hall with murder on their faces.

"Ladies," Ms. Ambrose cried, "raise hell!"

The archery club popped up from behind the rail on the balcony, arrows notched and bows drawn, their nightshirts making them look for all the world like Amazon warriors in tunics. They loosed a flurry of arrows to the screams and cries of the mob below. The mob retaliated with a blaze of raygun fire that blew chunks off the railing.

"Lacrosse team!" Hachi yelled. "Close quarters, attack!"

Screaming past Archie down the stairs came two dozen girls in wire masks and plaid skirts, their lacrosse sticks raised high. They flew into the stunned mob below, knocking away rayguns and torches and delivering a few good licks to men's heads and crotches. With the mob engaged on the ground, the archers popped up from behind the balcony again, firing at the attackers when they had a clear shot. Hachi and Meghan did the same with their rayguns from opposite sides of the room.

Archie saw a girl struck with the butt of a raygun and he was off down the stairs, the pelt draped over his head like a furry ghost. He grabbed the dazed girl up by the arms and dragged her to the stairs as the fight raged around him, rayguns *blaaating*, arrows *fffffffting*, lacrosse sticks clacking. An oscillator blast caught him in the back—*bzaaat!*—and he staggered. He felt the heat on his skin, but he wasn't dead. He wasn't even hurt. The pelt worked! It *must* have been the pelt that had saved him from his fall!

Archie dragged the girl to safety, where she was immediately tended to by some of the girls who hadn't been sent in to fight. Wading back into the battle with more confidence now, Archie let the raygun blasts and axes and torches hit him as he saved more of the fallen girls. With the Great Bear's pelt, he was invulnerable. If only a warrior like Hachi would wear it, she would be invincible!

Hachi's barricades kept the mob contained, but they were gaining ground. Soon they would be up the stairs and into the balconies, and from there they would be into the dorm rooms.

Fergus hobbled up with the beaming Cherokee girl on his arm as Archie pulled another student from the fray. "I've got a bit of charge!" he said. He rubbed his fingers together, and they crackled with lektricity. "I could stun the lot of them, I think, if only I could hit them all at once."

"The founder's statue!" Archie said. "If we tipped it over into the middle of them, Fergus could—"

"No," Ms. Ambrose and Hachi said together. "Nobody knocks Lady Josephine down," Hachi told them. Ms. Ambrose nodded curtly.

"All right then," Fergus said. "How attached are you to the chandeliers?"

Ms. Ambrose and Hachi looked up as one and seemed to agree that the chandeliers were expendable. Ms. Ambrose stepped up to the balcony rail as Hachi aimed her aether pistol.

"Ten Thousand!" Ms. Ambrose yelled. "Return to Greece!"

Somehow the girls still fighting below understood this meant retreat, and within moments they were backing up the stairs, still under attack from the mob. Hachi wasted no time. *Bzaaat. Bzaaat.* The chains holding the chandeliers snapped and their gas lines exploded, blowing upside-down craters in the ceiling. The chandeliers fell two stories and smashed to the floor, pinning the men at the front of the attack and forcing the others to climb over them to get upstairs.

Archie saw Fergus limping down the stairs and knew

he would never make it in time to catch the men on the chandeliers. Fergus seemed to realize the same thing, and he jumped on the banister and rode it down instead, his kilt flying. He hit the bottom of the rail and toppled off into one of the chandeliers with an *oof.*

"That's him! That's the one Edison wants!" a Pinkerton in the crowd yelled. One of them reached for him, but Fergus grabbed both chandeliers first. *Fzzzzzzzzzt.* Yellow-blue lektricity danced across the metal light fixtures, catching what was left of the mob in its death grip. The invaders kicked and thrashed, but Fergus held on until the last of his lektric charge had crackled away and all the attackers lay stunned. One or two had escaped Fergus' blast, but the archers in the balconies chased them off. The Battle of Lady Josephine's Academy for Spirited Girls was over. The home team had won.

Archie, Hachi, and Ms. Ambrose hurried down the stairs, followed by half the school. Fergus slumped against the base of Lady Josephine's statue, bruised and spent.

"Raise hell," he said with a grin as Archie and Hachi helped him to his feet. "I like that. It's a good motto."

To everyone's surprise—Fergus' most of all—Hachi gave him a kiss.

The doors banged open again and a new wave of men came pouring in. A First Nations man in a black uniform led the charge, an ivory-handled aether pistol in his hand. The archers in the balcony drew their bows.

"Nae, don't!" Fergus cried. "This'll be the cavalry, then."

Ms. Ambrose put a hand up, and the Amazons in the balcony held their fire. Sheriff Sikwai took a quick look around at the bodies on the floor and the girls in the balcony and holstered his gun.

"Get these men out of here and lock them up," he said. The deputies behind him stowed their weapons and started to drag the moaning bodies away.

"Sheriff," Fergus said by way of hello. He limped forward and put his hand out. The sheriff narrowed his eyes at him for a moment as if trying to decide if he knew Fergus.

"Fergus MacFerguson," Fergus said.

"I know who you are," the sheriff said, finally deciding to shake Fergus' hand. "I think."

Fergus frowned at that, but Ms. Ambrose was already there, offering the sheriff her hand. "Amelia Ambrose, headmistress. You're a bit late to the party, Sheriff."

"So I see. Sorry. We've had riots like this all over town tonight. We came as soon as we could, but it looks like you and your girls can take care of yourselves."

"We had a little help," said Ms. Ambrose.

Sheriff Sikwai nodded, staring at Fergus again. Archie looked to Fergus for some clue about why the sheriff was so interested in him, but Fergus seemed as mystified as anyone.

"All right then," the sheriff said, finally turning back to the headmistress. "We'll clean up for you. And I'll leave a couple of men at the door for the night."

"Thank you, Sheriff. My girls will sleep better for it. If I can get them to sleep at all." The balconies and stairs were filled with chattering girls animatedly reliving the battle.

"Oh, one more thing," Sheriff Sikwai said. He pulled a piece of paper from his pocket and unfolded it. It was a letterpress flier with a hand-drawn likeness of Fergus' face—black tattoos and all. Across the top the word WANTED appeared in all capital letters. "I don't suppose any of you have seen this boy, have you?" Sikwai asked.

The four of them stood stunned. Of course they'd seen him. Fergus was standing right there! Ms. Ambrose opened her mouth to speak, but she couldn't find words.

"The Pinkerton Agency delivered this by pneumatic post tonight. I expect they delivered one to every other sheriff in these parts too. Says here this boy's wanted for destruction of property, theft, and murder. Also says he's traveling with accomplices." The sheriff turned the flier around to read from it. "A boy with white hair, and a Seminole girl with a scar on her neck."

Fergus, Archie, and Hachi exchanged horrified looks.

The sheriff shook his head. "I don't know. Me? I look at this picture"—he looked up at Fergus again, his eyes narrowed like before—"and I just don't see a criminal."

"Neither do I, Sheriff," Ms. Ambrose said, cottoning on at last. "But we shall watch out for him, nonetheless."

"You do that," Sheriff Sikwai told her. "And you," the sheriff said, staring pointedly at Fergus, "you keep feeding the good wolf."

"Yes, sir."

The sheriff rounded up his men, and they herded the last of the dazed mob out the door.

"Your last name is MacFerguson?" Hachi asked him when the sheriff and his men were gone.

"Never mind that," Archie said. "Destruction of property? Theft? *Murder?*"

"I did bring that airship down, and there were a fair number of Edison's goons on it," Fergus allowed. "And I suppose Edison sees me as his property, in a way. Or what's inside me is, at least. Which I stole by running away."

"I don't think I should be hearing any of this," Ms. Ambrose said. "That sheriff's done you a great favor in giving you a chance to run."

"And letting us know more people will be after us," Hachi said. "We'll have to leave right away."

"Hachi Emartha, you must stay," Ms. Ambrose said. "We can protect you."

"No, you can't," Hachi told her. "And I'll just run away again."

"But your family has been so worried about you. Your aunt—"

"My aunt only wants me out of the way so she can take over my family's company."

"What company?" Fergus asked. "Hang on. Your last name is Emartha? As in, *the Emartha Locomotive and Machine Man Company?*"

Reluctantly, Hachi nodded.

"At least let us send you off with some food," Ms. Ambrose said. "Do you have any money? And we'll need to fetch your Tik Tok for you." The headmistress waved over another teacher, and students were sent off at a run.

"The Emartha Machine Man company that has skyscrapers in ten cities?" Fergus said.

"Not now, MacFerguson," Hachi told him.

"Thank you all," Ms. Ambrose said, shaking hands with Archie and Fergus. She hugged Hachi. "It was good to see you again." They separated, but Ms. Ambrose kept her hands on Hachi's shoulders. "I wish you had stayed with us and graduated, my dear, but even so, I know Lady Josephine would have counted you one of the academy's greatest successes. I know I do."

They hugged again, and Ms. Ambrose let her go. "I pray you find peace, Hachi—but I can at least rest well in the knowledge that you have found good friends."

27

Standing Peachtree's Union Station was still lousy with Pinkertons, so Archie, Hachi, Fergus, and Mr. Rivets slipped out of town to catch a train in the little Yankee village of Decatur instead. There was only one Pinkerton agent there, and Freckles the wind-up giraffe distracted him while Hachi laid him out cold with two quick kicks.

They found an empty compartment in a Pontiac sleeper car on an *Iron Chief* bound for Orlando, Florida, and Mr. Rivets kept watch for them while they slept. After everything that had happened, Archie expected to be awakened in the night by hired detectives or Edison goons, or maybe even a swarm of locusts. But when Mr. Rivets woke him gently the next morning, it was only to tell him the train had arrived at their destination.

Orlando was equally anticlimactic. There were no Pinkerton agents waiting for them at the depot, no mobs with torches and pitchforks, no hideous monsters. Just a dusty lane with a falling-down hotel, a small general store, and a combination horse stable/airship park/post office. Mosquitoes buzzed in their ears, and the air smelled of rotten citrus and horse manure.

"How quaint," said Mr. Rivets.

"I forgot you all came by airship the first time," Hachi said. She alone had gone to Florida the first time by train. "We'll need to rent an airship or a steam mule. It's too far to walk. Not if we want to get there before the full moon."

Fergus and Mr. Rivets headed for the horse stable/airship park/post office, but Archie stood where he was in the street.

Malacar Ahasherat was calling to him again. In broad daylight. While he was awake.

Jandal a Haad. Made of Stone.

Archie took a step toward the jungle. Toward the voice.

Jandal a Haad, the Swarm Queen said. *Mangleborn*.

He was almost to the line of trees at the edge of the town when something knocked him to the ground. He spat dirt as he struggled to get out from under Hachi.

"Ow! Hey! What did you do that for?"

"You were gone. I was talking to you, but you didn't hear me, and then you started to walk off into the swamp. Did you have another vision?"

Archie shook his head, trying to clear the fog that laid over his thoughts.

"No. No vision this time. Just a voice. The Swarm Queen's voice. Like my mom calling my name when she wakes me up in the morning. You didn't hear it?"

Hachi shook her head, a worried look on her face.

"Why is she picking on me?" Archie asked. His head hurt like he'd fallen on it.

"I don't know. But it's probably only going to get worse, the closer we get. You have to fight it, Archie. Remember your mantra."

"Right. Yeah," he said. *Save Mom and Dad. Save Mom and Dad*, he told himself as they went into the shop. *Even though they're keeping secrets from me.*

"No airships," Fergus told them when they joined him. "All they've got is a steam mule."

"That'll do," Hachi said. "I can get us there."

Archie wondered if he might be able to lead them there as well, just following the Mangleborn's voice. It was something he didn't really want to think about.

"Be twenty-five dollars a day," the surly old Seminole man behind the counter told them.

"Twenty-five dollars! That's criminal!" Archie said. "We could *buy* a steam mule for a hundred dollars!"

"Where?" the old man said. "You want a steam mule, it's twenty-five dollars a day, plus the price of coal."

They didn't have twenty-five dollars. They had spent most of the money Ms. Ambrose had given them on train tickets. They would have to walk, and they would miss the full moon. They would be too late to stop the Swarm Queen from rising.

"I guess we'll have to tell the prince the search is off," Fergus said.

"The prince?" said Archie.

"What prince?" asked the old man.

"A Nigerian prince. A *rich* Nigerian prince. He'll be so disappointed. But if we couldn't find one of the Seven Cities of Gold, at least we found the Fountain."

"The Fountain?" said Archie.

"The Seven Cities of Gold?" the old man asked.

"That's what the Nigerian prince hired us to find." He turned to Hachi. "We were so close."

"Yeah. Yeah, we were," she said.

"We were?" said Archie. Hachi kicked him in the shin to tell him to be quiet, but he didn't understand any of this.

"Atlantis!" Fergus said. "Just think of what we might have found there!"

The old Seminole spit tobacco juice into a spittoon. "You trying to tell me some Afrikan prince hired three kids to go looking for the lost city of Atlantis?"

"Well, we weren't kids when we started," Fergus said quietly, like there was anybody else around who might hear him.

"The Fountain . . . ," the old man said. "You don't mean . . ."

"The Fountain of *Youth*," Fergus said. "Why do you think I've got a bum leg at fourteen and Professor Dent here looks like he's ten years old and still has white hair?"

"Twelve," Archie said.

Hachi kicked him under the counter again.

The old man squinted at each of them in turn. "I don't believe you," he said finally.

Fergus sighed. "Do you have any mail waiting for Fergus MacFerguson?"

The old man pulled out a scrolled-up piece of paper. "Got one here for a 'Lord Fergus MacFerguson, Fifth Earl of Haggis, President of the Powhatan Geographic Society.'"

"That would be me," Fergus said. He took the note from the old man and skimmed it. "All right then. The prince wants us to return to New Rome. He's going to send another team. Airships, steam mules, cartographers, trackers. Dozens of men."

"But they'll all get a stake in the find!" Hachi said. "We were going to split our ten percent three ways!"

Fergus shrugged. "What can we do? We haven't got a steam mule."

"Lemme see that," the old man said. He read through the note. "Whoever finds this, they get a percentage?"

"That was our arrangement, yes," Fergus said. "But we're through. Thank you for your time. Mr. Rivets, we'll need train tickets back to New Rome. We're done here."

"As you say, sir," Mr. Rivets said.

They turned to leave.

"Ah ah ah—wait just a minute," the old man said. "Suppose I give you that steam mule. In return for one-fourth of your percentage."

"One-fourth!" Fergus cried. "That's highway robbery!"

"It's better'n zero, which is what you stand to get if you go back to New Rome and this here Nigerian prince sends down a new team," the old man said.

"He's got a point," Hachi said.

Fergus paced the small office like he was thinking it over, then finally relented. "Deal."

The old man clapped. "I'll get the steam mule ready for you!"

"And I'll write to the prince at once, to let him know our expedition is back on. You'll receive an official letter from him, granting you one-fourth of ten percent of whatever we find."

The old man hurried out to the steam horse stables, and Archie shook his head. "I'm so confused. What Nigerian prince do we know?"

"Our old friend Luis, from the sewers," Fergus said, scribbling a note to the prince. "I thought we might need a little leverage to rent an airship or something when we got here, so

I had Mr. Rivets pop off the train in Tallahassee and post a letter to Luis." Fergus finished his note and left it on the counter. "All right. Let's get out of here. I want to get as far away as we can before the old guy realizes our Nigerian prince wrote that letter on the back of a Cathay take-out menu."

It was late afternoon when they arrived in the clearing. The remains of the exploded equipment and the bent lightning tower Archie had destroyed still filled the glade.

Fergus brought the steam mule to a stop and let off its steam. "So. Here we are," he said. "Back where it all started."

Archie knew Fergus was just talking about when the three of them had come together for the first time a few days ago, but Archie couldn't help but think there was more to it than that. Their lives had all changed in some way in this clearing. They had all been reborn here. Edison's ceremony had turned Fergus into a lektric engine. Hachi's life had been transformed when strangers had come here and killed her father, turning her into a weapon of revenge. And Archie—Archie had lost his parents here too and started down a road he never thought he would travel. But there was something else about this glade. Archie didn't know how, or why, but he had an attachment to this place. A bond. To the clearing, and to the Swarm Queen. He had felt it before he'd ever put his hands into the green flames, and it had only grown stronger since.

They climbed down from the steam mule, and Archie went to the stone altar in the middle of the clearing. The surface of the ancient rock table had a maze of chiseled lines on it, something like the lines on Fergus' face. They all led to a small square hole cut straight through to the bottom of the table. Archie traced one of the lines with his fingers, imagining the blood of a hundred men flowing through the maze to its center. What connection did he have with this glade and this stone? Why did he feel as though he had been here before? And what, if anything, did it have to do with that scrapbook Uncle John had been keeping about him?

Jandal a Haad, Malacar Ahasherat whispered to him.

Archie looked up to find Hachi staring at him. He pulled his hand away from the stone altar.

"Sorry," he said.

"There are no bugs," Hachi said. "Here in the clearing. No bugs on the ground, and none in the air."

"That's a good thing though, innit?" Fergus asked.

"No, it's not," Archie said.

Hachi took Ms. Ambrose's aether pistol and oscillating rifle from the steam mule and tossed the pistol to Fergus. "You said we'd come back with an army, Archie." She activated the aggregator on her oscillator. "I only see three kids, two rayguns, and a machine man."

"We don't need an army," Archie said. "We're a new League. I know it."

"But there's only three of us," Fergus said.

"Three Leaguers can take down a Mangleborn," Archie told them. "The Seven fought *armies.*"

"So how do we get down there?" Hachi asked. "To where it's imprisoned?" A full, pink moon was rising in the late-afternoon sky; they had no time to lose.

"I didn't see where my parents went," Archie said. "It was dark, and there was a meka-ninja."

"What about this?" Fergus asked. He stood by a large stone set into a hill, a man-made thing like a wall or a door. The letters I and II were carved into it.

"One, two," Hachi read. "Two Roman numerals. Like the XX on the seal in our dreams. Twenty."

"One, two," Archie whispered.

Jandal a Haad, the Swarm Queen whispered. *Made of Stone.*

"Archie?" Hachi said, snapping him out of it. "Archie, focus. Remember your mantra."

"I'm sorry. Hachi, if I lose myself . . . if I forget myself . . ."

"That's not going to happen," Hachi told him.

"But if it does—"

"It's *not* going to happen," Hachi told him.

"One, two. Maybe they're coordinates," Fergus said, his mind not on Archie or Hachi but on the problem. "Or markers, like on a map. Does anybody have a map?"

"No," Archie said. "No, I forgot! Mom gave me a clue when we pulled that bug off her. One, two, buckle my shoe!"

"A nursery rhyme?" said Hachi.

"What you know as nursery rhymes began as ciphers created by the Mangleborn's Roman jailers," Mr. Rivets explained. "They are mnemonics. Simple ways for humans to remember the paths through the puzzle traps in the event that civilization falls and all written records are lost."

"You're saying nursery rhymes are . . . secret codes?" Fergus asked.

"In a way, yes, sir. But as times and languages have changed, many of the rhymes have lost their original meanings. The understanding and cataloging of these nursery rhyme clues is the work to which Master Archie's parents devoted their careers."

Just like Atlantis, going from the truth of a power station under a waterfall to the myth of a drowned civilization, Archie thought. *Or the Great Bear's father being a bear, not a six-legged monster with shark teeth and tusks for claws. Another part of humanity's hidden past.*

"That printer in New Rome, John Douglas. That's what he was publishing too—books full of nursery rhymes," Fergus said.

"Part of the Septemberists' mission is to keep old nursery rhymes in the public consciousness, so the codes are never forgotten," Mr. Rivets said.

"One, two, buckle my shoe," Archie said, trying to remember his studies.

"Three, four, knock on the door," Mr. Rivets said.

"The version my mother sang to me is different," Hachi said. "It's 'One, two, lace up your shoe.'"

They looked to Fergus, but he shrugged. "I heard it the same way as Archie."

"They both have to do with shoes," Archie said. "We have to look at our shoes!"

Archie bent down and started looking at the ground beneath his feet. Fergus and Hachi shared a skeptical look, then got down and searched with him.

Hachi poked into the dirt with her dagger until she hit something hard.

"There's something under here," she said. She cleared away the moist, woody loam and found more of the carved rock—and a brass plate about the size of a welcome mat.

"I told you! I told you!" Archie said. He knelt down on the plate, feeling around its edges. "This has to be something. A door, maybe."

"Hang on, I've got something," Fergus said. "It's a handle or a lever or something—"

"No, wait!" Hachi cried, but Fergus was already pulling it. The brass plate Archie was sitting on fell away, and he dropped into darkness.

28

Archie disappeared into the dark hole with a cry of surprise, followed shortly by a *thunk*.

"Archie!" Hachi cried.

"Ow," Archie said from the darkness.

"Archie? Are you all right?" Hachi called.

"Yeah. I don't think I broke anything. The pelt must have broken my fall again. Whoa, hey. Lights are coming on—"

Gaslights flickered on in the cavern, and Archie saw the floor and walls all around him were covered with brass picture frames.

"Hey—hey, it's that room we saw my parents in! Get down here!"

Mr. Rivets had already gone to the steam mule for a rope. Hachi shimmied down, then helped hold the rope for Fergus.

"I'll just stay up here and wait for you to get back then, shall I?" said Mr. Rivets. There was no way the rope would hold his weight.

"We'll be back before you wind down!" Archie called up.

"Just how long can he go without winding?" Fergus asked quietly.

The room they had dropped into was certainly strange. The walls, ceiling, and floor were all made of brass just like the picture frames, which were permanently attached.

"Looks like we're not the first ones to fall in," said Fergus. An old iron helmet lay in the corner, and he kicked it with his foot. It looked like something from paintings of the old conquistadors. Underneath it was a pile of bones, more metal armor, and a broken sword.

"Maybe Ponce de Leon found this place instead of the Fountain of Youth."

"Looks like he went down fighting, whoever he was," Hachi said.

"Aye," said Fergus, "but fighting what?"

"The Roman League built these rooms as a way of keeping the Mangleborn in and other people out," Archie said. "The Septemberists knew how to get through using the nursery rhyme codes, but nobody else did. I guess that didn't stop other people from trying."

Hachi saw something in another pile of bones and picked it up. It was a small pin with the Septemberists' pyramid eye on it.

"Guess they didn't *all* know how to get through," Fergus said.

"Remember, Master Archie," Mr. Rivets said from above, "the nursery rhymes have changed over time. The meanings may be very different now. You will have to think outside your programming, as it were."

"Brass," Archie said.

"Well, we got past one and two," Fergus said. "How many numbers are there in this nursery rhyme, anyway?"

"Twenty," Archie said.

Fergus groaned.

"At least now I understand why my parents made me memorize all those nursery rhymes," said Archie. He looked around the room for any clue as to what to do next.

"There," Hachi said. She pointed to the numbers III and IV etched into the metal near the ceiling.

"Three, four," Archie said.

"Three, four, cry no more," Hachi said.

"The one I learned is 'Three, four, knock on the door'," said Archie.

"So all we have to do is knock on one of these doors?" Fergus said. "That's easy." He knocked on one of the framed panels.

"No! Wait!" Hachi cried.

Too late. The brass door they'd fallen through in the ceiling snapped shut—*clank!*—and the door Fergus knocked on slid open. Something inside it began to click and whir, and all three of them took a step backward.

A clockwork cat the size of a big dog sprang from the opening. Its metal feet clattered on the brass floor, and its red eyes swept the room. Before he could even think to move, it sprang at Archie.

"Gah!" he yelled, dropping to the floor. He cowered under the Great Bear's pelt as the Tik Tok animal tore and slashed at him, its gears growling and screeching.

Fergus raised his aether pistol, but Hachi stopped him. "No! The beams will just bounce off the reflective surface."

"Do something!" Archie cried. "Ow! I can feel that! Somebody get it off me!"

"All right, I've got an idea," Fergus said. "All we have to do is—"

"Circus! Showtime!" Hachi cried. She leaped at the cat and sank her dagger in between the metal plates in the mechanical monster's side. The blade ground and jerked against the thing's clockwork insides, but it didn't stop it. The clockwork cat turned to slash at her. Hachi rolled back and kicked it away, throwing it into the wall with a clatter of metal. Her clockwork menagerie flew with it, fluttering around its head the way they had with Mr. Shinobi. The cat swatted at them like a real cat leaping for butterflies.

"Okay. Hold up. Here's what we do—" Fergus said.

Hachi leaped at the cat. They screeched and clawed and tore at each other, but the mechanical creature was too fast. Too wild. It bit and slashed through Hachi's defenses. It cut her arms, her face, her chest. She chipped away at it, making dents in it and fouling its clockwork, but she was losing. She fell and the cat pounced, but something jerked it back. Tusker! The little elephant had the tiger by the tail. He flapped his wings and dug in with his feet, slowing the Tik Tok cat down just long enough for Hachi to scurry back to her feet. She got ready for another attack, but the cat spun and snapped at Tusker instead.

Krunk.

The mechanical cat crushed Tusker in its metal jaws and spit out the pieces.

"*Tusker!*" Hachi cried.

Fergus snatched the Great Bear's pelt from Archie and tossed it over the cat like a blanket.

"Grab the corners!" Fergus cried. Archie dove for one side

of the pelt while Fergus picked up the other, and together they brought the ends up like a sack, the mechanical cat kicking and thrashing inside it. It was trapped.

Hachi dropped to her knees beside the little broken elephant. "Tusker! No, Tusker—no, no, no, no." She scooped him up in her hands, trying to see if he would be okay, trying to see if she could fix him, but he was smashed to pieces. Hachi wept—great, racking sobs that shook her. Archie and Fergus stood dumbly and watched, not able to let go of the pelt and not knowing what to say.

The rest of Hachi's clockwork circus were just as helpless. They fluttered around her trying to understand what was wrong with their companion. Mr. Lion paced back and forth in the air. Jo-Jo the gorilla grunted at Tusker like the elephant could still hear him. Freckles the giraffe prodded Tusker with her head, trying to get him to stand.

"Hachi, I'm so sorry," Archie said. The makeshift bag he and Fergus held sagged to the floor, and the mechanical cat's feet touched the ground through the pelt. It sprang into the air, still inside the sack, and Fergus lost his grip. Archie held on, desperately yanking it back down and slamming the pelt to the floor.

Krunk. The clockwork cat inside the bag stopped moving.

All three of them waited a breathless moment before speaking.

"Maybe it's playing cat-and-mouse," Fergus said.

Archie jiggled the bag, trying to get a reaction from it. Pieces of metal rattled around inside. If it was playing dead, it was putting on a pretty good performance. Archie flipped the sack open and jumped back.

The clockwork cat was smashed into a hundred pieces.

"It got what it deserved then," Hachi said. The sobs had stopped, but tears still ran down her face. She hadn't left the spot where Tusker had fallen.

Fergus examined the broken remains of the mechanical cat. "I thought the pelt was supposed to protect you from knocks and such," he said.

Archie frowned. Fergus was right. If the pelt protected who-ever or whatever was wearing it from harm, how had the cat been smashed inside it? Archie had taken far worse hits in the battle at Lady Josephine's, and there was no other way he could have survived that fall from the *Hesperus*. It didn't make sense.

The clockwork cat's door snapped shut and they all jumped. Archie looked around at the dozens of other doors and tried not to panic.

"There's gotta be fifty doors in here," Fergus said like he could read his mind.

"We'll never survive them all," said Archie.

"Nae," Fergus said. He knelt beside Hachi. "Especially not if you go throwing yourself at everything that says boo."

"I was—"

"You were getting yourself killed, is what you were doing," said Fergus. "You blame yourself for your parents dying, or for living when they didn't, both of which are slagging foolish, and now you've got a death wish. You might think you've got nothing to lose, but you do. You've got friends now, whether you meant to or not." He took the smashed pieces of Tusker from her reverently. "So I'm telling you straight out: That'll be enough of that. Either we all make it through, or none of us do. Aye?"

Hachi wiped the tears from her eyes. "I suppose if I wasn't around you'd be dead before the next puzzle trap."

"There's that too," Fergus allowed. "So no more flinging yourself into death's pointy teeth, right?"

Hachi nodded.

Fergus opened the pouch he wore at his waist and slid the broken pieces of Tusker inside.

Hachi whistled her circus—the three that remained—back to their places on her bandolier. She wiped her nose on the back of her hand and stood, scratching a deep mark on the door the cat had come out of.

"What'd you do that for?" Archie asked.

"So we don't open the same door again next time."

"All right then. So which door do we try next?" Fergus asked.

"Three, four, knock on the door," Archie muttered. "What did you say yours was?" he asked Hachi.

"Three, four, cry no more."

"Don't seem like they have much in common to me," Fergus said. "I wonder if we ought not to try one of those up around where the numbers are. More than likely one of them's the one that'll—"

"Shhh! No—be quiet. Be quiet!" Archie interrupted. "'Cry no more,'" he whispered. "Don't talk."

When they were all quiet, Archie put an ear to the panel beside him. "I hear ticking!"

Hachi tried one for herself and nodded.

"Same here," Fergus said.

"We have to find the one with no ticking behind it," Archie told them.

Together they moved through the room, listening for ticking behind the panels and scratching a line down each one where they heard something. Hachi used her dagger. Fergus used a screwdriver. Archie listened and scratched his lines with one of the claws on the Great Bear's pelt.

"Here. I think I've got it," Archie said, his ear to a panel in the floor. "I don't hear any ticking behind this one. You guys try."

Fergus went first, and shook his head. Hachi put her ear to the cold metal plate. Nothing. They all looked at each other. Between them hung the unspoken question: *Do we dare?*

"Archie, be ready with the pelt," Hachi said. She took up an attack position with her blade. "Fergus, you get behind Archie."

"Aye," Fergus said, limping for cover without argument.

Archie took a deep breath and nodded. Hachi knocked. The door flipped open. Everyone tensed. . . .

But nothing came out.

Hachi inched her way forward to peer down inside, then relaxed.

"It's a ladder," she told them.

Fergus clapped his hands. "All righty then! I can't wait to see what five, six will be!" He put his hands on Hachi's shoulders and guided her toward the ladder. "But you go first."

29

Hachi went first, followed by Fergus, then Archie. Fergus was slow going with his bad leg. He kept it locked straight, but it would slip and he'd have to catch himself, hugging the ladder again and again. He muttered colorful curses under his breath as they descended.

"Oy below," he said. "No looking up my kilt now."

Hachi snorted.

"Was that a laugh?" Fergus asked Archie.

"I think it might have been."

"The real Hachi would never laugh," Fergus said. "Quick, push her off! She must have one of them bug things on her neck! "

"Ha-ha," Hachi said. She helped Fergus down the last few steps of the ladder, and soon they all stood in a new room. It was small, rectangular, and all brass like the last, but there were no picture frames this time. The sides of this room were seamless except for a set of four dials on the far wall with something written above them in Latin: QVINQVE, SEX, NEC TIMIDVS, NEC AVDAX. Archie struggled to remember his Latin lessons with Mr. Rivets.

"There are no bones," Fergus said. "That's good, innit? Must not be too dangerous then."

"Or no one's made it this far," Hachi said. She had just taken a step across the middle of the room when the door they had climbed through slid shut and became part of the ceiling again. Something deep within the wall clanked, and the floor lurched and began to move. It slid slowly toward the wall with the dials on it, dragging them with it.

"Or they got crushed to powder down there in those gears!" Archie said. He pointed at what the moving floor was uncovering: massive, spinning gears that would chew them up if they fell in.

"Locked sprockets, do you see that?" Fergus said, pointing at the clockworks. "That's a gear train there. And look—it goes out underneath the walls. And there, that's a ratchet wheel! See how it disappears there? The whole place must be made of clockworks. We're only seeing a tee-ninsy part of it."

"We're going to be seeing a lot more of it if we don't figure out how to open the next door," Archie told him. He hurried across the room to where the dials were and started trying to decipher the writing with Hachi.

"*Quinque, sex, nec timidus, nec audax,*" Archie read aloud. "*Quinque, sex,* that's 'five, six.' Five, six, pick up sticks—that's what I was taught. But that's not what this says. *Nec timidus, nec audax.* Neither . . . scared? Neither audacious . . . ? Gah! We have to figure this out!"

"Five, six, neither fearful nor bold," Hachi translated easily. "It doesn't rhyme in Anglish, but it rhymes in Latin."

"Probably why it got changed to 'pick up sticks,'" Fergus said, half paying attention. He was still at the edge of the floor, watching the clockworks below. "Is that a tourbillon? Look at the size of it! That's absolutely brass!"

Archie ignored him. "The phrase doesn't make any sense! It doesn't tell us what to do!" He was starting to panic. The floor was more than halfway gone now.

"Oh, those Romans. Clever, clever lads," Fergus said. "You could use that pallet level as a seesaw, it's so big."

"Fergus!" Archie cried.

"There are four dials," Hachi said. "Each with one through nine in Roman numerals. All we have to do is turn them to the right combination. Five, six. Easy." She turned the dials.

"But that's only two numbers! There are four dials," Archie said. "That can't be it, Hachi!"

"Five, six, five six, then," Hachi said, and she turned the last two dials. Nothing happened.

"It's not that easy!" Archie told her. "The floor's past halfway!"

"Then we add them."

"Eleven doesn't have enough digits!"

"Eleven eleven then."

Still nothing.

"Oh no you didn't," Fergus said. "Oh, you did. But of course! How else keep all this working for a thousand years? Guys, you've got to come see this. *It's self-winding.* The whole place. The puzzle traps. The prison. Do you understand? It winds itself with an eccentric weight the size of—I don't know. Maybe the size of Standing Peachtree. I only saw the edge of it. It must use the Earth's rotation to—"

Archie grabbed Fergus and spun him away from the edge.

"Fergus! Fergus, we need to figure out this puzzle or we're

going to *die*, do you understand?" Archie saw a brown-stained gear and pointed to it. "That's not rust!"

Blood. It was blood on the gears, where someone had fallen in and been churned into ground beef.

"How did the wall get so close?" Fergus said. He shook his head like he was trying to clear it. *"Don't ignore what's right for anything.* I need that tattooed on me. All right. What have we got?"

"Five, six, neither fearful nor bold," Archie told him, hopping up and down. Hachi, meanwhile, was randomly spinning the dials, trying to luck into the answer.

"Right," Fergus said. "Neither fearful nor bold. That's the two of you, all right. What this needs is some cold, hard science." He looked at the Latin again. "What about all those numbers then?"

"We've *tried* five and six," Archie told him. He stamped his foot with a ringing *clang*. "And just about every combination of them we could think of!"

"Nae, nae, *these* numbers," Fergus said. He pointed at the V, I, V, and X in the first two words—QVINQVE, SEX. "V, I, V, X: five, one, five, ten. They're letters, but they're Roman numerals too."

Archie and Hachi stared at each other. Archie couldn't believe they hadn't seen it themselves.

"Five, one, five, ten!" Archie said. "Put that in!"

"There's no ten on these dials," Hachi told them. "Just one through nine."

Fergus glanced back at the spinning clockworks behind them. They were running out of floor.

"There's more numbers in the other words," he said. "More ones, fives, tens, Cs, Ds, Ms."

"Too many!" Archie said. "There are only four dials!"

"The dials only go to nine?" Fergus asked. "Add them. We have to add the numbers! Read them out."

Fergus kept a count in his head as Hachi read the numbers aloud. Archie backed up against the wall. They only had a yard or so of floor left. More of the gears below had brown stains on them now. They were *not* the first people to have gotten to this room, and if they weren't quick about it . . .

"Two thousand two hundred and forty-three!" Fergus yelled over the roaring clockwork. "Two, two, four, three!"

"Are you sure?" Archie asked. "That's not how you write two thousand two hundred and forty-three in Roman numerals."

"Just put it in!" Hachi yelled.

Hachi took the first two dials, Fergus the third, Archie the fourth. There was barely enough room to stand. If Fergus was wrong, if that wasn't the number—

Click! A little door slid open on the wall below the dials, and Archie now saw the tiny Roman numerals VII, VIII carved into the wall beside it.

"Seven, eight, don't be late!" he cried.

Hachi pushed Fergus and Archie through the door, then dove in behind them as the floor slipped away beneath the wall. They collapsed on the other side, breathing hard.

"That was not fun," Fergus said.

The door they had come through snapped shut. Something deep in the wall clanked, and the floor began to move *back* in the other direction—at twice the speed.

"Oh, you've got to be kidding me!" Fergus wailed.

Behind them, they heard the sound of more spinning clockworks as the floor uncovered another room full of deadly machinery.

"I think this is the exact same floor, just slid into the next room over," Fergus said.

Yes, Archie saw the place where he'd stamped his foot and put a dent in the floor.

Wait, how had he put a dent in solid brass?

Hachi was already standing, reading the words above the four dials on this wall. They were different this time. NOVEM, DECEM, ETIAM ATQVE ETIAM.

"I don't suppose that says 'Nine, ten, a big fat hen.'" Fergus said.

"No," Archie said. "Nine, ten—"

"—again and again," Hachi finished wearily.

They put in the same numbers as before, but no door opened.

"It's not working!" Archie said. "It's a different combination!"

"All right," Fergus told them. "Read me the new numbers, and let's do this again."

30

The Roman numerals in *"Novem, decem, etiam atque etiam,"* when added up, equaled four thousand six hundred and twelve. The answer reopened the door back to the room where they'd solved the first number puzzle. Archie worried that "again and again" meant they had to keep going back and forth from room to room, the floor always getting faster each time, but when they slipped through into the first room there was a new door open, with XI, XII written on a wall just beyond it.

Eleven, twelve, dig and delve.

A narrow spiral staircase led them down, down, down into darkness, surrounded on all sides by the clicking, whirring breeze of the giant clockwork machine that powered the complex. Its Roman builders had gone to a great deal of trouble to keep everyone but the League out, and their prisoner in. Archie's parents had made it this far too, and he had to believe the visions meant his parents were still alive. *Save Mom and Dad*, he told himself over and over again. *Save Mom and Dad. Save Mom and Dad. Save Mom and Dad.*

Gaslights flickered on as they reached the end of the spiral staircase. The stairs stopped a foot above the floor, which was moving. Not toward a wall, like the rooms above, but around in a circle: The stairs emptied out onto an enormous sideways gear that spun at the speed of a strong river. One by one they stepped onto the moving floor and peered out into a maze of moving gears, some turning lazily, others spinning like saw blades.

"We're more than halfway there," Archie said. "Now what?" His voice echoed in the vast chamber.

"Here," Hachi said. The numbers XIII and XIV were carved into one of the teeth of the gear they stood on.

"Thirteen, fourteen, start the machine," Archie recited. "But it looks like it's already started without us."

An empty space in the next interlocking gear rotated by, a place where the other gear had no tooth. Etched onto the gear where the missing cog would have been were the Roman numerals XV, XVI.

"Fifteen, sixteen, betwixt and between," Hachi said.

"Fifteen, sixteen, come out clean," Archie said. "Oh, slag. We're supposed to go down into those gears."

"I told you the whole place is clockworks," Fergus said.

"We'll be crushed!" said Archie.

"Not if we're quick," Hachi said. She saw the open tooth coming and crouched, ready to leap.

"Nae nae nae! Not this time," Fergus told her. "Those two gears are different sizes. The hole we saw before won't be the same this time. We've got to time the ratios just right."

"There has to be a trick to it," Archie said.

"Aye. We just have to have a basic understanding of clockworks. And be fearless, I suppose. Now . . . jump!"

Archie hadn't been expecting that. He was almost too late

jumping in behind Fergus and Hachi. He slipped in just as the gears closed around them, making a neat little rotating room.

"A little more warning next time!" he told Fergus.

"Now!" Fergus said, and again they were leaping into the free space where a gear had been forged with a missing cog. Hachi helped Fergus with the jump, putting an arm around his waist and helping support his dead leg. Archie hated not being able to help, but he had enough to worry about on his own. They jumped again, and again, Archie's leaps always sloppy and uncoordinated. One gear nipped at the Great Bear's pelt, but he pulled it away in time.

Fergus led them into another gear that was up and down, not side to side, and they had to slip out before they were dumped into the dark machinery below. Their next jump took them to another big sideways gear like the one they had landed on at the beginning, and they all took a minute to catch their breaths.

"We have to be nearly there," Archie said. "How far do you think we've gone down?"

"Ninety feet? A hundred?" Hachi guessed. "The stairs alone were something like four stories."

"Here's another set of numbers," Fergus said. He was standing near the edge of the gear. "Still fifteen and sixteen."

Archie flopped back onto the gear and closed his eyes, trying to muster the energy he would need for the next series of jumps.

Jandal a Haad, the Swarm Queen whispered in his head. Before Archie could repeat his mantra and focus his mind he was lost in another dream, the cavern inside the ancient puzzle traps dissolving around him.

Archie stood in a broad field. It was twilight, but the world was on fire—the grass, the trees in the distance, the wrecked hulks of clanker tanks and armored airships, everything burned. Ray-gun fire crackled in the distance, and the ground was strewn with the bodies of warriors from a dozen nations—Iroquois, Cherokee, Powhatan, Sioux, Muskogee, Yankee, and more. Archie panted, holding a twisted, shattered trunk of a tree that was impossibly huge in his hands. There was no way he should have been able to lift it, but he could.

On the horizon skulked the enormous, unnatural silhouettes of Mangleborn. Three of them, lumbering by, the earth shaking with every step they took.

Wham. Something smashed down on Archie's head and drove him into the ground, making a boy-sized hole in the earth. The force of it kicked him back up before he fell again with a thud.

"Sorry, Archie!" said a voice he didn't recognize.

He crawled to his feet. Arranged behind him were six people, all around his age. A thin, tattooed girl dressed like a pirate in tall black boots and a weather-beaten old coat, holding a glowing green harpoon. A masked Mexicano boy with an odd-looking turquoise aether pistol and a tin star on his vest. An Afrikan boy looking out of the enormous eyes of the ten-story-tall steam man that had pounded Archie into the ground. A shadowy girl crouching on the steam man's shoulder.

And beside them, standing together, were a boy in a kilt with black lines on his skin, his clenched fists crackling with lektricity, and a thin, scarred girl with a wave cannon in her arms and brass toys fluttering around her head.

Fergus and Hachi.

"Don't apologize," said Hachi. "Just kill him."

Archie woke screaming, swinging his fists. Destroy them. He had to destroy them all!

"Archie, Archie!" Hachi said. She leaned over him, slapping away his fists. "Archie, snap out of it! Remember your mantra!"

Archie felt sick, like he might throw up. The vision, the spinning gear, the cold, damp air of the underground cavern—it was all too much. He hacked and coughed, his head ringing like a hammer on an anvil.

"Get him to the center where it's not turning," Fergus said. Archie felt hands drag him to a place where the world, mercifully, stopped spinning. Hachi held him while he came back to his senses. Fergus passed by every few seconds, still standing on the gear that moved around them.

"What did you see, Archie?" Hachi asked. "You said our names."

"You didn't see it?" Archie asked.

"No. Just you. The Swarm Queen's just talking to you now. What was it?"

Archie squeezed his eyes shut, tears streaming down his face. He shook his head. He couldn't tell them. It couldn't be true. It hadn't happened yet. It wouldn't. Couldn't.

"Don't give in to it, Archie. Stay strong. You've got something to live for. Remember that."

"S-save Mom and Dad," Archie said, fighting the urge to throw up again.

"That's right. Deep breaths now, and keep saying that to yourself."

Archie did as Hachi told him. *Save Mom and Dad. Save Mom and Dad. Save Mom and Dad.*

But why had he seen those other people? Six of them.

Seven, including him.

The League of Seven.

He wasn't their Leader. He was their Shadow. And they were fighting him.

"Are you ready?" Hachi asked him. She helped him to his feet, and he took a tentative step onto the moving gear. He didn't feel too sick.

"We can wait," Fergus said. "We're perfectly safe here for the moment."

"My parents aren't," Archie told him. He had to focus. *Save Mom and Dad. Save Mom and Dad.* "I'm ready," he told them.

Fergus led them to the edge, and they waited for his signal to jump.

"Now!" Fergus said.

They dropped into the empty space between two cogs, then into a parallel gear, a tight fit for the three of them. Then down again, and a quick jump into another sideways gear. This one was a long wait. It felt wrong to Archie, like they had missed their jump. He was antsy. He could feel Malacar Ahasherat poking and prodding his brain like steam trying to force its way out of a boiler. *Save Mom and Dad. Save Mom and Dad,* he told himself. The gears around him ground on, and Archie couldn't help but feel that the complex didn't belong to the

Romans at all but to the Swarm Queen—a great living machine built to swallow Archie whole.

"Now!" Fergus yelled again.

Archie shook himself back into the present and jumped, but something grabbed him and yanked him back. The Great Bear's pelt was stuck under the edge of the gear!

"Archie, jump!" Hachi yelled. The space between his gear and theirs was going away. "Jump! Jump! You have to jump now!"

Archie tried to jump again, but the pelt wouldn't come loose. If he slipped out of it, left it behind, he could make it. But Archie needed it! Without the Great Bear's pelt he was useless!

"Archie!" Hachi cried. "Now! Now! It has to be now!"

Archie yanked as hard as he could. The pelt ripped free! He turned to jump, but the gears were closing. The space was too small. Too tight. He put his arm through, touched Hachi's outstretched hand, but had to pull it back before it was cut off.

The gears turned, the space closed, and Archie was alone.

"Archieeeeee!" Hachi cried.

Fergus pulled her away. "You can't do anything for him! He's gone now. He's gone!"

"Up! I'll climb up on top! I can pull him out—"

"You can't go up top. You'll be crushed. It's built to keep us in, don't you see? And the next jump's coming up any second now."

"No! We'll stay here. He'll come back around."

Fergus spun her around to make her look him in the face. "Hachi! We have to keep moving forward. Do you understand?

If we stay here, we'll be dead like him. The rotational speeds are different. If we don't take our one chance, we won't get another. Hachi, are you listening to me?"

Hachi batted his hands away and tried to turn, but there was nowhere to go.

"I'm sorry, Hachi. I'm truly sorry," Fergus told her.

The gap in the next gear began to open up.

"We can't give up. We have to go now. We have to keep moving or we'll be dead too," he told her. "Three, two, one—"

Screeeeeeeee! Fergus felt the gear grind beneath them, slowing down. *Trang!* Something big and metal snapped and clattered into the clockworks. *Sprang! Chink! Krunk.* Fergus knew the sound of a dying machine when he heard it. Something somewhere had broken or jammed or come loose, and the entire machine was falling apart, piece by massive piece.

Wham! The gear they were on buckled and the floor dropped away. Fergus fell, still clinging to Hachi. They slammed into a tilted gear and slid. Down, down, down they tumbled, left, then right, then straight down again as another falling gear took out the floor beneath them. It was happening so fast they couldn't see the next drop before they took it, plummeting as the great machine crumbled and disintegrated around them.

Whoomp. They hit a dirt floor. *Wrenk! Crunk! Shing!* Fergus grabbed Hachi and covered her protectively as an enormous gear crashed down on top of them.

Poom.

Fergus looked up, surprised he wasn't dead. The gear was wedged in above them, one end at their feet, the other propped on the cavern wall behind them like a lean-to tent. Pieces of the great machine clattered down on it like rain.

"Out, out!" Hachi cried. She half pulled, half dragged Fergus from under the gear as the weight on top of it finally made it snap. *Ka-thoom.* Dust and debris spilled out of the space where they'd been like an avalanche, knocking them both to the ground again.

Fergus was battered and bruised, and wouldn't be surprised to find out he'd broken a few bones. He checked to make sure Hachi was still breathing, then collapsed beside her, closing his eyes against the pain.

Suddenly Fergus wasn't lying on the floor in the puzzle traps anymore. He was standing in a dark field sometime in the future. What he was seeing hadn't happened yet, he knew, but it would. It felt real—as real as if Fergus were actually there.

There were bodies all around him. A boy with a tin star and a shattered raygun. A dead girl slumped over a branch in a nearby tree. A giant steam man ripped apart at the seams. A Karankawan pirate with a flaming green harpoon stuck in her chest.

And Hachi. Her clockwork circus smashed to pieces beside her broken body.

There was only one other person standing. Archie. Archie had done this. Killed everyone. Killed Hachi. Fergus knew it. Archie came closer, a wild, distant look in his eyes, and somehow, impossibly, he lifted one of the broken steam man's enormous brass arms over his head to bash Fergus with it.

Fergus felt his fists spark with one last charge of lektricity, but he let it go.

"Archie, mate. I can't do it. I can't kill you," Fergus told him.

"You should have," Archie said, and he slammed the giant metal arm down on Fergus like a hammer.

Fergus jerked awake. He'd only closed his eyes for a second. Beside him, Hachi was blinking too.

"Did you see it?" Fergus asked her.

"Archie," she whispered. "He killed everyone. He killed *you*. I was the only one left to stop him."

Fergus frowned. "Nae. *I* was the only one left."

Something clattered behind them, pushing its way out of the rubble at the base of the broken machine. It lifted a heavy metal beam out of the way and tossed it aside with a roar. Whatever it was, it was big and bad and coming their way.

"Hachi," Fergus said. "Hachi Hachi Hachi Hachi—"

She pulled Fergus to his feet, and they watched as rocks tumbled and a gear rolled out of the way. Hachi drew her dagger and Fergus summoned what lektric spark he had left, even though he feared neither one would be enough.

The thing worked itself free and pulled itself up out of the rubble, but it wasn't big at all. Bad, maybe, but not big.

It was Archie.

"Crivens," Hachi whispered, and she took a step back in fear.

31

Archie saw Hachi take a step away from him like she was scared. He didn't blame her. He was scared of himself. Who was he? *What* was he?

Jandal a Haad, the Swarm Queen's voice whispered. *The Stone Man.*

Fergus frowned at Hachi's fear and limped over to Archie.

"It's a miracle," Fergus said. "A blinking miracle. That bear-skin saved your life again."

Archie shook his head. He felt hot tears carve canyons down his dusty face. "No," he said. "No, you don't understand." He held the pelt up for them to see, but they still didn't get it. "It's not— Mom? Dad?"

Archie's parents stood at the far end of the man-made cavern Archie had seen in his vision on the airship, the room with the great iron buttresses and the huge stone well. They were here. Archie had made it. The top seal on the crypt was already open, as was another beneath it, but a third seal was opened just a few inches wide—just enough for lektricity from something below to crackle out of it, like it was ready to erupt. But all Archie cared about were his parents. His mother was still pushing buttons and turning dials on the great machine that kept Malacar Ahasherat's last seal in place while his father pounded on the clockworks robotically with a bent pipe.

"Mom!" Archie cried. "Dad!" He dropped the Great Bear's pelt and ran across the room to them. "Mom, Dad," he said, but they didn't hear him—or couldn't. They had smiles on their faces and glazed looks in their eyes from the bugs in their necks. "Hachi! Hachi, we have to get these things off them." Hachi hurried over.

"We have to keep them separated, or they'll try to stop us," Archie said. "I'll hold my mom. Fergus, you hold my dad."

Fergus put Mr. Dent in a headlock. Archie's father acted like he didn't notice, and kept banging away on the machine with his pipe. Fergus braced himself. "Got him," he said.

Archie took his mother's hands. "I'm sorry," he whispered to her, then nodded to Hachi.

She cast Archie a wary look, then slid her dagger under the bug on Mrs. Dent's neck. *Slurch.* Archie's mother screamed as the bug came out, and Fergus struggled to hold Mr. Dent, who tried to turn and stop them. Hachi pulled the bug out and squashed it, then quickly moved to do the same for Mr. Dent.

Archie's mom collapsed in his arms, and he sank to the floor with her, cradling her as she sobbed. Archie had never seen his mother cry like this before, had never seen his parents so weak, and it scared him.

"Mom, it's all right. I'm here now. I came back for you. We're going to get you out of here," Archie told her.

"No," his mother said through her tears. "Shouldn't have

come, Archie." She tried to lift herself, but she wasn't strong enough. Archie realized it must have been days since either of them had eaten or slept. "The Swarm Queen . . . ," his mother rasped. "Archie—you have to get out of here . . ."

"It wants you," his father said, still sobbing. He had fallen to the ground beside his wife, absolutely exhausted. "Malacar . . . Ahasherat . . . wants to use you."

"Use me? For what?" Archie said. His skin grew cold. "What am I?"

"We don't know," his mother said. She put a shaking hand to his face. "My beautiful boy. We don't know what you are."

Archie slumped back against the console. There were almost no other words his mother could have said that would have hurt him more.

We don't know what you are.

"The Septemberists brought you to us as a baby," his father said. "Asked us to raise you."

Archie reeled. *Adopted. I'm adopted,* Archie thought. Everything he'd known—his family, his life, the foundation of his world—it was all a lie.

"We didn't know . . . we didn't know you were . . ."

"Didn't know I was what?" Archie said, panic creeping into his voice.

His mother drew her hand back from his face, her eyes wide with fear. "Something else," she said.

Jandal a Haad, said a voice in the pit. They all heard it now. The ground rumbled.

"Seventeen, eighteen, the prisoner queen," Hachi said. She looked nervously at Fergus. "Nineteen, twenty, bar her entry."

"Archie, go. Go now. Run," his father told him. "Leave us. Save yourself."

"No! I can't. Just tell me what I am!"

"You're our son," his mother told him.

But he wasn't. Not really. He was something else. Archie looked from face to face, seeking answers no one seemed to have. Who was he? *What* was he?

Jandal a Haad. Made of Stone.

Hachi grabbed Archie by the shirt and shook him. "Are you with us? Archie, *are you with us?*" she asked.

Archie nodded, shaking himself out of it. *Remember your mantra*, he told himself. *Save your parents.*

But they weren't really his parents, were they?

"Fergus! Can you close that seal?" Hachi asked.

"See if I can't!" he said. He started flipping switches and turning dials on the console.

"All right," Hachi told Archie. "We're getting your parents out of here."

Archie helped her pick up his mother. She felt like she weighed nothing. She was so tired she had already passed out, her arms swinging listlessly as they carried her. They were three steps toward the rubble pile when something metal clattered in the shaft where the great machine had collapsed, and they froze.

An iron machine man lifted an enormous gear and cast it aside with a crunch that echoed through the cavern. The thing had a headless, bell-shaped body, with round porthole windows like different-sized eyes all over it. One side of it had two smaller arms, balanced against one larger arm on the other side. It walked on two spindly, piston-driven legs that *psssshted* as it walked, but the thing wasn't steam driven, at least not that Archie could tell. There was no boiler, no exhaust pipe, no smokestack.

Archie watched, mesmerized, as the thing stumbled down off the wreckage from the great machine like it had somehow been born from it. That wasn't possible, was it? Or was this one last defense the Roman League had left behind? Beside him, Hachi stared at the weird thing too.

"What is it?" she asked.

"Sing a song of sixpence, a pocket full of rye," the thing said with a strange voice like the crackle of lightning. "Four and twenty blackbirds, baked in a pie."

"*Edison*," said Fergus.

Archie took a step backward. "What? Inside that thing?"

"I think he *is* that thing. There's only room enough in there for a brain. I've seen inside it. If Edison's in there, that's all he is—a brain in a jar. The poor flange must have lost his body in the crash of the *Black Maria* after all."

Archie shivered at the thought.

"Brain in a jar, brain in a jar," Edison said. His mechanical body began dancing a clumsy little jig. "Big jar. Bad jar. Strong jar. Edison jar."

"Oh, and the suit never really worked," Fergus said. "Every brain they put in it went batty."

"*And you worked for this man?*" Hachi said.

"I don't anymore, all right?"

"Just get that seal closed!" Hachi said. She let Archie's mother back down. "Drag them over to a corner somewhere where they'll be safe," she told Archie.

"What are you going to do?"

"What I came here to do in the first place," she said. She drew her dagger. "Kill Edison."

Hachi ran straight at him, her flying circus—what was left of it—bursting from her bandolier. Edison's suit began to hum, and he raised the small pair of arms on his right side. Lektricity sparked between them.

"Hachi, no! Stop!" Archie cried. Too late. Lightning arced from Edison's iron hands to Hachi, blowing her off her feet.

"Hachi!" Fergus cried. He pushed past Archie, his tattoos rearranging themselves furiously. He raised his hands, and lightning leaped from him too. The crackling energy caught Edison's iron giant in the chest, but it didn't seem to hurt him. Edison danced a little jig, then turned and redirected the stream of energy toward the pit. The cavern shook. Rocks broke off the ceiling and smashed to the ground. The thing in the pit squealed, an inhuman sound that gave Archie goose bumps.

"When the pie was opened, the birds began to sing!" Edison sang crazily. "Wasn't that a dainty dish, to set before the king?"

"Stop! Stop!" Archie cried. "You're helping him! Fergus, he's just feeding it down to the Mangleborn!"

The ground rumbled again, and out through the narrow crack in the last seal came an army of insect men. The Manglespawn of Malacar Ahasherat, the Swarm Queen. They were part man, part insect: hideous things with sharp, spiky hair all over their bodies and powdery brown wings that fluttered in staccato. *Frum. Frum. Frum. Frum. Frum.* Their giant compound eyes glittered in the gas light of the chamber.

Fergus switched off his lektrical discharge and staggered

back into Archie, but the damage was done. The cavern was suddenly crawling with the things. They swarmed everyone, even Edison, attacking anything that moved.

"The seal!" Archie cried, running for Hachi. "Fergus, close the seal!"

Hachi's face and arms were black from the blast, and her hair and clothes were singed. Her Tik Tok animals hovered around her nervously.

Archie kicked at one of the moth men, knocking it away. "Hachi! Hachi, are you all right?"

She stirred, still groggy.

"Hachi, Fergus is closing the seal, but these moth things came up out of the ground! We need you!"

"Edison," she moaned.

"Edison's got some lektrical suit. I don't know how we're going to stop him. But first we've got to keep these moth creatures away from—"

Mr. Lion roared his little roar, and Archie looked up to see one of the moth creatures leaping at him, its jagged teeth aimed for Archie's neck. He ducked and closed his eyes.

Splurch.

When he opened his eyes again, Archie saw Hachi pulling her dagger out of the thing's chest. Yellow-green blood trailed from the end of her blade as the thing fell dead beside them.

"That is for Talisse Fixico, the potter," she said. Archie helped her to her feet, and she sent another moth man's head flying. "And that is for Chelokee Yoholo, father of Ficka." Her clockwork menagerie distracted another while she cut off its wings. "Hathlun Harjo, the surgeon." She gutted another. "Odis Harjo, the poet!"

Hachi fought her way toward Fergus to protect him, spouting her mantra as she slew moth men. Archie did his best to stay out of the way.

Edison's lektric stream stopped, and he put his hands up to dance among the insect men that chewed at his suit. "The king was in his counting house, counting out his money," he sang as he danced. *Crunch.* He stepped on one of the insect men, squashing it without seeming to notice. "The queen was in the parlor, eating bread and honey. . . ."

A clawlike green hand reached up through the crack in the last seal and grabbed the edge of the stone pit. Malacar Ahasherat was pulling herself up.

"Ferguuuuuus! Fergus, you have to close that hole!" Archie cried. He fell down and rolled out of the way as another insect man tried to bite him.

"I think I've got it. I think I've got it. Yes—yes!" Fergus yelled. He threw a switch on the console, and metal grated as the gears spun.

Over the pit that was Malacar Ahasherat's prison, the final stone seals pulled another few feet wider.

"Oh, crivens," Fergus said.

"Fergus! Fergus, it's going the wrong way!"

"I know! I know! I can fix it! I can fix it!" He turned dials and flipped levers like mad. The machine stopped, but the seal stayed half-open. "Just give me a second!"

Fergus didn't have a second. He'd drawn Edison's attention, and the madman's iron suit was dancing his way. "Fergus was in the garden, hanging out the clothes," he sang. "When down came Edison and pecked off his nose. . . ."

"Look out!" Archie cried. He pushed Fergus out of the way

just before Edison slammed his big left hand into the machine's controls. *Smash!* Edison pulled his iron fist from the wreckage of the machine and came after Fergus again, arm raised high to bash him.

"Hey! Hey, Edison! Look over here!" Archie cried, trying to distract him.

Edison swung around. *Wham!* The big arm caught Archie in the chest and threw him across the room. He hit the cavern's stone wall and fell to the floor with a sickening *thunk.*

"No! Archie!" Fergus cried.

Archie should have been dead, but he wasn't. Every bone in his body should have been broken, but they weren't. None of them. He looked himself over. His clothes were torn and ripped, but there wasn't a scratch on him, just like before. He didn't know why, didn't know how he had been born or where he had come from, but he understood the truth of his power now. There was no denying it anymore. He nodded and stood.

"Hey, Brain in a Jar. Is that all you've got?" he called.

Edison turned, just steps away from the retreating Fergus.

Across the room, Hachi stopped fighting insect men long enough to stare. "Archie? But how—?" Fergus was watching him too.

Lektricity crackled between Edison's two small arms, and he thrust them at Archie. *Kazaak!* Lightning caught Archie and two insect men who fluttered nearby. The insect men squealed and burst into flames, but it didn't burn Archie. The lektricity held him. Seared him. Burned his clothes. But it didn't harm *him.* It couldn't. He knew that now.

He took a step forward, pushing back the lightning.

"Twisted pistons," Fergus whispered.

Edison must have been thinking the same thing. The iron suit took a step closer and upped the amps.

"*Raaaaaaaaaaaaaa!*" Archie yelled, taking another step forward. "That's right. Let it all out. Burn it all up!" he told Edison. He took another step.

Edison might have been crazy, but he wasn't stupid. The lektricity stopped, and Archie staggered forward, no longer being pushed back. Edison charged him, his big arm windmilling. *Bam.* The blow knocked Archie to his knees, but it didn't kill him. It didn't crush his bones. It didn't break his skin.

Thoom. Edison stepped on him. *Boom.* Edison punched him. *Wham.* Edison smashed a broken gear on Archie's head.

Archie got up every time. It hurt a little. He felt pain, remotely, like the sound of a train in the distance. But none of it killed him.

Nothing could kill him.

Archie was unbreakable.

He had known it once and for all when he'd survived the gears of the puzzle trap. When he had fallen with the broken pieces of the great machine, been crushed a dozen times, and still climbed out of the rubble without a scratch. It hadn't been the Great Bear's pelt that protected him. It couldn't have been. He knew when it tore. When he had pulled it off and really looked at it. Seen, for the first time, all the gashes and cuts and raygun holes in it, hidden by the fur.

It wasn't the Great Bear's pelt that had saved him in the fall from the *Hesperus.* The pelt hadn't protected him from the raygun blasts at Lady Josephine's Academy. It hadn't shielded him from the crush of the gears when death had come for him up above. And death *had* come for him. Again. Archie had stood inside the empty cog, watching death come spinning toward him, but the massive gears hadn't chewed him up and spit him out. They had *choked* on him. The gears had closed in around him and squeezed him, but his body hadn't been crushed, hadn't been broken. None of it—not his shoulders or his chest, covered by the pelt, or his uncovered head and arms and legs.

The gears had closed in on him, locked tight around him, and squeezed him until he thought he would burst, but he hadn't. He clogged them. Stopped them. *Broke* them.

Because he wasn't human. He was something else.

He was unbreakable.

Edison tossed him into the air, and Archie fell to the floor with a thud.

Who was he?

An insect man jumped on Archie and bit him. *Crack*. The moth man came away squealing with a mouth full of broken teeth.

What was he?

Nunyanuwi, John Otter had called the Shadow. *The Stone Man.*

Jandal a Haad, rumbled Malacar Ahasherat. *Made of Stone.*

Mangleborn.

Monster.

"No. No, I'm not a monster," Archie said. "I'm not a monster!"

"Archie! Archie, remember what you're here for!" Hachi called to him. "Remember your mantra!"

Save Mom and Dad, he told himself. But they weren't his mother and father. *Maybe you were adopted.* That's what John Otter had said. The old medicine man had known, or guessed. *The Septemberists brought you to us as a baby*, his mother said. But they didn't know what he was. Where he had come from. Had Uncle John known? Is that why they were watching him? Studying him? Was he the child of a monster, like the Great Bear? Was even a part of him human?

Smack. Edison's big arm knocked Archie into the wall again. Rocks fell from the ceiling, burying him. When the last of the pebbles trickled down, Archie pushed his way up, unbroken. Edison's iron giant was waiting for him, dancing back and forth.

"So you're the Jandal a Haad," Edison sang. "Batty Blavatsky got something right! The Joke of Chuluota. But who's laughing now?"

"Wait, what did he say?" Hachi yelled, hearing the name of the village where her father had died. "Archie, what's he talking about? Did he say Chuluota?"

But Archie wasn't listening. He was staring at something on his arm, just beneath his torn shirt. A cut.

But not a cut.

A crack.

There was no other way to describe it. There was no blood. No muscle. Nothing pink inside. Nothing human. Beneath his skin, there was only gray, like stone.

There was a crack in Archie's arm.

32

Archie stared at the crack in his arm. *What am I? Who am I?*

Jandal a Haad, the Swarm Queen whispered to him. *Made of Stone.*

Mangleborn. Monster.

"No. No, I'm not a monster," Archie whispered.

The Shadow, Archie heard John Otter say.

"No," Archie said.

"Archie! Archie, remember your mantra! Remember why you're here!" Hachi yelled to him. She was surrounded by insect men. Drowning in them.

Save Mom and Dad, Archie told himself. *Save*—but he wasn't human. He was . . . something else, his mother said. They didn't know what he was.

A monster. *A* beast. *An abomination.*

Why hadn't his parents told him?

Not my parents. I'm not their son. I'm something else. I'm—

Jandal a Haad. Made of Stone. The Shadow.

Archie put his hands to his head. It felt like it was going to crack open.

A crack. There was a crack in him. Like a crack in a sidewalk. A crack in a stone.

The Great Bear. Heracles. Enkidu. The Golem. Always different, always the same, Malacar Ahasherat whispered. *Strongmen. Shadows. Monsters.*

"No!" he yelled. "That's not me. I'm not—I'm not a monster!"

"Sticks and stones can't break his bones," Edison sang again, his iron body doing a strange little back-and-forth dance. "But words can surely hurt him!"

Jandal a Haad.

Archie pulled at his hair. The Mangleborn's voice was unbearable. Visions of former League strongmen assaulted him, all of them raging monsters who had turned on their friends. Wave after wave of guilt and shame and agony. Relentless. His fists shook. His muscles clenched. He was a monster. He was a monster, and no one had told him. They had let him think he was a real boy, let him think he was normal, but all along he was something else. Something wrong. Something *evil.* He wanted to hit something. Wanted to smash things. Break bones. Crush skulls.

"Archie!" Hachi yelled. She fought her way over to him. "Archie, don't listen to it! You have to fight it, Archie. Fight it!"

"Shut up," he cried. He beat on his head.

"I need help over here!" Fergus said. He swung the lead pipe at a moth man and missed. Moth men swarmed Archie's unconscious mother and father.

Not my mother. Not my father. Not my parents—

"Sticks and stone can't break his bones," Edison sang.

Not the same, but the same. Always different, never different.

Hachi shook him. "Archie! Archie, you have to focus. Archie, listen to me!"

"Shut up! Just everybody *shut up!*" Archie roared. He backhanded Hachi, knocking her across the cavern. She hit the wall with a thud and slumped to the floor.

"Oy!" Fergus yelled.

Archie picked up a boulder twice his size and hurled it at Fergus. The rock missed him and smashed into the machine's console, destroying what was left of it.

"Archie, no," Hachi moaned from the floor. Her voice was weak. "Archie, you have to—"

"Just *shut up*. Just everybody *shut up!*" Archie yelled. An insect man buzzed in Archie's face, and he ripped an arm from its body and beat the thing to death with it. When there was nothing left of its arm he tossed the shreds aside and pulled a metal strut from the wreckage of the great machine, swinging it like a club at anything that moved. *Thoom. Thoom. Thoom.*

Your destiny, the Swarm Queen sang to him. *Your birthright. You are the Jandal a Haad. You have the strength of a hundred men.*

"Shut up!" Archie cried, cleaving an insect man in two with one swing. "*Shut up!*"

"Mantra," Hachi whispered. "Remember—"

Archie rounded on her, panting, heaving. Fergus was there, helping her to her feet.

"Save . . . your parents," Hachi told him.

"They're not my parents!" Archie yelled. "They can't be! I'm not human. I'm a monster!" He swung the great metal club at them, and the wall above Fergus and Hachi exploded into rock and dust. Hachi and Fergus limped toward the machine that sealed the tomb. Archie's parents were there too, awake again, and struggling to fend off the insect men.

Not his parents.

Archie lumbered toward them, dragging his impossibly big metal club along like a caveman.

"Archie. Please," his not-mother said. "We love you. It doesn't matter that you're—"

"What? That I'm *what?*" Archie cried.

Something else. Something not human. Made of stone.

Shadow. Monster. Jandal a Haad.

"Only words can hurt him!" Edison crowed, still dancing.

Not the same, but the same. Always different, never different.

"Archie, listen to me. It's the Mangleborn doing this to you. Malacar Ahasherat," Hachi told him. "It doesn't matter what you are. You're *Archie Dent*." She backed into the broken machine, beside the people he'd thought were his parents. "You're our *friend*."

"Archie, listen to her," his not-father said.

He was nobody's friend. Nobody's son. Everyone had lied to him. He was a monster.

"Shut up," Archie said wearily. "Please. Just—everybody *shut up*."

But they wouldn't shut up. None of them. Not the Mangleborn, not Edison, not Hachi and Fergus, not his parents. Not the voice in his own head that told him he was no different from the thing in the pit. That he belonged there with it.

But he would make them be quiet.

He would make them *all* be quiet.

Archie raised his club, tears streaming down his face.

"I just—I just need you to shut up now," he told them all.

Fergus ran away, but his not-parents and Hachi stayed where they were. Hachi drew her dagger, and Archie giggled through his tears. Like she could hurt him. Like anything could hurt him. He was unbreakable. He was—

Hachi stabbed his mother in the leg. Mrs. Dent cried out and crumpled to the ground.

"Mom!" Archie cried. He dropped the iron girder and fell to his knees to help her. "Mom! Are you all right?"

Hachi slumped back against the machine and held on to her stomach.

"You stabbed her!" Archie cried.

"You were going to bash her brains in with a big metal bar," Hachi said, her voice tired and weak. "After you did me and Fergus."

"Hi-yaaaah!" Fergus cried. He hobbled out from behind the machine with a lead pipe in his hands and whacked Archie in the head. *Clang.*

Archie didn't budge. He'd barely felt it.

Fergus looked at the bent pipe in his hands, then lifted it to hit Archie again.

"Stop. It's all right," Hachi told him. "He's back."

"Oh. Sorry, White, but you kind of went barmy there for a minute."

Archie tore off part of his ragged shirt, and his father helped him tie it around his mother's leg.

"Callous, but effective," Mr. Dent told Hachi. "I knew you were in there, Archie," he said to his son. "We didn't raise you to be a monster."

"I'm sorry," Archie said. "I don't know what came over me.

I—" He saw the crack in his arm again and covered it so the others couldn't see it. "I lost my head."

"Sticks and stones can't break his bones," sang an electronic voice behind them. "But they can hurt his friends."

Archie stood and turned. Edison's great iron hulk waited behind him, Archie's metal club in its hands. Edison raised it, aiming for Fergus. Archie stepped in front of his friend as the metal bar came flying down.

Krang. Archie caught it in his hands. He understood now. The Mangleborn had shown him. Archie wasn't just unbreakable. He was super strong. He always had been. Breaking little things all the time. Moving the Great Bear's stela. Turning the valve in Atlantis to flood the machine men. Leaving a dent in the brass floor of the puzzle trap room.

Archie had the strength of a hundred men, and he was going to use it on Edison.

Archie wrenched the metal bar from Edison's grip and whacked him with it. *Wham.* He dented Edison's big round dome. *Wham.* He smashed out one of the windows. *Wham.* He broke off one of Edison's arms. *Wham. Wham. Wham. Wham.* When the metal bar was bent beyond use, Archie tossed it aside and pounded on the iron suit with his fists.

"I'm not—" *Wham.* "—a monster." *Wham.* "You're—" *Wham.* "—the monster." *Wham.* "You're a brain—" *Wham.* "—in a big metal jar!" *Wham.*

Edison staggered back against the wall, his suit bent, broken, and fizzling. Archie pulled back his fist for one last punch, one that would tear the thing apart for good.

"Archie!" Hachi cried. "Archie! The pit!"

The floor rumbled. The low stone wall crumbled. Malacar

Ahasherat roared, a sound like a hawk's cry mixed with the buzzing of a million hornets, and up out of the pit rose the head of the real monster. The Swarm Queen. Archie felt icy, primeval fear course through him like it had in the glade when his hair had turned white, but this time he was ready. He had seen Malacar Ahasherat before in his dreams. Seen her inhuman arms and legs, her cicada wings, her fly-like, compound eyes. He was ready for her.

The Swarm Queen's giant wings fluttered as she tried to pull herself through the half-open seal on her prison. Her head turned, and her glassy eyes found Archie, mirroring him a thousand times back at himself.

Jandal a Haad, she said.

"My name," he told her, "is Archie Dent."

Jandal a Haad, the Mangleborn said. *Join me.*

"No thanks," Archie told her. "But I know someone who's dying to meet you."

Archie picked up what was left of Edison's broken iron body. It should have been impossible—a twelve-year-old boy lifting something so gigantic, so heavy. But Archie had the strength of a hundred men.

"Four and twenty blackbirds . . . baked in a pie," Edison warbled.

Archie trudged over to the pit, Edison held high over his head and sparking.

"When the pie was opened . . . the birds began to sing,"

"Always the same," Archie told the Swarm Queen. "You rise again, and the League of Seven always put you down."

Malacar Ahasherat lashed out at Archie with a tentacle made of swarming insects, but she was too late. Archie hurled

Edison's iron body on top of the Mangleborn, and they both fell back into the pit, Malacar Ahasherat screaming, Edison singing. The insect tentacle dissolved into a cloud of buzzing, skittering bugs.

"Fergus!" Archie yelled. "Seal it! Seal it now!"

"There's nothing I can do!" Fergus yelled back. He was desperately trying to operate the machine that controlled the seal, but it was too smashed. "Between you and Edison, you smashed the controls but good!"

"No!" Archie ran over to the machine. "What needs to turn? Where? Show me."

Fergus studied the clockworks with his tinker's eye. "There— that's the one that should do it. But the gizmo's broken. There's no way I can work it—"

Archie grabbed one of the cogs of the giant gear and pushed. The metal groaned, but it started to turn. Hand over hand Archie turned the enormous wheel, and the machine that controlled the seal on the tomb came to life. One by one the stone seals over the Swarm Queen's prison closed—*thoom thoom thoom*—and it was done.

Archie slumped to the floor, exhausted, and Hachi nodded at him.

"Better," she said wearily.

33

Edison had come by rented airship, which Archie and the others found tethered near the entrance. No one felt the least bit guilty about taking it.

"It's not like he's going to be needing it anytime soon," Fergus said. "Not where you threw him."

"About that, Archie . . . ," Hachi said.

Archie looked to his parents. They sat at a little fold-out table in the airship's cabin. Mr. Rivets had found food aboard the airship, and was plying them with chicken noodle soup.

"What am I?" Archie asked them.

"I told you, Archie," his mother said. "You're our son."

"But I'm not. Not biologically," he added quickly. The voice in his head was gone, but the fear and doubt remained.

"No," Mr. Dent said. "No, you're not our biological son." He reached out and held Mrs. Dent's hand. "We've never been able to have children of our own. The Society knew that, so when they found you, they brought you to us, to raise as our own."

"We were going to tell you we weren't your birth parents, Archie," Mrs. Dent said. "When you were older."

"Is that when you were going to tell me I was . . . I was a monster?" Archie said. He could feel the anger building up inside him, like steam pressure building in an engine. He took a deep breath. He couldn't let the anger control him. Not like before, in the pit. He could never do that again.

"You're not a monster," Mrs. Dent told him. "Never that, Archie."

"But we didn't know you were . . . so strong. Invulnerable," Mr. Dent said. "I promise, Son. If we had known, we would have told you. We could never have kept something like that from you."

"But you knew I was different. The Septemberist Society knew. Mr. Rivets knew. John Douglas knew. We found a scrapbook he kept, with pictures of me, and charts, and graphs. We lost it, but the Society was watching me. Measuring me."

"They told us you were the son of two Septemberists who'd been lost battling a Manglespawn in the South Americas," Mrs. Dent said. "John said there might have been some infection, some contamination, from the Manglespawn. They asked us to tell them if there was anything strange about you, but there never was. You were a perfect baby. Strong and happy and . . ." She put a hand to her mouth. "Never sick. Not once. You were never sick."

"We ordered Mr. Rivets not to tell you," Mr. Dent said. "But only because we knew you were adopted, and wanted to tell you in our own time."

"I am truly sorry, Master Archie," said Mr. Rivets. "It was never my desire to keep the truth from you."

"I know, Mr. Rivets," Archie said. He knew the machine man couldn't have lied to him if he'd wanted to, and that he'd been ordered to keep the secret. But still, he was glad to hear Mr. Rivets say he was sorry. "This couple John told you about. Were they my real parents?"

"I don't think so now," Mrs. Dent said.

No. Of course Archie's parents weren't human. Not both of them, anyway.

"We only learned you weren't . . . human . . . when we were connected to Malacar Ahasherat through those things on our necks," Mr. Dent said. "The Mangleborn read our thoughts. It saw we had taken you in as an infant and raised you as our own. But we shared its thoughts too. That's how we finally understood what you really were."

"Which is what, exactly?" Fergus asked. He and Hachi had been quiet, but listening.

"The Jandal a Haad. That's what it called you," Mrs. Dent said. "The man made of stone."

"But that's not right," Fergus said. "No man is made of stone. I mean, it's not physically possible. Look at him. He's got white hair, and pasty skin, and fingers and toes that wiggle."

"And a punch like a steam engine," Hachi said. "And an unbreakable body."

Archie knew there was one way to prove it, to show them he was truly, impossibly, made of stone. He'd hidden the crack on his arm from them because it made him a monster. He didn't want to show them. He wanted them to think he might be human after all, that he wasn't a monster. But how long could he hide what he was from his friends? From his parents? If they didn't help him figure out what he was, who could?

"Not totally unbreakable," Archie said. He put his hand to his shirtsleeve, but was still afraid to show them. To show them would mean to admit once and for all he wasn't human. That he was . . . something else. But he had to know what.

"Archie, what is it?" his mother asked.

Archie peeled back his sleeve and showed them the crack in his arm.

Mrs. Dent gasped. They stared at the crack, all of them, for what felt like hours, before someone finally spoke.

"Does it hurt?" Hachi asked.

Archie shook his head.

Fergus bent close to examine it. "Might be able to patch that with some mortar," he said. Hachi punched him. "What?" Fergus protested. "There's no sense in being all hush-hush about it now, is there?"

"Not in this room," Archie said. "Not between us." His meaning was clear: He wanted to talk about it with his family and friends. He needed to. But not with anyone else. Everyone nodded.

"We'll worry about the practicalities later," Mr. Dent said. "The first thing we're going to do when we get back is go straight to Philomena Moffett and find out what more the Society knows. We'll get answers for you, Son. For all of us."

Archie wanted to feel relief at that, but all he felt was a deeper, darker fear that the truth might be something he never wanted to know. Still, he appreciated the look of fierce protectiveness in his father's eyes.

"That would be brass," Archie said.

"Archie, we've told you repeatedly, we don't approve of you using that slang," his mother said.

"Crivens," Fergus said, laughing, "the boy's made of stone, and you're still worried about language?"

"Archie is a Dent," his mother said, "and the Dents are made of stronger stuff than stone."

Archie smiled. His mom and dad might not be his *birth* parents, but they were his family. They had raised him, and loved him, and he loved them too. Archie even let them hug him with Fergus and Hachi watching, though he'd squirmed out of hugs since he was seven. He didn't care if the *world* was watching now. He needed to feel human again, if only for a moment.

Because there was that crack in his arm to remind him that he wasn't.

"I'm ready to go home," Archie said. He turned the crank to raise the airship's anchor, and it snapped off in his hands. "I guess we know now why I'm such a klutz."

Fergus took the broken handle from him. "Here, I'll fix it."

"What about you?" Archie asked Hachi. "Will you go back to school?"

She shook her head. "I can't go back to that life. Not ever. Edison was the only lead I had for what happened to my father. I knew he was there that night twelve years ago, but I never could learn any of the other names. But he said something down there today: Batty Blavatsky. The Joke of Chuluota."

"What's Chuluota?"

"The name of the town where my mother grew up. The town that was wiped out the night the strangers came. I'm going to find this Blavatsky person. Find out if she was there, and who else was with her, and why. And then make them pay."

"I'll come along for the answers too," Fergus said.

"With which one of us?" Archie asked.

"With both of you, of course." He turned from working on

the anchor crank. "You don't think we can break up the team now, do you? There's no reason we can't get all the answers together. Besides," he said, "we've still got four more of our League of Seven to find, haven't we?"

Archie had been the one to argue that they were a new League, but in his heart he'd never believed it. Not until they defeated Malacar Ahasherat. That's what the League of Seven did: They put Mangleborn back in their prisons. They saved the world. Hachi was their warrior. Fergus was their tinker. And Archie—

Archie was their strongman. Their Shadow. He knew that now. Neither Fergus nor Hachi had said a word to him about when he'd turned on them, almost killed them both, but it was there, between them. Archie caught Fergus' eyes giving him the once-over before he finished fixing the anchor crank. Archie had seen that look before, in his dreams. In the eyes of Leaguers afraid of one of their own.

Afraid of the Shadow.

"Anchor's aweigh, sirs," Mr. Rivets said from the steering console. "Destination?"

"Home, Mr. Rivets," Archie told him. "We have a lot to do."

ACKNOWLEDGMENTS

Special thanks to my terrific editor, Susan Chang, both for her enthusiasm and her very useful Editor Talent card, to Bev Kodak and the YA Lit Track at DragonCon for first bringing us together, and to everyone at SCBWI Carolinas for bringing us back together again. Thank you to Emily Jenkins for reading an early draft and providing invaluable feedback, to Bill Householder for the loan of a bunch of Cthulhu mythos stories I hadn't read, and to H. P. Lovecraft himself for writing the super weird and creepy stories that inspired the Mangleborn. Thanks also to Thurber House in Columbus, Ohio, for putting me up for a month in the attic as the Children's Writer in Residence while I worked on *The League of Seven*, and to my fellow Bat Cavers and my great friend Bob for all their support. Extra special thanks as always to my wife, Wendi, and my daughter, Jo, for not jumping out of the family airship every time I said, "So, there's this one part of *The League of Seven* I need your help with. . . ." You guys are brass. And to steampunks everywhere—keep those boilers stoked!

Read on for a preview of
THE DRAGON LANTERN
Book Two of *The League of Seven*

Archie Dent dangled from a rope 20,000 feet in the air, watching the blue ribbon of the Mississippi River spin far, far below him. At that moment, he didn't feel scared, or dizzy, or angry.

He felt betrayed.

"Retrieving the Dragon Lantern will be a simple task for three Leaguers," Philomena Moffett had told him and his friends Hachi and Fergus. "For that's what you are. The first of a new League of Seven."

Simple. That's what the head of the Septemberist Society had called retrieving this lantern thing. Even though it was hidden at the heart of a Septemberist puzzle trap. On top of a giant helium balloon. Twenty thousand feet in the air.

As he hung from his safety line for what had to be the thousandth time in the last three days, all Archie could think was that Philomena Moffett had not been entirely honest with them.

"Haul him up," Hachi said. Her voice came through tinny and distant—and more than a little annoyed—in the speaking tube attached to Archie's leather helmet. Fergus had built the helmets special. A mouthpiece, which snapped on just below the brass goggles Archie wore, brought fresh oxygen to him from the tank on his back, and connected to Archie's ears were flexible speaking tubes that led to Hachi's and Fergus's helmets. All this was necessary—like the heavy, fur-lined coats and the spider's web of ropes and carabiners they wore—to scale the mountain-sized helium kite high up in the thin atmosphere that held Cahokia In The Clouds afloat.

Archie felt a lurch on his line, and then the familiar *yank-yank-yank* of Fergus's ratchet as he was lifted back up. Soon he was close enough to take Hachi's hand, and she helped him grab hold of the network of ropes that covered the vast canvas of the balloon.

"Archie, you've got to hang on better," Hachi told him.

Archie flushed in embarrassment inside his leather helmet. Hachi Emartha hadn't fallen off once in all the time they'd been at this, but that was to be expected. She'd spent the last three years of her life training to be the greatest warrior who ever lived. Everything she did was graceful, from eating her breakfast to killing Manglespawn.

What really embarrassed Archie was that Fergus McFerguson had only slipped and fallen twice, and Fergus had only one good leg! His other leg, hobbled by a meka-ninja, now had only two settings—loose and useless, or straight and stiff—which he controlled with a knee harness he'd built himself.

"I'm sorry," Archie said. "I wasn't made for this. I'm good at punching and being punched. Not hopping around like a monkey."

"Well, one of these times your safety line's going to give way, and then you'll really be sorry," Hachi told him. "You do not want to test Fergus's back-up plan."

"Oy," Fergus said. "The gyrocopters work great. Sure, they're better at going down than up. And they're maybe a little hard to steer. But they're better than falling straight down. Besides, there wasn't room for parachutes in the backpacks with all the oxygen and lamps."

Archie looked down again, but clouds obstructed his view of the ground. *I'm higher than the clouds*, Archie thought, and then he did feel a twinge of fear creep in.

"Archie doesn't need to worry about falling anyway," Fergus said. "He just hit the ground and bounced back up last time."

"From only half this height," Hachi reminded him. "And he's not totally invulnerable. We don't know what his limits are, but there's no reason to test them until we have to."

Archie shifted his grip on the rope, trying not to think about his fall from the *Hesperus*, trying not to think about how he was seemingly impossible to kill. Trying not to think about the crack in his arm.

The crack that showed he wasn't entirely human.

The crack that showed he was made of stone.

"Let's just get on with it," Archie said.

"Just a little farther, and then we wait for nightfall," Hachi said.

They were working their way sideways around the broad, gently curved side of the enormous helium balloon on the rope-like rigging that covered it like a giant net. Archie thought of the stuff as "rope-like" because it wasn't really rope—not like the twine rope he knew. It was made of something gray and shiny, like metal, but it stretched and hung like a fiber rope. The gray lines, just like the strange canvas-like material that held the helium trapped inside it, had been invented by Wayland Smith and Daedalus of the Roman League of Seven hundreds of years ago, and the world had yet to rediscover the secrets of their construction.

Fergus ran a hand along the glossy veneer of the canvas. "I can't get over this stuff," he said through the speaking tube. "Helium is so small it escapes from almost anything. Anything light enough to float, that is. But not this. It's been hanging up here in the clouds for almost two millennia."

"They had to make sure it wasn't going to fall," Archie said.

"Which you're both going to do if you don't focus," Hachi told them. "Next section. Go."

The ropes-that-weren't-ropes formed a grid of squares on the canvas-that-wasn't-canvas, like the latitude and longitude lines on a globe. They were just tall enough for Hachi and Fergus to stand in a grid square on the bottom rope and hold on to the top rope with their hands, but Archie was younger and shorter than both of them. Where they could crab-walk across, he had to lunge.

Fergus shuffled his way across the grid square to the next, his kilt flapping wildly in the freezing, howling wind. He'd at least had the sense to put on long underwear underneath it, even though the baggy red longjohns looked silly with his blue tartan kilt.

At last he was across, and it was Archie's turn.

"You can do this," he heard Hachi say.

Archie focused on the rope at the other side of the grid, took a deep breath of the fresh oxygen pumped into his mask, and dove for it. The wind caught his big coat like a sail and spun him, and he fell. He clawed out blindly with his hands and felt only canvas. *Zip!* He was sliding down again, falling, soon to be dangling from his safety line again—or worse—when at last his hand felt rope and he snatched at it. *Oof.* He slammed into the canvas as he stopped his own fall and hung there, panting, as he got his breath back.

"Better. Next grid," Hachi said, already moving along. "Don't forget to re-attach your safety line."

Archie closed his eyes and put his head against the canvas balloon. What was it his mother always said? *No rest for the weary.*

That they were here at all—three kids on a top secret, super dangerous mission for the Septemberist Society—was incredible by the looks of it. What kind of adults would throw children into the fire box like so many lumps of coal? And what kind of parents would let them?

But Hachi, the thirteen-year-old Seminole girl, had no parents to ask, and she had been on her own ever since their deaths. Fergus, the fourteen-year-old tinker, was on his own too. He had left his family's farm in North Carolina to apprentice with Thomas Edison, but had run away when he learned his boss was insane.

It was Archie's parents who had said no.

"He's too young," his mother had said.

"He's not ready," his father had said.

But then it had been pointed out to them that even though he was just twelve, Archie had the strength of a hundred men. Or so it seemed. And Archie couldn't get sick, couldn't be hurt, and couldn't die.

At least, nothing had killed him yet. And by all rights, he should have died at least sixteen times already. That he knew of.

And then there was the fact that this mission was all about where he had really come from. How he had come to be this way. In the end, his parents had to let him go.

Not that they were really his parents.

Archie jumped and almost missed the next rope. It took Hachi and Fergus both hauling him back up to keep him from falling again.

"*Focus,*" Hachi told him.

"*I'm trying,*" Archie said.

"No you're not," Hachi said. "Your mind is somewhere else. I can see it in your eyes. Stop thinking about how you're not real and focus on where you are and what you're doing. You know what happens when you lose focus."

Archie's face burned hot under his mask again. None of them needed any reminder about what happened when Archie lost his head.

Hachi stared at him until he met her eyes. She was hard and demanding, but she also knew what it was to be so angry it consumed you. So angry it ate you up and swallowed you whole, and you let it because deep down you *wanted* it to.

Archie nodded. "I'm okay. I'll be okay."

Hachi gave a curt nod back. "Tell us the nursery rhyme again while we climb."

Archie sagged. He'd repeated the rhyme a thousand times in the past two days as they'd tried to climb the balloon, but he knew what she was doing. She was trying to get him to say it like a mantra, to focus on the here and now.

"Twinkle, twinkle, little star. How I wonder what you are," he said, falling into the sing-song of the rhyme. "Up above the world so high, like a diamond in the sky."

Most nursery rhymes, it turned out, were codes. Riddles that, when unlocked, held the secrets to navigating the complicated puzzle traps previous Leagues had used to imprison the Mangleborn—the giant, unkillable, primordial monsters that woke from their slumber to destroy the world every time humankind discovered electricity. Sometimes too the puzzle traps were used to hide powerful artifacts, like this lantern.

Archie focused on the next jump, and made it. Not gracefully, but he made it.

"Well, 'up above the world so high, like a diamond in the sky' can't be anything but Cahokia In The Clouds," Fergus said.

Cahokia In The Clouds. A city built underneath a giant, kite-shaped helium balloon tethered at the edge of Illini territory by people who had no idea why the balloon was there to begin with. If only they really understood . . . But that was the job of the Septemberist Society: to keep the true horrors of the world hidden and buried. Or, in this case, hidden and floating.

The nursery rhyme clearly meant the kite-shaped balloon above Cahokia In The Clouds, and the twinkling star had to be the lantern they were after.

Lóngdēng. The Dragon Lantern. An artifact from the Mu civilization, which existed long before Atlantis fell and Rome rose from its ashes. Archie had no idea what the lantern was, or what it did. All Philomena Moffett had told him was that it held the answer to the secret of how he became whatever he was. That was enough to send him to the top of Cahokia In The Clouds to get it.

How I wonder what you are . . . Archie thought.

"You're losing focus again," Hachi told him.

Archie shook himself and nodded.

"Tell us the next part," she said.

Archie was the one who had all the nursery rhymes memorized. His Septemberist parents had made a point of drilling him on them as a boy.

"When the blazing sun is gone, when he nothing shines upon, then you show your little light, twinkle, twinkle, all the night," Archie sang.

This was where they had gone wrong for the past two days. Or so they now thought. Both times, they had attempted to scale the rope net during daylight. And why not? It was hard enough when you could actually see where you were going. But there were traps—dangerous traps—and they hadn't yet been able to find a way around them. Not by day. So they'd gone back to the rhyme. *When the blazing sun is gone, when he nothing shines upon, then you show your little light, twinkle, twinkle, all the night.* Now it seemed obvious: they were supposed to wait until dark.

Archie made one last leap, slipping and falling off the rope at his feet. He caught it as he fell and pulled himself up with a few choice comments into his oxygen mask. He heard Fergus snicker through his earpiece.

"Okay. This is where the traps start," Hachi said. Above them and to the right, Archie saw the ropes they had tried to climb. The ropes that had come loose as soon as their weight was on them, and sent them spilling off the balloon. Traps set to keep the curious out. If not for their safety lines, they would all be dead.

All but Archie.

"And . . . it's just about nightfall," Hachi said.

Hachi had timed it perfectly. Hachi, their war chief. It was still too light to see the stars, but the first of them would appear in minutes. In the meantime, Fergus, their tech wizard, lit the oil lamps he had mounted on the shoulder straps of their backpacks.

"Try not to get the lamps near your oxygen masks," Fergus said. "That would be bad."

"Bad how?" Archie asked.

"Boom bad," Fergus said.

"Good to know," Archie said.

The last of the red-orange sunshine drained away beneath the clouds, and their skyworld became the blue-black of night. There was a metaphor for Archie's new life in that, he thought. Waiting for the light to go away so he could work in the dark. But Hachi had told him to focus, so he put it away.

"All right," Archie said. "The 'blazing sun is gone.' Now what?"

They shined their lamps around, trying to see anything different about the rope maze around them, but it all looked the same.

"Wait a minute," Fergus said. He reached up and turned off his shoulder lamp.

"What are you doing?" Hachi said.

"Oh, brass! You've got to see this," Fergus said. "Switch off your lamps."

"Turn them off? But how are we supposed to see?" Archie asked.

Archie and Hachi did it anyway, and gasped. All around them, the rope net glowed like the tail end of a firefly.

"Phospholuminescence!" Fergus said. "Blinking brilliant! All day it absorbs the sun's light, and then it glows all night. We don't need lanterns at all!"

"But we still don't know which way to go," Hachi said.

For the past two days, they had made guesses. Bad ones, with painful results. But interpreting the second verse correctly had borne fruit, so Archie recited the third.

"Then the traveler in the dark, thanks you for your tiny spark. He could not see which way to go, if you did not twinkle so."

"So we follow the twinkling star?" Fergus asked.

They all looked to the sky. It was *filled* with twinkling stars.

"They're *all* twinkling," Archie said miserably.

"Not that one," Hachi said.

Archie and Fergus followed her finger to where it was pointing.

Below them, almost at the edge of the balloon's curve, was a single, small white light.

A tiny spark!

"Let's try something," Hachi said. "We've gone up from here, and we've gone sideways, but we've never gone down."

With practiced ease, Hachi released the catch on her safety line and rappelled down one place in the rope grid. As she landed on the rope below, the light beneath them went out.

"It's gone!" Archie said.

"Nae, it's not. It's just moved," Fergus said. "Look."

He was right. Among all the twinkling stars, there was only one that didn't twinkle — a tiny pin-prick of light at the far edge of the balloon, directly to the right of Hachi. She slid across her grid with the grace of a tightrope walker, her brown dress flapping underneath her fur coat, and stepped into the next one. The light stayed on, but shifted one grid farther away.

"*The traveler in the dark thanks you for your tiny spark,*" Archie said aloud. "*He could not see which way to go, if you did not twinkle so.* We need the stars to twinkle so we can follow the one that doesn't!"

"Come on," Hachi told them. "I'll stay one square ahead."

Archie and Fergus followed her, and Hachi waited for them to catch up each time she moved ahead. Right again, then up, up, and up, then left, then up again, and slowly they made their way through the maze toward the top.

"What's the rest of it?" Hachi asked.

"The rest of what?"

"The rest of the nursery rhyme."

"Oh," Archie said, focusing on his feet. "Let's see. Um, 'In the dark blue sky you keep, and often through my curtains peep, for you never shut your eye, 'till the sun is in the sky.' Then the rest of it is kind of the same. 'As your bright and tiny spark lights the traveler in the dark, though I know not what you are, twinkle, twinkle, little star.' Then the last stanzas are the first one over again."

"You never shut your eye 'till the sun is in the sky. So we've got until sun-up to get there. No problem," Fergus said.

"We've got until sun-up to get there *and back again*," Hachi reminded him.

"Oh. Aye. Moving right along then."

"Twinkle, twinkle, little star," Archie said. "Why do they twinkle?"

"It's the atmosphere," Fergus said. "The light from the stars gets all wonky when it comes through the air, making our eyes see it as a flicker. Doesn't work the same way for planets. They're closer, so they don't—"

Hachi screamed in their ears and spasmed, jerking back and forth on the rope in the next grid. Blue-hot energy crackled over her gloves and up her coat, sparking in the fur lining of her coat.

Lektricity!

"Hachi!" Fergus cried. He lunged for her and fell. Archie caught Fergus's safety line with one hand and hung on to the rope maze with the other, using his massive strength to keep Fergus from falling. As though he were lifting a wooden toy at the end of a bit of string, Archie raised Fergus back up to Hachi.

"Higher!" Fergus cried.

Archie lifted him up until Fergus could grab the rope that Hachi still clung to. As soon as Fergus touched it, the lektricity shifted from Hachi to him. Archie knew that right then, underneath Fergus's layers of winter clothing, the black lines that covered his friend's skin like tattoos were rearranging themselves, turning Fergus into a syphon for all the lektricity.

Without the lektric charge to hold her to the rope, Hachi's hands went slack and she fell.

"Catch her!" Fergus cried.

Archie fumbled for her safety line and caught it. Hachi jerked to a stop, and he hauled her back up.

Fergus pulled his hand away from the lektrified rope. The

blue-hot lightning followed him, finally disconnecting and slinking back into its hidden home in the rope.

"Crivens! I thought I could wait out the charge, but it kept coming! What's powering that thing?"

"Here, help me get Hachi back up," Archie said. She was awake, which was good, but she was still groggy. Archie lifted her higher, and Fergus helped Hachi get her hands back on the safe ropes in their grid.

"So," Hachi mumbled. "Planets don't twinkle."

"What?" Fergus said. "Oh . . . yeah."

Hachi punched Fergus, but there wasn't much strength in it. "You might have said so *before* I followed one."

Hachi leaned into Fergus, and he hugged her with one arm while he held tight to the rope with the other. Hachi and Fergus put their heads together, and Archie looked away. *Blech*. Hachi and Fergus had become close in their adventures together, and though neither of them said so, they were practically boyfriend and girlfriend. It always made Archie feel a little weird to see them when they got like this. But a little jealous of how close they were as friends too.

At last they separated. "I don't know how we're going to tell the difference between our guiding light and the planets," Fergus said.

"Planets move. The light doesn't," Hachi said. "We may not run into any more in the right position to fool us," she added, "but if we do, we'll wait and watch."

"And all the while get closer to dawn," Fergus said.

"We should be moving, not talking," Hachi said.

"Are you sure you're strong enough?" Fergus asked.

In answer, Hachi climbed up to the next grid.

"So, she's strong enough then," Fergus said to Archie, though of course Hachi could hear him too over the speaking tubes.

Together they climbed, sometimes moving up, sometimes side to side, sometimes back down, but all the while working their way around and up the giant dome of helium. The sheer vertical face of the balloon gradually gave way to the gentle slope of the top of the balloon, and they crawled along on hands and knees, still clinging to the ropes so the wind wouldn't tear them off.

Archie heard someone scream, and he froze.

"Crivens! What's that?" Fergus asked. "There can't be anyone else up here!"

But someone was up ahead of them. Lots of someones, from the sound of screams coming to them over the wind. It sounded like someone was being tortured.

"I can see silhouettes against the stars," Hachi said, crouching low. "Something's coming. Something's coming right at us!"

Archie ducked with Hachi and Fergus, then remembered he was the Heracles of the team. Whatever was coming, it was his job to meet it head on, so the others wouldn't be hurt. But that didn't mean he wasn't scared. Still holding the rope, he raised himself up, closed his eyes, and turned his head away.

"Honk-honk-honk!" the thing cried as it got closer.

Honk-honk-honk?

Something flapping and feathery smacked Archie in the face and he fell over, glancing up in time to see a big white bird launch itself off the side of the balloon and disappear into the dark night sky.

"It's birds," he said. "Geese!"

Fergus lit his oil lamp and shined it forward to have a look. The top of the balloon was covered with bird nests! There had to be hundreds of them, scattered here and there among the grid lines of the rope net that covered the giant balloon.

"You know what this means?" Hachi said.

"Aye," Fergus said. "If this thing is covered with birds, it's also covered with bird poop."

"No," Hachi said. "I mean, yes, probably, but that's not what I meant. Look at *where* they have their nests."

Archie scanned the nests, trying to see what Hachi saw. All he noticed was that the birds were packed into just a few of the grid squares, when they had lots more empty ones they could have been using. No—wait. He understood!

"Oh, brass! They're nesting in the grid squares that aren't booby trapped!"

"Exactly," Hachi said.

Sure enough, Archie was able to trace a path from where they stood all the way to the top, where something small and red glowed in the night sky.

The Dragon Lantern.

Starscape Books
Reading & Activity Guide
THE LEAGUE OF SEVEN
by *Alan Gratz*
Grades 4–8, ages 9–13

About This Guide
The questions and activities that follow are intended to enhance your reading of *The League of Seven*. Please feel free to adapt this content to suit the needs and interests of your students or reading group participants.

BEFORE READING THE BOOK:
Writing & Discussion Activities
The pre-reading activities below correlate to the following Common Core State Standards: (W.4-8.3) (SL.4-8.1, 3)

1. Ask each student to write about a time when s/he felt that a parent or other adult was treating them too much like "a little kid." What was the situation? In what way did they feel they were being treated childishly? What was the result? Describe the way in which they would have preferred to be treated. How do they imagine the outcome of the situation would have been different had they been treated in this way?

2. Invite students to discuss their experiences belonging to clubs or teams. What are the purposes and goals of these groups? How did they gain entry to these groups (e.g., sign-up, try-out)? How do group members work together? Are their groups successful in reaching their objectives? What groups do they see in the adult world (e.g., political parties, community organizations, book clubs)? In what ways do they see these groups as similar to, or different from, the groups to which school-age people belong?

Discussion Questions

The discussion questions below correlate to the following Common Core State Standards: (SL.4-8.1, 3, 4) (SL.6-8.2, 3) (RL.4-8.1, 2, 3) (RH.4-8.6)

1. The first chapter of *The League of Seven* introduces the "Tik Tok servant" Mr. Rivets. Describe the relationship between Archie and Mr. Rivets. Consider the high-tech devices you own or use. How might they be similar to and/or different from Mr. Rivets?

2. What do you think the author means when he writes "People didn't want to know there really were monsters in the world" (p. 19)? What kind of monsters does he mean? Do you think this statement holds true in our own world, too?

3. Explain the difference between "Mangleborn" and "Manglespawn." What types of creatures are the black bugs that attach themselves to Mr. and Mrs. Dent and other Septemberists?

4. Why do Archie and Mr. Rivets set the *Hesperus* on a course to Florida? What situation does Archie discover when he arrives? With what important people is he imprisoned?

5. En route to New Rome with Hachi and Fergus, the group stops to see the newly widowed Mrs. Henhawk. What promises are made and/or revealed in the course of this visit?

6. What animals are represented in Hachi's set of "clockwork gizmos"? Compare Hachi's five animals and their abilities to the seven abilities required of various League members as they have formed through history. In what other ways are the mechanical animals important to the story, both technically and symbolically?

7. New Rome seems to be an alternate history version of New York City. What features of the real city are recognizable in Archie's descriptions? What are the most significant differences between "New Rome" and the real New York?

8. Before Archie begins to understand his own role in the newly forming League, he is already the keeper of the "true" history

of the world and the person who shares legends and stories previously unknown to (or misunderstood by) Hachi and Fergus. Describe one or more of these stories, how it was originally understood by Archie's companions, and what is important about them learning the truth in the course of the novel.

9. Who is Mr. Tesla and how do Archie, Hachi, and Fergus find him? What does he reveal to them about the threat posed by Edison? How does the scene in Tesla's workshop show the dueling positive and negative elements of technological advancement? Can you apply your observations to a recent technological innovation in our own world?

10. Is the Great Bear's pelt truly invulnerable? Explain your answer.

11. What is Hachi's "mantra" as depicted in chapter 22? How might it relate to the concept behind the League? What does the mantra reveal to readers above Hachi's character and her motives?

12. Where is Lady Josephine's Academy? How is this location the scene of both a great deception and a great revelation?

13. On page 270, Ms. Ambrose bids her student farewell, saying, "I pray you find peace, Hachi—but I can at least rest well in the knowledge that you have found good friends." How might this be a wish you could make for yourself or offer to someone in your own life? Is there "peace" to be found in the League of Seven? Why or why not?

14. How do nursery rhymes relate to the Septemberists' mission? Has reading this novel made you reconsider folktales and legends you have been told? Explain your answer.

15. How do the three friends defeat the Swarm Queen? By what betrayals is Archie tempted?

16. What does Archie learn about his relationship to his parents at the end of the story? How might this change his understanding of the words "family" and "friends"? What might you say to him to help him cope with his new insights?

17. If Archie is the strongman/shadow figure, Hachi the warrior/fighter, and Fergus the tinker/maker, what other roles remain to

be filled to form a new League of Seven? What do you hope will happen in the next installment of the novel?

Research & Writing Activities

The research and writing activities below correlate to the following Common Core State Standards: (L.4-8.4) (RL.5-8.4) (RL.5-6.5) (RL.6-8.6) (RL.4-8.7) (SL.4-8.1, 3) (W.4-8.2, 7) (WHST 6-8.6)

1. Go to the library or online to learn more about the literary sub-genre of *steampunk*. Find at least three sources for your information. Use your research to create an informative poster that includes a definition of steampunk, a short history of the origin of the genre, and a list of some famous steampunk novels and/or movies.

2. The *setting* of a novel can loosely be defined as the time and place in which the story unfolds. In *The League of Seven*, the setting is an alternate history wherein some major world events took different turns—and yielded different outcomes—than they did in readers' reality. Alone or in small groups, identify events, geographical names, inventions, and historical figures that are represented differently in the novel than they are in your history books. Create a booklet entitled "A Guide to the Alternate History of *The League of Seven*," including maps; alternative biographies of historical figures, nations, and Native American tribal groups; short descriptions of specialized technologies, means of transportation, and other elements that are familiar yet different from the reality of the reader's world.

3. Go to the library or online to learn about ways the number seven, featured in the novel's title, has significance in many cultures. Consider researching the legendary Irish warrior Cú Chulainn, the Seven Gods of Good Fortune in Japanese mythology, or the biblical account of seven days of creation. With classmates or friends, create a mural, large mobile, or sculpture depicting the significance of *seven* across cultures and times.

4. Go to the library or online to research the sources of one or more

past League of Seven members to which Archie refers throughout the novel, such as Heracles, Hippolyta, Theseus, or Wayland [the] Smith. Write a one-page report comparing the history of this character as found in your research with the portrayal of the character in the novel.

5. "Square cogs" and "clinker" are just two of the many slang expressions specific to the world of *The League of Seven*. Make a set of at least a dozen flash cards featuring unusual terms from the novel. Test the "League" vocabulary of friends or classmates by quizzing them with the flash cards.

6. Create a PowerPoint or other multimedia presentation describing the origins of the League of Seven; the specific roles its members fill; the various individuals who filled these roles in the past; and the responsibilities of the Septemberists to the League.

7. Read a biography of Thomas Edison and/or Nicola Tesla. Then, prepare a brief oral report about their lives, relationship, and contributions to science, followed by an explanation of how these legendary thinkers of our history were changed in the alternate world of the League of Seven.

8. Imagine you are Mr. or Mrs. Dent (Archie's dad or mom) before the attack of the Manglespawn bugs, working on propaganda to keep the public safe. Create a colorful, annotated poster to help ordinary people remember why "lektricity" is dangerous.

9. Imagine you are one of a handful of Septemberists who has not fallen victim to the Swarm Queen's mind-controlling neck bugs. Write a letter to "Any Healthy Septemberist Out There," describing your understanding of what the bugs are doing and how they might be stopped. Include at least two black-and-white sketches with your letter.

10. If you could travel to the world of the League of Seven, what place would you most like to see or which invention would you most like to use? Would you stop in New Rome or Brasil? Would you ship yourself somewhere via pneumatic post? Create an outline-style travel itinerary for a visit to this alternate world.

Share and compare your itinerary with those of friends or classmates.

11. In the character of Fergus or Hachi, write at least four journal entries, including one recounting your first meeting with Archie; one discussing your life before joining the battle against Edison; one in which you consider whether Archie's revelations about the Septemberists and the League of Seven are true; and one in which you ponder what will happen to you and your new friends after the final scene of the novel.

12. In the character of Archie, write a journal entry reflecting on your recent adventures and describing your struggles with your newly discovered identities as an adopted child, as a possible Manglespawn and, perhaps worst of all, as the "shadow" member of a new League of Seven.

13. Using information from the novel, create a logo and slogan for the new League of Seven of which Archie, Hachi, and Fergus are all a part. And/or write a HELP WANTED advertisement describing the "open positions" in the new League and the abilities these jobs will require.

14. Author Alan Gratz commented that he began writing *The League of Seven* by "listing all the things that ten-year-old Alan would have thought were awesome." What do you think is awesome? Make a list of at least a dozen objects, images, place names, and phrases that pique your interest. Inspired by this list, write a 1-3 paragraph story idea, and a suggested title and genre (such as steampunk, fantasy, picture book, or graphic novel) you feel would best suit your concept.

JOIN THE
SEPTEMBERIST
SOCIETY!

www.septemberistsociety.com

ABOUT THE AUTHOR

Alan Gratz is the author of *Samurai Shortstop*, an ALA 2007 Top Ten Book for Young Adults. He began writing *The League of Seven* by listing all the things that ten-year-old Alan would have thought were awesome, including brass goggles, airships, tentacle monsters, brains in jars, windup robots, secret societies, and superpowers. (In fact, he still thinks all those things are awesome.) When he's not writing books like *The League of Seven*, *Samurai Shortstop*, *The Brooklyn Nine*, and *Prisoner B-3087*, he's usually reading other people's books or creating an awesome new costume for science fiction/fantasy conventions. Visit his awesome website at www.alangratz.com.